About the Author

Christy Hadfield works in academia as a biochemist researcher and adjunct professor during the day, although storytelling has always been a favorite pastime of theirs. They were born and raised in the Midwest where they still reside, actively supporting their queer community. They also enjoy other hobbies such as skateboarding, rollerblading, crocheting, and sewing.

Bella Books, Inc.
P.O. Box 10543
Tallahassee, FL 32302

First Edition - 2025

Editor: Heather Flournoy

ISBN: 978-1-64247-628-6

PUBLISHER'S NOTE

Dr. Margaret Morgan

Dr. Margaret Morgan

Christy Hadfield

BELLA
BOOKS

FRESHMAN YEAR

For almost an entire semester, Tess Stanford managed to avoid all contact with Dr. Morgan. This was a blessing, considering Dr. Morgan's notoriously awful reputation.

Technically, Tess was in Dr. Morgan's class, as the woman's name was listed on her class schedule. Dr. Morgan ran the introductory chemistry lab. She designed the class, developed the experimental protocols, wrote the grueling pre- and post-lab worksheets, and did all the final grading. She did not, however, teach. Rather, a collection of chemistry graduate students ran class time. So, Tess, like most of her fellow undergraduate classmates, had never actually seen Dr. Morgan during lab time. This was because the professor avoided freshmen like the plague. And yes, Dr. Morgan would argue, there was statistically significant evidence to suggest that freshmen did indeed carry more diseases than the average upperclassman.

Even though she did her best to avoid students, her horrid reputation preceded her. Therefore, everyone on campus knew of Dr. Morgan, and it was because of this reputation that Tess learned about the professor the first day she moved to campus.

Once the new freshmen were settled in their dorms, their RA called a floor meeting to address the agenda of the coming days. The freshman dorms were grouped mostly by major, to encourage connections in shared classes. Tess was a biology major, interested in pursuing research work, but she was lumped in with the other biology majors, most planning to pursue medical school. All first-year biology majors were required to take Introduction to General Biology, Introduction to General Chemistry, and the associated intro labs.

Because their RA was a chem major herself, when questions about the location of the intro chemistry lab came up, she pinched the bridge of her nose. "You all have to take the intro chem lab, don't you? I'm so sorry."

"Why? Is it hard?"

"It's Dr. Morgan. Have you heard about her yet? She's the devil. She's the lab coordinator, so she doesn't teach, but she does all the grading. I'm not supposed to say this, but I will anyway. She's an ass. She takes off points for the dumbest things, and any misstep in the lab, even something inconsequential, they'll kick you out. They don't give you any missed labs either, and if you're more than a minute late, they lock you out, no second chances."

Everyone fell silent. Tess glanced around the room, noting that all the premed students were visibly pale, mourning the death of their perfect GPAs. Tess wanted to be optimistic, but the class sounded like a real pain in the ass...just like this Dr. Morgan person.

"No, no, I didn't mean to scare you!" their RA quickly said. "Tons of freshmen survive that class every year and we have hundreds, probably, of students that move on to med school, so it's totally fine. You might leave with a few extra gray hairs, but you'll survive."

However, despite this initial introductory warning to the bio-chem professor, three weeks passed before Tess even *saw* Dr. Morgan.

Tess was adjusting to college life by then. She'd made a couple of friends. Her bond was solidifying with her roommate,

Kai, and there was a growing friendship with one of their floormates, Elle. Elle, too, was premed, so they shared classes, but she was already casting longing glances toward the English department.

"Just switch majors," Kai said.

"But what job could I do with an English major?"

"Ask them about it," Tess suggested. "I bet they have a whole list of careers you can do with an English major. Lists sound like a nerdy lit thing to me."

"You're rude." Elle laughed. "But yeah, maybe I can convince my parents that it'd be a lucrative career choice."

"*Lucrative*," Tess repeated. "You already sound like an English major."

"Omigod, stop!" Kai yelped, suddenly grabbing both Tess and Elle, jerking them to a halt.

"What?" Elle asked.

"That's *her*," Kai exclaimed breathlessly, pointing across the quad.

"Who?"

"Dr. Morgan!"

Tess followed Kai's line of sight, scanning the crowd, trying to make out which person was the notoriously awful professor.

"Where the hell are you looking?" Elle asked.

"She just came out of the chem building carrying a huge cardboard box."

Tess's eyes landed. Yards from them, on a different sidewalk, a woman stalked along carrying a massive cardboard box. Her hair was a dark brunette, pulled into a tight bun, and she wore a dark woman's suit. Sure, she looked professional, and perhaps a bit intimidating, but Tess was more surprised than anything.

"Wait, that's Dr. Morgan?" Tess asked in full disbelief. "Are you sure?"

"Yeah, I'm positive. I looked her up online. That's definitely her."

Even though Dr. Morgan was far from them and Tess could not make out subtler details, it was clear that Dr. Morgan looked *nothing* like what she had been picturing. She expected someone old and grouchy, a get-off-my-lawn type of old woman. Or maybe she'd pictured a warden of corporal punishment, ruler in hand for smacking students, her face ugly with a big, knotted nose. Or maybe she'd have fangs, and scales, and devil horns! Instead, Dr. Morgan appeared far younger than Tess expected, and she was striking, both in her looks and the way she carried herself.

Tess barked out her observation, stating, "But she's so—so young. And—and *hot*."

Both Kai and Elle stared at Tess curiously.

"Come on, don't look at me like that. I know the rumors. But you can't say, objectively, that she *isn't* good-looking."

"I mean, if you're into older women, I guess," Elle said with a shrug.

"Yeah, I mean, I guess I can see it," Kai agreed. "But I wouldn't dare try to compliment her. I mean, look." She gestured emphatically, and Tess turned back to watch Dr. Morgan.

Another student walked down the sidewalk toward Dr. Morgan, head down, looking at his phone. Tess couldn't imagine, despite Kai's urging, that it would be a problem. The sidewalk was plenty wide enough for multiple people. However, it quickly became clear that it wasn't wide enough for *Dr. Morgan* and another person.

The professor glared at the student. She yelled something— Tess could see her mouth move but couldn't hear—and the boy startled. He stopped, realizing who was approaching, then spun and sprinted away in the opposite direction. Other students noticed the commotion and also changed their trajectories to avoid Dr. Morgan. As Dr. Morgan continued, students parted around her, giving her a wide birth.

"Dang, she's terrifying," Elle uttered, shuddering.

Tess blinked, trying to process. "She's…bewildering…"

"You're treading on dangerous water," Kai said. "Sure, she's young—"

"I heard she's a kid genius, skipped a few grades," Elle supplied.

"And yeah, maybe she's got a good figure," Kai continued. "But with all the things I've heard about her, she is not worth it."

Tess considered the rumors she'd heard. Some of them, maybe, could be true, but surely most were made up. "What all have you heard?" Tess pulled her friends along as she continued walking.

"Well, I heard that the bio and chem departments, because she's in bio-chem, right, scheduled their weekly department meetings around Dr. Morgan *without telling her*, because they were hoping she wouldn't notice and wouldn't show up."

"I heard they deleted her from the department email list because they were sick of her showing up to events and ruining them," Elle said.

"I heard that Dr. Glower switched departments—and his entire tenure research plan—because his office was next to hers and he kept bumping into her until it was too much for him to handle."

"She only teaches graduate courses because none of the undergrads will sign up for her classes."

"That can't all be true!" Tess finally said. "I mean, if she's such a bad professor and everyone hates her, then how come she's still got a job?"

"Tenure stuff, I assume."

"Yeah, she's a crazy genius," Kai said. "I don't know much about her work, but I do know that she brings in a ton of funding and good rep for the school. That's why they're keeping her around, I'd imagine."

"I find it hard to believe," Tess admitted, "that someone could get this far being such a horrid person."

"She might not have always been bad," Elle suggested. "Some people get bitter with age."

"It doesn't matter, because she's a horrid person *now*," Kai concluded.

Tess glanced back over her shoulder, hoping to see Dr. Morgan once more. However, the professor was gone.

Tess set her gaze straight ahead. She wasn't sure if she believed the rumors, but she also didn't feel inclined to go out of her way to purposefully disprove the rumors, either. So, she decided it would be best to ignore the professor entirely.

And she did avoid Dr. Morgan...for almost an entire semester.

* * *

One more class...five finals...and then a monthlong break. That was all Tess was thinking about. It was bitterly cold outside, single digits with an even lower windchill. Day-old frozen snow covered the ground, piled where the sidewalks had been shoveled. Chilled to the bone against the frigid icy air, Tess fought her way across campus. She had tunnel vision for the warmth of the chemistry building and even contemplated breaking into a run, she was so desperate for relief.

Before she could, though, someone burst out of the chemistry building and Tess abruptly stopped. Ahead of her was Dr. Morgan, muttering angrily to herself as she stomped forward. Tess was frozen in place, too shocked to even remember the cold.

Dr. Morgan turned a sharp corner and ran straight into a boy who was running toward the warm relief of the indoors. When they collided, the boy tripped into a frozen snowdrift, falling flat on his face. The papers and lab books he had been carrying were cast out in a desperate attempt to use his hands to break his fall, and they all landed in the snow as well.

Dr. Morgan snarled. "Watch where you're going, you blind imbecile!"

The boy struggled to collect himself while Dr. Morgan just stood there, doing nothing to help. She huffed, tapping her foot, as if the collision inconvenienced her more than the poor struggling boy. Then she turned, staring straight at Tess, who was frozen a few feet away, watching with her mouth agape.

"What are you staring at?" Dr. Morgan harshly asked.

Tess blinked, coming back to her senses. She shook her head, trying to avoid confrontation, and stepped back as Dr. Morgan roughly shoved past her. Tess watched her storm off, still too shocked to process. Once the devil was gone, she turned to the snow-covered boy.

Tess extended her arm, helping the boy to his feet. Silently, she helped collect his papers. He gathered his things from Tess, shaking not from the cold, but with fear, and then nodded in silent thanks before running off.

Once he was gone, Tess looked back in the direction Dr. Morgan bolted. She pursed her lips, frowning slightly, and thought to herself what a horrid, horrid woman Dr. Morgan was.

* * *

Tess spotted Elle across the quad and ran to her, darting between students bundled in coats. They were a week into the spring semester, the January air still frigid. She called out to Elle, who was nose-deep in a book, grasping the object between her mittened hands.

"Elle! How are you? How was your break?"

"Oh, Tess," Elle replied jovially, glancing up. "It was great. I got to go home and see my family, but most importantly, see my dog. Was your break good?"

"Yeah, not bad. I also went home to visit family. My brother was annoying as usual, but he's not quite as bad now that we're getting older. What're you reading?"

Elle flipped the book over in her hands. "Just a book Dr. Greenwood let me borrow."

"Wait, isn't she the dean of the English department or something? You had a meeting with her, right?"

"She's the associate dean, actually, but yes. I have officially picked up an English major."

Tess was well aware of Elle's interest in literature. In fact, she had, with Kai's help, been part of the urging force to get Elle to email Dr. Greenwood in the first place.

"Well, congrats, although I think you're crazy. A science *and* English major."

"I'm definitely going to be busy, but it'll be good. Dr. Greenwood said she'll be my mentor, and she'll help me out. We've already talked a few times, and we kind of have this book club thing going on now? She lets me borrow a book, I read it, and then we just talk about it."

"Tell me about her. What's she like?"

"Well, her office is in the back corner of the English department building. That building is a straight-up maze. The corridors are claustrophobically tight, and they wind around in the most confusing ways. But in the back corner, the building opens up a bit, and there's Dr. Greenwood's office. She's got a Freddie Mercury poster on her office door."

"Good taste," Tess said, amused.

"Oh, I haven't even gotten to the best parts yet. Dr. Greenwood is a full-on *character*, and I mean that in the most admirable way. She's, um, like an eccentric off-grid aunt who does pottery and presses flowers in her field notebook, jotting notes into the margins of her well-loved books. She's got long gray-silver hair, usually pulled back into a loose ponytail, and she wears all sorts of bright colors and, frankly, gaudy patterns.

"Her office is exactly like her, vibes unparalleled. Every wall, except for the window and where her desk is, is covered in floor-to-ceiling bookshelves. She's got a bunch of old rugs covering the floor, all in clashing colors, overlapping and slightly ajar, and there's a super comfy sofa near the window with a mismatched and worn chair, both probably from two entirely different decades."

"She does sound like a character already. Clearly, though, you also meshed with her personality."

Elle nodded eagerly. "She's super nice. She was very excited about my interest in picking up an English major. She feeds my passion for literature, gets me excited about books and storytelling all over again. She's very inspiring."

"Well, clearly, she's already got you reading and discussing books for fun." Tess pointed at the book Elle was holding again. "What book is that, and why did she pick it out for you?"

"It's *Stone Butch Blues* by Leslie Fienberg. She said she teaches it in her upper-level queer lit class. I can't take it as a freshman, otherwise I probably would have signed up, but she said I absolutely have to take the class and, unable to wait, is letting me get a little preview of the material."

Curious, but mostly impressed, Tess stated the obvious. "So…she's gay."

Elle gave a knowing look. "It's probably why we hit it off so well. I mean, the Freddie Mercury poster was kind of a sign, but that could go either way. But when I was sitting in her office just looking around at the books she had…I mean, she has all the classics, obviously. But there were also a lot of books of very… *queer* origin. She loves her books hard. I mean, every spine was cracked, the covers were worn and flaking, and there were so many note markers sticking out that the books all swelled at their seams."

"Okay, she's just as obsessed with literature as you are. I get it. But coming from my smaller hometown, I've never encountered an openly queer professor before, so this is huge for me. Does she lead any groups, or can she mentor anyone?"

"She's very vocally queer on campus, despite all those old fuds on the board or whatever that *hate* it, which is another reason why I admire her so much. She's so visible. She's got a progress rainbow flag on her desk, and she wears a pin, and she has no hesitation talking about gay stuff all the time. That was actually how I found out about the queer lit class she teaches, because, you know how I can't keep my mouth shut, I just blurted out, 'I'm getting some pretty queer vibes from this office.'"

Tess laughed. "I assume she took your bluntness well."

"She did, thankfully. She said it was her intention to be so vocal and obvious about it, so she could create a safe space on campus for students like us. It feels really nice knowing her, that I can feel safe around her."

"And when are you taking her queer lit class?"

"Next year. It's only offered in the spring and usually it's only open to juniors and seniors, but Dr. Greenwood helped arrange my schedule so I could pick up some additional English classes over the next year so I'll have all the prerequisites to take it."

"You'll have to tell me all about it and how it is."

"I will, definitely. You should take the class too. You need an English credit to graduate anyway, why not take a fun queer class?"

"Well, with my science workload, I certainly won't have time to take it early. But maybe junior or senior year, like you were saying. If it fits my schedule."

"In the meantime, I'll just tell you more about how amazing Dr. Greenwood is." Elle looped her arm over Tess's shoulder, moving her as they began walking together.

* * *

Tess dreaded chem lab, and yes, she felt she had enough experience to confirm that the upperclassmen were not exaggerating. The labs were just as miserable as everyone said they were. They were so strict about the most pointless, anal things. Tess figured Dr. Morgan must be a sadist who got off on failing people. Because every rule, every grading principle, was in place to tear down students.

In lab they were forbidden from asking questions. It was silly, because for one, they were there to learn, and two, if students could ask questions, they would have avoided at least two chemical burns and one minor fire that year. But talking of any kind was forbidden, and when time was up, experiment completed or not, you had to be cleaned up and out the door, otherwise you lost an entire letter grade for every minute you stayed late.

Despite everything, Tess was getting by. Miraculously, her TA, who was a nice human being unlike stupid annoying ego-stroking Dr. Morgan, helped their lab section without docking points. The actual grading, however, was different because Dr. Morgan gave out the final grades herself. And Dr. Morgan, well…she had a stick up her ass. Every week Tess was bitter about losing points over stupid little things. But despite the annoyance, Tess realized something.

Dr. Morgan was consistent. She didn't just blindly dock points. Evidently, she had an exuberantly long list of requirements for each lab report. Failure to adhere to all meant a suffering GPA, but there was clearly a list of expectations being followed to a T. As the weeks went by, Tess was learning. Not so much about chemistry, but she was learning what Dr. Morgan wanted. She started her own checklist so she never made the same mistake twice. Although Dr. Morgan always found something wrong with Tess's lab reports, the seventy percents became eighty, and the eighties became nineties. It was a ridiculous amount of work, but Tess felt oddly smug every time Dr. Morgan had to write a better grade on her lab report. She desperately wanted *one* one hundred by the end of the semester, imagining Dr. Morgan's pained expression as she reluctantly wrote the 1-0-0.

Because Tess believed, despite the rumors, that if earned, Dr. Morgan would give out a one hundred percent. Her grading wasn't impossibly unfair, as evidenced by her consistent grading rules. She was just strict, and Tess was cracking her code.

Then one week, everything changed.

Tess shoved into the chemistry building but slowed as she neared the classroom, noticing that one of her classmates was crying hysterically in the hall. Tess stopped just behind the girl and listened as she pleaded with their TA.

"I can't let you in because your prelab isn't complete. You know the rules." Their TA's arms were crossed like a club bouncer.

"But that's an automatic zero," the girl wailed. "You know they don't let us have a dropped lab."

"But I can't let you in, unless—"

"I couldn't finish my prelab because my mother just died!" The girl sobbed harder. Tess's eyes widened. "I've missed so many classes because she got sick and then the funeral—but I couldn't skip lab today because I didn't get the paperwork filed in time for an excused absence. I just don't know how to do this one calculation. That's the only thing I don't have done. Please, I'm doing everything I can."

Their TA clearly felt horrible, but sneakily helping them out during lab was a lot different from breaking rules out in the hallway. Too many people were listening, frankly. Dr. Morgan could be right around the corner, and if he broke the rules, he could lose his job and then possibly his stipend for grad school.

"I'm sorry, but I just can't."

Tess stepped boldly up beside the girl. "We've got five minutes before lab starts, right?"

"Well, yes."

"Perfect. We'll be right back." Tess grabbed the girl by the arm and pulled her back down the hall a few paces. "I'm going to help you out, all right? I'll walk you through the problem. We have enough time before lab starts, but we must be quick."

"Okay." The girl sniffled, nodding resolutely. "It's just this one problem."

"Okay, yeah. Make sure you've got the correct molecular weight, since it's a compound. Yeah, you probably missed a zero, it should be bigger." Tess glanced at her watch while her classmate frantically scribbled on her paper. They were running out of time, but they were going to make it. "Just flip those terms so they cancel." One more quick calculation and then they'd run into lab and—

Dr. Morgan suddenly rounded the corner, immediately zeroing in on the two girls.

"My, my, what have we here?" The professor's voice was low and predatory.

Tess jumped slightly at the intrusion, and the girl beside her shook, shrinking back against the wall.

Dr. Morgan walked straight to them and yanked the girl's prelab from her hands. She looked at the paper, tsking as she shook her head. "Copying homework in the hallway...cheating on your labs...Of course, this will be an automatic zero." Then Dr. Morgan tore the prelab straight in half and threw the pieces of paper back into the girl's face. Immediately, the girl began sobbing uncontrollably. Dr. Morgan nodded, seemingly pleased with herself, before continuing off down the hall. "That's going on your student record, and the university takes academic dishonesty very seriously," she declared as she left the scene.

The girl fell to her knees, struggling to collect the pieces of her prelab scattered all over the floor. "I'm going to get expelled," she wailed. "I'm going to fail this lab and get kicked out of school, all on top of my mother dying and—"

Tess clenched her fists and snarled. "Yeah, well *fuck* her." The strength of her words caused the girl to cut off with a gulp. "She can't just…bully students. We weren't even doing anything wrong. We weren't cheating!"

"Hey, lab is starting," their TA shouted from the lab doorway.

Tess reached out and pulled her classmate up off the floor. "Hey, listen. Go home, calm down, and don't stress about lab, okay? After lab, I'm going to find Dr. Morgan and give her a piece of my mind."

"You—you have a death wish." The girl hiccupped.

"Maybe. But it's not right what she did. I don't give a rat's ass about her scary reputation. The way she treated us, *you*, isn't right. And it stops now."

The girl wiped her nose on her sleeve, standing more firmly. "You should just let it go. You'll only make things worse for yourself."

"I can't watch you get kicked out without saying anything."

"Girls. Tess. Lab," their TA called again.

"You need to go," the girl said. "I, um, well, thank you, for trying to help, I mean."

"Yeah, no problem. Now go home and rest." Tess darted into lab.

All of lab, Tess was fuming, but she did her best to keep a level head. She was still determined to get that one hundred, despite the odds. But in her downtime, she plotted. There was a lot she wanted to bark at the obnoxious woman, but she needed to remain mature, level-headed, and composed.

Once finished, she marched straight out of lab and right to Dr. Morgan's office. The university had been plagued by that bully for far too long. Enough was enough.

Dr. Morgan's office was in the back corner of the chemistry building. Every office door had a window which, according to university policy, was not allowed to be covered, so Tess could easily see into the office. The room was arranged with bookshelves along the back wall, and Dr. Morgan's desk was front and center. Sitting at her desk, facing the door, was Dr. Morgan, nose-deep in a stack of papers.

Tess firmed her stance, and with determination, she lifted her fist and knocked.

Without raising her head, Dr. Morgan glanced up over the rim of her reading glasses. She made eye contact with Tess and raised one eyebrow skeptically before raising her wrist and tapping on it to alert her to the current time. But Tess didn't care what time it was. Instead, she just knocked harder, refusing to stop banging until Dr. Morgan opened the door. Her message was received as the professor stood with a huff and walked to the door, opening it an inch.

"My office hours are over for today," Dr. Morgan stated firmly, immediately slamming the door shut again.

Tess blinked a few times, processing. Then, only further annoyed, she began to pound on the door again.

Dr. Morgan's head cocked slightly, but she continued ignoring Tess. She sat back down, flipping through papers as if nothing was happening. Irked, Tess continued to bang, escalating in force and speed. She figured that eventually the commotion would force an intervention, and if not, Dr. Morgan had to leave at some point. Tess's calendar was empty. She could stand there and bang for hours.

It didn't take hours. Only a minute later Dr. Morgan grew visibly tense, pressing hard against the pen in her hand. Her eye twitched. Then, her head snapped up.

"Go away," Dr. Morgan shouted. "I have office hours again tomorrow."

"I need to talk to you now."

"Unfortunate. Send an email."

Tess fought back a snarl. "I'm here now. If you'd just talk to me, I'd be done and gone already."

Dr. Morgan, again, continued to ignore her. She looked over her papers with more forced determination than before. Tess resumed her obnoxious knocking. She watched the muscles of Dr. Morgan's jaw tighten, her brow folding. Then Dr. Morgan let out a dramatically loud huff, flying up from her desk as she stormed to the door, jerking it open.

"Fine," Dr. Morgan snapped. "You're incessant and beyond annoying. But fine! Come in, speak your mind, then get the hell out of my office."

Dr. Morgan stormed back to her desk, falling down with another huff. Tess followed the professor in and stood by an empty chair, too angry to sit.

"It's about what happened in the hall before—" Tess began, but Dr. Morgan cut her off.

"Yes, you were copying homework. I won't forget your face in an hour. You are right in coming here, though."

Tess blinked in confusion. "I am?"

"Yes. It seems I forgot to take down your name to report you for academic dishonesty as well."

Tess nearly scowled, but instead of barking out the long list of insults she wanted to say, she bit her tongue and composed herself.

"No," Tess said evenly. "We weren't cheating. You jumped to conclusions and—"

"Do you take me for an idiot?"

"I—"

"I've been teaching for nearly a decade. I know cheating when I see it."

"Her mother just died!" Tess snapped, her emotions getting the better of her. In response to her outburst, a sinister grin grew across Dr. Morgan's otherwise calm demeanor, which only fueled Tess's bubbling anger.

Tess sank her fingernails into the skin of her palms, squeezing her fists as hard as she could. Clearly, Dr. Morgan thrived on riling others up. Tess wouldn't let her get the upper hand. She focused on her breathing before she spoke again.

Much calmer, Tess continued, "Her mother just died. It was sudden. She's behind because she missed lecture. The only reason she came today was because you were going to give her a zero since she didn't get the paperwork filed about missing lab…

paperwork that isn't flexible for emergencies. She only needed help with the math of one question, and I was just explaining the concepts so she could do the math herself. Just so she could finish the problem and get into lab. Have a little mercy and drop the lab for her."

Dr. Morgan was silent, studying Tess. Her eyes raked over Tess like she was her prey. Slowly she exhaled.

"What's your name?" Dr. Morgan asked.

Tess swallowed roughly. This was it. She might get in huge trouble, but she wasn't going to hide and cower under Dr. Morgan's wrath. Instead, she stood taller and held her head higher.

"Tess," she answered strongly. "Tess Stanford."

"Well then, Miss Stanford," Dr. Morgan said, tapping her fingers as she reclined slightly. "Your gall is perhaps somewhat admirable, but you're a fool nonetheless. Rules and procedures exist with good reason. Do you think we've never had a student lose a loved one during the semester before? We understand circumstance, but everyone must adhere to the same policies. Rules are rules, and collaborative homework is a strict no-no, regardless of extraneous circumstances."

Tess stared into Dr. Morgan's eyes. They were shining as if she were enjoying the exchange. Tess could practically *see* devil horns growing out of her head. Slowly, Tess's face fell. She shook her head slightly, averting her gaze. "I refuse to believe it," she muttered under her breath.

Dr. Morgan scoffed, almost laughing. "You refuse to believe that rules are steadfast and that you aren't immune to the consequences? How idiotic you freshmen are, I—"

Tess's nostrils flared in anger and her gaze snapped sharply back to Dr. Morgan. "No," she stated forcefully, cutting Dr. Morgan off. The professor pulled back, as if shocked Tess had such guts. Tess continued, ignoring her reaction, "No, I refuse to believe the rumors I hear about you. I'm sure you've heard them. I can't go a full day without overhearing someone talking about how awful a person you are. But you can't be that coldhearted. I don't believe it. I refuse to believe that you're as evil as they say you are."

Dr. Morgan raised a skeptical eyebrow. "Some rumors are true, Miss Stanford," she said evenly.

"No," Tess protested further. "You're better than that. You *have* to be. Being an educator requires some level of compassion. You could have any industry job you wanted, but instead you're here in academics, making less money. You're running an intro chem lab, you have to care—"

"It's time you leave," Dr. Morgan declared.

Tess startled, caught off guard by the icy point of Dr. Morgan's tone. The professor's stare grew deadly. Tess stepped back, every instinct inside her screaming to flee, but she remained. Holding her ground, Tess said confidently, "You should drop her lab."

"Get out," Dr. Morgan snapped. Her gaze hardened further as she growled out, "*Now.*"

Tess nodded once sharply before bolting out the door, not willing to risk it further. She scurried straight out of the chemistry building, heaving air into her lungs the second she burst free into the outside world. Adrenaline pumped through her veins, and she stumbled. Suddenly, she was crying.

She was in shock, probably, as if she just narrowly survived a near-death encounter. Finally, she understood why students would drop out after having to talk to that woman. And what was worse, she wasn't even sure her near-death experience had helped at all.

Tess held her hands over her mouth as she screamed out in frustration. Fuck chemistry, and fuck Dr. Morgan!

* * *

For the next week, Tess wore a brave face. She refused to be a statistic in the list of students Dr. Morgan scared off campus and she refused to cower with her tail between her legs. She went to class, head high, exuding fake confidence.

On Wednesday, Tess filed into bio lecture and sat down beside Kai and Elle in their usual front-row seats. She pulled out her notes while Kai and Elle deeply discussed video game lore. Up front, their professors set up for class.

Someone tapped Tess on the shoulder, and she turned around at the sound of someone saying, "Look at my grade."

Behind her was the girl from chem lab, the one who recently lost her mother and who was very recently traumatized by Dr. Morgan. She held her laptop forward, open to their online grade book for chem lab. Beside their lab from last week, where a zero should have been since Dr. Morgan tore the lab report in half, was instead a null grade. Tess's eyes widened. Dr. Morgan dropped the lab.

"An A! She dropped it," the girl confirmed. "I don't know what you said to her, but…you're a godsend. Whatever you did, it worked. Thank you!"

Tess nodded and muttered out a soft, "No problem," before she turned back around. Tess tried to focus on getting ready for class, but she couldn't. All she could think about was the girl's dropped lab.

It didn't make sense. Tess was positive that her conversation with Dr. Morgan went horribly, yet Dr. Morgan had listened to her. The devil incarnate did something nice. Well…her response was reasonable; she didn't deserve too much praise. But Dr. Morgan did drop the lab. She was seemingly capable of not being evil twenty-four seven.

Tess felt proud for standing up to a bully and helping a classmate. But still, the event plagued her. She had only heard negative things about Dr. Morgan, complaints about her strictness, her overall rudeness, but never anything nice. If Dr. Morgan was ever nice, surely there would be at least one teacher's pet praising her. Tess needed to know if anyone on campus liked Dr. Morgan, so she turned first to her friends.

"I'm sorry, what?" Kai looked at Tess peculiarly. "Did you ask me if I've ever heard anything *nice* about Dr. Morgan?"

"Yeah, I'm just curious." Tess shrugged, trying to act like it wasn't a big deal, like it wasn't consuming her every thought.

"I mean, she dropped that girl's lab," Elle cut in. "That's the only nice thing she's done."

"I just want to know if that's a once-in-a-lifetime thing, or if these rumors are just really blown out of proportion," Tess explained.

Kai gestured loosely to the front of the classroom where their intro biology professors were preparing for class. "Why don't you ask Dr. Marlow and Dr. Kemper? They'll have a professor perspective on Dr. Morgan."

"Are they even allowed to talk shit about another professor?" Elle questioned.

Tess watched their bio professors for a moment, contemplating. She really admired them. Over the year, Kai and Tess had grown close to the professors. They sat in the front row and chatted amicably with them, answering and debating more serious questions in class.

"I wouldn't want to put them in an uncomfortable position," Tess concluded.

"Because they probably hate Dr. Morgan too but wouldn't bash another professor in front of a student," Elle said with no subtlety.

"Anyway, I've just been contemplating it, but no one has anything positive to say. Everyone thinks she's an awful person who's never done anything nice ever."

"Except she dropped that lab."

"I know. It's driving me crazy. How could she be the worst person imaginable, but then she listened to me and dropped that lab? It just doesn't make sense."

"The nicest people are capable of evil on the worst days... maybe the evilest people are capable of good on the best days."

"Elle's right. You're never going to understand why she did it. But what's important is that you helped that girl. Cut your losses and be glad it worked out as well as it did."

"You're right," Tess admitted. She should let it go. She certainly couldn't confront Dr. Morgan again and demand she explain herself. That would be absurd.

* * *

Tess tidied her papers, waiting for her TA to check her out of lab. Another intro chem lab done, which was one lab closer to the end of the semester. Every week, finishing a lab felt like a blessing.

Tess stepped out of lab and retrieved her backpack from the lockers. The weather outside was nice, and she was hoping to meet up with Elle and Kai. She itched to escape outside to freedom. The gross chemical smell of the chemistry building always bothered her.

She started toward the main doors but then paused, remembering she needed to pick up a package. For efficiency's sake, she should leave the chem building through the side doors near the mail room. Tess course corrected, although there was one issue with her new direction: She had to pass Dr. Morgan's office.

It doesn't matter, Tess firmly told herself. As she neared Dr. Morgan's office, she noted that the lights were on. Her peripheral vision caught Dr. Morgan sitting at her desk, but she kept walking.

At the end of the hall, she shoved open the first set of glass double doors, the sun shining enticingly outside. She couldn't wait to meet up with her friends. Her hands settled on the handle of the next door.

Her feet stopped. She bit her lip.

Suddenly decisive, she turned and marched back into the chemistry building.

She paused at Dr. Morgan's office, hesitating, watching the professor through the window in the door. She needed to know, for her own peace of mind.

Tess raised her fist and knocked.

Dr. Morgan glanced up on reflex but immediately glanced away again, ignoring Tess. Tess expected as much, so she continued knocking.

After a spell of incessant knocking, Dr. Morgan said, "My office hours are over for today. I suggest you leave."

A bit irked at Dr. Morgan's stubbornness, Tess wanted to keep knocking just to annoy her. But she wasn't there to start trouble. Instead, she stilled her hand.

"I just wanted to say thanks."

Dr. Morgan glanced up, but then she looked away again without a word. Tess just stood there, watching. She took in the way Dr. Morgan sat, her posture, how she held her pen, how her reading glasses balanced on her nose. Dr. Morgan looked so normal… Under different circumstances, Tess would have no reason to be fearful of her. Actually, she wasn't scared of Dr. Morgan anymore, not now that she knew the professor was capable of good. That busted a crack straight through her terrifying act.

Eventually, Tess asked, "Why?" Dr. Morgan's hand stilled, frozen midwriting. "Why? That's all I want to know. Why did you listen to what I said?"

Another beat of silence passed, and Dr. Morgan remained frozen. Tess sighed. She wasn't going to get anything from Dr. Morgan. She turned to leave, but then she caught movement out of the corner of her eye and looked back into the office.

Dr. Morgan walked to her office door and pulled it open a crack in invitation before returning to her desk. Slowly, Tess pushed into the office. She stood, watching as the professor shuffled through papers.

"You're irritating," Dr. Morgan offered as explanation, her back turned to Tess. "I figured if I didn't listen to you, you'd be the type to come bang on my door every day until I caved. Really, I did it selfishly, so you'd leave me alone."

Tess let her words sink in, then she smirked. "Worked out well, huh? Considering I'm back here again."

Dr. Morgan stilled, tentatively turning to face Tess. "Yes, well…it was to be expected that you'd want answers."

Tess took her time digesting Dr. Morgan's appearance. She was gorgeous, truthfully. Her light blue eyes shone scarily, like daggers. Compared to her earlier fury, however, her eyes currently held a softer curiosity. There was an alluring glint shining in her eyes, a playfulness, something Tess never expected to see. Near instantly, Tess was addicted to it.

Before, Dr. Morgan just seemed like a rude jerk, carrying on an unnecessary ruse. But Tess was starting to see there might be more to the woman, just as she suspected. What Tess previously viewed as harsh intimidation, she now suspected was fierce confidence. Tess wondered what other character traits she might uncover in Dr. Morgan if she just pushed harder.

The two stared at each other. Other students would cower under Dr. Morgan's stare, but not Tess. Not anymore. Now Tess wanted to memorize every fleck in Dr. Morgan's eyes, every line on her face, every curve of her features.

Dr. Morgan broke their intense stare, turning away dismissively. Tess should have left, but she was too swept up in her new revelations.

"I knew they were wrong about you," Tess whispered. She wasn't sure if she'd intended to vocalize that or not, but now she felt bold. She continued, "I think you like intimidating people. It gives you a sense of power. Maybe it's how you choose to challenge students to better themselves, to grow thicker skin or stronger backbones, I don't know. But I knew you weren't all bad. You've got to have some compassion hidden in you somewhere."

"You're jumping to a lot of conclusions with no supporting evidence," Dr. Morgan retorted, but there was no bite. Her comment was soft, and with the way she was pointedly avoiding Tess's gaze, she seemed bashful. That reaction, Tess thought, was evidence enough.

"I think there's more to you than people give you credit for, Dr. Morgan."

Dr. Morgan looked at Tess with a slight shake of her head. "I think it's time you leave."

Tess didn't want to push too hard. But before she slipped away, her eyes involuntarily drifted to Dr. Morgan's hands resting on her desk. The professor wasn't wearing any rings... no wedding band on her left hand's ring finger.

As Tess left the chemistry building, she replayed their interaction in her mind. She could still vividly picture Dr. Morgan's beautiful eyes and could hear Dr. Morgan's commanding tone. She shivered, trying to control her arousal. Trying—and failing—to keep her fantasies from running wild, already imagining what that commanding tone would sound like in the bedroom.

* * *

Kai's and Tess's favorite pastime was friendly pestering their favorite intro biology professors. Dr. Kathy Marlow and Dr. Debbie Kemper were magnificent women and everything Dr. Morgan wasn't. They were compassionate where she was harsh, understanding where she was unyielding. They cared.

Tess wanted to believe that Dr. Morgan cared too. Maybe she didn't act very caring, but she was certainly capable. Tess felt her life mission was to prove Dr. Morgan had a receptively kind heart, but then she caught herself. Why did she care so much? Let bitter professors be bitter professors. She'd rate Dr. Morgan one out of five on ratemyprofessors.com at the end of the semester, graduate in another three years, and never give Dr. Morgan a second thought. It didn't matter.

But good professors *did* matter. Dr. Marlow and Dr. Kemper cotaught one of the intro biology classes and had done so for many years. Hundreds of students took intro bio every year, as it was a prerequisite for many tracks, so there were several sections offered. However, Dr. Marlow and Dr. Kemper's section was by far the most greedily sought after. Their classes were interactive and rewarding in ways normal lectures weren't. They treated their massive classes like small, intimate groups, learning every student's name. They nurtured creativity and collaboration. They also employed a handful of students that had already aced the class as teaching assistants to guide discussions, a coveted position.

Kai burst into the lecture hall and ran to the front with Elle and Tess hot on her heels.

"They're getting rid of the koi pond!" Kai exclaimed, rushing up to their bio professors. "What are they doing with the fish? Are they just going to get rid of them? Kill them?"

"Yes, crazy things they're doing," Dr. Kemper said, humming in agreement as she clicked around on the computer, bringing up the class slides.

"They can't just do that."

"We all signed a petition," Tess said. "They asked if students wanted to keep it, and we all voted to keep it."

"They don't care what students say at all." Kai huffed, frustrated.

"Well now, you don't know the results of that poll," Dr. Marlow said. "Sometimes funding comes with stipulations, so in order to build and expand, unfavorable things must be done."

"Maybe if you protested," Dr. Kemper suggested.

"We could chain ourselves to the trees around the pond so they can't dig it up."

"Please stay safe," Dr. Marlow said, ushering the girls to their front-row seats.

In many ways, Dr. Marlow and Dr. Kemper complemented each other. They were both married and mothers to several. They were supportive, always encouraging their students and getting to know them personally. However, Dr. Kemper was more gregarious, and Dr. Marlow more reserved.

Throughout the year, Kai and Tess had spent a lot of time with their biology professors outside of class. Initial trips to office hours as attentive students turned to curious discussions which shifted into casual chats. They'd drop by unannounced, whenever, to tell the professors about their day.

Kai shared her grandiose ideas about improving the school or society in general. She'd chat about her classes or rant about chem lab. Dr. Marlow told them to look on the bright side; Dr. Kemper agreed with them and even sometimes called Dr. Morgan names that Dr. Marlow never approved of. When Tess landed herself a lab position spring semester, she was humbly bashful, but Kai insisted on bragging. They were all extremely happy for Tess.

Tess couldn't imagine college without their deeply personal relationships, and she feared what would happen after they finished the intro class.

Dr. Marlow began class with, "We have a fun announcement to make. We're looking to hire new TAs for next year. There's an application online, so please, if you're interested, apply."

Kai jabbed Tess in the ribs. "We're getting those positions, right?"

Tess wasn't sure she was cut out for tutoring freshmen and leading class discussions, but working alongside the bio professors for the foreseeable future did sound amazing.

"Come on, please? It'll be so much fun."

Tess's gaze locked with Dr. Kemper, and Dr. Kemper shot her a wink.

"Okay, let's apply," Tess said, nodding with confidence.

SOPHOMORE YEAR

"Ready for our first baby bio TA meeting?"

Tess eyed Kai curiously. "Baby bio?"

"It flows off the tongue. Alliteration, or whatever Elle would say."

"I don't think freshmen appreciate being called babies."

"That's how it works. You start at the bottom of the food chain. We're like older siblings now. We help the freshmen, but we also tease them."

"Fair."

Just as Kai and Tess could derail the professors' office hours with their own antics, so could they derail the weekly TA meetings. It was fun, though, getting to know everyone through friendly banter. Their professors' personalities shined even more during TA meetings. Dr. Kemper brought snacks and often derailed the conversation as often as Kai did. Dr. Marlow laughed along with everyone, but she was the only reason they ever accomplished any work. The TA meetings would soon become Tess's favorite time of the week.

When they arrived at the meeting, Tess's attention fell on the professors. Dr. Marlow looked drained, Dr. Kemper looked frustrated, and their tones matched.

"Yes, I know, but I think it's a bad idea," Dr. Marlow said. "It would be better if we kept the meetings separate. Sure, there are plenty of universities pairing their bio-chem program between the biology and chemistry departments. But chem complained for years until we gave them bio-chem. So, I find it a bit distasteful that now they're begging for our help."

Dr. Kemper scoffed. "Don't be absurd. She'd never beg."

"What are you two talking about?" the senior TA asked.

"We're getting an extra weekly meeting, a codepartment meeting to discuss the bio-chem program," Dr. Kemper explained.

"But chemistry just took over bio-chem my freshman year."

"They can't handle the biology, but god forbid Margaret ever listen to reason. Or—oh no!—be wrong."

"Are you talking about Dr. Morgan?"

Margaret. Tess pictured Dr. Morgan's dark hair and striking blue-gray eyes. She imagined calling her Margaret. It made her even more human to have a first name.

"Yes, she's insufferable," Dr. Kemper snapped, but then she looked at Dr. Marlow sheepishly. "I'm sorry, but she is, and you know it. She makes it impossible to have a civil conversation about anything. She's always argumentative and combative. Meetings with her are the worst. We didn't get a single productive thing done today because they told her they're moving her office to the biology building, and she threw such a massive hissy fit the whole meeting was shot."

Tess's ears grew hot. "She's moving over here?" She fought to keep her voice as level as possible, feigning disinterest.

"Yes. The bio-chem major isn't getting much traction, and they think the more inviting hands-on approach of the biology department will help. What better way to advertise inclusivity than to have the head of bio-chem over here in the newer biology building?"

"I forgot Dr. Morgan's the head of the bio-chem program," one junior said. "My freshman roommate switched majors when he learned she was in charge of the program."

"I think the move will be good for the program…good for her too, maybe," Dr. Marlow admitted. "But I don't want to be her guinea pig while she learns her manners."

"I don't know why she's complaining so much," Dr. Kemper said. "I know it's not what Margaret wants—she was very vocal about her displeasure—but this building is way nicer than the chem building. She's getting a huge upgrade."

"I get that they want our good attitude to rub off on her," the other junior said, "but I'm with Dr. Marlow. I don't want to endure her while she's learning her manners. Her attitude is terrible. I think they should just appoint a different head, someone that not everyone hates."

"Unfortunately, her name is worth more," Dr. Kemper admitted with so much effort that it looked physically painful. "Margaret is…next-level smart. It makes sense for the university's image that she's leading a department. I mean, the board practically wet themselves they were so excited when she expressed interest in bio-chem. I'm sure that's why they gave the program to chem in the first place."

"Regardless, I'm dreading having her in the same building as us."

"Not just the same building, but the same *floor* as Dr. Kemper."

"When is she moving over here?" Kai asked.

"Trying to plan when you need to start taking the back staircase up?" the senior joked.

"I'd imagine she'll be settled in by the start of next week."

Tess survived intro chem lab. She passed the only class she had to take with Dr. Morgan. Her interactions with the grouchy bio-chem professor were a thing of the past. And yet, something pulled at her.

* * *

"Want to go pester Dr. Kemper?" Kai asked Tess after class Monday morning.

"Sure, might as well."

They headed upstairs to the second floor where Dr. Kemper's office was, but then Kai gasped. "Crap, I forgot I need to print out my homework before class. I need to run to the library. Wanna come with?"

"Nah, I have class over here next, so I'll just hang out. Maybe I'll stop by lab and plan some experiments," Tess replied, waving Kai off.

Alone, Tess stood in the hallway, contemplating. She should go get some lab work done while she had the time. Or she could go chat with Dr. Kemper as they'd originally planned. She glanced down the hallway. Nothing looked different, but something felt different. Decisively, she headed down the hallway, checking the name plates on the office doors as she went.

On the opposite side of the floor from Dr. Kemper's office, Tess found Dr. Morgan's new office. That entire section of the biology building was void of undergraduate students, which was odd, considering the other sections were always packed with students chatting and studying.

The bio-chem professor's general demeanor might have been enough to deter most students, but not Tess. Tess found the professor distant and mysterious, like a puzzle demanding to be solved. For someone with a steadfast reputation for being icy, why would she suddenly go against her nature, listen to Tess, and kindly drop that girl's lab last semester? There was something more to Dr. Morgan.

As Tess neared the office, she found the door was cracked open about half a foot. She glanced inside. The space was far nicer, and larger, than Dr. Morgan's previous office, enough room so that her desk was to the side of the door, out of view. Straight in was a two-person couch with a coffee table facing the door, illuminated by a huge window. Unlike her office in the chem building, this space was more nicely decorated. There were several potted plants, a few art pieces, and colorful pillows on the sofa.

After inspecting the room, Tess glanced back toward the desk where Dr. Morgan was sitting, working furiously. She was grading a stack of papers, clearly unimpressed with the students' work.

"Unbelievable," Dr. Morgan grumbled under her breath. "Didn't you learn anything in undergrad?" She furiously scribbled with her red pen, muttering further profanities. She was clearly stressed and hardly making any progress, nitpicking every little detail.

She was cute, all frustrated like that.

Tess knew how to grade. It was one of her TA jobs, and she graded a graduate exam for her principal investigator last year. Confident in her abilities and wanting to ease the frown lines from Dr. Morgan's face, Tess reached up and knocked gently against the open office door.

Dr. Morgan jumped slightly, clearly too distracted to notice how long Tess had been standing there. When she looked up, a scowl grew across her face. "I'm busy," she stated harshly, and then quickly added, "*Obviously*. Shut the door on your way out."

Tess ignored Dr. Morgan's comments and instead stepped forward. "Are you grading exams?"

"I would be if you weren't interrupting me."

"Would you like some help?"

For a split second, Dr. Morgan seemed caught off guard. Her eyes widened and she stilled her writing. But then she recovered and huffed. "There's a reason I'm grading these myself. I can't trust incompetent TAs to grade when my own PhD students barely have a single brain cell."

"I could still help though. I've got experience grading. If you have a grading key, I'll just follow along."

"Grading keys are for professors who don't know their own material."

"All right." Tess shrugged. "I don't need a key. I'll just follow the ones you've already graded, and if I have questions, I promise I'll ask."

"I don't want you asking," Dr. Morgan stated bitterly. "There's a reason I don't teach undergrads. Explaining basic concepts is repetitive and dull."

"Who says I don't know the basic concepts?" Tess was becoming irked by Dr. Morgan's stubbornness.

"Are you a senior?"

"No."

"Then get out of my office."

Tess stayed, unfazed by the sharpness but irritated by Dr. Morgan's obstinance. But Tess was obstinate too, so she reiterated her suggestion. "Are you sure you don't want help? You could take a break, and I promise I'll grade every bit as harshly as you do. Scout's honor."

"Get out," Dr. Morgan snapped harsher.

Tess wanted to push. She wanted to snap that Dr. Morgan was being ridiculous, refusing help. She wanted to prove that she was more than capable of grading some papers. But…she deflated, realizing that what she *actually* wanted was to steal a glimpse of that kinder side of Dr. Morgan. Was last year a fluke? A one-off? Getting through to that side of Dr. Morgan, if it truly existed, would take more patience and strategic planning.

Tess nodded, retreating from the office.

* * *

Dr. Margaret Morgan was on a mission, dragging a box of chemistry notes to the dreaded biology building. The place where annoying premed kids congregated, where ecology students tracked in mud, and where there was an overall lax attitude about proper procedure that drove her mad.

Reaching the quad, she concluded, based on the lack of students, that it was the late afternoon, meaning there would be few annoyances around.

"Margaret!"

Well…some annoyances, then. Margaret scowled. She continued walking toward the biology building, defiantly ignoring her name.

"Blasted, Margaret, I said wait up!"

Margaret slowed as it dawned on her that it was Friday, the day of her friendly get-together of dinner and wine. Anyone else

Margaret would have blown off. But this was heartbroken Amy who needed a friend.

Dr. Amy Greenwood was loved by some and a headache to many. She fought to make campus a safe space for queer students, pioneering the women's and gender studies program. To those students, visibility mattered. Being an openly gay professor meant she naturally fell into a mentorship role for queer students. When the old white men of the English department scoffed at her Queer History and Literature course, she kept fighting for those students.

Margaret could hear Amy stubbornly saying, "We've been around since the beginning of humankind. Our community has influenced every aspect of the world's culture. You simply can't have history without the gays."

Above all else, Amy believed in what she taught, and she believed in spreading positivity, adopting a happy-go-lucky demeanor. At times Margaret found herself almost envious of the ease with which Amy could be so outgoing and friendly. However, last summer had been particularly hard on Amy, forcing Margaret out of her comfort zone.

Margaret had met Amy back in college, but they fell apart, realizing they wanted different things. Amy wanted monogamous love and stability…Margaret was looking for passionate, heartbreaking flings. But they reconnected a few years back, realizing they'd settled in the same city. By then, Amy had found her soulmate. Margaret listened over coffees as Amy explained the magical romantic affair she'd nurtured for years, then later shared quips with Amy's partner, Susan, over dinners. But then, after nearly twenty years together, on the first day of summer, Susan had walked out.

Not knowing who else to turn to, Amy had evidently chosen Margaret, as the biochemist was suddenly caught in a whirlwind of sobbing phone calls, Amy absolutely desperate for distraction. At first, Margaret just showed up, went over to Amy's to be a presence so she wouldn't have to face the hollow emptiness of her house alone. Then, she offered actual distractions: wine nights, movies, card games. To fill the awkward silence while

Amy cried in her arms, sometimes Margaret would include tiny details about her own life. And so, they had become somewhat close "friends," as Amy would call it, and now Amy seemed better, her spirits higher, rejuvenated by the new semester.

"You didn't say wait," Margaret deadpanned, turning to face Amy.

"What?" the other woman asked, panting, bent over with hands on her knees.

"You never said to wait, you just called my name." There was a twinge of humor to Margaret's tone.

"The 'wait' was implied." Amy stood up straight then, pressing her hands to her hips.

"I'd hate to assume." Margaret smirked.

Amy frowned but then scoffed in recognition. "Are you teasing me? I didn't think you had a humorous bone in your body."

"I don't know what you're talking about." Margaret turned sharply then and continued to the biology building while Amy tripped after her. "What are you doing over here? Our routine is to meet at your place at seven."

"I had some free time, so I thought I'd spend it with my friend."

Just as Amy said this, a student passed them. He noticed them too late and startled, dipping away. Margaret scowled.

"Must you be so friendly?" she snapped. "I have a reputation to uphold."

"Mmm, yes, that big, mean, scary reputation of yours." Amy rolled her eyes. "We'd certainly hate for your students to learn that you actually care about them."

Margaret narrowed her eyes sharply. "If you keep sprouting lies, I'm locking you out of my office."

"Oh, your office! I need to see your new space. You set up the plants I gave you, right? And the artwork?"

"I'm stuck in the biology building." Margaret huffed with distaste. "I should at least try to fit in."

"Making your office homey and inviting is hardly specific to the biology department. We fine arts individuals have a leg up on all you grouchy STEM people. I would like a tour though. The building was recently updated, wasn't it?"

"Yes, because it *caught fire*," Margaret said, appalled. "You'd think of all the science buildings, it would be the chemistry building going up in flames…flammable chemicals, exothermic reactions. But no, the biology building caught fire because of their lax safety. Someone is going to get seriously hurt over here."

"I thought it caught fire because of some faulty wiring."

"Well, if they didn't stack cardboard boxes full of flammable loose papers everywhere, maybe the fire would have been contained in the furnace room."

"Well, either way, it looks nice now. Ooh! Is this your office?"

"Yes, come in."

"Maybe you do have a taste for interior design. It's nice in here. Not as maximalist as I like, but very neat and orderly, just like you. I love the brightness of the plants. And this couch is"— Amy flopped down—"heavenly. I could nap here." She glanced around. "The artwork I gave you adds a little something extra, but nothing is personal."

"Personal? It's a work office."

"You haven't got a single picture of a loved one. Not a picture of your lover, or your family, or even, god forbid, your best friend." Amy waggled her eyebrows.

"That's because I haven't got any of those things in my life."

"Oh, I know you haven't got a—hey!" Amy snapped once her friend's words registered. "I am too your best friend. Oh, you're teasing me again. I swear, Margaret. You listen to me. If you ever let me take a picture of you, I'd have it framed and sitting on my desk, I promise you that."

"It's unnecessary clutter."

"It shows you have a heart."

"I have no such thing."

"Lies!" Amy said, but then she laughed. "You're horribly obnoxious."

"Relax for a moment while I finish unpacking this."

While Margaret worked at unpacking, Amy took to annotating a novel, one she taught in her queer literature class. Margaret knew she'd read the book many times before, could possibly quote certain passages from memory, but also knew skimming through the familiar pages comforted her. Her "comfort books" were a topic that had come up plenty over the summer.

The sun started setting, casting a warm glow into the office space. Margaret started leafing through papers, scribbling down notes. She would have been content working for the rest of the evening. Both women were easily swept up in their work. Maybe that was why Susan had left Amy. Maybe that was why Margaret didn't have anyone waiting for her at home either.

"Do you want to go to the bar?" Amy asked abruptly, breaking the hours of silence that had stretched between them.

Margaret's routine was to go to the bar on Saturday, and she greatly disliked breaking her routine. However, Amy's presence was a welcomed change. She could shift her bar trips to Fridays. But should they? Margaret enjoyed entertaining new partners to forget old ones, but Amy wasn't like her.

"Come on, please." Amy pouted. "I just want to talk to someone, casually, maybe. I just…" She paused and fixed Margaret with a determined stare. "I'm lonely, Margaret, and I miss having sex."

Margaret raised a surprised eyebrow and snorted, finding Amy's wording amusing. "I'm more than willing to help, but I know how attached you get. I don't want you getting hurt."

"I don't even remember how to flirt." Amy sighed, sinking further into the couch. "But I'm an extrovert, and I need more."

"I suppose we could go to my local spot. I'm close with the owner. We could have some drinks, maybe find some women to chat with."

"Yes, that. That's precisely what I need right now."

"All right."

* * *

Tess wanted to get to know Dr. Morgan better, so she needed to figure out something to chat with her about. The one thing she knew Dr. Morgan loved without arguing was science, particularly her own research work. Which meant all Tess had to do was learn Dr. Morgan's research, study it enough to be vaguely competent, and then she was in.

At the next TA meeting, before the biology professors arrived, Tess seized the opportunity.

"I heard some comments about Dr. Morgan's research," Tess said nonchalantly. "It sounded interesting. Do any of you know what her work's about?"

"Genetic disease research, I think," the senior said. "She does pharmacology and drug discovery work."

"She does a ton of o-chem," one of the juniors said, groaning. "I don't understand how anyone can do organic chemistry. That shit's a different language, I swear."

"I love working in Dr. Logan's lab, but I don't know. If I had the time to work in two labs, I think I'd want to do research in Dr. Morgan's lab," Tess said.

"Geez, do you have a death wish? Her grad students are the most miserable people I've ever seen."

"Yeah, and she has a super high turnover rate. She forgets that we're students. Mistakes are part of learning, but she doesn't let people make mistakes. Be glad she doesn't take undergrads, because she'd absolutely slaughter you."

Tess felt an insistent need to defend Dr. Morgan's research. "Okay, but the work is still interesting."

"Whose work is interesting?" Dr. Marlow asked as she stepped into the conference room with Dr. Kemper.

"We were just talking about Dr. Morgan's research," Kai said.

"Ah, yes, well...she does great work, that's for sure. Her research is interesting, and I will admit she gives fantastic chalk talks. But don't let anyone know I was going around complimenting her."

"She's smart and does great work, but she's just holed up in her office all the time," Tess said. "I get that she's not really a team player, but it's like she doesn't even try..."

"She's probably just busy," Dr. Marlow said. "I'm sure her plate is full of grant applications, writing papers, and building the curriculum for bio-chem."

A workaholic. So Tess was definitely on the right track. Talking about Dr. Morgan's favorite thing—work—would be her best shot.

A week later, after trudging through Dr. Morgan's published research papers, Tess finally felt confident enough to approach. She found Dr. Morgan in her office, working as usual. Tess wasted no time and knocked on the ajar door.

Dr. Morgan paused, but only to shoot Tess a look of contempt. "Oh, it's *you* again," she said. "I suppose telling you that I don't have office hours now isn't going to help."

"No, it won't, because I already know you don't have office hours right now. May I come in?"

"No."

Despite Dr. Morgan's answer, Tess stepped into the office. She glanced around, noting some new scribbles on the wall-mounted whiteboard. There were drawings of organic reactions, and Tess recognized some details from her review of Dr. Morgan's research.

Dr. Morgan watched her almost curiously but remarkably said nothing and didn't fight her to leave. After a moment, she turned back to her work, ignoring Tess.

Noting Dr. Morgan's distraction, Tess picked up some papers from her desk. She scanned the writing, realizing she was holding either notes or data from Dr. Morgan's research.

"I've been reading up on your research," Tess said, breaking the silence. "I won't claim to understand all of it, but I find it interesting."

Without missing a beat, Dr. Morgan stated icily, "I don't accept undergraduates on my research team." Then she harshly snatched her papers out of Tess's hands.

"Oh, I know." Dr. Morgan cocked her head to Tess's response. "I mean, I'm not looking for work," Tess explained. "I'm already working in a lab. But I still find your work interesting." She pointed at the whiteboard. "That's the molecule you discovered, right? For the cancer drug? And those are the reactions to get the chemical properties you need? That's my understanding, anyway. I'm sure there are a lot of details I'm missing."

Dr. Morgan reclined, folding her hands in her lap as she finally gave Tess her full attention. "What do you want?"

Tess shrugged. "I'm just wasting time before my next class… Beats sitting around twiddling my thumbs."

Dr. Morgan frowned. "Well, you're keeping me from my work, so kindly leave."

"Are you kicking me out?" Tess asked innocently.

"Considering I told you to not come in in the first place, yes."

"I don't want to be too much of a bother, but I hope someday you'll tell me about your work. I keep asking other people, but they only know bits and pieces. I'd much prefer an explanation from the source."

Dr. Morgan didn't say anything, so Tess just nodded and turned. As she reached for the door handle, Dr. Morgan called to her.

"Miss Stanford?"

Tess's heart stuttered, and she froze. Up to that point, she thought Dr. Morgan didn't remember her. She figured Dr. Morgan thought she was some random, annoying undergrad. But Dr. Morgan did remember her, and even more, she remembered her name!

Tess's lips curved into a grin as she turned in the doorway. "Yes?"

Dr. Morgan did not match her giddy excitement. "Shut the door on your way out."

* * *

Margaret had asked that blasted man in room 314 for buffer two hours ago. That was annoying for several reasons, the first being that she had to ask for help and the second being that the man had a terribly chatty, distracted nature. Every minute she spent without the blasted buffer made her more irate.

She desperately missed the chemistry building. In her home department, she knew where everything was and she had keys to every supply closet. But in the biology building, the blasted biology department lived off some unwritten code where doors that definitely should have been locked weren't, and doors that were locked, no one had keys for. And the undergraduates, blasted undergrads, were permitted to do lab work unsupervised, which meant they moved around supplies, lost things, and the absolute worst: contaminated things.

Regardless, she needed the blasted buffer, which she couldn't get herself, so she needed the man from room 314's assistance, like it or not. Out of patience, she flew down the halls in a fury, trying to locate the blasted man anywhere, since he wasn't in his office. She didn't know his name, didn't care, but she knew his face. As soon as she had the blasted stock from him, she'd lock it up because she was never going on a blasted scavenger hunt again.

As always, the biology building was full of students. Margaret's saving grace was that the biology students were terrified of her and avoided her. It made her life easier, with fewer distractions. Except when she had to hunt down annoying professors for chemicals they should have finished mixing up hours ago.

Margaret spotted him down the hall, walking away from her. He was a shorter man with crystal-white hair, very charismatic, who clearly would rather chat than work. As Margaret chased him, she noticed he was conversing with a student, but she hardly cared. Her objective was to get the buffer. When she reached him, she shot out her hand and bumped his shoulder while harshly snarling, "Hey!"

The man turned, and he had the gall to grin widely, as if they were buddies and he was happy to see her.

"Ahh, Dr. Morgan, hello," he said, seemingly oblivious that he was ignoring her chemical request. "We were just talking about you. It seems my research assistant has taken quite the liking to your work. I hope you aren't going to steal her away from me. She's my best worker."

Although she didn't care who it was or why they were talking about her, Margaret's eyes involuntarily looked at the student beside him. She paled, if only slightly, in realization.

"Hi, Dr. Morgan," Tess said meekly. Or teasingly…it looked like she was biting back a smirk.

Margaret refrained from rolling her eyes. Of course it was Miss Stanford, the only person on all of campus that she just couldn't avoid. And, of course, this girl was distracting the man, keeping him from getting her the buffer.

"You need the buffer solution," Tess said, to Margaret's surprise. "Dr. Logan was telling me about it. I'm sorry I distracted him."

"We were discussing the results of her latest experiment, and it's looking fabulous," the man—Dr. Logan, evidently—said. "The results got me excited, and we started talking about next steps and well, time flies when you're having fun." He stopped to laugh heartily, but Margaret didn't find it funny. He glanced at his watch. "Oh, yikes. I need to get to the med campus."

"The *buffer*, Dr. Logan," Margaret finally cut him off, a frill of distaste in her tone.

"I can get it for you." Tess spoke up happily, uttering an even worse suggestion.

Margaret tried to rectify the spiraling situation. "It isn't a standard stock solution—"

"Tess is extremely chemically literate," Dr. Logan stated proudly. "She's absolutely, without a doubt, the best on my team, and only an undergrad! Anyway, the recipe is on my desk, Tess. I'm sure you can work out the ratios."

"Of course."

"All right, perfect. I'll catch you tomorrow, then."

Ruefully, Margaret looked at Tess and found her watching her with that bashful yet slightly cocky smirk that was basically her signature look. Margaret couldn't decide if she despised Tess's smirk or found it alluring.

When neither moved initially, Tess spoke up. "Well, are you going to come supervise, or do you trust me enough to just mix it up and bring it to your lab?"

"Trust you?" Margaret scoffed. "Absolutely not. I'll supervise."

"I figured." She was still smirking.

"Well, get on with it," Margaret barked, feeling uneasy just standing there.

They went to Dr. Logan's lab, and Tess got to work. As Margaret did with her own students, she hovered, carefully watching everything. Usually, her students were intimidated, second-guessing themselves and making mistakes. The cowardly behavior annoyed her.

But as she watched Tess, Margaret begrudgingly admitted to herself that Tess was competent. Her hands were steady, and her measurements quick but exact. Tess had a knack for lab work. Although Tess seemed unaffected by Margaret's presence, she was also seemingly aware that Margaret would want to know each measurement she took, as she spoke every step out loud. Margaret double-checked everything, but it was all exact.

"So that's sixty-four—"

"It's fifty-six," Margaret harshly interrupted, correcting a simple multiplication error. She expected her correction to finally break the fragile façade Tess had built.

Instead, Tess chuckled. "Oh, you're right, fifty-six. I never was any good with eights."

Margaret frowned slightly, blinking in confusion. No worries, no tears, no fear…just competent calmness and an ability to laugh, even when wrong. The longer Margaret watched, the more outrageously angry she grew. Because she realized she might not…mind Tess. But that was absurd. Because Tess was just a stupid undergrad, and undergrads were annoying.

Tess held the filled jar in her outstretched hand. "All done."

Margaret snatched the jar, grumbling about courtesy and time management before she turned and fled without so much as a simple thank-you. In her own lab, she looked at the handwritten label on the side of the jar, with the chemical composition and the date, along with the initials *TS*. Tensing, Margaret shoved the buffer at one of her grad students, and they scurried away with their tail between their legs. Margaret nodded contentedly. That was how students should react to her, not whatever game Tess Stanford was playing.

* * *

Three days later, Margaret was still thinking about Tess. She could still picture the cocky grin on Tess's face as she handed the buffer over. Undergrads, especially anyone younger than a senior, shouldn't be that competent. Half the time she was fighting with her graduate students, some already with master's degrees, just to get them to perform the most basic of tasks. It was absolutely annoying that she couldn't stop thinking about Tess, some undergrad, and her elevated skills.

Margaret was definitely working in her office and was not at all just sitting at her desk playing over her interactions with Tess in her mind, when, without preamble, Tess crashed straight into her office. Margaret startled, bewildered momentarily that she had thought so hard about Tess she manifested her physically, before realizing with contempt that the student had just come to bother her again. Before she could retort, Tess flung herself down on the couch and pulled out a sandwich.

Margaret stared at her in disbelief. "What are you doing?"

"Eating lunch," Tess declared, propping her feet up on the coffee table. Margaret opened her mouth to question this further, but Tess rushed on before she could. "I have class soon in this building…not enough time to go back to the dorms, but too much time to just loiter. I usually sit in the front lounge, but it was packed today. I just needed a place to sit. That's all."

"And you chose my office, of all places?"

Tess gestured to the couch she was sitting on. "You have an entire sofa you aren't using," she replied, as if it were the simplest thing in the world.

Margaret huffed. "Yes, well, I'm busy, *working*, and you're interrupting me."

Tess shrugged. "Don't mind me." Then she pointedly flipped through some homework papers, ignoring the professor.

"Get out of my office," Margaret forcefully stated when she saw Tess was only further settling in.

"No."

Caught off guard, Margaret frowned, working her jaw. Finally, she snapped, "What do you mean, 'no'?"

"I mean, no, I'm all right staying here, but thank you."

Margaret continued working her jaw angrily, but after a moment she turned back to her work. She aggressively flipped through papers, bitter Tess wouldn't listen to her, grumbling under her breath.

For a while, they worked in silence. Margaret didn't have time to argue. She needed to work. But Tess's physical presence was still too much of a distraction, and her defiance continued to irritate Margaret so that her annoyance grew.

Margaret abruptly slammed her fists down, startling Tess. "Must you chew so loudly?"

Tess stilled her chewing and then, seemingly self-conscious, roughly swallowed. But she crossed her arms defensively, stating, "I don't chew loudly. I'm sure you chew the exact same."

"What are you talking about?" Margaret was perplexed by Tess's defiance, insisting on being contrary to every point she made.

Tess pursed her lips. "I guess I'll have to bring you lunch so we can test my hypothesis and see which one of us actually chews louder."

"I don't have lunch with students."

"Not even for science?"

"The audacity to suggest that something this frivolous could be counted as science!"

Tess's eyes sparkled with a playful glint, and she smirked.

Margaret realized, shocked and bewildered, that Tess was… teasing her. Tess was riling her up for her own entertainment, and what was worse, it was working. With another huff she turned away from Tess and her stupid sandwich and returned to her work, determined to ignore her.

Tess didn't keep eating, but Margaret still heard Tess flipping through papers and she could feel her presence, which was entirely too distracting. She couldn't stand it. Annoyed, and with her fists clenched, Margaret stood exasperatedly and demanded Tess leave.

"This is ridiculous! You can't just invite yourself into a professor's office and stay as long as you'd like."

"Well, you didn't kick me out."

"I didn't—I told you multiple times to leave," Margaret said desperately, but she sobered and sucked in a deep breath. Tess was getting under her skin. No one got through her impenetrable walls close enough to pinch and prod. Students especially would never, could never. She wouldn't allow it.

Tess smirked, evidently enjoying herself far too much.

"So you *said*," Tess responded dramatically, milking her act. "But it's not as if your actions are backing up your words."

"What are you implying?"

"I just mean, kick me out if you want me gone so badly. And I mean literally, not just chatting about it."

"You're insufferable."

Tess reeled on Margaret, pointing an accusatory finger at her. "Your threats are empty," she shot back. "You have everyone on campus cowering, but I'm figuring you out. You're a lot of bark but very little bite, and frankly, I happen to not mind barking."

Margaret's anger rose. She was growing increasingly frustrated that Tess wouldn't listen to her, being obstinate, distracting, and obnoxious. But she was also nervous because she knew that what Tess said was true. If Tess was left unchecked, it could become disastrous.

"Leave," Margaret said, harnessing every bit of her power to sound threatening. "Now!"

Slowly and very leisurely, Tess packed up her things.

"I'm heading out. Not because you said so, but because my class is starting soon, and I don't want to be late."

Margaret continued to scowl as Tess paused in the doorway and turned back with a smirk, that same infuriating smirk that was driving her crazy.

"See you tomorrow, Dr. Morgan," Tess said, then she dipped away.

Margaret moved to shove her office door shut, but she froze. "See me—wait!" she shouted, registering Tess's words. But Tess was already gone.

*   *   *

Margaret had been in a bitter mood ever since she took Amy out to the bar. That Friday was full of bad spirits, as Amy would say. Margaret didn't believe in that. She was just mad at herself.

A woman had been poorly flirting with Margaret all evening. She was attractive, but the conversation was dull. Which was unfortunate, because that was why they were there—so Amy could talk to women. Amy met a fellow bookworm, and the two were engrossed in boring talk of literature. Margaret downed another drink, desperately needing to blow off steam.

Eventually, she sought out the woman from earlier, the attractive one with dull conversational skills. She found her in the bathroom with her tongue down another woman's throat. Margaret moved to leave, to find another willing participant, but the new girl reached toward her.

"Hey there, don't be shy."

The dull blonde also regarded Margaret, who was watching the pair curiously, contemplating. "Hi again," she said. "Join us?"

It had been years since she'd last had a threesome; they weren't really her thing. However, the invitation was tempting… But then her phone rang, a crying Amy on the other end. Which was how the night ended—with Margaret consoling her friend instead of entertaining a one-night stand…or a threesome.

The following weekend, Margaret returned to her usual routine of going to the bar alone on Saturday night. She fucked a young woman senseless in the bathroom, leaving her cross-eyed in satisfaction, and then she went home with an older woman—Gail—who was good company the rest of the evening.

"Come here," Gail requested, arms outstretched, her naked form illuminated by the moonlight.

Margaret hovered at the foot of the bed and wiped off her chin. She shook her head slightly and stood, retrieving her clothes.

"Really? You don't want to cuddle, or lounge, or anything?"

"I don't cuddle." Margaret turned and walked toward the door.

"Wow, you really are a stone-cold bitch, huh?"

Margaret scowled. "Pardon? Did you not just have a good time, or was your screaming all for show?"

"Of course I had a good time," Gail said. "You're great in bed. You told me as much when you were seducing me. But you're awful at the human side of things."

"I'm not looking for a human connection."

"Yeah, clearly. Way to make a girl feel used."

Margaret just left then without another word. Gail wasn't the first woman—nor would she be the last—to call Margaret cold. Her lovemaking was cold on purpose. She performed to scratch an itch, nothing more. But Gail implying she wasn't human stung.

All week, the harsh words lingered. They cost her a fling with a stunning brunette, and when a questioning woman shot her down for the first time in years, Margaret nearly lost it. Returning to her own bed alone left her more than one type of frustrated.

Margaret never failed. She always made the discovery, got the grant, published the paper. She always got the girl. But now she didn't get her chemistry building office, she hadn't gotten laid, and a meddling undergrad was worming her way in uninvited. So, Margaret was pissed, the icing on top being the codepartment meeting with the biology department.

"Next order of business," the biology chair said. "Margaret, I'm afraid this pertains to you."

Margaret fixed him with a stare.

"I want you to partner with a biology professor to finalize the bio-chem core."

"Absolutely not," she immediately replied, crossing her arms.

"Absolutely *yes*," he copied her. "The bio-chem department is a dual-department core. You are the chemistry faculty, and you will be partnered with a biology professor."

"Who then?"

"I was thinking Maxwell—"

"I'm actually going on sabbatical soon—"

"Right, then, Alice—"

"We have a very tight deadline—"

"Well, if Terry—"

"I'm already teaching several classes; I don't think I'll have time—"

Margaret grinned impishly, enjoying as the performance of feeble excuses stroked her ego.

Amidst the desperate pleas, Dr. Kemper slammed her palms down on the table. "She doesn't want a partner in the first place, so let's stop wasting our time. Let her organize the entire core herself. She made her bed, let her sleep in it."

Margaret nodded contentedly in agreement. Though she disliked the entire biology department, she didn't mind Dr. Kemper. That woman had gall and wasn't afraid to speak her mind.

In response, the chair gave in, muttering, "Fine, never mind, then."

Once the meeting adjourned, Margaret slipped to the back to pour herself a cup of coffee. As she did, she overheard the chair ranting about an unwillingness to compromise in academics, too many big-headed britches in one room. Good. Maybe if she was a big enough pain in the ass, they'd send her back to the chem building, where everyone understood her better and the chemical smell soothed her.

In the hall, Margaret's skin prickled when she realized how many students were in the biology building. The place was packed, for whatever asinine reason. She snapped at every student in her way, their chatting mind-numbingly loud, wastes of space loitering like cockroaches. Slowly, students vacated, realizing the foul mood she was in. Students that remained slunk into corners, lowering their conversations to whispers, watching out of the corners of their eyes.

Her bad mood grew tenfold when she saw that one obnoxious student: Tess Stanford. Tess who was good at pushing buttons and Tess with her unbearable smirk! Margaret could shout every unpleasant remark that had been running through her mind all day, finally putting Tess in her place. She would run away with her tail between her legs, and she'd never bother the bio-chem professor again. That was what Margaret wanted: peace and solitude. It was high time Tess stopped challenging her.

As Margaret neared, she realized Tess was with two other students who were whining about intro chem, so they were undoubtedly freshmen. Complaints about chemistry were not okay. She'd have to give them all a piece of her mind.

"I wish you were a chem lab TA instead of a bio TA, because you'd make lab bearable," the one said.

Margaret paused. Tess was a biology TA?

"My friend was kicked out because she accidentally broke a beaker. You would have just cleaned up the glass and not said anything."

Margaret hovered behind a potted plant as the students paused near a lounge.

"I hate Dr. Morgan," the other freshman ground out. "I can't stand her. I mean, god forbid you even try to get to class in this building, because she's always lurking somewhere, waiting to snap at you."

"She does! It wears you down, always getting yelled at. She's so nasty."

"I bet she gets off on making others feel horrid. I bet she loves being rude and nasty to everyone."

Margaret had had enough. She moved to make true everything they said about her, but before she could, Tess said something that made her freeze.

"Dr. Morgan isn't a bad person," Tess said softly. "She's capable of kindness...will listen to reason when pushed. Maybe if you weren't always talking bad about her, she'd be nicer to you."

"I can't believe you're standing up for her."

"I'm not excusing her bad behavior. I know she can say extremely hurtful things and she has a lot to work on. I'm just saying it goes both ways. She wears you down with her bad comments…maybe all the rumors wear her down too. Just think about it, all right?"

The freshmen contemplated before one sighed. "Okay, you're right. I shouldn't be bad-mouthing people. I don't know if my opinion will change, but I will be more careful about what I say. I'm sure having the entire campus against me wouldn't feel great."

"That's all I'm suggesting. No one is a fully bad person, and certainly no one starts out evil. She's human, just like us. We all have things we need to work on, and we all do things that are bad. Anyway, come on, let's work on your bio worksheet."

Tess ushered the girls into the student lounge. Margaret fell farther back into the shadows.

Why would Tess defend her? Tess was much more difficult for Margaret to intimidate, but that didn't mean Margaret treated her any differently. She'd snapped at Tess, yelled at her, and certainly never done anything nice for her. There was no reason for Tess to say something positive about her.

What was worse, Margaret couldn't decide if she appreciated it, or if she despised Tess even more for not cowering like everyone else.

* * *

Margaret tended to keep her past in the past, bottled up, locked behind secure walls, packed away neatly in the farthest corner of her mind. However, since she'd been spending so much time with Amy as of late, she couldn't help but think of the past they had together.

They first met in college. Margaret was an undergraduate and Amy was in graduate school. They didn't meet at college; they attended different universities, studying vastly different topics. They met at a Pride rally.

Amy was with several friends. Margaret was alone. She used to wear a black leather jacket then, one soft from years of wear. It made her feel sexy, but also safe. She remembered locking eyes with Amy across a restaurant late one evening. Margaret was decimating an opponent in bar billiards at the time, and Amy was a drink or two in, unabashedly flirting. The events that followed grew hazy with time, but that evening sparked a very passionate, though short-lived, fling. But it was clear their relationship never would have worked long term.

Margaret, even in her younger years, was emotionally hardened. The death of her parents during high school devastated her, and she was taken in by her abusive homophobic relatives. While Amy tried to love her, she couldn't mend Margaret's heart. And Margaret didn't want her to.

They broke off their mainly sexual engagement with no bitterness and went their own ways. Margaret now knew that shortly after, Amy met Susan and moved on. Margaret focused on her work, got her degree, set up her lab, and started teaching. She, too, moved on in other ways and rarely thought back on Amy.

Until fifteen years later when Margaret was grabbing food between meetings at the campus café when someone ran straight into her.

"Watch where you're going!" Margaret scolded.

Her assailant immediately apologized, but Margaret wasn't listening, too busy staring at eyes that once regarded her passionately, soft lips she'd once caressed, and long hair she'd once run her fingers through, now turned gray with the passing of time.

"Amy?"

"Margaret?" Amy questioned just as softly. "What are you doing here?"

"I work here."

"So do I."

They just stared at each other until Amy broke, smiling as she loudly said, "We have so much catching up to do! How have you been?"

From there came the occasional meetups, coffee between meetings, dinners at home. They were friendly but not friends. They didn't get that close until the heartbreak, when Amy needed Margaret to coach her through how to live again. When Amy was sobbing uncontrollably, Margaret uncomfortably babbled about anything she could think of. After Amy chastised her that the science talk was not helping, Margaret started sharing various tidbits of her own life. That was how they grew close.

Margaret was still very much a lone wolf, someone who kept only a couple of friends at max and liked to act like she didn't even have that. Her regular sexual romps continued. She frequented bars and went home with a different woman every weekend.

"I never bring them to my house," Margaret had said. "I want to escape when we're done...but it's impossible to get a satisfied girl out of your bed if she doesn't want to leave. If we're at her house, I can just leave her in her own bed and escape myself."

She hadn't dated anyone since Amy and pointedly said she didn't want to. She liked the changing, nonserious companionship, separate from her own life.

They worked better as friends with complementing differences. Margaret was literal, a glass-half-empty type who didn't understand the point of being nice for no reason. She was a scientist. She lived by empirical evidence guiding the natural world. In her book, there was no time for feelings and philosophy.

Amy, however, loved a good metaphor, saw her glass as half full no matter what, and based every decision on feelings. She was very convinced there was a ghost in her house, which Margaret scoffed at. Still, Amy made Margaret come over and help her burn cleansing sage, listening to Margaret grumble about the "lack of scientific validity" the entire time.

Their greatest similarity was their workaholic tendency. Amy was easily absorbed into knitted words immortalizing human emotions, and she loved conversing with others, each person's mind a universe of beauty. Her own mind swam with the puzzles of literature, her heart pounded for inclusive mentorship, and her fingers itched to flip the pages of worn, banned books. That was why she was always late. There was always something beautiful and addictive pulling her in.

Margaret was also fully absorbed in work, but in different ways. She hated conversation. Her debates were short and to the point, not open for discussion. Though Amy worked diligently, she wasn't a perfectionist like Margaret. For Margaret, every little detail had to be perfect, every bit of work flawless.

Maybe that was the difference between their disciplines. Literature was romantic and fluid, science was sharp and cold, as Amy had mentioned once before.

At precisely five till seven, Margaret knocked on Amy's door. They relaxed into each other's company, drinking wine and snacking on cheese.

"I was shocked when he said Oscar Wilde was straight. The man wrote an entire gay novel, for crying out loud!" Amy howled with laughter.

Margaret stared at the wineglass she held. She didn't even crack a smile. Amy reached out to poke at Margaret.

"What's wrong?"

"Hmm? Oh, nothing."

"What are you thinking about, then?"

"What? No, I just—yes, what he said was absurd. You've grilled me plenty on the life of Oscar Wilde, and if you read *The Picture of Dorian Gray*, uncensored, of course, then obviously what a ridiculous conclusion."

Amy rolled her eyes at Margaret's long-winded explanation.

"No, come on. There's something on your mind. Tell me," Amy said before adding, "Please."

"It's nothing, really."

"Margaret, share." Amy fixed her with a serious expression.

"It's just that…I have a problem."

Amy's eyebrows raised. Margaret experienced issues— seldom did chemistry work without issue. But science problems made Margaret passionate, not downcast as she was currently.

"Explain," Amy stated.

"It's a problem with a student," Margaret admitted.

"You always have problems with students," Amy immediately barked out, seemingly unable to help herself. When Margaret fixed her with her signature glare, Amy burst out laughing. "Okay, I'm sorry, but you know I'm right. You're always complaining about their incompetencies. But please, share. Which of your grad students messed up this time?"

"It's not one of my grad students. She's an undergrad."

"Oh?" Amy sat up straighter, fully intrigued. "What crazy thing happened in lab this time?"

"No, I—" Margaret nervously ran her hand through her hair. "She's not in any of my classes, that's the problem. She has no reason to engage with me and yet…I can't escape her."

"Wait, so, there's some undergrad with no direct relation to you, but she, what, just keeps talking to you?"

"Yes."

Amy burst out laughing at Margaret's ghastly expression. "You know, Margaret, the average person is friendly and likes to chat."

"But not with me. I've spent years curating the perfect persona so I can avoid all frivolous wastes of time, maximizing my productivity. Up to this point, everyone's gotten the memo, but not this girl. I don't know how to get it through her thick skull."

"You aren't nearly as heartless as you pretend to be. Maybe this student is more observant than her average peer and she just happened to notice your notorious reputation is all a façade."

"It's not a façade. It's who I am."

"You've spent so long practicing your persona that you believe it's real now. But I know you aren't really like that. We regularly have fun interactions."

"You're different."

"What is this student trying to talk to you about? Chemistry, the weather, her life?"

"She first tried discussing my research, as a mutual point of interest, I suppose. But now…well, it's less what she talks about and more so that she keeps barging into my office, even when I tell her explicitly to not come in. The other day, she sat down on my couch and started eating lunch, as if it were a completely normal occurrence! No matter what I said to her, she wouldn't leave."

"That *is* bold," Amy admitted, "but maybe she's just used to that level of familiarity with other professors. Maybe she crashes into other professors' offices and figured she could do the same to you. I mean, you do have a very nice couch in your office."

"I don't—"

"Or maybe, it's the opposite. Maybe she's shy."

"Shy? She busted into my office!"

"Maybe she was seeking out peace and solitude. I mean, sure, you were in your office, but in general your office is quiet and would offer a good reprieve. Besides, why are you so butt hurt? It's not like you were using your couch, surely."

"Whether I was using the couch or not is not the point. The point is that she invades my space uninvited and doesn't care that she's annoying me."

Amy looked knowingly at her friend. "I think you're just upset that your scare tactics aren't working on her."

Margaret looked down at her lap, muttering, "I overheard her the other day. She said something about me."

"Oh, a new insult?" Amy asked.

Margaret was well aware that everyone knew of the rumors, and Amy in particular disliked the bad-mouthing and had been very vocal about it, but Margaret protested her response, hating when others fought battles for her. Amy now kept her tongue bit, for the most part.

"No. She was with a couple of freshmen that were going off on me. But this student, this girl I can't seem to escape… she defended me. She suggested that I was bitter because the bad-mouthing got to me, that it hurt me. She said I wasn't a bad person, that I'm…capable of kindness. Isn't that peculiar?"

"First off, I like this girl," Amy said. "The things people say about you are atrocious, so I greatly admire her ability to recognize that and point it out to others. She's got a good heart."

Margaret continued to toil over the strange occurrence. Amy sighed lightly and sat forward, resting a hand on Margaret's knee.

"Margaret, dear, she's right, you know. You can be pretty lovely. It was right for her to stand up for you like that."

"But I don't deserve it. The things people say about me aren't unfounded—I deliberately act like that so people stay out of my way. It cuts down on distractions so I can maximize my time efficiency for work. But because of this, I've been nothing but horrible to her. I never gave her a reason to believe that I was good. Why would she defend someone who's treated her so awfully?"

"It's perplexing. Humans are innately selfish creatures. We prefer revenge over mercy and compassion…but doesn't that just speak volumes to this kid's character?"

"She's a fool," Margaret grumbled. "It makes no sense."

* * *

Orgo lab was only marginally better than intro chem. It was still difficultly rigorous, but it wasn't run by Dr. Morgan, so everything was more casual. They were allowed to talk and work collaboratively, which was great because Kai and Tess were in the same lab section. Their current protocol was crystal purification. Supposedly, it was finicky, and their TA told them to not expect crystals.

"Most of you will end up with nothing, but don't panic. You didn't do anything wrong. The coordinators gave you a difficult structure to purify. Just do the steps, see what happens, and turn in whatever you get. We aren't docking for poor yields."

The lab required good time management. Kai focused hard and wasn't much for chatting. Tess tried to stop dreaming about their upcoming break and focused.

To Tess's pleasant surprise, something precipitated out of solution, so she got product, although she doubted it was very pure. She cleaned up and called her TA over to check it out.

"Oh, you got so many crystals," the TA said. "What was your percent yield?"

"Like, ninety-two? If I did the math right."

"Wait, you got all that product?" Kai's mouth hung open when she noticed the vial.

"Yeah, but I doubt they're very pure…" Tess muttered, suddenly bashful.

"No, they are, they're beautiful," their TA said. "This is really impressive. It's difficult to get product this pure even on easy reactions."

"Oh, um, thanks."

"Everyone, come look at this." The TA gestured for the other students to come over. "This is what you want when you do a purification."

"I can't believe you managed that," Kai said, slapping Tess's arm. "How'd you do that?"

Tess shrugged. "I don't know. I just followed the procedure."

"It's meticulous attention to detail," the TA said. "You must be extremely accurate with your measurements and temperatures. I'll show the lab coordinator. He'll be impressed."

"Sounds like you're going to be the talk of the chem department this week!" Kai teased.

* * *

Intro chem lab administrative duties found Margaret back in the chemistry building. She was doing inventory, a grating task since undergraduates were seemingly incapable of returning supplies to their proper homes. That, and the glassware was dirty. She'd once again need to stress the importance of proper lab checkouts. Students shouldn't be cleared to leave until everything was clean, even if they ran over time and lost points. It was important they learned proper time management skills, and it was a safety issue if the chemical residue reacted with something in the future.

"Ahh, Dr. Morgan."

She turned, noting another chemistry professor. She preferred the formal use of titles in the chem department over the first names used in the bio department.

"Do you have a free moment? I'd love to show you a crystal purification, if you have time."

"Sure," Margaret replied, more than happy to oblige him. "What did you purify?"

"Not me, a student." He grinned cheekily as they entered the other lab space. "Orgo lab did purifications this week."

"Same compound as last year?"

"Yep."

"And a student managed a remarkable purification? I seem to remember only two students got product last year, and both were horrifically contaminated."

"Yes, and we figured it would be just as bad this year, but one student did it."

"I remember when I helped you write that lab…We spent a week trying to get it ourselves."

"Yes, so you know how fickle the measurements and timing are."

"Of course. We never figured a student could manage it."

"Well, this student did, a ninety-something yield. Beautiful results from a sophomore. I think she's a bio major. Maybe we can convert her to chemistry—bio-chem. I think you'd enjoy her. Look at her crystals, truly beautiful."

Margaret rolled the vial between her fingers, watching the pure white flakes fall. Truly, it was remarkable. Beginner's luck, maybe, but clearly this student had a knack for details. She would make a great chemist…

She spun the vial to read the name written on the side: T. Stanford… *Tess* Stanford. Margaret's stomach constricted. Her mind betrayed her, flashing images of that student, with her obstinate attitude, too-big heart, and obnoxious, unbearable smirk.

* * *

Tess was roused from her studying by someone pounding on her dorm room door. When she opened it, Elle was there, flushed like she'd been running. She was vibrating with excitement, and finally, it hit Tess what was going on.

"You had your first queer lit class today, didn't you?" Tess asked, excited to hear about Dr. Greenwood and the class she desperately wanted to take.

At Elle's eager nod, Tess ushered her straight into the room. Kai was lounging on a beanbag chair with headphones on, but she perked up slightly when she saw Elle enter the room.

"Yes, we had our first class today, and it was amazing. Better than I could have ever expected," Elle gushed. "Dr. Greenwood was wonderful as always. I mean, I've been seeing her like once a week at least because there's always books I want to talk to her about, or ask for her opinion on certain writing styles and tropes, and sometimes we just end up chatting about our lives. So, we're pretty close."

"Did you do that icebreaker you were talking about?"

"What icebreaker?" Kai asked, leaning forward toward the others.

"Oh, so, apparently Dr. Greenwood does this every year. It's our introductory assignment. She sent us an email before class saying that the word 'queer' has multiple definitions. In our modern era, it was reclaimed by the community after being used as a slur against us, but before it was a slur, it meant something weird, or unusual, or unique. Something queer was just different from the norm. So, for our first assignment, we had to think of something queer about us, something uniquely special about us, to share with the class.

"She was very inclusive too. I mean, I'm like ninety-nine percent sure everyone in class is gay. But just in case, she said, 'Regardless of any identities we do or don't have, you are all a bit queer. There's nothing wrong or shameful with that, it's just personal uniqueness.' That's why she asks students to do this exercise. And then she started us off with her queer fact."

"What was her queer fact?" Tess asked. Kai nodded, eagerly interested as well.

"That her house is haunted."

Tess and Kai looked at each other, unsure if they ought to laugh or not. But Tess, unable to contain herself, snorted.

"I know," Elle said, "but she was very serious. She said she's tried cleansing the house and rearranging things, but there's something stuck. She also said that if anyone had any suggestions, she'd happily take them. And one of the student's queer facts was that they were Wiccan, and they had, like, a whole list of suggestions."

"Well, what was your queer fact?" Tess asked.

Elle froze, glancing almost nervously toward Kai.

"Is it that bad?" Tess laughed.

"No, it's just like, telling a bunch of strangers isn't that big of a deal, but you're both my best friends so I care a lot more about your opinion of me."

"Your queer fact is not going to make me think less of you," Tess said. "I mean, we're all a little bit queer, that's the whole point of this exercise, right? So, Kai and I have our own weird queer tidbits as well."

"Yeah, we aren't going to judge you."

"Ah, well." Elle rubbed at the back of her neck. "I told the class that back in middle school, I used to write *Sonic the Hedgehog* fanfiction."

Tess and Kai were silent for a moment before Kai burst out, "That's it? Dude, I never wrote fanfiction, but I have read every single Bella and Edward fanfiction to date. Including all the super weird shit."

"God, I'm surrounded by a bunch of nerds," Tess affectionately teased, rolling her eyes.

"The funny thing was, actually, someone else in the class immediately spoke up and said that *Sonic the Hedgehog* fanfiction was how they discovered the existence of gay people, a little blue hedgehog kissing a two-tailed fox twink." Both Tess and Kai burst out laughing. "And then Dr. Greenwood asked what *Sonic the Hedgehog* was, and we spent like twenty minutes showing her clips online."

"Clips like…memes?" Tess asked.

"Oh yeah. Like the weird, super roasted, far-corners-of-the-Internet stuff."

"I can't wait to take this class, it sounds like so much fun!"

"Yeah, I'm going to enjoy it a whole lot."

* * *

Tess's presence became a staple in Margaret's life. Twice a week, around lunch, Tess barged in, plopped down on the couch, and munched or did homework until she needed to go to her next class. Margaret still complained. She couldn't let Tess think she was growing fond of her. However, she kept her door open just a crack, never shut and locked, so Tess could always come in. A nagging part of her figured Tess knew this, that she was smart enough to connect the dots on her own. Still, it thrilled her.

Once again, Tess burst into Margaret's office. This time, however, she dropped a paper bag onto the desk. Tess flopped down and pulled out a sandwich, acting as if nothing different had happened.

"What…is this?" Margaret asked, skeptically prodding the bag with the end of her pen.

"Lunch. Remember when you told me I chew loudly, and I said I bet you didn't chew any quieter?"

"Perhaps…"

"Well, I figured we could test it. So, chop, chop. Start eating so we can figure out which of us chews louder."

This felt like crossing a line, so Margaret lied. "I already ate."

"One bite won't kill you. It's for science."

Margaret scoffed. "Calling this science is insulting to scientists worldwide."

"Sounds like pretentious mumbo jumbo."

Margaret shook her head, refusing to give in. However, she was curious. She had a specific palate—a "picky eater" is what Amy called her. She just knew what she liked and didn't feel the need to change up good routines. Ordering for her was bold considering the likelihood she'd disapprove.

The bag was from the on-campus café, one she frequented herself. Her order was the same every time she went: half a bowl of chicken and wild rice soup with half a tomato caprese sandwich, extra tomatoes.

She pulled out a paper bowl and popped off the plastic lid, revealing chicken and wild rice soup. Her empty stomach jumped, but she fought off a reaction. Next, she pulled out a sandwich and unwrapped it to reveal a tomato caprese. She hesitated. There was no way. Hesitantly, she lifted the top slice of bread, holding her breath.

There were extra tomatoes.

Tess eagerly watched Margaret, failing to fight back her grin. "It's your favorite, I believe," she smugly stated.

Margaret looked at Tess. "How did you…?" she began but couldn't piece together a full sentence.

Tess shrugged, focusing on her own lunch. "I've just seen remnants on your desk every now and then."

"The extra tomatoes?" Margaret managed to ask, swallowing roughly when her throat caught on the last syllable.

Tess looked at Margaret, smirking, and winked. Margaret was caught off guard by the wink and how annoyingly cute it had been. She looked back down at the sandwich, her stomach rumbling. Finally, she took a bite, sighing into the familiar and delicious flavor.

After a moment, Tess said, "You definitely chew louder than me."

Margaret wrinkled her nose. "Your evidence, Miss Stanford?"

Tess pulled up a cheap phone app. It was supposedly a decibel meter, though it was obviously fake. Still, the image of a meter ticked and sputtered.

"A decibel meter," Tess said. "Look, one thirty!"

"That's as loud as a jet engine taking off. I think you've been scammed."

"One fifty!" Tess giggled. "Dr. Morgan, you'll burst my eardrums with your chewing."

Something fluttered in Margaret's chest at the sound of Tess's giggles. Instinctively, she wanted to jump on the defensive and scold her. Instead, she turned away, her face feeling flushed. She choked out, "Haven't you a class to get to?"

"Oh, crap!" Tess knocked her things to the floor as she hastily scrambled up. In a blur, she rushed for the door.

As Tess slipped across the office threshold, Margaret said, "Thank you. For lunch."

* * *

"Don't go causing too much trouble," Dr. Kemper called after Tess and Kai as they left her office.

"Our protest will only mildly inconvenience the administrative staff," Kai said back.

"Oh, hey, it's Elle," Tess said as they rounded the corner, noting their friend who was nose-deep in a book. "Elle!"

"Hey, what's up?" Elle asked, her head snapping away from her book.

"I'm livid at our stupid university," Kai complained.

"Oh, the adjunct professor thing? Yeah, that's messed up."

"I heard some of the upperclassmen are organizing a protest. I think we should help. We do have an orgo exam coming up, but I think I'll be all right."

"Yeah, because Ms. Social Justice here is an organic genius." Tess scoffed. "I could study for the full week straight and still get a C."

"Oh, hush. You're doing better in orgo than you did in gen chem."

"Except chem *lab*, because Tess is obsessed with Dr. Beelzebub herself."

"Hey, don't call her that," Tess scolded. "Dr. Morgan is sweet, once you get to know her."

"You *don't* know her. You annoy the shit out of her, but you said yourself that you hardly talk. That's not really knowing someone, is it?"

"Okay, fine, I don't know many personal details about her, but I know she's a creature of habit who never changes her food orders. I know she has two pencil jars, and she'll go ballistic if you put the wrong pen in the wrong holder—"

"Speaking from experience, are you?" Elle laughed.

"I had to borrow a pen once, and god forbid I didn't look where I was putting it back!"

"She sounds like a pain in the ass."

"She can be in the most infuriating ways, but I think that's why I find it so fun. I like poking fun at her, lightheartedly. Really, though, I think she's lonely. As in, she's been alone so long she doesn't know how to handle affection, lonely. But humans crave companionship and friendship."

"Are you saying you're friends with Dr. Morgan?"

"I'm saying I'd like to be."

"You're crazy," Kai said.

"What book are you reading?" Tess deflected, poking at the book Elle was holding. "Is that one for your queer lit class?"

"Yep, it's *Maurice*, by E. M. Forster. The class is great. I adore Dr. Greenwood. She's actually kind of going through it right now though."

"Oh? What happened?"

"Well, I didn't want to pry too much, but she mentioned in her office the other day that her partner of like twenty years walked out on her at the beginning of summer. I didn't really ask for details beyond that, because I didn't want to pry, like I said. I just gave her my condolences."

"That sounds awful. Was she married?"

"I don't know…I don't remember ever seeing her wearing a ring. She was with a woman though, I know that much. I think she's doing okay. She's very outgoing and friendly. I'm sure she's got plenty of support."

"Well, I know you really care about her, so I hope she's well. Kai and I care about Dr. Kemper and Dr. Marlow, so we'd feel the same way if they were hurting."

"*And*," Kai stressed, "for some asinine reason, you also care about Dr. Morgan."

"I'd hardly feel bad if she was hurting. It'd just be karma," Elle grumbled.

"She is hurting. I just told you two she's lonely," Tess said. "I swear I'm going to crack through to her, and when I do, you'll both see she isn't so bad."

Kai looked at Tess pointedly. "I think you just want to bone her."

"Wait, what?" Elle howled with laughter.

Tess's cheeks flushed. "No, it's…well, it's not just that."

Both Kai and Elle roared with laughter.

* * *

Sitting and watching Dr. Morgan, while Tess pretended to work on homework, was a guilty pleasure. She always wore her dark-brunette hair in a tight bun. Tess wondered how long it was. She imagined pulling out the tie, running her fingers through the hair as it cascaded down. Tess would trace her eyes along Dr. Morgan's strong jawline, imagining trailing kisses and nipping little bites along her perfectly smooth neck.

Tess wanted to know her better. She tried to make small talk, but Dr. Morgan was huffy about interruptions, making conversation difficult. Tess, maybe foolishly, cared about her, but she wasn't convinced the professor cared for her.

Dr. Marlow and Dr. Kemper always asked about Tess's life, curious to get to know her. Dr. Morgan, however, never asked about Tess's life. Tess wasn't convinced the professor knew anything about her beyond her name and grade level.

"You're thinking too loudly."

Tess blinked out of her thoughts and looked at her. The professor was staring at her, blue eyes blazing.

"What?" Tess uttered, feeling like she was in a haze.

"I don't know what you're toiling over, but you're doing it so loudly I can't hear myself think," Dr. Morgan said, but there was barely any bite to her words. Tess could almost hear a cautious curiosity…but that was probably just wishful thinking.

"What's your favorite color?" Tess asked.

Dr. Morgan rolled her eyes. "Not this again."

"Why can't you answer the simplest question?"

"Because it's not a simple question. Simple questions are basic facts. What's two plus two? Four. That's simple. Asking for someone's opinion, their thoughts and feelings, isn't simple."

"It's one color, for crying out loud."

"Burgundy."

Surprise caught Tess, but only until she registered the shirt she was wearing. "You only said that because it's the color of my shirt and it's the first thing you saw."

"Is now a bad time to tell you that I like your shirt?"

Tess frowned. She looked at Dr. Morgan quizzically. "Are you joking with me?"

Dr. Morgan turned sharply back to her work. "Such frivolities are a waste of time."

Tess smirked giddily. "No, you were, that was a joke."

"I don't know what you mean."

After a moment, Tess said, "I like blue."

More silence followed with not so much as a grunt of acknowledgment from the professor. Dejectedly, Tess picked up her homework papers.

"You have a knack for chemistry. I'd hate to see your potential wasted," Dr. Morgan abruptly said.

"What are you talking about?" Tess felt like she had whiplash.

"You have a knack for chemistry," Dr. Morgan said again. "I think your skills would be better served elsewhere."

"What are you saying—or implying?"

"Switch your major to bio-chem."

Tess immediately felt defensive, the professor's comment striking a nerve. "You don't even know what I want to do with my degree, so how do you know a bio major isn't best?"

"Any job requiring a biology degree could more easily be obtained with a bio-chem degree."

"And how do you even know that I'm good at chemistry?" Tess asked, her tone growing sharper.

"I don't give out many A's in intro chem lab," Dr. Morgan said, "and even fewer students seem as motivated to fight so diligently to improve their grades."

Tess exhaled slowly. She fought all of freshman year for that one hundred percent, and although she ultimately fell short of her goal, she still worked her ass off. Realizing that Dr. Morgan had noticed her efforts, had perhaps been eagerly awaiting each new lab report to see Tess's improvements, made her feel fuzzy and lightheaded. Still, she never expected Dr. Morgan to remember her name, since they were all just annoying freshmen to her.

"You also managed extremely pure crystals with impressively high yield in your organic lab. Surely you understand how impressive that is."

"Yeah, I'm a good scientist," Tess said confidently. "But I'm a biologist, and that won't change."

"Fine. Waste your potential, see if I care."

Tess fought back a snarl. "Chemists aren't better than biologists. Maybe someday someone will knock you upside the head and you'll realize you're no better than anyone else." Then she stood, grabbing her things in a wave of anger, and stormed out of Dr. Morgan's office.

The absolute gall of that woman.

* * *

"Why are you in such a foul mood?"

Tess glanced at Kai. They had finally reached the last organic chemistry lab of their entire academic careers, a partner lab Tess and Kai were working on together.

Tess knew she was stewing and hardly paying attention but refused to admit it out loud.

"I'm not in a foul mood," Tess said.

"You are, and you've been in a bad mood since—oh my god! Are you still miffed because Dr. Morgan told you chemists are better than biologists? Really? We all know she thinks she's superior. She drives Dr. Kemper and Dr. Marlow mad constantly. Give it a rest."

Tess pursed her lips in annoyance. "I don't know what you're talking about."

"Stop denying it. You know I'm right."

"Okay, fine. Maybe I am miffed. She's so frustrating. She told me I was good at chemistry, but biology uses a lot of chemistry anyway, so it's not like I'm wasting some hidden talent I have."

"That's just how she is, though. All she cares about is chemistry, so she saw your chemical mixing skills and figured you could be doing better work for the chem department."

"I hate the chem department," Tess grumbled. "It always smells gross and toxic over here, and all the professors are standoffish. I love the biology department. It's where I'm happy. Besides, I want to do biomedical research. A biology degree is way more applicable to that."

"Here, do this step while I prep the next one."

"Sure. And I get it. I shouldn't expect anything else. It's just that…I thought she might care about me, that's all. Just a little compassion from a mentor to a mentee, you know?"

"She's not your mentor. She's just a university employee that you bother a lot."

"Okay, but you know what I mean. Dr. Marlow and Dr. Kemper would still care about us even if we weren't their TAs."

"That's fair."

"But clearly Dr. Morgan doesn't actually care about me, because she doesn't care about my aspirations. She didn't even ask. Just, bio-chem is better, never mind the meaningful research work I'm already doing. She doesn't care."

"Are you done with that step?"

"Yeah."

Kai started the next step and Tess sighed, looking around the mostly empty room. They were allotted one dropped lab—their lowest grade—so half the class left immediately after check-in, going home after attendance. Tess wanted to do the same, but Kai and her perfectionist self wanted to try for full credit.

The guys at the station next to Tess and Kai suddenly took off their aprons and goggles.

"We're out of here," one said.

"Did you finish already?"

"No, but we're sick of waiting around for this to boil. It takes forever. We're just going to let this be our dropped lab and get out of here. Later! Have a good break."

Tess threw back her head and groaned. "That could be us."

"Gosh, they didn't even clean up. They must really not care about their grades," Kai replied. "Actually, this could save us time. See if they got to step nine and already measured out their base buffer."

Tess peered into the hood next to her, noting a beaker with *BUF* written on it. She grabbed it and turned back to their own hood.

"Here. Do you think it's the right amount?"

"Measure it in that graduated cylinder and see."

Tess did as Kai suggested and noted that the amount was correct. "Yeah, it's the right amount. Here, use this."

"Nice, just pour it into that beaker while I add the other stuff."

"Yeah, no problem." Tess slowly began pouring.

"Anyway, back to your whole Dr. Morgan issue," Kai said. "I think you might have to accept that she's not that nice. I don't think she's going to lose her superiority complex anytime soon. Hold the beaker so I can pour the mix in."

"I know I'm just being foolish, thinking she might care." Tess sighed, taking hold of the beaker. "I don't know why I'm so determined to make her out as a nice person. I mean, I'm sure she's capable, but why should I subject myself to her abuse in the meantime?"

"Exactly. Capable or not, she's not being nice now, and there's nothing to say she'll have a change of heart and start trying."

"I guess that's true too. Besides, I honestly don't—"

"Holy shit, Tess, the beaker!"

Tess's eyes flew to the beaker she was holding, realizing it was violently bubbling. She dropped it on instinct, and both girls turned away from the hood right as the beaker exploded into a mess of chemicals and broken glass. Tess and Kai both screamed, then their TA screamed, and Tess, off-balance, fell to her knees.

Their TA immediately rushed over. Kai apologized profusely, noting the fizzling mess in the hood. Slowly, Tess stood. She focused for a moment, then looked down at her arm, which stung horrifically.

"My...arm kind of hurts," Tess said.

It was nearly summer, so Tess was in short sleeves, leaving her forearms vulnerable to the explosion. As she looked over her arm, she noticed there was a shine of liquid residue that was clearly irritating her skin.

The TA grabbed Tess by the apron, jerking her to a sink. She turned the water on and shoved Tess's arm straight under the cold spray.

"What chemical did you get on you?" the TA asked.

"We were adding the base buffer mix to the nitrogen dioxide, but then there was that reaction, so it must not have been the chemical we thought it was and…" Kai rambled, clearly panicking. But she stopped and reached out, grabbing Tess's shirt. "Shit, Tess. Your shirt looks wet. Did it get on your side too?"

"What?" Tess asked, in shock. She tried to turn and look at her side, but her arm started pulling out from under the water and their TA shoved her back under the spray.

"Okay, you need to get to the safety shower. Now," the TA snapped, finally just jerking Tess away from the sink and out into the hall. "Kai, call safety and the lab coordinator."

"On it!" Kai saluted, running for the emergency phone.

Tess stumbled as her TA dragged her to the hallway safety shower, already dreading her fate. She hesitated. "Are you sure the shower's necessary?" Her arm hurt, but surely it wasn't that bad.

"Yes. Get under that showerhead immediately, and strip!"

Tess tumbled forward under the metal showerhead, and the TA jerked a solid plastic shower curtain around her. Then, the TA tugged a chain and freezing water burst out, drenching Tess.

Tess gasped, instantly shivering. She tried to focus through the discomfort, methodically removing her clothes, careful not to invert them against her skin. She stripped to her underwear, but she'd be damned if she stripped any more. She'd rather suffer a chemical burn than stand butt-ass naked in the stupid chemistry building.

She stood shivering beside the pile of her soaking wet clothes. It was difficult to not pull her arms close to her body, but she knew she needed to maintain direct spray on her aching arm. Her side felt fine though, her clothes probably saved her.

Against the loud onslaught of freezing water, Tess tried to listen to what was happening. She heard Kai clamoring on about how emergency services were on their way but the lab coordinator didn't answer the phone. Their TA instructed Kai to run upstairs and find anyone that was trained in safety.

In the momentary quiet—other than the pouring water— Tess looked down at her arm. It would likely scar, but it wasn't bad enough to need a skin graft or anything that serious. She tried to peek at her side but couldn't see anything, so she felt with her fingers. Nothing was overly sensitive. Likely, her side was fine. Sick of the cold shower spray, she stepped back and stood so that only her arm was in the water.

Tess heard fast-approaching footsteps. Then Kai shouted, "I'm sorry in advance, but she's the only person I could find."

"I'll grab a robe for Tess," their TA said.

"Out of the way!" someone yelled. Before Tess could react, the privacy curtain was jerked back a foot.

Suddenly, Tess was eye to eye with Dr. Morgan. Tess hardly thought of covering herself. Instead, she froze, staring wide-eyed and standing soaking wet in only her underwear. Dr. Morgan's eyes dropped, and Tess blushed, until she realized the bio-chem professor was just looking at her red and raw arm.

"Is it just your arm?" Dr. Morgan asked.

"I think so," Tess replied, shivering.

Dr. Morgan looked charged. She sounded livid, like in one of her foulest moods, but she didn't seem simply mad that her day had been interrupted, or even angry that something so idiotic had occurred in lab. Instead, she seemed genuinely worried. It made Tess's head spin, and she suddenly didn't feel stable.

"Show me your arm," Dr. Morgan said, jerking the chain to stop the flow of water.

Immediately, Tess felt warmer, no longer in the direct freezing spray. When Dr. Morgan roughly grabbed her wrist, inspecting the injury, she felt even warmer.

"Here," Dr. Morgan instructed, jerking a robe from the TA's hands before shoving it at Tess. "Put this on and come back into lab. You need to keep running water over your arm, but you'll be far more comfortable doing that in a sink."

Tess nodded numbly, taking the offered scratchy robe. It provided minimal comfort other than no longer being almost nude, but she was still wet and cold. Dr. Morgan grabbed her shoulders and maneuvered her into lab, depositing her at a sink.

Tess rinsed her arm as she watched Dr. Morgan storm around the room. Her classmates shrank back, eager to stay out of the way. Kai was the bravest, staying close to Dr. Morgan, wanting to help.

"What chemical was it?" Dr. Morgan asked.

"We, um, we don't…"

"I don't have time for your stuttering. Show me the beaker."

"It exploded—"

"*Show me!*" Dr. Morgan shouted.

Kai, shaking, scurried to the hood. The beaker was shattered, and the reaction, spilled all over the hood, was still fizzling. Kai feebly tried to explain what happened, admitting their stupid decision to mix unknown chemicals from another group. Tess thought that admission was particularly brave because she knew Dr. Morgan would throw a fit and lecture them about how stupid they were.

By then, the safety team arrived. One team member was on the phone, directing an ambulance, while several others swarmed Tess. They inspected her arm and fussed over her, but she only cared about what Dr. Morgan was doing. She muttered out short answers to their questions as she craned her neck to look for the professor.

Dr. Morgan added various chemical drops to the frizzling mess in the hood. She realized the professor was testing to see what was in the concoction that burned her.

"We need to know what chemical burned you so we can better neutralize it," one of the members of the safety team stressed.

"I don't know what it was. We were—"

"The burns are from nitric acid," Dr. Morgan declared forcefully, coming up to Tess abruptly. "You added *water* to nitrogen dioxide."

"What morons label their water as 'BUF'?" Tess said, annoyed at the other lab group, but also annoyed at herself for trusting them.

"What morons mix unknown chemicals from other groups?" Dr. Morgan snapped in response.

Tess fixed Dr. Morgan with a look, but she knew the professor was right. It was dumb what they had done, and she was paying for their stupidity.

"The ambulance is outside."

"Hurry, time is of the essence with burns," Dr. Morgan said, ushering Tess along with the safety team.

"But I don't have any of my things! I need my phone and wallet and—"

"What's your friend's name?"

"What? Who? Oh, Kai."

"Kai! Bring Tess's things."

"Do I even need to go?" Tess asked. "My arm isn't even—"

"You're going," Dr. Morgan stated with finality. "The school is responsible, you needn't worry about cost. Focus on getting your arm properly treated."

Tess worked her jaw in irritation, bothered by the way Dr. Morgan kept dictating what she should and shouldn't do. She was still bitter about the "chemists are superior" conversation. Dr. Morgan was an annoying know-it-all.

"Text me," Kai said, sliding up beside them. "Call me when you're done. I'll pick you up."

"Thanks, Kai."

The safety team loaded Tess into the ambulance and the EMTs started dressing her arm. Tess thought it was all very excessive. If the school wasn't paying for the ambulance ride, she would have just walked away and dealt with it herself. Although judging from the commotion outside, Tess wasn't sure Dr. Morgan would have let her leave.

Dr. Morgan was creating a scene. She was shuffling around, fussing over every detail, and fretting, almost like a worried mother. She commented on everything, demanding they treat Tess differently if she didn't agree with their methods. Slowly, Tess's anger dissipated.

Just as they were about to close the ambulance doors, Dr. Morgan appeared at the back.

"I'll follow you to the hospital."

"Is that customary?" Tess was skeptical.

"They're going to have to properly neutralize the burn, and I'm going to insist they—"

"Hey," Tess stated more firmly, her expression softening. Dr. Morgan stopped rambling and looked up, meeting Tess's eyes. "Do you always go to the hospital with a student after a chemical burn?"

"N-no," Dr. Morgan stammered. "There's paperwork to be filed and messes that need proper cleanup, but I'm not your lab coordinator, and I can—"

"I'm fine, then," Tess said calmly. "And I will continue to be fine."

"I—"

"Really, I'm serious. Go back to whatever you were doing before Kai interrupted you."

Dr. Morgan's eyebrows tipped down, but she relented and took a step back. "Your lab coordinator is worthless. Lab coordinators should always be in the building during lab hours, for reasons just like this."

"It's a good thing you were around, then."

"Yes, well..." Dr. Morgan stepped back fully as the EMTs reached for the handles of the ambulance doors. "Maybe this will teach you to not mix chemicals all willy-nilly."

Tess snorted as the doors shut, closing her off from Dr. Morgan. Her arm hurt, but even so, her chest buzzed with warmth. She hadn't been wrong: Dr. Morgan did care. If she didn't, there was no way she would have fretted, would have been willing to give up her afternoon and take time away from her work to go with Tess to the hospital, just to ensure she was okay.

She did care. Tess was convinced.

JUNIOR YEAR

"I can't believe you survived Dr. Morgan's wrath from a chemical spill," one of the new sophomore TAs said. "That's terrifying. She scares the daylights out of me."

"Did she chew your head off? Threaten to expel you?"

"Hardly." Tess scoffed.

"That happened to someone in our class," one of the senior TAs said. "They spilled something when Dr. Morgan came by, and I never saw them again."

The TA team was leaving the first lecture of the semester and paused at Dr. Kemper's office while she collected her things. Dr. Marlow continued down the hall, questioning if they should have their start of the year meeting in the conference room.

One of the sophomore TAs suddenly yelped, "Oh, yikes." They shrank back toward the stairwell. Another squealed, "It's Dr. Morgan!"

The senior TAs shoved into Dr. Kemper's office. Kai hurried after Dr. Marlow toward the conference room and toward Dr. Morgan, who had just rounded the corner. Kai dipped behind Dr. Marlow, using her as a human shield.

Dr. Morgan stalked forward, her mind preoccupied.

As Dr. Marlow passed her, she pleasantly said, "Good morning, Dr. Morgan."

In response, Dr. Morgan scowled. However, she did reply with a terse, "Dr. Marlow," in acknowledgment.

Kai pointedly kept her head down until they slipped into the conference room. Then it was just Dr. Morgan fast approaching Tess, who was standing outside of Dr. Kemper's office. Tess locked gazes with Dr. Morgan, giving an inviting, somewhat teasing, smile while waving.

"Hello, Dr. Morgan. Enjoying the start of the new school year?"

Dr. Morgan froze a few paces back. Her scowl turned into a curious and pleasant expression. She opened her mouth, the corners daring to spike into a smile, but then she noticed the two sophomore TAs cowering nearby. The scowl returned.

"What are you gawking at?" Dr. Morgan snapped at them. "Learn some manners this year." Then she shoved past Tess harshly, disappearing down another hall.

"Are you insane?" one sophomore asked. "You said hi to her. I thought she was going to bite your head off."

Tess fought to keep from rolling her eyes. "I'm not afraid of Dr. Morgan."

* * *

Margaret was on her way to the departmental comeeting when she passed by Dr. Debbie Kemper's office. She didn't care about the biology professors and certainly didn't keep tabs on them, but she still noticed, as she approached, that the door looked closed but was actually sitting just shy of the frame. Because of this tiny gap, she could hear two people inside carrying on a conversation.

She certainly wasn't nosy, too busy to care about whatever the biology professors discussed in their offices. But she took pause as she passed because she heard her own name escape from the office.

"Did you see Margaret?"

Margaret stopped, noting the name plaque beside the door. Of course it was one of the professors Tess was close with. It seemed like she couldn't escape Tess, or her acquaintances, no matter what she did.

She was about to keep walking again when she then heard the same person ask, "And Tess's response?"

Slowly, Margaret took a step back so she could listen better.

"I think I heard Tess saying hi. That's what they were going on about at the meeting, right? About Tess's bravery?" This voice was different, likely that other professor Debbie was always with. They cotaught classes or something, or else were just very close friends—Margaret couldn't quite tell, nor did she care.

"Yes."

"I was mainly concerned that we set up the office-hours schedule."

"There's something going on between them." This was Debbie, and she said this statement with gusto, as if proud of her conclusion.

"Who?"

"Margaret and Tess."

"What?"

Margaret's heart stuttered. The same word bounced around in her head, though with more hostility. *What!*

"Dr. Morgan, the bio-chem professor, and Tess, our TA."

"No, yes, I know who you're talking about. I don't understand why. You think there's something going on between them just because Tess said hi? I don't follow."

"Yes, precisely," Debbie stressed. "When you passed Margaret, Kai was literally hiding behind you. That's the behavior I expect from students around Margaret—hiding, cowering. Sage and Ila, for example, both slammed themselves into the stairwell to hide. Students fear her, Kathy."

"Okay, and your point?"

"So, Margaret passed you in the hallway, and you said hi to her because you're suicidal—"

"I'm nice."

"Yes, and we love you because of it. But all our TAs scampered away to avoid Margaret except Tess. Because Tess, unlike all the other students, said hi to Margaret as well."

"Well…Tess is also nice."

"Sure, of course. Tess is wonderful. But there wasn't any hesitation with her comment."

"Comment? She said hi."

"And she asked if Margaret was enjoying the new school year. That's more than you even offered in greeting."

"Still a common thing to ask."

"But even more perplexing was Margaret's response. Remember how she responded to you?"

"She greeted me. I hardly see—"

"Please." Debbie scoffed. "She was scowling the entire time, acting like your comment was a waste of time."

"Well, probably, knowing Margaret."

Margaret scowled.

"But when Tess addressed her, Margaret stopped. And she didn't lash out at Tess. I thought she might actually smile."

"She does smile, you know."

"Sure, sadistically! But I'm talking just a pleasant, genuine smile. Like she was happy to see Tess."

Margaret pulled back from the door abruptly. She didn't have *feelings* for Tess. She wasn't *happy* to see Tess. What a preposterous accusation. Irritated, she stormed away to the meeting so she wouldn't be late.

In the boardroom, she poured herself a cup of coffee and made her way over to the table, still stewing. How dare some biology professors speculate about her life. How dare they insinuate there was something between her and Tess.

"Howdy, Margaret."

Margaret looked up abruptly, only to find Debbie waving at her. She walked up with her colleague before plopping down right beside Margaret.

"What do you want?" Margaret growled.

"Kathy and I were just talking about our marvelous TA team this year, and it got me thinking. Have you given any more thought about having TAs in the bio-chem department?"

"For lab. You can't expect a lab course to run smoothly with only one professor, not that I'd expect either of you to know, since your research is void of a laboratory." She meant for this comment to cut. She was aware the other two professors researched pedagogy, giving out surveys rather than doing experimental benchwork.

"I meant in the lecture classes, of course," Debbie said, countering flawlessly. "Kathy and I published a paper last semester detailing the benefits of having TAs in class. You should read it. Modern pedagogy is just as important as the scientific benchwork. We are, after all, an institute of learning which someone running an entire curriculum should know."

"I find your use of undergraduates wasteful."

"They're anything but, actually. Our TAs are amazing, and the students love having mentors so close in age. There's something very magical about a team of undergrads. They're exceptionally passionate and bright."

"I don't recall asking."

Debbie ignored Margaret and continued anyway. "We love hearing about Kai's passionate grand schemes. Tess too—she's bright and wonderfully curious, extremely smart. So friendly…I can't help but think she's a bit enamored with you."

Margaret inhaled her coffee, hacking aggressively. "What did you just say?" she snarled once she could suck in air again.

"Just that Tess talks about you a lot," Debbie said dismissively. "Do you know her? Tess Stanford? I don't think she's taken a class with you, so I doubt—"

"Of course I know Miss Stanford! She's the worst student here."

Motherly protection evidently flared in Kathy, the other professor, as she shouted, "How dare you? Tess is a brilliant young woman. She does marvelous work, always going above and beyond, always—"

Margaret held up a hand, silencing Kathy midspeech. "I never said she wasn't. Miss Stanford is brilliant and well-skilled. I merely meant that she has no respect for her superiors and is, without a doubt, the biggest headache in my life. Do me a favor and give her extra work. Maybe then she won't find herself in my office every other day."

The biology department chair arrived then, immediately diving into the meeting agenda. Margaret turned away sharply, crossing her arms, still stewing.

* * *

Tess ran her fingers along the bedsheet hem. She looked across the studio apartment's void of darkness, finding it unnerving. She missed walls. Slowly she rolled over and watched the peaceful rise and fall of her bedmate's chest as she slept. She was an art student at one of the other local universities. Tess crashed into her painting setup playing frisbee with Elle and a foster dog at the park and insisted on buying her dinner as an apology.

Tess tried to reason that the woman was nice, though they had vastly different views on life. They did both like cats, though, not that it was something worth building an entire relationship over. Tess wasn't trying to build a relationship anyway…probably. Sure, she'd been flirting, but she was cute! The apology dinner went well, because it was an apology and not a date, except it was a date, and ugh, why was dating so difficult?

After dinner, when they were standing in the parking lot, the woman said, "I bet you miss your cats back home. Would it help if you got to cuddle a cat tonight?"

"That depends."

"On?"

"On if I also get to cuddle the cat's owner." Then Tess leaned in and kissed her.

Tess sat up in the unfamiliar bed in the unfamiliar studio apartment. Glowing eyes stared back at her. So that was the aforementioned cat she'd been too distracted to properly meet.

The sex had been nice. Tess didn't sleep around much but had enjoyed a handful of hookups since starting college. This woman was adorable, and though she still didn't know her well, the time they'd spent together was also nice. Under normal circumstances, Tess would have fallen asleep cuddling, woken to more tender kisses, and left with the promise of a second date. But the circumstances weren't normal, and that wasn't what Tess wanted.

She was semiromantic and dreamed of finding her one person, but until then she was just enjoying life, having fun experiencing. Casual hookups had entertained her plenty, but something was shifting. Tess realized, with growing annoyance, that it wasn't what she wanted anymore. But admitting what she actually wanted? That was something else entirely.

Tess untangled herself and slid out of bed. As she dressed in the dark, she watched her bedmate's steady breathing. She crept toward the apartment door, watching for the cat, and carefully slipped out. Breathing easier, Tess made her way back to the outside world.

It was only around midnight when Tess slipped into her on-campus apartment that she shared with Elle. Kai accepted a resident assistant position and had to room with the other RAs, though she came by often, which was how Tess found her friends that evening, playing video games.

"Oh, you're back?" Elle commented offhandedly, whooping when she beat Kai in their game. "I thought you'd sleep over. I mean, it was a date, right? She seemed interested in you, and you said she was super cute, so…figured you might get laid."

"I did."

"Was it…bad?" Kai eyed Tess suspiciously.

"No, it was fine—"

"High praise." Kai scoffed.

"No, I mean, it was good. She was wonderful," Tess said, quickly correcting her statement. "It's just that…I'm not looking for anything long-term, so I just left afterward. It was just—"

"A one-time hookup for fun. I get it."

Tess retrieved a glass of water and stood watching her friends boot up another round of the game. Elle decimated Kai again and shouted in triumph while Kai watched her fondly. Interesting. Kai was clearly letting Elle win.

"Want to play a round, Tess?" Elle asked.

Tess noticed that Kai seemed disappointed, so she waved Elle off. "No thanks, I'm just going to head to bed."

In her room, Tess stared at the ceiling. She thought about kissing that woman, how when she ran her fingers through her blond hair, she wished it were brunette, and how when she licked along her jaw, she wished it were sharper. She remembered how her name sounded tumbling from the woman's lips, and how she wished her voice was rougher, more demanding. The woman was too nice. Tess wanted sass, a sarcastic and flat remark, a lighthearted insult too. When she was running her hands over the woman's soft curves, tracing kisses down her body, she wished she was an entirely different person altogether... someone older, with a doctorate, that Tess could bury her face against and whimper out *Margaret...oh Margaret.*

Tess swallowed hard. What she was thinking—and feeling— was horribly dangerous, but that made her want it more. However, her remaining thread of self-preservation screamed at her to avoid Dr. Morgan until she got over this little fixation. She should listen to that voice.

* * *

Margaret tapped her pen impatiently. It was past five on Friday and therefore officially the start of another weekend. That meant it had been two full weeks and Tess hadn't stopped by her office once.

Not that she cared.

Because Margaret didn't care. All she'd wished for was a break from Tess's obnoxious interruptions. Debbie and Kathy probably took her words to heart and doubled Tess's TA workload. It would do Tess well to have more work to focus on. She'd spend less time just sitting around, twiddling her thumbs, and wouldn't have the time to barge in unannounced. That was better for everyone involved, absolutely.

But for Tess to not stop by even once in two weeks? Oddly uncharacteristic.

Of course, Margaret hadn't seen Tess all summer, either. It was an odd adjustment. Her working routine remained the same, but it felt hollow. She realized she missed Tess's interruptions. It startled her to miss something. She missed Amy at times, but the last people she'd missed so viscerally were her parents.

She forced in a sharp breath at the memory.

Refocus.

She missed Tess's interruptions. They messed up her routine, but the interruptions were regular, and they became the new routine. Now she was bitter that the interrupted routine was being interrupted again. Margaret hated disruptions to her routine.

The transition to summer had been abrupt. The last time Margaret saw Tess was when the ambulance doors closed. She was unnerved by the racing of her heart and her instinctual desire to drop everything and follow Tess to the hospital. It felt almost personal, which it wasn't. It was just work.

Margaret knew Tess was okay, because she heard Kathy and Debbie carrying on about the incident. There was worry, scolding, and relief. Sometimes Margaret liked those two obnoxious biology professors. Tess deserved good mentors like them.

Margaret spent an absurd amount of time thinking about Tess. Thinking of Tess in her absence was an even worse distraction than her physical interruptions. Tess was an enigma driving Margaret crazy. Why would she refuse to leave her alone, and then disappear without a word over summer?

Eventually, Margaret adjusted, falling back into her old routine. Then one day, Kathy insisted on greeting her, and suddenly Tess was there. Tess, with her wavy golden hair and sun-kissed skin, with her shining hazel eyes and her signature smirk. Margaret realized, suddenly, just how much she'd missed Tess, growing excited at the prospect of more interruptions and more time spent together. She almost let her guard down, but then those obnoxious sophomores were cowering by the stairs and Margaret knew she couldn't be vulnerable in the biology building where she was foe, not friend.

But maybe in the safety of her office, behind a closed door, she could. So, Margaret waited for Tess to grace her with her presence.

But Tess never came.

Margaret tried to act like it didn't bother her. That was why she didn't let her walls down. When she let people in, she always got hurt. It was good Tess was finally done with her. She didn't have friends, and she certainly didn't want an undergrad clinging to her.

Usually, the building was empty late on Fridays, but that Friday, a noisy commotion distracted her. She figured she should at least track down the culprits and tell them to be quiet, so she followed the noise down to the conference room. Inside sat Debbie and some graduate students, all laughing.

"Some of us are trying to work in this building," Margaret snapped, "which is impossible with the way you lot are carrying on."

Debbie sucked in a breath, trying to stop laughing. She looked at her companions with a knowing expression. "And hello to you too, Dr. Morgan."

Debbie's tone caused several others to giggle, drawing Margaret's attention to the other side of the table...where she noted two undergraduates she recognized. There was Tess, whose appearance made her mouth go dry, and there was Tess's friend from the incident in lab, Kai.

Insults leapt to the tip of Margaret's tongue, but before she could release them, Tess said, "Dr. Morgan, you cut your hair!"

Margaret fought to counteract the way Tess's words made her face heat up. She hadn't thought about her haircut since she got it a few days ago. The length of her hair became annoying, so she lobbed it off at her shoulders. But now the bob was too short to properly pull up into her signature bun, so she'd left it down.

No one else had acknowledged the change. When people kept their eyes averted, they didn't notice changes in her appearance. She didn't want compliments anyway. They were pointless, an annoying schmoozing tactic.

Why, then, did it feel like she was dying when Tess smiled at her kindly and said, "I really like it. I think it suits you"?

"Did I ask?" Margaret barked out defensively. She felt wobbly, like she wasn't in control, and she hated it. She turned to Kai. "Get ahold of yourself and stop wheezing like a dying dog. Keep the noise down!"

* * *

The door slammed behind Dr. Morgan, and Tess pinched her hands between her knees.

Plan "Avoid Dr. Morgan" had been going decently well, but she hadn't expected to see her with her hair down and short. Dr. Morgan looked infinitely more gorgeous with her short bob. What Tess wouldn't give to run her fingers through that hair, to grab a fistful and pull, arching her head back, to lean down and nip, to kiss—

"I think you rendered her speechless," Kai squealed. "Did you see how she froze up when you complimented her?"

"I know, I think she was blushing." One of the graduate students chuckled.

Tess gave an indifferent shrug. "I just thought she looked nice, and the words were out of my mouth before I could stop them."

"The cut does suit her," Dr. Kemper agreed. "She looks like an actual woman now as opposed to her drill-sergeant-tight bun."

"Maybe she'll be nicer now that her hair isn't pulled so tight," Kai said. "Release some tension, you know."

Tess shifted uncomfortably. She was feeling a lot of tension, all of which she was dying to release…the source just several offices down the hall. She really shouldn't. But that haircut! And Dr. Morgan's piercing eyes, and her commanding stance, and—

Tess stood somewhat roughly, forcing out a casual laugh. "I'm going to grab a drink. I'll be back."

She stopped outside Dr. Morgan's mostly closed office door. She'd done so well not bothering the professor for two weeks. She shouldn't break good habits.

Slowly, as if she still hadn't convinced herself, Tess pushed open the office door.

Dr. Morgan was just sitting at her desk, absently twirling her hair around her finger. When she saw Tess, she released her hair like it had burned her.

"What do you want?" Dr. Morgan snapped. "Come to tell me how rude I was to interrupt your fun little party?"

Tess's eyebrows bent inward, and she frowned, shaking her head. "No." Her voice was far softer than Dr. Morgan's. "I just…came to ask how your summer was." When she said this, she kicked the door shut behind her, hoping her intent to stay within the isolated bubble was clear. She sat down on the couch.

"As if you care," Dr. Morgan grumbled.

"I do care." Tess's response was immediate, automatic.

"Lies," the professor snarled in accusation, a fury in her eyes Tess hadn't witnessed since freshman year. "You come here pretending you care only because I interrupted your evening. We aren't friends. You don't want to talk to me. You don't care."

Perhaps Tess had been selfish. She wanted space to save herself but hadn't considered how Dr. Morgan would be impacted.

Tess grew bold. "You're upset I didn't come visit yet." She watched a flicker of pain shoot across Dr. Morgan's eyes. She knew she was right. Dr. Morgan was so easy to read now.

"Get out of my office. I have work to do." Dr. Morgan turned sharply away from Tess, but her bite was gone.

"I do really like your haircut," Tess said, making no move to leave. "A lot, actually." She bit at her lip. "And just so you know, I did think about barging into your office. I just wasn't sure you wanted me around."

"I don't."

Tess stared at the back of Dr. Morgan's head, since she was pointedly focusing on her computer and not Tess. The tone remained soft, just feigned disinterest. Tess missed the banter, the verbal fight but clear permission to stay. It was their thing. No, they weren't friends, but they could be, easily. If they only talked more…

"I went home over summer," Tess said. "I worked at a grocery store, a new chain. My brother, he just finished high school, worked at the local grocery store. We acted like enemies. He was on the home front, I was the enemy invading the town. He's a better bagger, but I have better customer service skills. We called it a tie, but only because I didn't mention the raise I got. Doesn't matter. The competition was what was fun."

Tess paused and waited to see if Dr. Morgan would contribute. There was nothing, but she was listening, so Tess continued.

"I went to the lake a lot, that's why I'm so tan. I really like water sports, sports in general. My brother and I were always outside doing something growing up, throwing a ball around, running races, stuff like that."

After a beat of silence, Dr. Morgan said, "I published a paper this summer." She shyly turned toward Tess, and Tess beamed at her.

"I saw. I also saw that the drug you developed was approved for clinicals."

Dr. Morgan's eyes narrowed. "Were you…keeping tabs on me?"

Tess shrugged, but the truth was, she had been. Late nights, she fueled fantasies, imagining Dr. Morgan's body. Every time Tess caught sight of the scar on her arm, she remembered Dr. Morgan's piercing eyes regarding her with full concern.

"My burn healed nicely." Tess held out her arm as bait to show Dr. Morgan. Too far away to see, Dr. Morgan was forced to approach. She took Tess's arm in hand. Tess's breath stuttered.

"You could have lost your arm," Dr. Morgan stated harshly. "Or something worse, with the explosion you caused."

"Luckily we were working in the hood."

Dr. Morgan squeezed Tess's arm and then roughly shoved it away. "You're a reckless fool."

"You were worried about me."

Dr. Morgan stated skeptically, "I thought you were always saying that deep down I just must care about my students."

Tess nodded, confident that Dr. Morgan at least cared about her. Surely that compassion could extend to others in time. She patted the space beside her then laughed softly at Dr. Morgan's bewildered expression.

"Sit with me? I—I missed you."

"Absurd," Dr. Morgan said instantly, defensively crossing her arms.

Tess dipped her head, somewhat embarrassed. "I did. And I do."

"Fine." Dr. Morgan gave in with far less protest than Tess was expecting. "However, this doesn't mean that I like you, or frankly even tolerate you, and it doesn't mean I want you here, since you're still a distraction," she grumbled, almost like an afterthought.

Tess looked over at her. "No, of course not." She smirked. "What else did you do this summer?"

"I worked."

"Didn't you do anything fun? I mean off campus, because I'm sure you could go on for hours about how fun chemistry is."

"I don't do fun things, Miss Stanford."

"I don't believe that."

"Believe what you want," Dr. Morgan replied curtly. However, she then quickly added, "Did you do anything else over break?"

Tess grinned widely, over the moon that Dr. Morgan was amenable to conversation.

* * *

Tess Stanford was becoming a new type of problem.

At first, Tess was just a headache: boisterous, demanding, and so annoying. But now, Margaret was growing fond of her.

Margaret reasoned it was only because Tess cared. No one else cared, but that was her own fault. She purposefully kept her heart locked up, buried deep behind walls, out of pure self-preservation. She kept everyone at arm's length, only regarded them when necessary, and when she fell victim to the needs of her biology, she found women in bars looking for one-night stands.

But in the past year, the walls started crumbling. The first chip came while comforting Amy last summer. It was awkward at first, but Margaret started craving affection, wishing for attention and intimacy even though it terrified her. Opening up to Amy was safe, but beyond her, Margaret fought to keep her walls up. Then Tess crashed in, being too much and not enough all at once, leaving Margaret desperately wanting more.

It was confusing. Clearly, she wanted something more from Tess. But what? She wasn't sure what she could take, what Tess would be willing to give. Maybe nothing. Maybe everything. Margaret couldn't figure out which would be worse.

Margaret knew she longed to run her fingers through Tess's hair. Tess's sun-kissed skin beckoned her, to touch and learn how soft it was. And that smirk! Margaret wanted to kiss that smirk right off Tess's smug face. She wanted to pin Tess down and make her understand that Margaret wasn't soft or loving, that she only took, used, and abused. She needed Tess to understand that she was evil. Tess was too good. She'd corrupt her, and hurt her, because that was what Margaret did.

But Margaret also wanted to make Tess beg and whimper. She wanted to know what kind of unholy sounds she could pull from Tess's throat.

"You're fidgeting." Amy huffed.

Margaret glanced up from her beer bottle, looking at her friend, who was sitting across from her at a table in her favorite bar.

"If someone's caught your eye, go," Amy said. "You don't have to stay here and babysit me."

Margaret glanced around. In truth, she'd barely noticed the strangers, attractive or not. She'd stayed in her office chatting with Tess until seven, and then she met Amy at the bar. However, the alcohol wasn't drowning out the screaming in her mind.

In lieu of answering Amy's earlier comments, Margaret tipped her beer bottle toward the bar. "Jimmy's shift just started. I'm going to say hi."

"I'll come with and grab another drink."

As they approached the bar, Jimmy called out, "Mad Dog!" in greeting.

"Hi, Jimmy," Margaret replied, automatically handing him her empty bottle as he passed her a freshly opened one.

"I've barely been in a minute, and already several women were asking about you. Oh, and hello, Amy," Jimmy said. "You know, there's a Susan here, lamenting about her lover of twenty years."

Amy paled. "What?"

Jimmy pointed behind Amy. She turned to see her ex sitting alone nursing a drink.

"Now's your chance to get some closure," Jimmy said.

"I guess."

"Go," Margaret urged. "But if you sleep with her again, I'll end you."

Amy nodded, making her way over to her ex. Margaret watched them for a moment, then she turned back to Jimmy.

"Keep an eye on her," she instructed. "Don't let them leave together."

Jimmy saluted. "Sure thing, captain. Go mingle. I can see you salivating over that cutie."

Margaret wandered off. She wasn't sure which woman Jimmy was referencing, but she spotted at least a dozen attractive women. A hunger settled at the base of her stomach. She loved sex, loved dominating women, in complete control of their pleasure as they came undone at her fingertips.

She spotted a table occupied by three women. Two were engaged in conversation, the other clearly left out, third-wheeling. She made eye contact with Margaret and grinned innocently, but Margaret could tell she was anything but.

Easily, Margaret slipped into place beside the receptive woman. The woman boldly plucked Margaret's beer from her and took a sip, making a show of her mouth. She dipped her tongue to catch a droplet on her lip, and heat surged low in Margaret's belly.

"If you'll excuse me for one moment," the woman said, running her fingers down Margaret's arm. She sauntered over to the restroom.

Margaret paused to glance back at Amy. She was leaning too close to Susan with a whimsical look on her face. Margaret should have intervened, but the sparkle in her friend's eyes reminded her of Tess. Angrily, she stood, storming toward the bathroom. She needed to get Tess out of her head immediately.

Margaret found the woman standing at the sinks, leaning forward so that the bottom of her short, tight dress crept up, exposing the lower curve of her butt cheeks. Margaret stepped behind her, caught her eyes in the mirror, and ran her hand from thigh to ass, squeezing as she leaned in and sucked at the woman's neck.

The woman spun and Margaret lifted her onto the counter, their kisses all teeth. Margaret ran her tongue along the woman's neck again, palming at her breasts. She reached into the woman's dress and pulled out one of her tits, dipping to suck a nipple into her mouth. The woman threw back her head, moaning. She pressed between the woman's thighs, rubbing at wet silk as she canted into her.

Margaret bit the nipple in her mouth, trying to elicit a yelp, but she only received a heated groan in response. The woman smelled overly fruity, and her perfume was cheap. It wasn't right. *She* wasn't right.

Margaret's nostrils flared. She jerked her into one of the stalls. She shoved her against the wall and fell to her knees, hiking up her dress, shoving the silk panties aside with her thumb. She dove in tongue first, nuzzling. The woman moaned and tugged at Margaret's hair, but it was light, and she was sighing, not begging. Margaret couldn't find her footing, couldn't get the heated passion she needed. Frustrated, she shoved back, standing abruptly. The stranger looked at her quizzically but didn't fight the loss of contact.

Furious, Margaret stormed out of the bathroom. She collapsed on a barstool with a huff and jerked a drink straight out of Jimmy's hand, immediately chugging half of it.

"Hey, that was for a table," Jimmy said, though unbothered, and he immediately worked at repouring the drink. "What's wrong?"

"I'm suffering."

"I can tell. Want to talk about it?"

Margaret mumbled out a few automatic excuses. She stared at the drink she'd grabbed, displeased with the taste, but she took another large gulp anyway. Mostly, she was frustrated with herself.

"I think I know what's going on here," Jimmy said after observing his friend for a few moments. He leaned on the bar counter and pointed an accusatory finger. "You've got your eyes on someone specific...someone who isn't here tonight."

"You're being absurd." Margaret's answer was instantaneous.

"Am I? It's surprising, sure, seeing Mad Dog in love."

Margaret scoffed. "I'm hardly in love. Lust, if anything. I don't think I'm capable of love."

"Lust, huh?"

"It's entirely physical."

"But there is someone specific, then."

Margaret sighed, admitting defeat. "Yes, there's someone. My...fixation on her has grown suddenly and intensely. I find myself comparing every potential partner to her. Apparently, no one else lives up to my expectations."

"Expectations are dangerous," Jimmy pointed out. "Your special girl might not live up to your expectations either."

"Of course, but at least I'd know."

"What's stopping you from making a move?"

Margaret hesitated, drawing her finger through the condensation of her glass. "It's easy meeting a stranger at the bar and slipping into bed with them, but with someone in my daily life...That's more complicated, isn't it?" Her gaze drifted back to Amy then, and she stood abruptly. "Excuse me, I have a friend I need to save."

Margaret stomped up to Amy and pulled her friend back harshly, afraid the two women were about to kiss.

"We're leaving," Margaret stated low in warning.

"But we were just—"

"Leaving," Margaret stressed, cutting Amy off.

"She can make her own choices, Margaret. She's a grown woman," Susan said.

"You don't get to do this. You lost every right when you broke her heart," Margaret snapped. "You hurt her. You don't get to hurt her again."

"You're…right," Susan admitted. "I'm sorry for approaching things how I did."

"It's fine—"

"It's not fine. Come on. We're leaving."

"Bye, Susan," Amy uttered as Margaret pulled her toward the exit.

The two professors shoved out of the bar, Margaret a ball of furious energy and Amy a bundle of sadness, entirely occupied by their own feelings.

* * *

When Tess met back up with Kai after the TA meeting, Kai teased her. "A two-hour water break? Were all the water fountains on campus broken?"

"Ha ha, I clearly got distracted. Stop working on homework and let's hang out."

"Sure, if you fess up."

"To what?"

"You went after Dr. Morgan, didn't you?"

Tess colored. Kai laughed harder.

"You've got it bad for her, huh?"

"I'll buy you ice cream if you stop talking about this."

"Deal."

They found themselves back at Tess and Elle's apartment. Elle went out with a friend from the English department, so they had the place to themselves. Tess reclined in her bed, tossing a stress ball into the air and catching it repeatedly while Kai sat at her desk.

Eventually, Kai asked, "Do you think it's a date?"

"What?"

"Elle and her friend. Do you think it's a date?"

"To a gay bar? Don't you usually go to gay bars to meet people?"

"Yeah, but if there's a drag show, I would consider that a date. Do you know the friend she went with?"

"Not personally, but she's been at the apartment a few times."

"So, it's a girl."

Tess sat up fully, looking at Kai. "What is this? What's going on?"

"Nothing."

"You like her," Tess stated.

"No."

"Yes, you do. You're blushing."

"No, I don't," Kai snapped, somewhat forcefully.

Just then, the front door flung open, and Kai startled, nearly falling off the chair. Within seconds, Elle was in the doorway, heaving and panting.

"Oh my god, you guys, oh my god," Elle said, heaving in gasps of air.

"Where's your friend?" Tess asked, mostly for the benefit of Kai, who was doing a poor job of discreetly looking behind Elle for the mystery girl.

"My—what? Oh, Lucy. She went home. The gay bar was kind of lame. We thought there'd be dancing, but it was mainly just drinks…and kind of expensive."

"Why are you so amped then?"

"Because!" Elle exclaimed. "You're never going to guess who we saw at the gay bar."

"Who?"

"Dr. Morgan! We saw Dr. Morgan at a gay bar downtown."

Tess's heart stuttered, and Kai shot her a knowing look. Tess glanced down at the ball she was holding and rolled it, feigning disinterest. "So?"

"So?" Elle whined dramatically. "So, the devil incarnate is a lesbian."

"Just because you saw her at a gay bar doesn't mean she's gay," Kai pointed out.

"I couldn't even believe we saw her in public." Elle continued to breathe excitedly. "She looked so different, I almost didn't recognize her. And, yes, Kai. She could be bi. But! It makes so much more sense that Dr. Morgan isn't straight."

"Does it?" Tess asked. She felt the need to crawl out of her own skin, but she fought to keep her voice neutral.

Kai smirked. "If Dr. Morgan likes women, that means you have a chance with her."

Tess's façade dissolved into a horrific red face so intense she could feel it, which she buried in her hands.

"Whoa." Elle giggled. "I knew you found her attractive, but you've got a full-blown thing for her, huh?"

"I do not have a—a 'thing' for Dr. Morgan."

"You're saying that if Dr. Morgan was interested in you, which she could be, because she might not be straight, that you wouldn't want to get it on with the mysterious and aloof bio-chem professor?" Kai asked.

"She's hardly aloof. She's an asshole," Elle said.

Tess fell back on her bed, tossing the ball above her again. "Don't be ridiculous. I'd never stand a chance with Dr. Morgan, wanted or not."

"You would," Kai said, her tone full of merriment. "You most absolutely would bang Dr. Morgan, given the chance."

"I get it. She's not my type, but I get it. She's attractive in a 'stomp on me with your stiletto and spit on me' kind of way."

"Was she there with anyone?"

"I think she left with a woman, but I didn't get a good look because I was too blown away that I was looking at Dr. Morgan, out in public, at a gay bar."

Tess clenched her fist and missed the ball, which smacked her in the face. She jerked up, trying to play it off. She had no right to be jealous of what or who Dr. Morgan spent her free time doing. But she *was* jealous, especially if Dr. Morgan did fancy women and Tess had an actual chance...

* * *

"The puppy's a nightmare!" Dr. Kemper said. "My daughter swore she would train the dog, but she got bored after a week, and I'm left picking up the pieces."

"She's so cute though," Kai said, heart-eyes about the black-and-white, floppy-eared puppy dog.

"She's a terror, is what she is," Dr. Kemper reiterated.

"You need puppy classes," Dr. Marlow stated.

"Elle works with dogs."

"Oh, Elle. She picked up an English major, didn't she?" Dr. Kemper asked. Tess and Kai both nodded. "Good, she has a knack for literature. But she works with dogs, you say?"

"She volunteers at the shelter, and she walks and trains dogs part time."

"I'll have to ask her for help, then."

After class, Tess and Kai graded in the professors' offices, which turned into casual chatting until the professors needed to head home. They walked out together, the professors to the parking garage, the girls toward the on-campus apartments.

Suddenly, Dr. Kemper held out her arm to stop everyone. "Oh no, it's Miss Stick Up Her Ass."

"Don't call her that," Dr. Marlow scolded.

"Well, she's been an extra pain lately. Remember the codepartment meeting last week? Stop defending her."

Tess glanced toward Dr. Morgan. The bio-chem professor was struggling to balance several packages as she navigated campus. The others kept walking toward the parking garage, but Tess hesitated.

Elle saw Dr. Morgan at a gay bar...possibly flirting with women, possibly into women. She needed to know.

At the top of her lungs, Tess shouted, "Dr. Morgan!" Then she sprinted away from the others, as she shouted again, "Dr. Morgan, wait up."

With ease, Tess slid up beside the professor and smiled as she snatched several packages from Dr. Morgan's arms.

"Here, let me help," Tess said.

Dr. Morgan blinked in surprise before her face hardened. "Really? Now you're bothering me outside of my office?" Her comment only made Tess smile larger. "I'm perfectly capable of carrying those, you know."

"Of course, but that doesn't mean I can't help."

Dr. Morgan eyed Tess oddly, and then, in a fit of obstinance, jerked the packages away from Tess. "Stop being difficult and give me those. Now get out of here."

"And if I don't? You're being the difficult one." Tess emphasized her statement by playfully shoving Dr. Morgan's arm.

The physical contact seemed to cause a shift in Dr. Morgan. The professor grabbed Tess's wrist harshly. They stood frozen, less than a foot apart, with Dr. Morgan's hand clamped on Tess's wrist. They stared at each other, blazing blue eyes meeting equally fierce hazel. Their breathing became ragged. Tess fought to keep the strength in her stance. She almost caved under the pressure of Dr. Morgan's touch, which she desperately craved.

Dr. Morgan shoved Tess's arm back. Another beat passed, their stares still linked, but then she turned sharply and practically ran away. Tess remained frozen, her breathing erratic. She was just barely able to breathe normally again when the bio professors and Kai caught up to her.

"What was all that about?" Kai teased, smirking.

Tess fought the blush that was trying to crawl up her neck. "She just looked like she needed help," Tess muttered, rubbing at her wrist. Her skin still felt like it was on fire.

"Don't feel bad. She hates needing help," Dr. Marlow said.

"Your wrist okay there?" Kai asked, still teasing.

"She's just in a mood, that's all," Tess said, finally releasing her wrist. "Hey, I, um, forgot that I need to print some stuff. I'll catch up with you all later." Then Tess fled for the library.

* * *

Her every-other-day intrusions shifted to daily lunches, which shifted into interruptions whenever Tess had any free time. Between classes, Tess did homework in the bio-chem professor's office. In the evening, she returned. Work shifted into casual conversation that lasted until Dr. Morgan finally, almost begrudgingly, admitted that she needed to leave.

Tess wasn't sure when Dr. Morgan let her invade her space more readily, if there was a conscious choice that was made, or if it was just the natural flow of their relationship. Still, even though Tess saw Dr. Morgan upward of four times a day, every day, Dr. Morgan still always fought Tess's presence with empty threats. As ridiculous as it was, Tess didn't want Dr. Morgan to stop. The protests maintained some semblance of boundaries. If Dr. Morgan ever invited her in with open arms, like Dr. Marlow and Dr. Kemper had, Tess wouldn't survive.

Tess dropped a steaming carryout container on Dr. Morgan's desk. "If you weren't such an obsessive workaholic, you could get food for yourself, and we could stop having these dinner dates."

Dr. Morgan scoffed. "I seem to remember telling you to not get me food." She cautiously opened the container and scoffed louder. "Calzones are a poor man's pizza."

"Why? Because they can eat them on the go? I'd call that an efficient man's pizza, or an obsessive workaholic's pizza."

"What's even in here?" Dr. Morgan poked at the calzone suspiciously. "If there are black olives in here, I'm kicking you out for good."

Tess laughed. "I'm well aware of your hatred for black olives." She watched as Dr. Morgan took a cautious bite. She was clearly pleased, and Tess silently celebrated the victory.

Over the next hour, the two worked independently in content silence save for the occasional question from Tess, the offhanded response from Dr. Morgan, or her regular grumblings about the incompetencies of others. When Tess finished her homework, she faked work to appear busy. She knew if Dr. Morgan noticed her just staring, she'd more adamantly kick Tess out. So, Tess was careful to appear occupied, occasionally stealing glances.

Dr. Morgan was gorgeous, nibbling absently at her lip as she focused. What Tess wouldn't give to bite Dr. Morgan's lip, to feel the other woman's tongue trace across her own lips. She could kiss her. Would Dr. Morgan fight her? How thoroughly could she kiss back? Tess wanted to find out.

Tess cleared her throat. "Have you ever heard of O'Charlie's downtown? I hear it has good food."

Dr. Morgan's typing fingers stilled. "Why?" she replied with another question, her tone neutral.

"I was just wondering if you'd been before, if the food was good, or how the drink prices are," Tess said nonchalantly. "Kai's turning twenty-one, and we're trying to find a good bar."

"Um, yes, it's a good bar." Dr. Morgan's response had less poise than usual. "I've been a few times. I'd recommend it."

Tess almost smirked, but she pressed her lips into a thin line. She asked, as casually as she could, "Did you know it's a gay bar?"

"A common misconception."

"What?"

"It's not marketed as a gay bar and wasn't opened as one," Dr. Morgan explained. "It's just…a certain crowd gathers there, so it's gotten a reputation."

"Well, we'd fit in fine. Kai's bi and Elle's super gay," Tess said confidently. "Anyway, mind if I play some music?"

* * *

The tips of Margaret's ears were hot, irritated that Tess's orientation was the only one she failed to mention. When music started emanating from Tess's laptop, she grew more annoyed. It was electric pop noise, utter garbage.

"Turn that off immediately," Margaret snapped.

Tess eyed her, a playful glint in her eyes. "Make me."

Tess's challenging tone sparked a fury of emotions in Margaret: anger, irritation, and frustration. Tess was toying with her. It drove her mad. She was up in a flash, and charged at Tess, grabbing for the laptop, but Tess turned and flung herself down the couch.

Margaret huffed. "You're annoying and obstinate."

"This is good music," Tess objected.

"It's trashy noise." Margaret lunged again, this time diving to her knees on the couch. She crawled after Tess, grasping for the laptop, but Tess kept shoving herself farther down the couch and out of reach.

Then Tess jerked, setting the laptop on the coffee table. Margaret turned sharply and realized they were very close, face-to-face.

Tess was on her back with Margaret leaning over her. Acutely, Margaret was aware of Tess's hand hovering at her side. She was very aware of how heavily they were both breathing. And she was extremely aware of the burning ache in her lower stomach.

Tess smirked contentedly, as if this had been her plan all along, wearing the exact smirk that had been teasing Margaret for months on end. Tess arched up, her eyes pleading, and Margaret broke.

She surged forward and kissed that obnoxious smirk straight off Tess's face. She came at Tess all teeth with sharp, nipping pain, harshly shoving Tess down before cupping the back of her neck to pull her close. She bit her lip and ate the cry Tess released. Then, with a rough shove of finality, Margaret pulled back, standing away from Tess, licking her lips.

She waited for Tess to bolt, convinced she'd proven once and for all that she was wicked, rough, and unkind. But then she met Tess's eyes.

Abruptly, Tess leapt off the couch and reconnected their lips with equal desperation and force. Margaret fell back in shock, and Tess balled her fists in her shirt, clinging on for dear life. She dragged her tongue across Margaret's lips and her mouth opened in a gasp, their tongues colliding.

How foolish Margaret had been to think Tess wouldn't want her with the same extreme desperation. How had she been so blind? Misinterpreting the months of longing looks and teasing, flirting. They'd been dancing around this for months.

Margaret spun, hoisting Tess up on her desk. Items went flying, but for once, Margaret didn't care. All she cared about was kissing Tess Stanford and sucking the absolute life from her. However, Tess fighting to remove Margaret's shirt turned the professor's rational brain back on.

Tess was far too eager...too demanding. Margaret tried to pin her wrists to the desk, but Tess fought her hard. They struggled, each fighting to dominate. Of course, Tess wouldn't be submissive in the way Margaret required. Nothing about Tess's personality suggested submissive. Margaret stumbled back a step.

Tess surged forward again, but the professor stopped her. Jimmy was right; expectations were dangerous. But at least now she knew.

"We can't do this," Margaret said, serious but soft. However, Tess didn't seem to get the message, so she firmed her tone. "You need to leave." Margaret stepped farther back and crossed her arms.

Tess clearly wanted to protest, as her jaw was working wildly, but instead she simply nodded, slid off the desk, and retrieved her things. Margaret, who was used to tear-filled fits when she turned down women, expected waterworks that never came. Tess's reaction, or lack thereof, confused her.

Tess broke the heavy silence while standing in the doorway. "Good night, Dr. Morgan."

Margaret shifted uncomfortably against the ache between her legs. She wanted to stop Tess, drag her back, and claim her like all her nerve endings were screaming at her to do. But this was Tess, at school, and things were complicated.

When Margaret shut her office door behind Tess, she hit the wood with her fist, cursing.

* * *

Twelve days.

She wasn't counting...but twelve days.

Twelve days had passed since the kiss, the lapse in judgment, and she hadn't seen Tess since. Obviously, this was a good thing. She wanted to hurt Tess so she'd stop worming her way past the protective barriers. She needed Tess gone before it was too late...too late for Margaret to save herself.

But in all the times she'd imagined the scenario, she never once considered Tess might like it.

They wouldn't work in bed. Margaret liked fully submissive girls. She needed her partners pliable because she couldn't be vulnerable. She didn't like being touched in the bedroom.

Horrid memories played through her mind of her uncle backhanding her, screeching that he'd get those perverted thoughts out of her mind. She shuddered.

No. She liked pleasuring other women, worshipping their bodies without emotional attachment, purely physical connections. She couldn't give up her control and relax into their touches. She didn't trust like that.

So, yes, Margaret liked her partners submissive, which Tess wasn't. They would clash, and Margaret would grow distant, and they would both end up displeased. Margaret did not subject herself to mediocre sex. She was right to turn Tess away after only kissing.

Kissing deeply, passionately, hungrily.

It was legal. Their age difference was a bit much, but Tess was twenty-one, not a child. There was nothing in her contract forbidding her from sleeping with a student, providing she didn't have immediate control over Tess's grades, which she didn't. But it would inevitably complicate things. It already had. She hadn't seen Tess in twelve days.

Not that she was counting.

Margaret needed to move on. She'd turned Tess away. Yet, she was still irrevocably turned on from their encounter. She needed to bed another woman. The sooner she could fill her senses with another woman, the sooner she could get over Tess. Yet for some reason, picking up a stranger sounded exhausting. So, when Amy said she didn't want to return to the bar that weekend, Margaret was relieved.

When Amy swung open her door, already holding a glass of red wine, she looked at Margaret perplexedly. "Are you all right?" she questioned, sidestepping to let Margaret in.

"I did something foolish." Margaret bolted inside, heading straight for the alcohol.

Amy followed, watching as Margaret poured herself a glass of wine and downed the entire thing in a heaving gulp before pouring another.

"What happened?" Amy asked, cautiously taking a sip of her own wine.

Margaret groaned. "Do you remember that girl who was always bothering me?"

"That one sophomore, right? Although, well, I guess she's not a sophomore anymore. You haven't mentioned her in a while I assumed she'd stopped bothering you. But now I suppose that's not the case."

Margaret turned with an expression of dread. She could see Amy fighting to not roll her eyes at the dramatics. But then Margaret said, her voice heavy and eyes wild, "I kissed her."

Amy choked and her eyebrows shot straight to her hairline. She downed the rest of her wine, letting the liquid settle before she spoke.

"Okay, well, now what?"

"I haven't seen her since."

"Did you sleep with her?"

"No."

"Was she…okay with the kiss?"

"Very." The edges of Margaret's lips curled into an almost pleasant smile, but then she snatched her wineglass and downed another gulp, smoothing out the edges of her grin.

"You aren't really the kiss-and-dip type, though. You're a kiss-and-finish-the-job type. So, why didn't you sleep with her?"

"Conflict of interest."

"What conflict of interest? She's a bio major, so she's not under your supervision. She's legal, I'm assuming. And the university doesn't have anything against such relationships, provided there aren't conflicts of interest…which there aren't."

"I didn't consider the implications until a full day later, which is unacceptable. I shouldn't let my guard down like that without reviewing all possible consequences."

"No, you probably shouldn't, but you did. And you stopped. Why? Did she stop you?"

"No, I did…because I realized we wouldn't be compatible in the bedroom."

Amy scoffed. "I find it very hard to believe that you wouldn't be compatible with a receptive girl, especially since I know how experienced you are. And don't you dare say it's because she's inexperienced. I know damned well that you love being a woman's first."

"I don't think she's inexperienced…she kissed far too well. But maybe that's the problem. She knows what she wants and demands it too harshly."

"Oh, I see. She's not submissive enough for your fragile domme persona."

"Don't mock me."

"Let me repeat what I asked earlier. Now what? You seem distressed that you didn't sleep with her but also say you don't want to. I don't understand why you're acting like this."

After several moments of contemplation, Margaret sighed. "I don't know what I want, Amy. That's the problem. She used to bother me every day, and now it's been two weeks since I last saw her. I can't tell if I'm angry, or disappointed, or glad…all I know is that I'm discontent."

"So you miss her."

"Yes, I suppose, her presence at least," Margaret admitted. "But it's because of this fixation. That's why I kissed her. But I know we aren't compatible now, and clearly she's avoiding me, so it's over. I'm sure by Monday, I'll be over it."

"Right…"

Amy's skepticism was called for. Margaret was not, in fact, over it by Monday, and her temper exploded. She left disaster in her wake, screaming at students, throwing a fit. When the codepartment meeting rolled around, she was ready to kill.

"That's why I thought it would be helpful to have an information session for the bio-chem department. I don't think it gets advertised enough because not everyone knows—"

"If they don't know that bio-chem exists, they're too stupid to survive the program anyway," Margaret snapped. "Information sessions are a waste of time."

The chair rubbed his temples. They'd been going on like that for nearly an hour. Margaret came up with a pessimistic remark to counter everything said, related to her or not. She didn't care if it was grating and exhausting—the other professors were acting like imbeciles.

"Margaret," the chair said, squeezing his hands together in prayer. "Just because some of us don't like socializing with students doesn't mean that information sessions are a waste of time, nor does it mean that an information session wouldn't greatly benefit your program."

"It's not like she could host anyway, because no one would come," Debbie said, mostly under her breath, but she clearly wasn't trying to hide her comment.

"Got something to share with the class?" Margaret sneered.

"Yeah, actually. You're a terror to the students here," Debbie shouted, her patience having run dry. "Why does everything have to be a headache with you?"

"Hey…" Kathy stated in warning.

"No, I'm sick of this! What's the matter with you? You're being even more impossible than you usually are, which is saying a lot. Maybe you need a time-out—"

"Oh, a time-out. Real classy," Margaret snapped.

"Ladies," the chair clamored.

"You're all incompetent fools, everyone in this department. I wish I never had to move into this stupid building, and I wish I never had to come to these dumb meetings." She shoved her chair back and stood hotly. "I have more important things to do than sit here and listen to this idiocy."

Before Margaret could storm out of the room, Debbie also shot out of her chair. She shouted, "Yeah? Well, we have a TA meeting to get to." She grabbed Kathy's hand, jerking the woman up with her. Margaret and Debbie shoved out into the hall with poor Kathy pulled along behind them, and both women stormed off in opposite directions down the hall.

* * *

"She drives me crazy!" Dr. Kemper shouted as she shoved into the lab. "She's so immature."

All the TAs were already there. Their amicable conversations died as the professors stormed into the room. Tess looked up at them, already sensing who they might be talking about.

"Yes, I know, I know," Dr. Marlow chanted, trying to sound soothing. "But you can't let her get under your skin. She's fueled by your outbursts."

"Oh, I know it. That's the most frustrating part. I'm sorry everyone." Dr. Kemper took a deep breath to calm herself. "Our codepartment meeting with you-know-who didn't go so well today."

"Dr. Morgan's been in a terrible mood for the past two weeks," the senior TA said.

Tess chewed at her fingernail, lost in contemplative thought. If Dr. Morgan was feeling even half the pent-up frustration that she was feeling, that could easily cause such a foul mood.

But Tess wasn't avoiding Dr. Morgan this time. She was plotting.

Tess, embarrassingly enough, had nearly come undone just kissing Dr. Morgan. It was glorious. Yes, Dr. Morgan stopped them, but Tess wasn't taking that as final. There was so much tension between them. Dr. Morgan had kissed her first, so surely she wanted it just as badly. Tess needed a way to further break the professor's resolve, but she couldn't plan while in Dr. Morgan's presence because then her own resolve would break.

But Tess would be back.

* * *

"Please, Tess, I desperately need your help."

Elle stood in the apartment doorway with two dogs on leashes.

"What did you do this time?" Tess asked.

"I told the animal shelter that I'd take Tulip so she could get out and decompress," Elle explained, gesturing toward the white bully-mix. "But I totally forgot that I'm dog-watching for my regular client today." She gestured down at a dog that looked like a young German shepherd and golden retriever mix.

"And you need my help because…?"

"Because these two morons don't know how to walk on leashes and keep getting all tangled, which is how I got this." Elle gestured down to her scraped knee. "I only have them for a few more hours and I want to take them to the park to run out their energy. I just need you to walk one of them so we can get to the park in once piece."

Tess laughed, taking one of the leashes. "Of course I'll help."

"Thank you so much."

The girls and dogs headed off through campus. They slipped into one of the older neighborhoods in the greater downtown area, making their way to the nearest park.

"How's Dr. Greenwood doing?" Tess asked as they walked. "Do you see her much now that you're done with her class?"

"She's good. I saw her Friday, actually. She's trying to take down the wallpaper in her guest room because she heard that negative energy can get stuck in the fibers."

Tess laughed sharply. "If spirits can get stuck in wallpaper, surely they could get stuck in drywall too."

"Yeah, well, I don't share her weird beliefs in the supernatural either, but that's what she's doing."

"I signed up for her queer lit class next semester—I don't know if I ever told you."

"That's awesome, you'll love that class. Casper, whoa, stop!" Elle said as the golden-German-retriever-shepherd took off after a squirrel, darting straight into the road.

Tess stopped on the sidewalk, waiting with Tulip as Elle fought to regain control of Casper. She noticed they were coming up to an intersection.

"I'm going to go push the walk button so we don't have to wait through another light," Tess said, tugging at Tulip to get the little dog walking again.

Tess walked to the intersection, her attention on the crosswalk. She pressed the pedestrian button but was immediately jerked back as Tulip darted forward, barking. Tess swiveled, realizing that a jogger had run up on them. She tried to pull Tulip back, but Tulip ran around the jogger, knotting the leash around her legs. The jogger made a sort of undignified yelp.

"I am so sorry!" Tess exclaimed, cheeks flushed in embarrassment, jerking at the leash to untangle them. "She's a shelter dog. It's her first time walking on a leash."

When Tess finally managed to jerk Tulip back by the collar, her eyes panned up the jogger. The woman was wearing dark-brown leggings that hugged deliciously sculpted legs, and a cropped white shirt. The top layer of her short hair was pulled back into a tiny ponytail. Then Tess noticed the piercing blue eyes staring at her, and she let out an undignified squeak herself.

It was Dr. Morgan. Out jogging on a Sunday afternoon. Wearing skintight leggings.

They hadn't talked in three weeks. The last time they were together, they'd kissed.

"You should have better control of your dog," Dr. Morgan stated.

Tess's eyes raked back over the professor's body. She didn't even try to hide her actions. Her once-over ended, meeting Dr. Morgan's icy eyes once again.

"She's not my dog, she's a shelter dog," Tess reiterated. "I'm helping Elle."

Dr. Morgan's attention was drawn toward Elle, still struggling with Casper.

"You aren't hurt, are you?" Tess asked.

"Hardly."

"Good."

There was a charged pause. Dr. Morgan continued to watch Elle and Tess continued to stare at Dr. Morgan. Tulip tried to bolt forward, but Tess tightened her grip on the collar. Neither woman moved.

"What are you doing over here?" Tess then asked, her voice suddenly soft, as if it were a secret.

"I'm going for a run," Dr. Morgan replied in the same tone she used when someone said something stupid. Tess pursed her lips in annoyance.

"Clearly. I just meant, why here? Do you live around here?"

"Yes," she said, then sidestepped around Tess.

Tess turned as Dr. Morgan took off at a sprint, running across the street as the signal changed. If she hadn't been there with Elle, hadn't been holding on to a dog, she would have chased Dr. Morgan, pulled her behind a tree, and kissed her senseless.

Leggings? How was Tess supposed to function after seeing Dr. Morgan in skintight leggings?

* * *

Friday, Tess was making a move. All week, her thoughts were consumed by Dr. Morgan. She had to do something. But she couldn't corner Dr. Morgan until Friday because she wanted the buffer of the weekend, and Tess couldn't see Dr. Morgan before then because she would absolutely lose it herself.

Except on Wednesday, Kai interrupted her plans.

"I need you to come with me to this event on Friday, and I need you to bring Elle," Kai said.

"What event?"

"A banquet to recognize department-nominated students. They pick students who get the best grades, who show initiative in class, or who are doing great research work," Kai explained. "You know it's just an excuse for the university to invite parents so they can get donations."

"Okay, so invite your parents."

"No, because it's lame. I'm only going because they're catering a full dinner, a whole free buffet. I'm not making my parents take off work for this. But I still get two guests, so you and Elle should come."

The catered food would be fantastic…but sucking on Dr. Morgan's lips and burying herself between her thighs would be even better.

"I would…I absolutely would," Tess said quickly, "but I was already—"

"Please? I really need you to get Elle to come."

"Dude, just ask her. Elle loves free food, so obviously she'll go."

"But I need you there as a buffer. I can't just ask Elle." Kai's cheeks were red.

Tess took pity on Kai. "Okay, fine. I'll come." However, she held up her hand when Kai's face lit up. "But only if you admit you have a crush on Elle."

"I don't—a crush? That's crazy, I mean—"

"I don't have to come…"

"No, okay, fine! I like Elle, and I want to dress up nice, and sit close to her, and eat dinner together."

"All right. We'll come, but I'm leaving early so you can have some one-on-one time, maybe finally tell her how you feel." And then Tess would go find Dr. Morgan as originally planned.

On Friday, the girls did themselves up for the event. Tess, wanting to go all out to seduce Dr. Morgan, borrowed one of Kai's old prom dresses, a deep purple gown with gold accents, tight at the top and flowy at the bottom. Kai even did everyone's makeup, and they were all looking spectacular and hot.

The event was hosted in the school's ballroom, filled with circular tables. While Kai and Elle were engaged in flirtatious banter, Tess looked around the room. At the head table, she recognized the university president and the biology department chair. But one specific woman at the table caught Tess's attention.

Dr. Morgan.

She wore a black fitted suit. Her short, dark hair was pulled into an updo, held by pins that Tess longed to remove. The president was trying to converse with her, but she seemed uninterested. She kept angling herself away, and he kept edging closer, completely oblivious.

"I'll grab us drinks," Elle said. "I assume you want a lemonade, Kai. Tess, what would you like?"

Tess's eyes darted to the drink table, then back to Dr. Morgan. "I'll just come with you."

She boldly bolted toward the center of the room, weaving between tables with purpose. Elle scampered after her, dodging guests with far less grace, muttering out apologies.

Tess walked straight up behind Dr. Morgan and not so subtly bumped her shoulder. Tess continued walking, though, acting oblivious to the collision, and she went to the drink table. She grabbed water for herself and took a sip while Elle picked out hers.

Tess discreetly looked over her shoulder at Dr. Morgan. When she noted that the professor's eyes were on her, she turned more fully. Tess smugly noted that Dr. Morgan's mouth was slightly agape. Feeling emboldened by the obvious want in Dr. Morgan's expression, Tess winked, watching as Dr. Morgan visibly swallowed hard. Pointedly, Tess snatched up another water glass.

"You good?" Elle asked.

"Yep."

Elle gestured vaguely, letting Tess take the lead and walking a few paces behind her.

Tess stopped tantalizingly close to Dr. Morgan and reached over her shoulder to deposit one water glass on the table. Then Tess leaned into the professor's ear and whispered, "Feeling a bit parched, Dr. Morgan?" She pulled back as quickly as she had come and turned sharply, walking back to her own table before Dr. Morgan could react.

As they neared their own table, Elle darted around Tess and grabbed her shoulder.

"Hey, um, sorry, but what the fuck was that?"

Tess smirked impishly, sneaking another peek at the head table. Dr. Morgan still stared at her, but she was too far away to make out the nuances of her expression. Tess flipped her hair over her shoulder as she turned back to her friends, feigning disinterest.

"Wait, what happened?" Kai asked.

"Tess handed Dr. Morgan a drink, but it was super flirty," Elle explained.

"Wait, you what?" Kai asked again, but with extreme intrigue now. "Are you going to make a move?"

Tess bit her lip as she ran her finger along the rim of her glass. "Oh, I'm making a move all right."

"Yeah right. As if." Elle laughed.

"Yeah, sorry, Tess, but I have to agree with Elle. I mean, she's a bit out of your league."

"We'll see."

This was the perfect opportunity. There was no denying the blatant want in Dr. Morgan's eyes. Tess knew she looked damned hot; that was the intention. Now, she just had to seal the deal.

Eventually, they broke for food. As they fell into the buffet line, Tess fought the urge to look for Dr. Morgan.

Tess was fishing out meatballs when a presence stepped behind her and a warm hand pressed into the small of her back. Tess turned slightly, and her eyes locked with an icy blue-gray gaze. Dr. Morgan leaned toward her, and Tess's breath hitched.

"Careful, Miss Stanford," she drawled. "We wouldn't want you getting sauce on this gorgeous dress of yours." The professor's voice fell to an octave entirely too low for the public space they were in. Then Dr. Morgan was gone, disappearing into the crowd.

Tess ground her teeth together. She focused on filling her plate, then turned from the buffet. Dr. Morgan was already seated, but she looked tense, trying to deflect the conversation being thrown at her. Tess figured she would be more than amenable to leaving.

Leisurely, Tess strolled toward Dr. Morgan. She stalked past the table, gaining her eye. Then she reached out and subtly ran her fingers across her back, up her shoulders, and to her exposed neck. Tess received her desired reaction when she felt Dr. Morgan's sharp intake of breath. Then, Tess treaded back to her friends.

Kai and Elle were engaged in conversation, which Tess barely paid attention to as she let her fantasies unfold in her mind. She imagined how she'd undress Dr. Morgan, how Dr. Morgan would undress her, how they'd come together, everything.

"She's leaving," Elle said as they finished eating. "Looks like you missed your chance."

Tess spun, catching a glimpse of the bio-chem professor as she slipped out of the ballroom. Dr. Morgan looked back for half a second, eyes locking with Tess, before she was gone.

Tess hastily grabbed her phone and shoved her handbag at Elle. "Bring that home for me," she said, quickly standing. "Now's my cue."

"You can't be serious. This isn't going to work."

"Dr. Morgan will eat you alive," Kai warned.

"Yeah, I hope she does," Tess replied.

Elle let out a snort of laughter as Tess strode toward the exit.

As Tess slipped out of the ballroom, she noticed Dr. Morgan disappearing down the hallway toward the bathrooms. Tess picked up her pace, and when she passed an alcove, someone grabbed her and jerked her back. Tess spun, colliding with Dr. Morgan, and they came together with a feverous passion.

They lapped into each other's mouths. Dr. Morgan bit Tess's lip and pulled before she dipped and grazed her teeth along Tess's jaw. "You're such a fucking tease," she said, her voice husky, "wearing that tight dress." She dropped her arms and cupped Tess's ass, jerking her closer.

"I didn't even know you were going to be here."

"Liar."

Tess scoffed. "You're so full of yourself."

"It doesn't matter. Since you found out I was here, you've been teasing me." Dr. Morgan reconnected their lips, then broke to suckle Tess's neck again. "You know exactly what you look like in this dress. You were flaunting, expecting me to keep my hands to myself—"

"Oh, that was never my intention." Tess was unable to stop the whimper that tumbled from her lips. "I intended to tease you, yes, but for you to keep your hands to yourself? Absolutely not." Tess pulled back just enough to fix Dr. Morgan with a solid stare. "Take me back to your place. Now."

Dr. Morgan stilled. "We can't. This won't work."

"Why?"

"Because I…have certain preferences about who I fall into bed with."

Tess cocked her head. "You're the one kissing me right now, pawing at my ass, and you're saying you're not interested—"

"Not that I'm not interested. We just...wouldn't be compatible. We're both too controlling."

Tess whipped her head back. "You think I'm too dominant?"

"I prefer a more submissive partner."

"Hmm, submissive." Tess contemplated the word. She leaned forward again and licked along Dr. Morgan's jaw, unable to stop herself.

"Yes," Dr. Morgan said, but the word came out disjointed, like it was difficult for her to focus. Still, she dug her nails into Tess's shoulder. "Yes," Dr. Morgan said again. "I prefer a submissive partner, and unfortunately, you've too big and bold a personality. This won't work."

Dr. Morgan tried to pull back then, but Tess shoved at her, and Dr. Morgan stumbled into the wall. She opened her mouth and snapped, "See? That's exactly what I mean!"

Tess silenced her by licking her way up Dr. Morgan's neck, around the curve of her jaw, and up, pulling Dr. Morgan's earlobe into her mouth. Tess paused and whispered into Dr. Morgan's ear, hoping her warm breath sent a shiver down Dr. Morgan's spine.

"It's true, I suppose, that I have a bold personality in my day-to-day life, but that's hardly a reflection of what I'm like in bed." Tess pulled back, her expression pleading, tipping her head to invite Dr. Morgan to suck at her neck again. "The things I want you to do to me...I want you to pin me down. I want you to mark me, abuse me, make me yours." She pressed her center more firmly against the professor. "Please, Dr. Morgan. I need you." Tess let out a pitiful and needy whimper. "I need you to fuck me senseless, Margaret."

It was the first time Tess had ever called her by her first name. Tess did it on purpose, to elicit a reaction, and she figured Dr. Morgan knew that, but she still received her desire response.

Dr. Morgan grabbed Tess harshly and snapped, "It's Dr. Morgan."

Tess whimpered again. "Yes, Professor," she said, but then she gasped sharply when Dr. Morgan squeezed her harder. "I mean, Doctor. Yes, Dr. Morgan."

Dr. Morgan's lips curled into a sinister snarl, and she grabbed Tess's wrist, pulling her straight out to her car.

* * *

Margaret lived close to campus, but that hardly made the charged car ride shorter. Neither said a word, they just stole electric glances at each other. Margaret performed an effortless parallel park in front of an old and beautifully kept building. However, Tess didn't have time to admire the architecture.

Margaret wasted no time, chasing Tess up the front porch steps, grabbing her wrist to pull her up faster. She unlocked the door and shoved Tess inside, kicking the door shut before she pinned Tess against it.

A lamp in the adjacent room cast a warm glow over the threshold, but they were otherwise in the dark. Margaret fondled her, her fingers lightly tracing skin before pressing in the pinpoints of her short nails. Tess moaned into her mouth. Then Margaret hiked her knee between Tess's legs and Tess threw her head back in an involuntary groan.

Tess was shaking. Margaret smelled delicious, like spice and musk. Her tongue and fingers were intent and experienced. Margaret rocked against Tess, and Tess whimpered again. She raked kisses up her neck and licked around her ear. She pressed her knee firmly against Tess's center as she whispered, "The sounds you make are delectable." Then Tess shuddered, went rigid, then limp, grasping at Margaret, who simply pressed Tess more firmly against the door to keep her standing.

Heat flooded Tess's cheeks, her breathing erratic. She couldn't believe she'd come, in a matter of seconds, just making out with Margaret. Embarrassed, she dipped her head and covered her face with her hand.

Margaret stilled, though she remained pressed close. Tess waited for a snide comment, or even for Margaret to kick her out. Instead, she said, "I'd hope someone as young as you has better stamina."

Tess shivered. "I'm sorry, you just got me so worked up…"

Margaret bit her earlobe. "Good. Catch your breath quickly because I'm absolutely not done with you."

Tess released a shaky, eager breath. "I hope you know I don't plan on leaving until I can't stand."

"That can easily be arranged."

Margaret stepped back slightly, checking that Tess could support herself before she stepped away entirely. Margaret pulled her jacket off, tossing it on the floor before she undid her shirt buttons, staring at Tess with a ravenous expression. Tess shivered under her gaze. Margaret shucked off her white shirt, standing before Tess in only a lacy black bra. Tess balled her hands into fists. She so desperately wanted to touch, but she was letting Margaret be in charge. Instead, she simply stared at her cleavage, imagining what it would be like to suck the tender flesh there.

"Come here," Margaret instructed. Tess immediately stepped forward, letting Margaret tug her into her arms. Their mouths met again as Margaret pulled Tess backward.

They tumbled into a bedroom and Margaret spun Tess. She kissed down Tess's exposed upper back and sucked, then bit, and flicked her tongue across the tender spot she'd created. As she continued kissing and nipping at Tess's neck, Margaret slid down the zipper at the back of the dress and slid her hands around Tess's sides before slinking up her front. Tess wasn't wearing a bra, so she cupped her breasts and pinched Tess's nipples between her fingers.

"Ah, fuck." Tess groaned, throwing her head back and arching her chest deeper into Margaret's hands.

In a graceful swoop, Margaret knocked the dress off Tess so that the garment pooled at her feet. She spun Tess and grabbed her behind the head to kiss her again, stepping forward and shoving Tess down onto the bed. Tess gasped as she fell backward, bouncing up onto her elbows, dying to chase the other woman's touch.

But Margaret held her hand up and stated, "Stay," in a low growl, which had Tess settle. Margaret turned to the bedside lamp and flicked it on, regarding Tess with a pleased smirk. "I want to see you."

"And do you like what you see?" Tess asked, lying contentedly exposed for the other woman.

Margaret hummed approvingly.

"This is all for you, Margaret."

Margaret cocked an eyebrow. "Doctor."

"Yes, Dr. Morgan."

Margaret tutted, though nodded approvingly. She stalked up to the edge of the bed and settled between Tess's legs. She stared down hungrily, running her fingers along Tess's legs, swooping with each pass closer to where Tess wanted her, but never close enough. Tess groaned in frustration. At her verbal protest, Margaret crawled on top of Tess.

"You're beautiful," Margaret said, dipping to kiss Tess. "Your complexion is flawless...too perfect. I intend to rectify this issue."

Confused, Tess opened her mouth to ask for clarification. But before she could, Margaret dipped and bit, sucking hard at the top of Tess's breast, and Tess let out a hiss.

Margaret pulled back and looked down at her handiwork. "Much preferable," she declared, repeating the same action on Tess's other side. Tess hissed again and arched toward Margaret's mouth. "Do you like it when I mark you like that?"

"Yes, absolutely."

Margaret continued down Tess's body, kissing, biting, sucking, and licking a trail, leaving little bruises in her wake. The lower she went, the wigglier Tess became. Tess grew impatient, feeling the slickness pooling between her legs.

Margaret dipped her fingers in the waistband of Tess's underwear and pulled, Tess lifting her butt into the air to speed up the process. Margaret, however, stilled and waited until Tess settled before she slowly, way too slowly, pulled the underwear off. Then, she crawled atop Tess again, running her fingers along Tess's jaw. She lowered her lips to Tess's ear, pressing their chests together as Tess canted up toward her, dying for friction.

"Do you want me to fuck you, Miss Stanford?" Margaret asked, her voice commanding.

"Mmm, yes, Dr. Morgan."

"Do you want me to eat you out until your legs shake?"

"Yes."

"And pound you until you can't stand?"

"Fuck, yes, please."

"Please what?"

"Please, Dr. Morgan, fuck me, hard, do whatever you want to me. Please!"

Margaret nodded and bent, inhaling the scent of Tess's need before she leaned forward and lapped, her tongue flat and her stroke long. Tess jerked and moaned at the contact, grasping at the bed cover, whimpering as Margaret began to tease her. She licked lazy circles around Tess's entrance, dipped into her, then licked straight up to her clit.

Tess threw her head back, groaning. Margaret's tongue, and her warm breath right at her center, felt so good. Unimaginable. Tess gasped as she grazed across her clit again, circling it, sucking at it. She was going to come again. Oh, fuck she was going to come again.

Margaret stilled and pressed her tongue flat against Tess, pausing, before pulling back. Tess whined at the lack of contact, but then Margaret pressed at her center and a finger easily slipped in.

"Oh, fuck." Tess groaned as she settled into the new feeling.

"Can you take another finger for me?"

"Yes."

Another finger joined the first, thrusting, and then Margaret dipped her head and ran her tongue against Tess's clit.

"Oh fuck, don't stop." Tess canted her hips up. "Oh fuck, I'm going to—"

Margaret curled her fingers and Tess was gone, her head spinning.

Tess collapsed fully, panting. She forced her eyes open, desperate to see the beautiful woman who had just given her one of the best orgasms of her life. Her muscles clenched happily as Margaret pulled out her fingers, and then Tess watched as she sat back, fixed Tess with a stare, and sucked her fingers clean of Tess's juices.

Need spiked in Tess again. She scrambled up, flinging forward, and kissed Margaret with reckless abandon. Margaret fell back, clearly not expecting the ravenous kiss, but Tess pulled at her, loving the feeling of naked skin under her fingertips, and balanced them more firmly in their embrace.

As they kissed, Tess removed Margaret's bra. She gazed at her breasts, suddenly very glad for the light in the room, and cupped them greedily. She'd imagined touching Margaret in such a sensitive spot for ages, and now that she finally could, she was beside herself. She leaned forward and gently kissed the tender flesh, then trailed her tongue down, desperate to suck a nipple into her mouth.

Margaret shoved her back hard. As Tess fell, Margaret went with, hovering over her again. Determined, however, Tess stretched her neck up to kiss Margaret's breasts again. Margaret tsked and shoved Tess down more firmly.

"I'm not done with you," Margaret declared.

"No, you certainly aren't, but I'm dying to worship your chest. Humor me for a minute, will you?"

Tess reached her arms forward, because Margaret was still holding her down, keeping her head away, and grazed her fingertips along the tender flesh, biting her lip in wonder at how amazing it felt. But then Margaret grabbed her wrists and flung Tess's arms up, pinning them above her head.

"I'm not finished with you," Margaret repeated, her face mere centimeters from Tess's. "It would do you well to listen."

Tess fixed Margaret with a challenging glare and replied, "Yes, Margaret."

Margaret squeezed her wrists tighter, and Tess gasped loudly. Then Margaret dipped and bit her collarbone hard, causing Tess to hiss.

"Okay, fine, yes, Dr. Morgan."

"Better."

Margaret released Tess's wrists and pulled back, pressing another passionate kiss to Tess's lips. While she was absorbed in the kiss, Tess lifted her arms, cupping Margaret's breasts again. Margaret shot back, sitting on Tess's hips.

"Miss Stanford," she hissed in warning.

"Sorry, wandering hands," Tess replied with mock innocence.

"Unacceptable."

Margaret removed her belt. She stared straight at Tess as she looped the leather in on itself. Tess cocked a curious eyebrow until Margaret dropped the looped belt over Tess's hands, tightening it, tying her arms together. She grabbed her wrists by the belt constraint and flung her arms over her head, pinning her down again.

"Keep your arms above your head," Margaret warned. "Otherwise I'll tie you to the headboard."

Tess pointedly picked her arms up and draped them over Margaret's head, loosely trapping her in her embrace.

"Cheeky," Margaret said, huffing.

She slipped out from Tess and slid off the bed, retrieving something from the dresser. When she returned, she snapped a thick black rope between her hands.

"On your knees."

Immediately Tess spun, flaunting her ass in the air. Margaret paused before smacking Tess, hard, open palmed, on her ass cheek.

"You've been a bad girl. Do as I say."

Tess purred, smirking happily. "Yes, Dr. Morgan." She bit her lip.

The black rope looped around the belt restraint and through a post in the headboard. Then Margaret instructed Tess to look straight ahead and wait.

Tess did as she was told, the anticipation making her shudder. Then the bed dipped behind her.

"Spread your legs," Margaret commanded, pressing her thumbs against Tess's inner thighs. Tess jumped, flinging her legs out farther. Margaret grabbed her ass and squeezed each cheek into her hands. One hand released her, then something hard pressed against her center.

Tess sucked in a deep breath, greedily aware of the strap-on. She slammed her ass backward, trying to force the dildo inside, but Margaret pulled back, chuckling lightly.

"Eager are we?"

"Please, Margaret, pound me."

"It's Doctor—"

"I need your cock inside me, now."

She heard Margaret suck in a sharp breath. Then the dildo pressed into Tess and slipped inside. Margaret held Tess's hips as she thrust, slow at first, then working to a faster pace. Tess slammed her hips back to meet each thrust with more fervor.

"Oh, fuck, Margaret, your cock feels so good inside me." Tess groaned, whimpering and moaning with each thrust.

Margaret pressed her hand into Tess's back. "You're taking it so well," she whispered, voice deep. The sound only made Tess needier.

Tess's head fell to the bed, no longer having the energy or focus to keep it up, and unholy sounds tumbled from her lips.

Margaret was so good in bed.

Tess's eyes fluttered open. She must have dozed off, entirely spent, though her chest still buzzed in postcoital bliss, so she couldn't have been out for long. She stretched languidly. She had never been more thoroughly shagged in her entire life.

She rolled over, realizing she was no longer tied up, and a blanket was draped over her. Margaret stood beside her dresser, removing the strap-on harness. She was naked as well, truly beautiful. As Tess traced her eyes over smooth pale skin, she realized abruptly that she wasn't satisfied. She might never be satisfied, not now that she had seen the goddess naked, not when she could still feel a slickness between her legs, and certainly not when she hadn't even gotten a taste of the other woman. It was time to rectify that.

Lazily, Tess reached out, her arm dangling over the side of the bed. "Margaret," she said, her voice slightly hoarse.

Margaret cocked an eyebrow at Tess's pleading and smirked slightly. She stalked toward the bed, watching as Tess's gaze tracked her body. When Margaret was close enough, Tess reached out and wrapped her arms around her waist, tugging until Margaret caved and crawled back into bed.

"Not yet satisfied?" Margaret asked, kissing her.

"Mmm, hardly," Tess hummed. She pushed gently against Margaret, grinning when she conceded and fell onto the pillows.

She crawled up Margaret, reveling in the feeling of their naked skin touching. She nuzzled against Margaret's jaw and sucked at her neck.

Margaret felt tense, as if only humoring Tess momentarily, but Tess needed to worship her. She wanted to explore her body, build her up, and send her crashing back down.

As Tess kissed and sucked at Margaret's neck, she listened to the subtle hitches of breath and paid extra attention to those areas. She continued her ministrations until she elicited a needy whimper from Margaret. Then, she kissed up and sucked at her earlobe before she spoke.

"I wasn't completely truthful earlier," Tess admitted. "It's true, I can be and do very much enjoy being submissive in the bedroom. However…" Tess jerked, grabbing both of Margaret's wrists before pinning her arms above her head. Margaret fought against the sudden restraint, but Tess held firm. "I'm actually a switch." Still pinning Margaret, she leaned down and nipped at her neck. "And I do believe it's my turn to make you beg."

"Miss Stanford…" Margaret's tone was a clear warning.

Tess pulled back. She kept Margaret's wrists pinned but used her free hand to grab Margaret by the throat. She pressed her fingernails into the tender flesh and then dragged her hand down Margaret's center. Tess released her wrists and dipped her head, dragging her tongue along the red lines she had just clawed down Margaret's abdomen.

"You're beautiful, you know, absolutely stunning." Tess punctuated her words with nips and kisses. "I love when you're in control, when you're demanding and know exactly what you want. But I also want to see you relinquish that control. Relax. I want to watch you come undone."

Margaret flushed, pressing up on her elbows. "It isn't that easy," she managed to gasp right before Tess pulled a nipple into her mouth.

"Lie down and let me worship you." Tess slowly pushed Margaret back into the pillows. "Let me give you just a fraction of the pleasure you gave me."

Tess kissed her, lazy and deep, running her hand back down Margaret's body. She pressed her fingertips into Margaret's upper thigh, waiting until she relaxed under her. Then her hand slipped deeper, and she ran her fingers through wet folds.

They both inhaled sharply at the touch. Tess couldn't believe how wet Margaret was.

"Look at me," Tess said softly, noticing that Margaret had scrunched up her face. She stilled until blue eyes regarded her. "Yes, there you go. Absolutely gorgeous. You're doing great."

Margaret whimpered pitifully, like a woman on the precipice. Tess's chest swelled, amazed that she was allowed to witness such a vulnerable side of Margaret.

Tess moved her fingers again, lightly circling, watching and feeling as Margaret's breath grew heavier. "I'm going to eat you out. Can you let me do that to you?"

Margaret nodded roughly.

"Perfect," Tess said, smirking. "Good girl." Margaret purred, letting out a short gasp.

So, the big, mean bio-chem professor had a praise kink. Tess pressed her lips together to suppress her grin.

She slid down Margaret's body, settling between her legs. She breathed in the heady scent, then canted downward and licked. Margaret was quiet, clearly censoring herself, but Tess remained determined.

"Let me hear you, Margaret," Tess said, her warm mouth vibrating against Margaret's center. "Can you do that for me? Can you let me hear you? Don't hold back." Tess licked over her clit, and Margaret let out a deep moan. "Yes, good girl, just like that."

Tess pressed a smile into Margaret's center when she heard her gasp, "Fuck."

Tess continued her ministrations, Margaret's moans and grunts growing louder. She shook in Tess's arms. She had to be close.

"Can you come for me?" Tess asked, flicking her tongue quickly. Wordless groans and gasps answered her. "Margaret, be a good girl and come for me," Tess said, her tone demanding.

Margaret tensed and gasped. "Oh fuck, *Tess!*"

Tess licked Margaret down from her high, swallowing roughly, her own heart pounding. That was the first time ever that Margaret had called her by her first name. Margaret finally called her Tess in the throes of passion, naked in bed, with Tess's face between her thighs.

Margaret was going to be the death of her.

* * *

Margaret stood at her kitchen island, cradling a steaming coffee mug. She was wrapped in a silk robe to ward off the ever-growing cold of the incoming winter season. Unable to sleep, she got up around five, leaving Tess sleeping peacefully, undisturbed. Still, Margaret wasn't tired. She felt rejuvenated. Last night had been…wonderful.

But that was the issue. She built walls around her heart decades ago, so thick she no longer knew if they were defenses or who she truly was. The walls, her rules and boundaries, hadn't been poked in years. It was safe that way.

Yet, Tess smashed through all her protective barriers in a single night.

The last woman Margaret let touch her was Amy. However, their fling was brief because her heart had already been marred by her homophobic aunt and uncle.

Your father would hate you! She could still hear her uncle screaming. *He would be ashamed of you, embarrassed to call you his daughter. You should be glad he died before he ever had to know his kid was a dyke.*

She could never trust another person after he violated her, stripping away any sense of comfort she had with intimacy. Learning that the people she trusted didn't care about her destroyed her sense of trust beyond repair. She couldn't be hurt like that again. She wouldn't survive.

Margaret had her routine. She loved the company of other women, but she had rules. She was the one doing the pleasing. Sure, it turned her on, but she didn't need them to touch her. All she needed was to be their source of pleasure. She'd leave them spent and return home. Sometimes she'd punish herself with the lack of release because she didn't deserve it. Other times she'd touch herself with feverous desperation and cry herself to sleep because she was worthless and horrible and didn't deserve such pleasure.

Most girls that Margaret slept with didn't challenge her rules. She'd sleep with pillow princesses, or leave her companions so spent they could barely move. No one ever fought her.

Then there was Tess.

Sure, Tess was overall more demanding than most women Margaret brought to bed. But if she had been firm or, god forbid, talked to Tess about her hesitancy, Tess never would have pushed. But Margaret didn't want to say no. It was easy to let Tess kiss her, getting lost in the sensation. That hadn't happened in...forever. She couldn't remember the last time she'd been comfortable enough to let someone try to bring her to orgasm. Even when there were opportunities, Margaret could never let her guard down enough to plummet over the edge.

But Tess had done it.

Tess was good in bed, but that wasn't what impressed Margaret, wasn't what she was standing in her kitchen toiling over. It was that Tess was sweet enough to lessen Margaret's discomfort to the point that she eagerly let Tess nestle between her thighs. And god, it was amazing. She'd forgotten how wonderful it could feel.

Margaret heard shuffling and turned. Tess sauntered out in one of Margaret's shirts, just barely long enough to cover her bare ass. She looked thoroughly shagged: beautiful and glowing. Margaret loved the messy hair, swollen lips, and smell of sex. If she didn't have her steadfast no-morning-sex rule, she might have been tempted for a second round.

"Morning," Tess hummed. She stepped up beside Margaret and watched the rising sun.

Margaret's eyes drifted to the curve of Tess's buttocks. Maybe she could break the no-morning-sex rule...but there was also her no-sleeping-with-the-same-girl-twice rule, which was more serious. Twice meant a pattern with expectations that would lead to complications.

Tess leaned forward on the counter, pressing back her ass, and Margaret inhaled sharply as more skin was exposed. Tess faced her, fully smirking, and Margaret jerked her gaze away. Tess was tempting her on purpose, and it was working. That wouldn't do. Margaret was a one-night-stand kind of woman. She didn't do relationships of any kind. She barely tolerated friendship as it was.

"Got any food around here?" Tess questioned, pulling Margaret from her thoughts.

"Coffee," Margaret replied dryly.

"That's not food." Tess turned, rooting around the kitchen. "Don't you eat breakfast? It's the most important meal of the day."

"Some studies beg to differ."

"Well, I like breakfast. Ahh, yogurt." She brought her prize to the island counter. Margaret reached to her side and pulled open a drawer, retrieving a spoon that she silently handed over.

Then, the two stood in silence. Margaret sipped her coffee. Tess ate the yogurt.

Just as Tess was fishing the last bit of yogurt from the container, Margaret said, "I need to take you back to campus."

"Already?" Tess asked curiously, licking the spoon clean.

Margaret swallowed hard. "Yes. I have a lot of work to do, and I'm not about to let you infiltrate my home the way you've infiltrated my office."

"Careful," Tess teased. "I know where you live now."

Margaret glanced down. "You need to change. You aren't stealing my clothes either."

"But I wore a dress. It's uncomfortable and sleeveless. I think it's cold outside. Just let me borrow some clothes, please? I promise I'll return them Monday."

"And risk one of my coworkers witnessing that exchange? I think not."

Tess fixed Margaret with a look. "Ugh, fine."

Instead of further protesting, Tess changed back into her dress. She was struggling to reach the dress's zipper when Margaret stepped up behind her and pulled it up with ease. She left her hand lingering on Tess's back for a beat longer than necessary.

As her hand fell away, Tess said, "I think I prefer you unzipping my dress, as opposed to zipping it."

Margaret was pensive. "You can wait for me in the kitchen. I need to get dressed."

* * *

Tess watched Margaret for a moment before nodding, respecting her boundaries as she trailed out to the kitchen. When Margaret reemerged, she looked put together, ready for another day of work.

The car ride back to campus was tense in an entirely different way than it had been the night before. Last night they were impatient and eager. Now, they held on to every lingering moment, trying to delay the inevitable.

Margaret pulled to the side of the road about a block from the edge of campus. Tess looked around, confused at first, but then she recognized where they were.

"Well, here you go," Margaret declared.

"Seriously? We're so far away," Tess complained. "Can't you drop me off any closer?"

"And risk someone seeing? Absolutely not."

"You're being unreasonable."

"Just because we slept together doesn't mean you're afforded special privileges." Tess opened her mouth to protest, but Margaret cut her off. "I never would have brought you to my house had I thought you too stupid to realize this."

Tess pursed her lips in annoyance but kept her mouth shut. Still, she didn't move to get out of the car, she just watched Margaret for a moment. Margaret looked on edge, picking at her finger and tapping the fingers of her other hand against the dash, refusing to look at Tess. Neither spoke.

Then Margaret said, still looking out the windshield, "This can't happen again." Her tone was firm, but even so, she didn't sound convinced that she meant it.

Tess turned more fully toward Margaret, though she was still being ignored. "I had a good time. A great time, actually."

"I only do one-night stands."

"I understand."

Margaret looked at Tess like she expected a scene, especially since Tess had never been good at listening to her. Instead, Tess nodded in understanding, hoping to keep the connection from last night by further defying Margaret's expectations. She certainly wasn't done with her, but she knew this wasn't the time to push.

She did, however, favor her with the smirk that seemed to drive Margaret crazy. "Can I at least kiss you goodbye?"

"Absolutely not."

"But if you don't grant me a final kiss now, I might demand one later."

Margaret frowned but leaned across the console and captured Tess's lips. The initially chaste kiss deepened quickly, and by the time they pulled apart, both were panting.

Tess could feel the pleading expression on her own face, but she still didn't fight Margaret. That wasn't the winning play. She just smiled softly and said, "I'll see you Monday, Margaret…" before she slipped out of the car.

"Dr. Morgan," Margaret harshly stated.

Tess shot Margaret a wink as she slammed the car door shut.

It wasn't until Tess reached her apartment that she remembered she didn't have her keys. Hoping Elle was either up already or wouldn't sleep through her knocking, Tess reached up and banged on the door.

Graciously, the door swung open, but to reveal Kai, not Elle.

"Oh my god, you actually did it. You slept with Dr. Morgan," Kai said.

"Umm, hi, Kai," Tess said as she stepped inside, bewildered. "What are you doing over here so early?"

Kai blushed profusely but was saved by Elle dashing out of her room.

"I can't believe it," Elle said. "There's no way."

"But look at her neck," Kai declared, pointing. "There's no way she did that to herself."

Tess's eyes widened, and she instinctively brought her hand up to shield her neck. She darted into the bathroom, looking in the mirror. Margaret wasn't kidding when she said she wanted to mar Tess's perfect skin. Tess was covered in marks all over her neck and along her collarbones, and little bruises littered the top of her chest.

"You look like you got beat up with all those bruises," Elle said, leaning against the doorframe of the bathroom.

"Those aren't bruises, they're hickeys," Kai said, correcting Elle. "You're having that dress cleaned before you give it back to me."

"Did you have a good time? Was she good in bed?"

"Mind-blowing," Tess uttered breathlessly. "I don't know how I'll survive never doing it again."

"Who says it has to be a onetime thing?" Kai asked with a shrug. "If Dr. Morgan's into it, go for it. Life's too short to miss out on amazing sex."

"Kai, do you still have that really good concealer kit?" Tess asked. "I cannot face Dr. Kemper and Dr. Marlow looking like this."

"Yeah, I'll grab it for you."

Kai darted out of the apartment, and Tess turned to Elle. "So, what did you two get up to last night?"

Elle flushed. "This is crazy. Did you know Kai likes me?"

"Oh, she does?" Tess managed to say with a mostly straight face.

"Yeah, we came back here after dinner, to hang, but then she kissed me."

"You seem happy."

"Yeah…I am."

"So, did you sleep together?"

"No!" Elle replied hotly, her face now a deep crimson. "I just lent Kai some clothes to spend the night—just sleeping."

"Sure. But do you want to sleep with her?"

The front door flung open again and Elle quickly said, "Shush, quiet!" just as Kai ran back, makeup in hand.

* * *

"Good morning, Debbie. Happy Monday. Kathy"—Margaret nodded toward the other woman—"lovely day, isn't it?"

"Umm...yes..." Kathy answered hesitantly. Debbie appeared too flabbergasted to respond with the way her mouth was hanging open.

Margaret paused, sorting through various papers. "Have either of you read the newest edition of *Frontiers*?" she asked, pausing on a copy of the journal.

"No, I haven't grabbed a copy yet," Kathy replied.

"Here, you can have mine. Let me know if you find any particularly interesting articles and I'll be sure to check them out."

"Umm...all right..."

"See you around. Have a good week." Margaret exited the mail room, her head still down as she flipped through her mail.

As she left the room, however, she paused, remembering that she needed to make a copy. She turned back but slowed, overhearing the biology professors talking about her.

"What in the world was that?"

"I...honestly don't know. I think Margaret was being nice?"

"That's impossible. Flip through the journal she gave you. She probably scribbled insults in it."

"No, it's clean. I think Margaret just woke up on the right side of the bed for once. I hope it lasts."

"Don't get your hopes up. I bet she's a sourpuss by lunch."

Margaret frowned at Debbie's last response but found herself giddy still, the memory of Tess too wonderful to bring her mood down. She decided her copies could wait and instead headed back to her office to be productive.

* * *

Margaret wasn't surprised when Tess poked her head in later that Monday. Of course, she still acted disinterested to keep up their farce. But truthfully, she was giddy to see Tess again. It was dangerous and confusing, but it felt good.

"Not you again," Margaret said, rolling her eyes when Tess appeared in her office doorway. "I'm busy. Go away."

"Yes, it's me again. Lovely to see you as well," Tess retorted, looking entirely unbothered by Margaret's farce. She pushed into the office and shut the door behind her, then fell onto the couch, sighing blissfully.

Margaret bit back a grin. She was proud to see Tess still beaming, happy that *she* had been the one to do that.

"Dr. Marlow and Dr. Kemper said you were being nice today. Are you feeling all right?"

"Very. Are you?"

"Very," Tess mimicked. "And how's your neck doing?" she commented cheekily. "You look dashing in that black turtleneck, but you rarely ever wear one."

Margaret's hand reflexively shot to her neck, pawing at the knit fabric covering it. She noticed Tess's seemingly clean neck then, narrowing her eyes and fighting the urge to pin Tess down and wipe off the makeup she suspected covered the evidence. She wanted everyone to know what she'd done to the sweet, innocent bio TA, but keeping it a secret was much more important than bragging.

"Anyway, I just wanted to check up on you, but I have a lot of work to do, so I need to get going."

Margaret pulled a disgruntled face. "Check up on me? I'm perfectly capable of taking care of myself."

"Of course," Tess replied. She eyed Margaret somewhat oddly, leaving her uncomfortable that she couldn't tell what Tess was thinking. "I'll...see you later. Although, this week is a nightmare. I don't know when I'll have time to come see you again."

"I think I can manage without your presence for a week. In fact, it might be my most productive week yet."

"Good, then. Make use of your time and publish another paper." Tess winked as she dipped away.

Over the next several days, Margaret and Tess caught each other's eyes in the hallways or across the quad, but neither approached. When Margaret first saw Tess in passing, she felt warm and suspiciously eager, but when Tess never acknowledged her beyond a gaze, Margaret realized she had been holding on to hope.

She wanted to sleep with Tess again.

But that was against her rules. They'd never come together again because Margaret wouldn't ask or beg for seconds. However, the regret bittered her mood. This was why she didn't let people in, didn't get close to others. She couldn't let her guard down again.

* * *

Dr. Kemper walked in on her gathered TAs, unhappily declaring, "Well, I reckon the era of 'Happy Dr. Morgan' has ended."

"Codepartment meeting that bad, huh?" Kai asked.

"Oh, yes, dreadful." Dr. Marlow groaned.

"We didn't get a single productive thing covered," Dr. Kemper continued. "She's back to being contrary to everything, snapping at everyone. She's so tense. She should take up kickboxing to get out her pent-up frustration."

Kai discreetly elbowed Tess. "Maybe you should pay her another visit and help release some of that tension?"

"I don't know what you're talking about."

Every time Tess saw Margaret around campus, she wanted to leap into her arms, pull her lip between her teeth, and rip her shirt off. But even if Tess could convince the professor to break her one-night-stand rule, it would never be on a school night. So, Tess played it safe with simple smiles. But the tension was driving her crazy.

After the meeting, Tess and Kai hung back and continued chatting with the bio professors.

"How's the puppy training going?" Kai asked.

"Oh, well, she's still a nightmare, but a slightly more manageable nightmare." Dr. Kemper chuckled. "Kai, tell your girlfriend thank you. The training is helping immensely."

Kai went red in the face, stuttering out, "My—my girlfriend?"

Dr. Kemper regarded her quizzically. "Are you and Elle not…?"

"We're *talking*," Kai ground out.

Tess rolled her eyes, siding with Dr. Kemper. "They're basically dating."

"Basically and actually are two different things," Kai said, protesting hotly.

The conference room door slammed open, startling everyone as a fuming Margaret appeared.

"There is a horribly obnoxious, high-pitched beep coming from your lab, and if you don't stop it—"

"Oh shit, Cal's experiment!" Dr. Kemper exclaimed, leaping up immediately. She raced straight out of the room, shoving into Margaret as she fled.

Tess sucked in a sharp breath. The sight of Margaret fuming, with that fire in her eyes, sent a shiver through her body. She couldn't keep seeing Margaret around campus, ignoring what they'd done, leaving it in the past.

Tess stood abruptly and marched up to Margaret. She snapped harshly, "Your office. Now."

Tess saw Margaret's anger subside into confusion, a look of vulnerability to her expression. She watched Dr. Marlow shrug and Kai cover her mouth to suppress a laugh. Margaret turned sharply then and stalked toward her office, Tess following.

"How dare you speak to me like that, and in front of other professors, no less!" Margaret slammed her office door shut behind them. "You have no right talking to me like—"

"I can't handle this." Tess shot forward, harshly shoving Margaret into the closed door. She kissed her with reckless abandon, moaning into Margaret's mouth.

Margaret's response was eager. She shoved her leg between Tess's, giving herself leverage as she flipped their positions. Tess didn't fight, only whimpered as Margaret sucked at her earlobe. When she dipped and bit her neck, Tess let out a hiss.

"I don't do relationships," Margaret growled, her voice low in warning. "I only do—"

"One-night stands, I know. But I can't only do this once, and clearly, you can't either."

"No." Margaret's voice was firm.

Tess smirked deviously. "No, you can't only do this once either?"

"Stop it."

"Stop what?"

"That smirk of yours. It drives me crazy."

"Oh, does it? Then, good. Because listen. All week you've been driving me crazy. Do you have any idea how insanely attractive you are?"

Tess leaned forward, trying to capture Margaret's lips again, but she pulled back.

"No, we are not doing this. Absolutely not."

"Please," Tess whimpered, still trying to nuzzle against the other woman. "I need you."

"You don't need me. It's just an influx of chemicals in your brain, your body reacting to mine because it remembers our time together. But it's temporary...fleeting."

"We're all just a bunch of chemicals," Tess mocked, huffing. "That's so very bio-chem of you. Maybe we are. I'm not here to debate philosophy with you. It's just, chemicals or not, I can't help the way my body reacts to yours."

"You'll get over this fixation."

"Not unless you sleep with me again."

Margaret hesitated only for a millisecond, but it was enough for Tess to attack. She snaked her arms around Margaret's back and sucked hard at her neck in the exact spot she knew made Margaret weak.

Margaret grabbed Tess's neck with her hand, shoving her against the door, hard. Margaret's breathing was heavy, irritation and heat behind her movements. Tess loved the roughness. She was practically withering on the spot.

"Margaret, please," Tess said, begging.

Tess pushed against the hold and immediately Margaret released her, though she remained close. Tess bit her lip, whimpering, shaking under the intense and wanton look in the other woman's eyes.

Tess closed her eyes and let out a shaky breath, trying to compose herself.

"You don't understand what you do to me," Tess whispered, slowly opening her eyes. She traced her hand down Margaret's arm, grabbing her wrist tightly.

"The things you do to me…" Tess restated, pulling her hand closer. "You make me feel such powerful, explosive things. Feelings I barely know how to handle." She cupped Margaret's hand in her own and pressed Margaret's fingers under her shirt, running Margaret's fingers along her abdomen. "You fill me with such need and desperation." Then, she slipped both their hands into the waistband of her pants.

Margaret inhaled sharply when Tess pressed her fingers into dripping wet folds.

"Do you feel that?" Tess asked. "You make me that wet, Margaret. That's all for you."

Tess's knees gave out when Margaret suddenly took control, sinking her fingers straight into her. She pressed into Tess and captured her lips, so Tess's gasp died in their mouths. She pressed forward, thrusting. Tess's head rolled back. She was going to come at school in the biology building at the hands of the notorious bio-chem professor.

But then, Margaret was gone, the air harshly cold in her absence.

Tess popped her eyes open, whimpering unhappily.

"No, stop, don't complain," Margaret stated. "We're going back to my place. Right now. I simply refuse to take you in my office like some randy teenagers."

Tess suppressed an eager grin, nodding rapidly. "Well, hurry up, then," she purred.

* * *

"You're leaving. Now."

Tess pursed her lips. "Seriously?"

Margaret propped herself up, the bedsheet dipping dangerously low, revealing more cleavage. Tess salivated at the sight.

"This was already an exception," Margaret said. She tilted Tess's head up with her finger, so Tess's gaze met her eyes instead of her cleavage. "This will not happen regularly…and to prevent it from becoming routine, you cannot spend the night."

Tess raised a challenging eyebrow. "Who said we were done?"

"I seem to recall someone begging me to stop, something about not being able to walk tomorrow…"

"Okay, yes," Tess admitted. "But postcoital cuddles account for at least sixty-nine percent of a sexual encounter."

Margaret snorted. "And just where did you get that absurd statistic?"

"Personal experience," Tess murmured, pleased that Margaret got the joke. She reached for her, trying to wrap her arms around her, but Margaret fought her off. Tess let out a huff, crossing her arms. "Women tend to prefer a more intimate experience, you know, which is improved by cuddling."

"Some women, perhaps." Margaret eyed her warily.

"When was the last time you gave cuddling a chance?"

"It's pointless intimacy, I don't—"

"Regardless, you haven't cuddled with *me*. Don't knock it till you try it."

Margaret slowly shifted, turning toward Tess, and reluctantly, making a huge fuss out of it, she opened her arms, inviting Tess over.

"Only so you shut up and leave faster," Margaret said with warning as Tess slid up closer to her.

Tess pulled against Margaret, nuzzling her neck. Margaret squeezed her tighter.

"And if we happen to fall asleep…" Tess purred softly.

"Not"—Margaret reached down and pinched Tess's bare ass check—"going to happen."

"Oww," Tess yelped, jerking back slightly. She frowned at Margaret. "What is your deal? Cuddling is objectively nice."

"Stop talking."

"Margaret—"

"Shh."

Tess wanted to argue more, but she was quite comfortable cuddled against Margaret. She settled down again, resting her head, the warmth of the other woman's body lulling her to sleep. Small victories, she thought to herself as she nodded off. Small victories.

* * *

Parked a block from the edge of campus again, Margaret drummed her fingers on the steering wheel, staring straight ahead. Tess gazed out the passenger window, refusing to get out of the car. She'd already protested the distance and been met with a snappy remark, and yet she remained, just sitting there.

Though silence stretched between them, Margaret's mind was screaming.

She had three resolute rules for women and sex.

First, she didn't do relationships, so she only had one-night stands. There was no attachment. That was why she never had morning sex either. Daylight was too real. She specifically never slept with the same woman twice, because that was a pattern, a type of relationship, and Margaret did not do relationships.

Second, she never let another woman touch her. It was too dangerous to let her guard down. She never felt safe enough to trust.

And three, she didn't cuddle. Cuddling was intimate, just as Tess said. Cuddling was too close to caring, too much like opening a door to heartbreak. Intimacy was too dangerous.

For twenty years, the rules held. But now, Tess crashed into her life, obstinate and refusing to listen, and she shattered all three of Margaret's rules in a week flat.

Why was she being so lenient with Tess?

Tess touched her. Tess thoroughly, multiple times now, fucked her. Tess cared about her, for whatever asinine reason, and that was sufficient for Margaret to feel safe enough to trust Tess to touch her. Tess cherished her like she was something beautiful and deserving…even though she wasn't. Margaret was disgusting and ugly, inside especially, and she didn't deserve any of the tenderness Tess afforded her.

And they cuddled. Margaret couldn't remember the last time someone embraced her that way. But Tess wanted to. She genuinely enjoyed being close to Margaret and Margaret didn't know how to process that information.

They kept getting closer. That was bad, because Tess was bound to catch feelings, but Margaret couldn't love. She wasn't capable. She'd break Tess's heart, and she already felt bad about it, but it was inevitable, and—

"We should do this regularly."

Margaret cautiously turned toward Tess. "We most certainly cannot." She felt sick to her stomach.

"I know you only do one-night stands, but we've already done this twice, and…I can't just stop. You've ruined me. You're too good in bed. I can't do it justice myself. And trust me, I've tried. All week. But I can't get any relief, it's so frustrating."

Margaret swallowed roughly. She really shouldn't but it was so easy to let Tess touch her, and it felt so good. "I am loath to admit this, but you are…very much adequate in the bedroom yourself." Tess smirked wildly, and Margaret let out a huff. "Don't let that go to your head, Miss Stanford."

"Then, look. If you're enjoying yourself as much as I am, why should we stop?"

"I only do one-night stands because I don't do relationships. I don't do feelings, and repeat offenses are—"

"I don't want a relationship either," Tess cut her off. "I just want sex."

Tess's hazel eyes shone hopefully. Margaret shifted uncomfortably, turning back to the windshield, unable to meet Tess's gaze any longer.

"We can meet up every Friday, just as we've been doing," Tess said. "I can come to your office after the TA meeting, and you can take me to your place from there."

"What if I'm still working?"

Tess rolled her eyes. "Fine. If you're still working, I'll just do homework in your office until you're ready to leave. Happy?"

Margaret hesitantly turned back to Tess. "Every week?"

"Unless you'd like more often," Tess cheekily teased, smirking.

Margaret's eyes narrowed. "You know that smirk drives me crazy."

"Then do something about it."

Margaret grabbed Tess across the console, attaching their lips in a fury. Tess yelped when Margaret pulled her into her lap, but she melted against her, straddling her. Minutes later they parted, panting wildly.

Tess was the first to find her voice. "If you keep kissing me like that, I'm not going to make it to Friday."

Margaret popped open the car door and dumped Tess out.

"Friday," Margaret said. "But you aren't spending the night."

"Of course not. Just like I didn't spend the night the last two times."

Margaret slammed her door shut, fixing Tess with a glare. But Tess, clearly feeling emboldened by their now-to-be repeating bedroom habits, just burst out laughing.

* * *

When Tess slipped into her apartment, feeling like she was on top of the world, she found both Elle and Kai sitting at the kitchen table eating cereal, and they all regarded each other with deer-in-the-headlights expressions.

"Uhh…hey guys," Tess uttered, quickly making to dart to her bedroom.

"Whoa, hang on," Kai said. "Get your butt back here and sit down. I want to hear the tea."

"Yeah, what are you doing over here?" Tess asked as she backtracked.

"We were hanging out, and you never came home last night, so I told her she could stay over," Elle answered.

"Not that tea, I'm talking about you and Dr. Morgan." Kai refused to accept Tess's misdirection. "What's up with that stunt you pulled, dragging Dr. Morgan back to her office on a leash?"

"Also," Elle said. "You never came back last night and you're just now slipping in wearing the same clothes you wore yesterday…I'm not great at math, but I'm pretty sure two plus two equals you slept with Dr. Morgan again."

Tess shrugged nonchalantly. "Yeah, so?"

"So! My roommate is regularly bedding the school's in-house devil. That's hardly nothing."

"We're hot, we're horny, we're good in bed together. It's hardly a problem."

"Yeah, it's not a problem, it's just crazy," Kai said.

"Is it going to be a regular thing now?" Elle asked. "I mean, when you don't come home at night, can I just tell our RA you're out getting pounded, or do I need to report you as a missing person?"

"We agreed to meet every Friday, so...I won't be around Fridays anymore, if that answers your question."

"Wait, 'agreed to'? Every Friday?" Kai questioned. "Tess, are you in a friends with benefits with Dr. Morgan?"

"Sure, I guess."

"*Tess!*"

* * *

"What's the deal, Margaret?"

Margaret glanced up from her mimosa and looked at Amy. She shrugged, feigning disinterest, and glanced back down at the menu. "I don't know, Amy. What's the deal with Sunday morning brunch?"

"It's so, come Monday, I don't break down your office door demanding answers. You've blown me off two Fridays in a row now."

"Last Friday, I told you I was busy. And this Friday, as I detailed over text, something urgent came up. You're an English professor, I figured you could read."

"Hilarious, Margaret. You never followed up on what urgent thing came up and I want answers."

"I was just...busy," Margaret replied, hoping her answer was cryptic enough.

"All Friday night?"

"Yes."

"And Saturday?"

"That morning, yes, I was busy too."

"Busy with what?"

"Just a...pressing and urgent...matter." Margaret paused, recalling every sinful thing she did to Tess. "I took care of it though," she added then, the sounds of Tess's undoing still fresh in her mind. Then she remembered kissing Tess feverishly in her car Saturday morning. "Well, it's more of a reoccurring issue now. I won't be able to meet up with you on Fridays anymore. I'm sorry. But we can meet up Saturday evenings or we can make Sunday brunches our new thing, if you'd like."

"You're blowing me off for this, and you won't even tell me what it is," Amy snapped. She crossed her arms protectively over her chest. "If you want some space from me, you can just tell me. I know I've been a lot ever since the breakup."

"No, Amy, it's not that," Margaret reassured. She reached across the table and grabbed Amy's hands, squeezing them. "It's got nothing to do with you, I promise. I enjoy being this close and having you in my life as a friend." Amy glowed happily at Margaret's difficult confession. Margaret rolled her eyes, pulling back. "There's just something going on and I'm not entirely sure how I feel about it, but..."

"Tell me about it?"

"Well...all right." Margaret gave in. "Do you remember that one student who was giving me quite the headache? The one that I—"

"Kissed?" Amy deadpanned. "Yes, I remember." She pulled her mimosa closer and took a sip.

Margaret pursed her lips but continued, "Yes, well...I slept with her."

Amy coughed and spat her drink across the table, right into Margaret's face.

"Amy!" Margaret gasped, flailing for a napkin. She fixed her friend with a glare.

"I'm sorry," Amy stated, gasping herself. "But you can't just drop that so nonchalantly. Geez, no wonder you were busy this Friday."

"No, this happened a week ago."

"Oh, okay, well…what kept you busy this last Friday?"

"I slept with her again."

Amy's eyes widened. "Are you feeling okay?"

"I'm fine…I think."

"Then what is this? What's going on?"

"I don't know," Margaret replied truthfully. "I thought one time to scratch the itch, but it didn't alleviate the tension. If anything, it made it worse. Then Friday she dragged me to my office and jumped me, declaring she needed more, and I just… caved."

Amy grinned. "The sex must be good, since you went back for seconds."

Margaret flushed but ignored the comment. "We agreed to keep doing it, every Friday, which is unfortunately why I can no longer—"

"Every week?" Amy gasped again, although this time, luckily, she didn't spray mimosa out of her mouth. "You're telling me that you're going to sleep with her, one, singular girl, every week, regularly? Wait, Margaret." Amy fixed her with an accusatory glare. "Are you in love with her?"

"No, don't be absurd!" Margaret snapped. "This is entirely physical. There are no feelings, no relationship happening."

"Your friends with benefits is most certainly a relationship that is most certainly happening."

"There is no friends with benefits! I'd have to be friends with her for that, and I most certainly am not her friend."

"Margaret, honey. She hangs out in your office almost daily and you just chat. That's friendship, no matter how hard you try and deny it."

Margaret scowled. "We're done talking about this. I just wanted to explain why we can't meet up on Fridays anymore. But we will still spend time together, I assure you."

"I expect regular updates about this girl."

"Absolutely not."

"Yes—"

"There won't be any updates because it's just sex. And I'm not detailing my sex life to you, Amy."

"Ugh, fine."

* * *

Margaret, the poster child of poise, was fidgeting during the codepartment meeting. Her mood wasn't good, nothing like her chipper mood two weeks prior, but she'd certainly been in fouler moods. She'd been strikingly silent throughout the meeting. She didn't cut anyone off, didn't even call anyone stupid. She was just silent, restless, and kept glancing at the clock.

The chair said, "Because of that, we're passing the pharmacology class planning to Mitch. He spent his postdoc working on drug discovery, so he'll be a great fit for the job." He paused, glancing cautiously at Margaret. "Nothing against you, Margaret. I'm not diminishing your drug discovery work. It's just that...well..."

"Dr. Castor has a stronger biology background," another professor quickly said.

The chair was nervously sweating. Clearly unnerved by the silence, he said, "Thoughts, Margaret?"

"Hmm? Oh, yes, fine, give the planning to Dr. Castor."

The room was stunned, but Margaret, oblivious, just checked the time on her watch again.

"So, you're fine with us giving the class to Mitch?" the chair asked in disbelief. "You're completely fine giving him the work you've already planned and just moving on?"

"Yes. I said as much. Are you deaf?" Margaret snapped then, much closer to her normal self. "Is that everything? We're a minute over time."

"Umm, yes, that's everything. Meeting adjourned."

Margaret stood immediately and turned pointedly to the two intro bio professors. "Keep your TA meeting short," she stated accusatorily. In explanation, she added, "Your TAs have a bad habit of being overly obnoxious, so I want them gone as soon as possible. And I need Miss Stanford when you're done with her. Send her straight to my office once the meeting's over. Don't keep me waiting."

"All right..." Debbie muttered.

* * *

At the TA meeting, Tess was just as fidgety, and it was just as unusual coming from her. She loved the TA meetings. She was normally attentive, dedicated, and outgoing, not withdrawn and distracted.

Once the meeting was over, Tess flew down the hallway. When she reached Margaret's office door, she realized the door was fully shut, but before she could knock, the door jerked open. Margaret grabbed Tess by her shirt and pulled her into the office, spinning as she forcefully shoved the door shut behind them. She attached their lips with forceful desperation, and then slowly and gently she pushed Tess's backpack off her shoulders, softly lowering the bag to the ground.

"Thanks for not breaking my laptop." Tess laughed against Margaret's mouth.

"Stop talking. Your biology professors don't know the meaning of a short and concise meeting."

Tess moaned under her touch. "Are you done for the day?"

"Yes."

"Good. Then let's get out of here."

* * *

Sex with Margaret was addicting. Her commanding nature left Tess aching. That was what initially caught Tess's interest. But the sex was addicting because Tess got to witness Margaret giving up control.

The rest of campus only saw Margaret as some inhuman monster, but Tess knew better. Margaret acted tough and aloof but was actually a softie who enjoyed the sort of friendship Tess was building with her. Every day, bits of her hard exterior would chip away.

Their first many times regularly falling into bed together, they were insatiable. Mouths had to slot together, clothing had to be shed. Margaret would pull a rippling orgasm from Tess before she could blink, and she'd spend the rest of the night playfully fighting to get Margaret to let her touch her.

Why was Margaret so stubborn about letting Tess touch her?

Obviously, Margaret enjoyed herself plenty; she kept coming back for more. Maybe it was just another one of her obstinate, stubborn things. Tess didn't mind. The challenge made it all the sweeter when she finally managed to pin her down.

Tess realized quickly that Margaret had a wide breadth of experience. Every week Margaret found another way to tease and deliciously torture Tess until her head was spinning. Tess wanted to spar with her, jab for jab, when she wasn't in a fully submissive mood. So, she started reading up on sex.

"Did you know there are different kinds of orgasms? And you can have multiple at the same time?"

Margaret glanced across her office at Tess. "I thought you were doing homework."

"I am, kind of. I'm studying."

"Studying orgasms? Why? You aren't in the Developmental and Sex Biology class."

Tess shot Margaret a curious look. "How do you know what classes I'm taking? Did you memorize my schedule?"

"Of course not, what a waste of effort," Margaret shot back. "You just talk about your classes plenty, so it's easy to remember."

"What classes am I taking, then?"

"This is also a waste of time."

"You're just chicken because you don't know."

"Fine. Mondays, Wednesdays, and Fridays, you TA for the intro bio class, physics at ten, molecular biology at one, ending with history at three. Tuesdays and Thursdays you have evolutionary biology at ten, spend the early afternoon working in lab, and your physics lab is at four fifteen. Oh, and your TA office hours are Tuesday and Wednesday evenings at seven with Kai."

Tess was surprised. "How do you have all that memorized?"

"I told you, you mention things and details fill themselves in—"

"Do you have a photographic memory?"

Margaret ran her fingers through her hair. "Maybe, slightly, it isn't a big deal."

"It's a huge deal," Tess said. "I think that's amazing."

"It's more so a curse."

Tess stilled, concerned as she took in Margaret's sudden melancholy demeanor. This was a glimpse into the cracks, a hole in the icy exterior. Tess wanted to stick her fingers into the crevasse and pull.

"Hey. You can talk to me, you know."

"It would just be nice if I could forget some things. Anyway, I don't wish to discuss this further. Continue your sex research while I type this up."

They wouldn't discuss Margaret's photographic memory curse for quite some time, but Tess still utilized her new discovery.

"Watch me, Margaret," Tess said as she straddled her. "Commit this to memory. I never want you to forget the time we spend together."

Tess went up, eager to grind down her hips again, but Margaret caught her and shoved her backward, pinning her against the bed as she kissed her roughly. She lined the dildo up and thrust back into her.

"You know damned well I won't be forgetting any of this," Margaret declared, sucking at Tess's neck. "And I don't want to, either. You are beautiful, Miss Stanford, and insanely attractive when you come undone in my arms. But as wonderful as those memories are, I much prefer reexperiencing them in real time."

"Oh, me too," Tess eagerly said.

That was another thing about sex with Margaret. Tess, as much as she loved the formality in the bedroom, took up a personal quest to get Margaret to call her by her first name. Getting Margaret to say *Tess* was a rarity. Her name had only tumbled from Margaret's lips a handful of times, always as she hovered on the precipice. Tess was obsessed with how wet Margaret got with a little praise. Surely she got compliments regularly—she was a scientific genius, after all—yet praise spilling from Tess's lips in the throes of passion was what got Margaret off. It was so uniquely special.

It would have been easy to let their sex get to her head, but Tess remained diligently focused on her schoolwork. Still, she never canceled their plans. The only time Tess was even remotely tempted to cancel was the weekend before finals, because she should have been studying. But self-care was important, and having sex with Margaret was the best self-care.

Tess let it slip, though, when Margaret's tongue was sliding down her neck. "I really should be studying for finals, but you're such a good kisser."

"More than just a good kisser," Margaret replied cockily. "When are your finals?"

"Molecular and evo are both on Monday. It's fine though, really."

"As a professor, I'm obligated to ensure you study."

Tess pouted. "Come on. You aren't going to kick me out, are you?"

"No, I've got a better idea. Come on."

Margaret pulled Tess into the bedroom where they continued with impatient and desperate hands until Margaret nestled between Tess's thighs. She licked up the length of Tess's heat.

"Tell me everything you've learned in molecular biology," Margaret said, her warm breath hitting Tess's most sensitive spot.

"Wha—what?" Tess wiggled, seeking out friction.

"Molecular biology recall. Start."

"Okay, um, we learned all the methods to sequence DNA."

"Good." Margaret licked her. "Tell me what they are."

"Sanger sequencing was first, a breakthrough. Then there were second generation methods, and now we have third generation."

"How do they each work?"

Tess continued, fighting to focus on biology recall while Margaret ate her out. Whenever her mind grew fuzzy in ecstasy, Margaret would stop. She'd pull away from Tess's center and hold her hips down. Then once Tess could focus and kept talking about biology, Margaret would resume her ministrations.

This moved into evolutionary biology, with Margaret behind Tess with a strap-on. When Tess stumbled over her words, Margaret would freeze and punctuate the wrong answer with a slap to Tess's ass cheek. Then the thrusting would resume once Tess got back on track.

Tess got the highest score on both of those finals, not that Margaret needed to know. Or maybe she did. Maybe that was going to be Tess's new preferred method of studying.

Then, it was winter break.

Tess wasn't sure she'd survive. They hadn't missed a single week, but now they were facing a dauntingly long three-week break.

Tess grew bashful leading up to their last Friday together. She wanted, desperately, to explain to Margaret how she wasn't sure she'd be able to survive without their weekly sex, but that seemed much too desperate. She didn't want to scare her into thinking she had grown codependent. Because she hadn't... The sex was just fantastic, and she didn't want to stop.

Instead, Tess tried to play it cool.

"I'm driving home Sunday," Tess whispered into the darkness of the room.

Margaret was curled into her, warmth engulfing her like a safe cocoon. She wondered if Margaret heard her. She wasn't sure the other woman was still awake.

But then, after a moment, Margaret spoke. "What time are you leaving?"

"Eight in the morning, probably."

"Good. Traffic should be light."

Tess realized she wanted Margaret to protest, or admit she'd miss their sex too. Tess couldn't understand what was going on with her head. Maybe she *was* getting too clingy. Maybe the break would be good. Because this wasn't serious, and Tess didn't want it to be.

"Make sure you get enough sleep before you leave," Margaret said after a moment. "And...drive safe."

In a flurry of limbs, Tess flipped them and furiously attached their lips. It was searing, and raw, and Tess gasped when they pulled apart.

"Let me have your phone number. Please," Tess begged. Her hand was on the side of Margaret's face, holding her still and gazing into her eyes.

The phone number had been a point of contention. Tess gave her number to Margaret before they'd even kissed, but Margaret threw the note away. Once they started having regular sex, Tess tried again—for logistical reasons—but Margaret always refused. Tess decided not to push. Sometimes, Margaret got this look in her eyes like she was one second from fleeing, and Tess didn't want to know what would happen if she pushed too far.

But Tess needed this. She kept her eyes locked on Margaret's crystal-blue eyes, bracing for a no that never came.

Instead, Margaret asked, "Why?"

"No, not why," Tess complained. "You're too good at arguing, you counter all my points."

"Get better arguments, then."

Tess scowled. "You're infuriating."

Instead of fueling the argument, Margaret rested her hand atop Tess's, the one cradling her cheek.

"Why are you so insistent on getting my phone number, Tess?"

Tess's heart pounded. That was the first time Margaret had ever called her by her first name during normal conversation, not during an orgasmic release. Tess wanted to scream. How could this woman drive her so crazy with just a simple sentence? It wasn't fair!

"Because I'll be gone for three weeks," Tess said in a rush, "and I need to be able to sext you or I won't make it."

Margaret's eyes darkened. "You're going back to your parents' house for break?"

"Yes."

"And you're going to call me—when? In the late hours of night, so you can listen to my voice while you touch yourself, fighting to keep quiet so your family won't overhear?"

Tess felt the flush of her cheeks and dipped her head, breaking their intense gaze.

"Or you'll text me, detailing all the filthy things you wish you were doing with me?"

"Y-yes." Tess's voice wavered with need.

"You naughty, filthy girl."

"Fuck, Margaret!" Tess exclaimed, punctuating her point by straddling Margaret's lap. Their mouths met again and Tess ground desperately against Margaret's thigh. "Yes, god, yes, absolutely. I will. I need to."

Margaret pressed their foreheads together, listening to Tess whimper as she built herself up.

As Tess came crashing down, Margaret grabbed her tightly and whispered into her ear, "You can have my number, then."

* * *

Tess was bubbling over with excitement for the spring semester. Of course, she was desperate to see Margaret again—that was a given—but she was also finally taking Dr. Greenwood's class. She already knew all the books they'd be reading because Elle kept her constantly updated, and she was more than excited to finally meet the professor Elle wouldn't stop gushing about.

Thanks to college, Tess was being exposed to more and more queer spaces where she could find and make new friends. She knew the Queer History and Literature course attracted others within the community, so Tess was extra excited to be in a queer space where they could discuss books about their history and community.

Just as Elle had to do, Tess's first assignment from Dr. Greenwood was to reflect on the original meaning of the word queer and, on the first day of class, share something queer about herself. Although Tess had teased Elle about her icebreaker, Tess found herself growing more and more anxious and embarrassed as the time neared to share her own queer fact. It felt monumental to share such a raw and honest part of herself with a room full of strangers.

When Tess walked into the classroom, Dr. Greenwood was already there, front and center. The desks had been arranged in a large circle, and Dr. Greenwood was in the middle of the circle, sitting on top of one of the desks. She was exactly as Elle always described. Her long gray-silver hair was pulled back in a loose ponytail. She was wearing brightly colorful tartan dress slacks paired with a floral print shirt that did not match yet shockingly seemed to coordinate perfectly with the pants.

Tess took a seat on the opposite side of the room from Dr. Greenwood. She was absolutely going to introduce herself to the professor properly at some point after class, but for this first meeting, she simply wanted to observe. Others trickled in. Tess knew several of the other students in the class from various other queer events on campus, or even just from other classes. They all sat down in the circle and waited for Dr. Greenwood to begin.

"We'll begin with our icebreakers," Dr. Greenwood explained. "You know, this is maybe my favorite exercise of the entire semester. I love this. Everyone is a little bit queer. That's the beauty of humankind. Plus, having an odd little fact about all of you helps me remember your names." She winked.

Of course, Dr. Greenwood started them off. "Hello, everyone. My name is Dr. Greenwood, and my queer fact is that my house is haunted." Tess grinned slightly. She had heard plenty about Dr. Greenwood's haunted house woes through Elle, who had passed on stories about spiritual cleansing rituals, tearing up floorboards, and redoing drywall to try and dispel the spirt. "My ex let the spirit in with all her negative energy," Dr. Greenwood said, by way of explanation. "At first, I wanted the spirit gone. I mean, who wants to live in a haunted house? I didn't know its intentions! But now, I actually think I'm starting to relate to it. I mean, maybe the spirit is just lonely like me. Maybe that's why it's appeared, so we could come together, two broken hearts looking for companionship. Being dead might be quite desolate."

The hesitant and quiet mood of the room seemed to lift from there, giving students the opportunity to relax and feel comfortable to be more open themselves. They bounced around the room through roll call as everyone else shared their unique queer tidbits.

Then, it was finally Tess's turn. When Dr. Greenwood called her name, she raised her hand slightly and answered, "Here."

"Hello, Tess," Dr. Greenwood said. "So, what's queer about you?"

"Well, I'm convinced that dolphins will someday take over the world."

"Very interesting." Dr. Greenwood smirked. "Would you be willing to elaborate?"

"Absolutely."

Tess had tortured Margaret with this fantasy tale before. It was based in logic. Dolphins were highly intelligent creatures, often interacting and communicating with humans, and their potential reach had been documented in pop culture on numerous occasions.

"The only reason they haven't taken over the planet yet is because they're stuck in the water and don't have fingers," Tess once explained smugly while lying in Margaret's bed. "But they're plotting, and the second they can figure out how to breach land, it's over for us."

"You're joking," Margaret deadpanned.

"Why would you think I'm joking? You're not a creationist by any means. If intelligent life evolved once, it's highly probable it will evolve again."

"Yes, of course I believe that. But it won't happen in our lifetimes, not even the lifetime of humans, and certainly not of dolphins. At best, a distant descendant of dolphins will evolve intelligence. That's how evolution works."

"I know." Tess dipped to kiss Margaret. "But it sounds cooler to say that dolphins will take over the world, not that someday thousands of years from now a newly evolved creature will develop intelligence."

"We aren't sensationalizing headlines, we're scientists. We should stick to the facts."

"What's wrong with a little sensationalizing?"

Margaret rolled her eyes dramatically. "Everything."

Tess noted, as they went through the syllabus after their queer introductions, that Dr. Greenwood had office hours that afternoon. She wasn't sure office hours would start already on the first day of class, but since the English department building was near the on-campus housing, Tess thought she might as well swing by that afternoon. She waited outside Dr. Greenwood's office door for a couple of minutes, looking at the Freddie Mercury poster still hanging on the door. Sure enough, not long after, Dr. Greenwood rounded the corner and nearly tripped over Tess.

"Hi, Dr. Greenwood. I didn't mean to startle you."

"No, no, it's all right," Dr. Greenwood said as she opened her office door. "I should be the one apologizing. I wasn't expecting anyone."

"I wasn't necessarily expecting you to show up," Tess replied honestly. "But I was in the area, so I figured it wouldn't hurt to swing by and check."

"All right, well, come in. Tess, right?"

"Yep, that's me."

"Why don't we sit and chat for a bit," Dr. Greenwood offered, gesturing toward the couches. "What brings you to my office today, Tess?"

"I'm in honors," Tess explained, getting straight to the point. "I was hoping to take your class as dual credit."

"Yes, you can do honors credit. No problem. You'd just have to write an extra critical paper or two. We can finalize details later. For now, I'd like to get to know you better. What's your major? What do you want to do?"

"Biology. I want to do research. I might work in industry, or I'll go for a PhD. I haven't decided yet."

"What do you do when you aren't studying?"

"Well, most of my time is dedicated to school-related activities. I work in a lab, and I'm a TA for intro bio. But I also volunteer at an animal shelter with my roommate, who, speaking of..." Tess paused. "It's Elle. I live with Elle. I told her I was starting your class today, and she told me to say hi."

Dr. Greenwood's eyes widened. "Elle?" She gasped. "Oh my gosh, so, you're the elusive roommate of Elle. It's great to finally meet you."

"And you're the spunky queer lit professor that everyone, particularly Elle, never stops talking about." Tess felt giddy. She could already tell why Elle liked Dr. Greenwood, and she could sense them getting along well and growing closer as the semester went on. She certainly hoped she could develop a close relationship with Dr. Greenwood like she had with Dr. Kemper and Dr. Marlow.

"Tell me about yourself. I want to know everything," Dr. Greenwood prodded.

They spoke for a while, just chatting. Tess spoke of her ambitions and interests, answered all of Dr. Greenwood's curious questions, and the conversation flowed naturally. Eventually, the topic shifted to literature and the class. Tess was less confident about that topic.

"I do kind of struggle with literature," Tess admitted. "It's just so subjective. I mean, there's symbolism, which can change based on the time and culture, and hidden meanings to things I can never seem to pick up on. That's why I'm more comfortable with science. In science, everything is proven by repetition and observation of measurable facts."

"You know, I have a friend who's in the sciences. She's told me almost the exact same thing before. She said that this world I live in, my world of literature, is too colorful. That she needs her black-and-white laws that never change, things that aren't influenced by emotion. But isn't it that emotion which makes us human?"

"Well...I'm determined to figure it out," Tess replied. "I want to understand literature better, to understand this colorful world of emotion that Elle is so in love with, and that you, too, love. I might just need a lot of help along the way."

Dr. Greenwood laughed. "And that's where you differ from my friend. I can never get her to open her heart—she's too stubborn. But if you're open to it and ready to fall in love with prose, then it would be my honor to guide you on your journey."

"I can't wait."

* * *

"Did you miss me?"

Margaret tipped her head down to hide her instinctual grin. She shrugged, feigning disinterest. "I found myself with fewer interruptions. I'd hardly consider that a problem," she replied, her tone neutral.

Tess slipped into the office, pulling the door shut behind her. She set a paper bag down on Margaret's desk, then settled on the couch.

"Well, I missed you over break," Tess said. "I found myself thinking about you…wishing you were around…"

Margaret recalled the purely sexual content of the phone call they shared just days earlier. She was plenty aware that Tess had been thinking about her; she had been thinking about Tess too. She made sure to detail to Tess every sinful thing she planned to do to her the second she was back.

However, she chose not to comment on Tess's setup. Instead, she investigated the food. She hadn't asked Tess to bring her food. She never asked. Yet, Tess continued to do it.

After a minute of deliberate chewing, Margaret regarded Tess. "I don't suppose you're still free Fridays?"

"I am. And I finish classes at noon, so I can come by whenever you want. My schedule's pretty open this semester. I can crash here every day."

"That's entirely too much. It's my office, Miss Stanford, not yours."

"I can stop by between every class."

"Find a hobby."

"You'd miss me."

"I wouldn't."

Tess grinned wildly. "So, what did you do over break? I saw family and friends. We baked cookies, decorated gingerbread houses, and it snowed."

"I didn't do much."

"You celebrated the holidays though, right?" Tess inquired. "Christmas, surely. I know you're an atheist, but I assume you still subscribe to the consumerist holiday. It's hard to avoid."

"Yes. I spent Christmas with…a friend."

"Whoa, a friend?" Tess gasped, being purposefully dramatic.

"Yes. That's what I said."

"I didn't think you had friends."

Margaret huffed. "I see you're just as insufferable as ever."

Tess shrugged. "So, you spent Christmas with a friend. Are family dinners too confrontational?"

"I don't have any family left."

Tess frowned. "Margaret...?" she muttered with concern.

Margaret shrugged and shifted in her seat uncomfortably. "My parents died when I was in high school. My aunt and uncle took me in. It...didn't work out. I've been on my own for so long, I don't really think twice about it."

Tess tumbled over and crashed into Margaret with a powerful hug. She practically fell into her lap, nuzzling her face into her collarbone.

"This is...unnecessary." Margaret's arms were stiff, refusing to hug Tess back. "Release me."

Tess listened, but she hovered and reached out, cupping Margaret's cheek. "It's heartbreaking that you don't realize how sad that is," she whispered. But the exchange was entirely too intimate, and Margaret felt panicked, trying to put space between them. Luckily, Tess picked up on her discomfort and pulled away completely, giving her space.

"Anyway," Margaret said, clearing her throat. "My friend's family lives across the country and she rarely sees them, so we decided to celebrate together. Everything worked out fine."

"Fine," Tess echoed. "The holidays aren't supposed to be 'fine.' They're supposed to be joyous and memorable."

"I'll admit, it was a bit boring without your constant pestering."

Tess beamed. "I knew you missed me."

"Yes, well, can you be quiet? I have work, and it's impossible to focus with all your blabbering."

"Of course, Margaret."

"And stop calling me that."

"It's your name, isn't it?"

Margaret regarded her challengingly. "Only off campus... and only if you're lucky."

"Okay, fine, *Dr. Morgan*."

* * *

As their weekly hookups continued through the spring semester, their initial desperation lessened to slower, all-encompassing meetups. Tess was just so open and safe that Margaret found herself adding tidbits to their conversations before she even realized it.

The sex was still a necessity, obviously. But the nature of their meetings was shifting. Last semester, they crashed into each other like starving dogs. Sometimes, they still went after each other with such desperation. But as they got to know each other better, they began to value the companionship just as much as the sex, and they found their patience. They were going to sleep together—they did so every week and weren't going to stop—so, they didn't need to be so frantic.

As repayment for all the food Tess brought Margaret, the professor started cooking them dinner. Eating together was only for metabolism reasons—not because it was fun to laugh with Tess, sipping on wine while they chatted about their days. Because they weren't doing it for the enjoyment of each other's company. That was far too much like dating. And they didn't date, because neither was looking for a relationship.

One night, Tess found a collection of card and board games. Margaret had them for game nights with Amy, but once Tess found the stash, she wouldn't stop pestering Margaret about playing. Eventually, Margaret gave in. Tess was relentless. That was how their friendship started—with Tess banging on her office door nonstop until Margaret was forced to listen—and it was how their friendship was to continue, evidently.

They settled in the living room around a board game. Very quickly, Tess discovered, like with all things in life, that Margaret was hypercompetent.

"Not fair! You have to be cheating!"

"How could I cheat? I rolled a three."

"Ugh! This whole game you keep rolling the exact number you need. And—" Tess paused, looking at Margaret. Margaret was snickering, trying to tamp down her grin but failing. "Oh, you are cheating! I am so livid with you." She fell to her knees and crawled toward Margaret. "But…I am also extremely turned on by your cockiness."

"Come here, then," Margaret said. She pulled Tess into her lap and kissed her, letting out a breathy moan when Tess ran her fingers through her hair, tugging gently.

"I love your short cut. I'm glad you've kept it. I adore how dark and shiny your hair is. It makes your eyes glow."

Tess jerked the fistful of hair she was holding, arching Margaret's head back. Margaret loved the feeling. A grin of contented happiness twinged with want spread across her face involuntarily. Tess's eyes sparkled as she gazed into them, and then Tess dipped and kissed her senseless.

When Tess pulled back, still fondly gazing at Margaret, she said, "You know, you're something else, Maggie."

Margaret fought against Tess's hold, trying to lean in and bite Tess's neck. She was so focused on her task that it took a moment for her lust-hazy brain to register what Tess just called her. When the words did sink in, she sat straight upright and frowned.

"Maggie?" Margaret questioned curiously.

Tess hummed, already leaning in to kiss Margaret again. But Margaret pulled back.

"*Maggie?*" she asked more incredulously.

"Yes, Maggie, short for Margaret," Tess explained. "Don't you know how nicknames work?"

"I don't have a nickname."

"Well, you do now."

"You can't just give me a nickname, that's—"

"That's exactly how nicknames work."

"You shouldn't be calling me Margaret in the first place, let alone Maggie."

"Ooh…that's really unfortunate, then, because I happen to call you Margaret, and now Maggie, rather often."

"Miss Stanford!"

"Maggie!"

"Tess!"

Tess burst out laughing. She buried her face against Margaret's shoulder as her chest heaved and Margaret threw her head back, groaning dramatically.

* * *

Margaret hated change. She liked routine and consistency, so watching her world change around her, completely out of her control, was not something she enjoyed. She didn't like it when she found out her mother had cancer, watching her get sicker, unable to stop it, and then she was gone, and her dad was gone, and then she had to move to another house. Her aunt and uncle didn't actually love her, so she was all alone, but at least back then she was in control. But now, first she had to move into the biology building, and then Tess wouldn't listen to her, and now Tess was part of the routine. But the rules and boundaries of their routine were starting to blur.

Margaret hadn't been to the bar in almost six months. She found that she didn't want to sleep with anyone other than Tess. Not because she had defined a monogamous relationship with Tess—they were casual and would remain as such. But all she thought about was Tess, and all she looked forward to was Tess.

They hadn't *really* discussed boundaries, nothing beyond saying it was casual. Therefore, Margaret assumed their arrangement was open. She didn't figure Tess would say anything, or even care, frankly, if Margaret took in other partners. Not that she was the type to let anyone else tell her what she could or couldn't do. But she didn't want to. All that need and want was now reserved for Tess.

Their sex was plentiful. She could tease and satisfy Tess so deliciously, and Tess could do the same for her. It was wonderful, relaxing, and fully satiating. Margaret couldn't even look toward another woman without immediately comparing her to Tess.

Which was a very dangerous game to play.

She was friends with Tess. They never defined that situation either, but they were. She liked having Tess in her life. She trusted that Tess wouldn't hurt her, and that let her be freer. Margaret deeply enjoyed the time she spent with Tess, whether they were naked or fully clothed, it didn't matter. Tess brightened her day.

Which was how Margaret suddenly realized, with dread, that she had broken her unspoken fourth rule.

Never fall in love.

* * *

"I need to talk to you. Right now," Margaret said, flinging open Amy's office door.

"I sense the urgency, but what's the—" Amy gasped, noticing the time. "Crap, I'm going to be late to this meeting. It's in the library…can we walk and talk?"

"No! I can't talk about this with others around, I—"

"So, I'm guessing this is about that girl you're hooking up with." Amy smirked humorously. Margaret grew pale. "Oh, lighten up, Margaret. We can talk this evening. In the meantime, walk with me to the library."

"Fine."

As they wound their way out into the damp spring air, they seemed in stark contrast to each other: Amy, a beacon of colorful sunshine, waving at others, and Margaret, glowering and stewing.

"You're like an intimidating guard dog," Amy scolded.

"Is that a bad thing?"

"We're giving textbook light and dark contrast. Actually, one of my students just wrote a paper about the juxtaposition of light and dark metaphors in literature." Amy paused. "You know, I actually think you'd get on well with this student. She's in my queer lit class this semester and she reminds me of you. She's a science major, so my class hasn't exactly been easy on her—"

"I know, you put the science kids through the ringer. You do the same to me, or try to, anyway."

"Yes, well, she's putting in far more effort to understand literature than you ever have. Although I swear, I'll make a poetry lover out of you someday. My point is, though, I think the two of you would get along."

"I don't get along well with any students."

"No, you don't, except in the case of your very special girl."

"Amy, I can't—"

"With your glowering, you're keeping everyone so far away, it doesn't matter."

"I don't like my personal business being paraded around like cheap gossip."

"I am doing nothing of the sort." Amy gasped, appalled. "Gosh, you're in a sour mood. What happened?"

"It's just…well I'm afraid that…I've grown a bit fond of her…" Margaret whispered, terrified and appalled of the emotions she was feeling.

"That's wonderful!" Amy exclaimed, clasping her hands together gleefully. "Explain why you look terrified."

"Because I am. I used to only care about myself, because no one else had my back. But now I care about you, which has been wonderful, and now there's this student…I mean, it's preposterous! How could I go from—"

"Shush, *you're* being preposterous," Amy stated sternly. "Honestly, you're being silly. It's not—"

"Dr. Morgan!"

Margaret froze, grabbing Amy's bicep forcefully, jerking her to a stop as well.

"That's *her*," Margaret forced out. "Turn around. Hurry. We can go around—"

"Dr. Morgan! Wait up."

Amy spun, her eyes frantically scanning the crowd. Just as Margaret was turning to go toward the back entrance of the library, a girl darted out of the sea of students and ran straight up to them. She very boldly caught Margaret around the waist, pulling her into a tight hug.

Amy's eyes went huge. "Tess?"

Margaret promptly shoved Tess off her.

"Oh, hi, Dr. Greenwood." Tess beamed, turning to the other professor. "I didn't realize you knew Dr. Morgan."

"I didn't realize you knew her either…"

"Well, she'll claim she doesn't know me, or that I'm just a major headache in her life," Tess said, and then she winked— *winked!*—at Margaret. "But she is actually rather fond of me, believe it or not. And I'm fond of her too, truthfully."

"I'm sure she'd say the same about me," Amy replied, eyeing her friend. Margaret was trying, and failing, to fight off the blush that was crawling up her neck.

"Enough of this," Margaret finally fought out. She spun, stalking away. Amy followed, and Tess skipped after them.

"How long have you two known each other?" Tess asked.

"We were friends back in college, actually," Amy answered.

"Wait, college?" Tess reached around Amy to playfully smack Margaret. "You mean, you've had a friend since college and you pretended you didn't have any friends?"

"Don't you have a class you need to get to?" Margaret asked, growling unhappily.

"Yes, I do, Miss Know-It-All." Tess turned back to Amy. "I do want to know about this friendship, though. Another time. I'll see you in class, Dr. Greenwood. Goodbye, Dr. Morgan."

Immediately, once Tess was gone, Amy spun on her friend. "You're kidding me. You're sleeping with Tess Stanford?"

"Shush!" Margaret snapped in panic. "Why say her name like that, like she's someone special?"

"Because she is someone special! Other than the fact that she managed to melt your ice-cold heart, she also happens to be a very lovely person. Tess is the student I was talking about. Truthfully, she's my current favorite student, and—"

Margaret rolled her eyes. "Of course she's your favorite."

"She is because we've had marvelous discussions together. But she's even more so my favorite now that I know it's her who's got you so whipped."

"I am not whipped."

"You are too. I can't believe she hugged you. You don't even let me hug you, and we're best friends."

"Yes, well."

Margaret wouldn't meet her friend's eyes. She felt bashful and sheepish, fearing that her friend could see right through her. Unfortunately for her, a dawning realization seemed to coalesce in Amy's mind at that precise moment.

Amy pointed accusingly. "I have to get to this meeting, but the second you're done with work today, you're coming straight back to my office and we're talking about this."

"No, it's—"

"No protesting. We're talking about this today."

"Fine."

Margaret regretted approaching Amy to discuss her current dilemma and found she'd prefer to crawl in a hole rather than return to Amy's office that evening. Still, she knew Amy was just as stubbornly persistent as Tess, so she wouldn't be wiggling her way out of this conversation.

* * *

Perfectly on time, Margaret returned to Amy's office. She was agitated.

"This department is ridiculous," she said as she stalked in, taking a seat on the couch. "You're the only person still here, and it's barely five. We've got people in the chemistry building until eight or later every night."

"Yes, well, some of us understand the importance of a healthy work-life balance. Anyway, let's talk about something other than work, shall we?"

Margaret sat rigidly but broke a moment later, her shoulders falling.

"I guess you want to talk about Tess," she practically grumbled.

"Yes, I do." Amy nodded eagerly. "When were you going to tell me that you're in love with her?"

Margaret coughed, her face growing a brilliant red. "I most certainly am not."

"You most certainly are. Don't lie to me, Margaret," Amy scolded. "She hugged you—in public, no less—and you didn't even snap at her. You tolerated—"

"Yes, tolerated, that's hardly—"

"That's more than you let anyone else do. You keep that bubble around you, but you let Tess in easily. You're completely right. You have grown fond of her…rather very fond of her."

Margaret let out a shaky breath. "I mean, I do. Have feelings, I mean." She swallowed hard, unable to properly articulate her feelings. She took a moment to compose herself. "However, nothing will come from what I'm feeling. We've both been clear about our casual intentions."

"You realize feelings can change? Clearly, since your own feelings have. You should probably revisit that conversation about boundaries, have a quick check-in."

"She'd never feel the same way," Margaret said dejectedly. "How could she fall for someone so much older, harder, and emotionally unavailable? She wouldn't. I'm snappish and standoffish, bitter and cold. She could never care for me...not in that way."

"You could be right. She might not be interested. But people can surprise you too. You should talk—"

"Absolutely not." Margaret's heart pounded at the mere idea of speaking to Tess so openly. "It doesn't matter, it would never work out anyway. She's young with her entire life ahead of her... I'm old and stubborn and stuck in my ways."

"Stop calling yourself old, it makes me feel worse," Amy said. "Maybe it's not the most common of situations, but age-gap relationships do work."

"Tess told me she's only interested in sex. I would never betray her trust by letting my foolish feelings get in the way. Besides, the sex is entirely too good to risk."

Amy pursed her lips. "You're putting up walls. That never works. You're going to get hurt in the end anyway."

"It doesn't matter. I've survived heartbreak before, I'll survive it again."

"Oh, Margaret, this is entirely too sad. You finally have someone in your life who makes you happy."

"You make me happy—"

"Beyond me, Margaret. I want you to get what I experienced with Susan, even if it wasn't forever. I want you to get some of that. Because love is beautiful and wonderful, and you deserve—"

"I don't deserve anything!" Margaret reared on Amy, snarling. "You hear what people say about me. I'm a horrid monster, the devil incarnate. I'm not a nice person. I don't deserve happiness."

"I know you believe that," Amy stated firmly, "but I don't, and I never will."

* * *

"I want to introduce you to this guy."

"A weird opener," Tess said, eyeing Kai suspiciously. "I know I'm not dating anyone, but come on. You know I only like women."

"No, I know that," Kai said, playfully smacking Tess on the arm. "I didn't mean it like that. You know how GSA had that social that you couldn't come to because you were too busy banging the brains out of our resident bio-chem professor?"

"My Fridays are occupied." Tess shrugged, unapologetic.

"I went to the social, though, and I ended up chatting with this super nice freshman. He's in our bio section. I told him to come to office hours this week."

"He should. Our office hours are a lot of fun."

"That's exactly what I said. Anyway, his name is Caleb, and he's been struggling. He's stuck in the girls' dorm because you know our school won't allow cogendered housing and—"

"Wait, what? The girls' dorm? But—oh, wait, is he trans?"

"Yeah, exactly."

"And they stuck him in the girls' dorm? That's awful."

"We should boycott, right? It won't help Caleb this semester, though. But I figured we could, in the very least, help him out with biology, and I'm trying to use my RA powers to finesse something."

"We can definitely help him with biology. I can't wait to meet him."

Caleb had a spunky, charismatic personality. He also was failing biology, probably because he did more chatting than studying. But in his defense, he had a lot of other crises going on in his life.

"The office hours tonight were really helpful, but I don't know," Caleb said. "My grade is pretty bad. I think it's going to take a lot to pull me out of this one."

"If some extra one-on-one tutoring would help, we could do that too," Kai said. "We tend to hang out periodically throughout the week, so if you wanted to come hang, we could just also talk about biology."

"Yeah, and if you hang out at my apartment, Kai's girlfriend also happens to be a pretty smart bio major too."

"Okay, yeah, I'm definitely going to take you up on that offer," Caleb said.

"Fantastic. Can't wait to see you around."

And so, under the guise of tutoring, Kai and Tess befriended Caleb, who needed friends and allies much more than he needed help with biology.

* * *

The next time Tess shoved into Margaret's office, she paused, realizing that Margaret was not sitting at her desk as usual. Instead, she was sitting on the couch. Tess, to her knowledge, was the only one who ever sat on that couch. Certainly Margaret never did.

Tess pressed her hands to her hips. "You're in my spot."

Margaret glanced up from some papers. "I seem to remember this being my couch, not yours."

Tess watched momentarily as Margaret returned to her reading. Tess could tell from her expression that she wasn't impressed with the article. It was striking how well Tess could read the other woman. It was to be expected since they spent so much time together, but it still hit Tess hard when she realized she didn't have such a close relationship with anyone else.

Sensing that Margaret was about to bark at her about loitering and gawking, Tess turned, shut the door, and walked over. She nudged her. Margaret ignored her. With a huff, Tess fell onto the couch, landing halfway on Margaret's lap. Margaret scowled, but Tess looked up at her through her lashes, and Margaret gave in, shifting over. Tess smirked proudly in triumph and reclined.

"Why are you sitting over here today?" Tess asked. "You never sit over here."

After a short pause, Margaret said, "My back hurts." Tess raised her eyebrows. Margaret, admitting a weakness? Unheard of.

"Turn around. I'll give you a massage."

"That's not necessary."

Tess noted the very matter-of-fact tone Margaret defaulted back to when she was uncomfortable.

"My friends say I give the best massages," Tess replied, resting her hand on Margaret's arm. "But even if they didn't, you of all people ought to know what magic I can work with my fingers."

Margaret opened her mouth to further protest, but Tess dropped her hands to Margaret's hips, squeezing gently but emphatically.

"Fine," Margaret said, giving in.

"What hurts the most?"

"My lower back."

Tess grazed her hands over Margaret's back, across her silken shirt, and pressed firmly into her lower back. She continued to push until she felt her relax. Then, she lightened her movements, feeling impish. After a while, her massage reached the desired effect when Margaret, lost in herself, let out a breathy moan.

"Glorious," Tess whispered, equally as breathy, right into her ear.

Margaret tensed and pulled away, clearly coming back into herself. She cleared her throat. "Thank you. That was…nice… adequate. My back feels much better now."

"Anytime."

It was weird to think how much had changed in the three years they'd known each other. At first, Tess tried to avoid the admittedly attractive woman, mainly because she could recognize Margaret's temper. But then she learned that Margaret was capable of caring for students. How could everyone hate Margaret, not a single person able to recognize her ability for good, other than Tess? She was a mystery that Tess wanted to solve. Of course, now that she knew Margaret better, she knew she was quite capable of caring, of compassion, and that she wasn't just some soulless demon. She even had friends.

They settled, the blush fading from Margaret's cheeks. Margaret continued reading and Tess pulled out some homework, but she was having a difficult time focusing. If the massage had been in private, it would have ended much differently. Just sitting beside her in her office, Tess longed for the other woman just inches away.

Tess set her homework on the coffee table, slipped her shoes off, and turned to face Margaret, tucking her feet up on the couch. She wiggled closer and snuggled against Margaret's side, laying her head down in Margaret's lap.

"Wha—what are you doing?" Margaret snapped, but her voice wavered in confusion.

"Taking a nap." Tess yawned. "Wake me up before two? I don't want to miss my class."

"On me?"

"Well, you're taking up the whole couch, and you stole the two pillows—"

"I need the support. My back hurts."

"Regardless, you're comfortable."

"No, but—you can't just—"

The protests died on Margaret's tongue as Tess snaked her arms around her waist. Margaret bit her lip, looking down at Tess cuddled against her. Slowly, Margaret lowered her arms and rested them against Tess's back.

"I suppose one time won't hurt," Margaret whispered. "But, certainly, do not make a habit of this."

"No promises."

* * *

"Hi, Dr. Greenwood. How's it going?"

"Tess. Come in. Things are going well. How are you doing?"

"All right." Tess plopped down on the mismatched couch. "I know we just finished a paper, but I was hoping we could discuss the reading. I think this is a pivotal moment, but I can't make out the meaning. I was hoping that talking through it would help."

"We can definitely talk about the reading, but there's something else we need to talk about first."

"Oh," Tess uttered, caught off guard. She stopped reaching into her backpack and instead sat back. "I, um, is this about the honors work? Because I'm almost done with the first draft, and I hadn't planned to talk about it, but we can if you'd like—"

"No, this is unrelated."

"All right."

Dr. Greenwood folded her hands across her lap. "You're sleeping with my dear friend Margaret."

Immediately, Tess panicked, but she fought to school her expression.

"Sorry, what?" Tess said as innocently as she could manage, but her voice pitched higher, giving her away even if Dr. Greenwood hadn't already known the truth.

Dr. Greenwood quickly said, "You aren't in trouble. Sorry, I didn't mean to scare you."

"I—but…how do you know?"

"Margaret's my best friend, Tess. We talk," Dr. Greenwood explained simply. "I've known she was sleeping with a student since the start, although I didn't know it was you until you ran into us the other day."

"Oh…I…well this isn't going to be a problem, is it? Since you're my professor and I'm…sleeping with your best friend."

"Well, you aren't sleeping with me, so it's hardly a problem."

"Okay. I appreciate that, a lot, really. I like your class, and also, it's past the drop date."

"Don't worry about it."

Tess nodded, staring down at her hands. She could feel Dr. Greenwood observing her in silence until she looked back up.

"You don't need to play the protective friend," Tess said. "I know my relationship with Margaret is a bit unconventional, but I do genuinely care about her. She's my friend too."

"I can tell—or…I could tell, just from that small exchange between you two. Sorry for how blunt I was. I just wanted you to know so things won't be awkward in the future. Like, if I showed up at Margaret's house one evening, and you were over there. I'd much prefer we're on the same page now."

Tess let out a small, somewhat forced laugh. "Yeah, I guess that's a good point."

"Would it be horribly nosy of me if I asked what you see in her?" Dr. Greenwood asked, a playful pitch to her words. "I love Margaret, I do, but she does come off pretty cold, hard, and dryly sarcastic. She's not always the easiest person to get along with."

"No, not always. But...she's a caring person, in her own way, if you know what to look for. Sure, she can be blunt and demanding, but that confidence is infuriatingly attractive."

"I'm glad someone's finally seen her for who she truly is."

"So, you've known Margaret since college, but how did you meet? I'm just curious. Did you go to the same school?"

"No. I was in graduate school while Margaret was in undergrad," Dr. Greenwood explained. "We met at a Pride rally."

"A Pride rally? What year?"

"Early nineties."

"Were celebrations like that even commonplace back then?"

"Yes and no. If you were in the community and knew where to go, we were everywhere. It wasn't so commercial as it is now, but we were there, rallying and fighting."

"How did it feel when they legalized gay marriage? I was a teen, and I wasn't out back then, so I didn't celebrate much. But I could imagine that for you...I don't know."

"It was wonderful, getting recognition as people, that we could have the same basic human rights as everyone else. I was in a committed partnership at the time, but we never married. I had friends that did, though, and it was amazing."

Tess worried her lip before hesitantly asking, "Can I ask why you never married?"

Dr. Greenwood shrugged. "Hindsight is twenty-twenty. I think Susan always wanted an easy escape. But at the time we were happy and didn't feel the need to change our lives."

"I remember Elle mentioned you'd recently left a twenty-year relationship..."

Dr. Greenwood nodded. "I've mostly made my peace with it now. Sometimes, people just grow apart."

"I'm sorry."

"Don't be. I'm happy I got to love her for as many years as I did. Anyway, back on topic. My friendship with Margaret. College is good for us queers, usually. We get out of our toxic parents' houses, leave behind friends with preconceived ideas of us, and we get to spread our wings as individuals, find like-minded people and a community where we can be ourselves. My family's an open-minded bunch. It wasn't ever an issue. Margaret's family was…not so understanding."

"Didn't Margaret's parents die when she was in high school?"

"Yes. Did she tell you what happened?"

"No. I'm surprised she told me at all, actually. It's just…she's so sad sometimes. I'm sure that loss was really difficult."

"It was. I won't betray her privacy beyond that, but yes. Losing her parents was hard on her, and then her aunt and uncle, who she went to live with after, did not make her life any easier."

Tess went silent, very curious but not willing to probe Dr. Greenwood for secrets. She respected Margaret's personal life and her desires to share or not share those details. "So, did Margaret go hog wild in college?" she asked instead.

Dr. Greenwood laughed. "I met her two beers and a blunt in. I fell for many of the same charms you have—her self-assuredness, her confidence, her demand for excellence, all that."

"Wait, you…fell for?" Tess tensed, feeling suddenly protective, unsure where these feelings were coming from.

"Yes, we hooked up, a bit of a fling," Dr. Greenwood answered. "For a short spell we dated, but we realized we weren't compatible and split ways. Are you all right with that? That Margaret and I have a history?"

Tess became aware of herself then, blinking wide-eyed, surprised by her own instinctual reaction. "I, um, yes, of course," she said, deflating. "I just, well, I feel I need to ask, are you okay with me sleeping with her now?"

Dr. Greenwood burst out laughing. "Absolutely. That ship has long since sailed. When we ran into each other here on campus, we rebuilt our friendship then, but nothing more."

"You're sure?"

"I don't feel anything romantic or sexual toward Margaret, I assure you. Even back when we were young, she kept her heart very guarded. She's still a lone-wolf type, distant, bedding women for the experience but unwilling to spend enough time with anyone to gain any sort of emotional attachment."

Tess frowned. "Does she...sleep around a lot?"

"Truthfully, yes, she used to," Dr. Greenwood admitted, speaking slower, as if she were carefully picking each word. "She'd go to the bar and leave with a different woman every weekend."

"Explains why she's so good in bed."

"But she hasn't gone out since she started sleeping with you, at least not to my knowledge."

Tess nodded firmly. "Okay, good, because if she was sleeping around, I'd make her get checked more often. Wow, every weekend, huh? Is it bad that I feel proud that I manage to keep her content now?"

"I'm impressed myself. Although I think it's more than just your skills. I think she likes your company."

Tess smiled. "I like her company too."

"Good. Now then, let's discuss this week's reading."

* * *

When Tess left Dr. Greenwood's office some thirty minutes later, she ran straight back to her apartment and burst in screaming for Elle. She slid to a stop in Elle's doorway and, picking up on the urgency, Elle gave Tess her full attention.

"Dr. Greenwood knows!" Tess declared, chest heaving.

Elle frowned. "Dr. Greenwood knows what?"

"That I'm sleeping with Dr. Morgan."

"I—whoa, okay, hang on. How does she know?"

"Because Dr. Greenwood is friends with Dr. Morgan."

"Friends?" Elle asked incredulously.

"Yes, friends! They've known each other since college."

"I didn't know the devil had friends."

"She's not the devil—"

"Yes, because you're sweet on her."

"That's not the point," Tess grumbled.

"But friends, really? Dr. Greenwood and Dr. Morgan?"

"Yes, but that isn't even all. They dated in college."

Elle's eyes widened even further in shock. "Dated? They dated?"

"And Dr. Greenwood confronted me about it. It was mortifying, having a professor call you out on your sex life. Especially because, I mean, yes, we've been getting to know each other better, but I wouldn't say we're particularly close, so I went to her office hours for normal class stuff and she was all, 'Before we discuss the reading, I know you're sleeping with Dr. Morgan.'"

"Well…you are," Elle stated. "I mean, it was only a matter of time before people started figuring it out."

"I know." Tess deflated. "I assume they're close. I just don't want it to be weird, or for it to be a problem."

"Well, if it bothers you that much, just stop sleeping with her."

Tess's head snapped up, eyes blazing. "No!"

"Why so dramatic?" Elle asked with a shrug. "I mean, so the sex is good, but there are other women. This is casual, right? But don't you want to settle down someday, and surely not with Dr. Morgan. So, you'd have to stop eventually, right?"

"I—" Tess shut her mouth abruptly.

What was she doing? Did she want a serious relationship? She didn't a year ago when she first started sleeping with Margaret, although she did want to settle down someday. But Margaret wasn't girlfriend material.

Well, she could be, possibly. Tess cared about Margaret and certainly, in private, she cared about Tess. Although her aggressive mood swings had lessened, Margaret was still prone to angry outbursts and snobbish comments. Tess didn't want those characteristics in a long-term partner. However, was it possible that Margaret was shedding those distasteful traits of her icy exterior? With more compassion and guidance, tasteful nudging from Tess in the right direction, could she become the type of person Tess could fully fall for? Was Tess willing to wait it out, willing to put in all that work with no guarantee of success? If she wasn't, should they even continue sleeping together? Tess didn't want to give up the sex, or the companionship, but now that Dr. Greenwood knew, things might get complicated.

"I need to talk to Margaret about it," Tess concluded, mostly to herself.

"Who's Margaret?"

"Sorry, Dr. Morgan."

"Oh my god, you're on a first-name basis?"

Tess scoffed, fixing her roommate with a funny expression. "Elle, I've been knuckle-deep in her and you didn't think I'd call her by her first name?"

"Okay, well, I've never slept with a professor before, so how was I supposed to know the etiquette?"

Tess laughed. "Yeah, okay, fair."

* * *

Margaret had to admit that the couch was rather comfortable and perhaps she shouldn't have been so stubborn about not sitting on it before. The cushions were soft, and the lighting was good for reading. But what made it most enticing was that Tess could sit right beside her.

Margaret tried to ignore Tess. She did everything in her power to maintain the walls she built years ago. But it was futile. Margaret was desperately running around with a bucket of mortar, resetting bricks just as quickly as Tess was sledgehammering them down.

In her office, Margaret liked their farce. She focused on work and ignored Tess as long as possible. Viewing it as a challenge, Tess pushed closer. She'd stab at Margaret's sides or pinch her arms. Sometimes, she'd bite an earlobe or suck on Margaret's neck until she was forced to acknowledge her.

Or, in her less mischievous moods, Tess would wiggle her way into Margaret's arms. Those were the moments Margaret realized she was most screwed: when her heartbeat picked up—not out of lust, but something deeper—and she grew irritated with her heart's betrayal.

That evening, Tess settled on the latter, cuddled against Margaret's breastbone. When Margaret glanced down, she noticed a gleam of admiration in Tess's eyes. Her pulse quickened. She swallowed roughly and looked away, afraid she might get lost in the hazel orbs and her own eyes would reflect back, spilling her secrets.

They stayed like that for a long while. Tess had finished her homework ages ago and was just waiting for Margaret to finish her work. But Margaret kept rereading the same lines, unable to focus. Still, she didn't move. It was the most comfortable position she'd ever been in, with Tess cuddled against her. She noted it was nearly nine at night. How had it gotten so late? When did their impatience die back?

It was safer before…when she'd sleep with one woman and leave before the light of day. But now, everything was unsettled, and Margaret felt seasick with the world shifting around her.

"Did you tell Dr. Greenwood that we're sleeping together? Or did she just happen to discover it?"

Margaret startled, Tess's voice abrupt in the otherwise quiet office. Then, it took her a moment to comprehend who Tess was talking about.

"Oh, you mean Amy," Margaret stated, clearing her throat. "I told her I was sleeping with a student. I never mentioned your name because I assumed she didn't know you. I might not have told her more, except that before you, she and I always met up on Fridays, a girls' night of sorts. Amy went through a bad breakup and needed a friend. It morphed into regular wine-and-game nights."

"Oh," Tess said. She was quiet, then she muttered something into Margaret's abdomen.

"What?"

She was met with another equally muffled answer.

"Sit up and talk to me," Margaret snapped. "You're in physics. Surely you know how sound works. I can't hear you when you're talking directly into my shirt."

Tess jerked upright, eyes squinting. "Dr. Greenwood told me that you two dated," she said, voice fully clear, eyes locked on Margaret as if challenging her to deny it.

Margaret didn't understand. "Yes, we did." Still, the stare. "So? What's your point?"

"So?" Tess mimicked with animosity.

"That was two decades ago, I don't even…" Margaret shook her head, still confused. "What is this?" she finally asked.

"What? N-nothing!" Tess's cheeks reddened.

Margaret cocked an eyebrow, questioning, "Jealousy?"

"Don't be ridiculous!"

Margaret smirked then, realizing her hunch was correct. "It is. You're jealous."

"Am not."

"Are too."

Margaret reached out and snaked her arm around the back of Tess's head, pulling her closer. She ran her teeth along Tess's jaw, then dipped and sucked at her pulse point, listening to the whimper that escaped Tess's lips.

Margaret pulled back slightly. "You don't have anything to be jealous about. I have no interest in Amy. None whatsoever. I rather like bedding you weekly, believe it or not."

"I know." Tess moaned. Her voice was breathy as Margaret tugged her shirt collar down, nibbling at her collarbone. "I just…I didn't realize you had an ex you're so close with, and I know you're a bit of a player, so I just—"

Margaret jerked back. "A player? What on earth did Amy tell you?"

"No, I just meant—she said you used to go to bars and pick up different women every weekend." Margaret opened her mouth, but Tess cut her off. "Don't try to deny it. You're too good in bed. I know you're experienced."

"I wasn't going to deny it. I don't tend to lie," Margaret stated lowly, feeling defensive. "Why is this a problem now?"

"It's not. This is casual. I just want to hear it from you. Do you go out Saturday nights after we've slept together and pick up another woman?"

"If I said yes?"

Tess pressed her lips together. "Then you better be getting tested for STIs. I don't want to catch something."

"I'm not, truthfully," Margaret said, deflating. "Since we started sleeping together, no, I haven't slept with anyone else. I would never jeopardize your health. Surely you know that?"

Tess dipped her head. "Yes, of course. Maybe I was jealous, thinking there was more to you that I didn't know about. I'm glad you have other friends, truly. But maybe I'm just a bit jealous that I'm not your only friend, even if it's silly."

"It is silly, but a bit cute, especially when you get flustered."

"Stop." Tess attempted to protest, but she was giggling too much. Margaret moved to kiss her, but Tess stopped her, flinging her hands up. "Wait!" She gasped. "You could have told me that you were busy on Fridays. I can't believe you blew off your best friend just to have sex with me."

Margaret rolled her eyes. "Amy is fine. We meet regularly on Sundays for brunch now. She's hardly being ignored."

"Positive?"

"I even, sometimes, go visit her on the fine arts side of campus. So, yes, I'm positive that I'm not neglecting my friend."

"You better watch out, because I live closer to the fine arts side of campus and I'm becoming friends with Dr. Greenwood, so I might start crashing her office too."

"Better hers than mine," Margaret teased.

"You don't mean that."

"No, I don't." Margaret punctuated her statement with a solid kiss. "I think it's past time for us to head out, don't you think?"

"Yes, let's get going."

* * *

As Tess headed up to Margaret's office Friday evening, she noted that Debbie was still in her office. It was odd getting onto a first-name basis with her professors. Margaret...well, that was inevitable and a lot different than her other professors. Debbie and Kathy, though…they wanted their team to feel closer, to eliminate the formal titles and power rankings. They were all working toward a common goal, to help the freshmen learn intro bio, and so with time the TAs began using the professors' first names outside of class.

"Working late?" Tess popped her head into the office.

"Oh, Tess, hi," Debbie responded. "Yes, unfortunately. What are you still doing here?"

"Oh, just hanging out with some friends and studying."

"Well, don't spend your entire weekend studying. Take some time off to relax too."

Tess pressed her lips together, already imagining her time with Margaret. "Oh, I'll definitely make time to relax. Have a good weekend."

"You too, Tess."

Their evening was no different than it usually was. Margaret was still working when Tess got to her office, so they sat for a bit in their own respective areas, stealing wanton glances at each other. When their need built up to a deliriously high level, they left the building, practically racing for the parking garage where Margaret was parked. They chased after each other giddily, unaware and uncaring of their surroundings.

It was already dark outside, and campus was officially in weekend mode. Commotion emanated from the main part of campus. There was clearly some event happening, the rumbling of distant music a telltale sign.

Across the street, a group of girls ran by in short dresses and heels, squealing. Farther down the sidewalk, a group of boys in shorts and backward caps laughed loudly. No one was paying attention to anyone else. Tess, speed-walking after Margaret, reached forward and pinched her side.

"Hey," Margaret snapped, reeling on Tess. Her look, however, was needy. Tess shivered.

When they reached the parking garage, Margaret got her revenge, diving on Tess.

"Maggie! S-stop! That tickles." Tess giggled, squealing as she tried to wiggle away from Margaret's invasive hands. Margaret, however, did not stop, running her nimble fingers around Tess's sides toward her stomach. "No, stop." She attempted to sound scolding, but her giggling tone came out too playful.

"Stop calling me that ridiculous nickname, and maybe I'll stop."

"Maybe?" Tess asked incredulously. "Maybe isn't good enough, Margaret." She turned, poking a finger straight into Margaret's breastbone.

By then they had reached Margaret's car, and in protest Margaret had cornered Tess against the closed passenger door. She leaned in closer to Tess, close to her lips before tipping toward her ear. "Watch yourself, Miss Stanford," she said, her voice low and sinful.

Tess moaned, practically melting under the intensity of Margaret. She fisted her hands in Margaret's shirt to keep her close despite her earlier protests.

"Fine." Tess's voice was barely more than a whisper. "I won't call you Maggie."

"See? Now was that really so difficult?" Margaret took a step back.

"For the next hour," Tess added coyly.

Margaret narrowed her eyes, firmly pressing her lips together. Then she grabbed Tess's arm, pulling her forward before she opened the passenger car door. "Get in." She shoved Tess toward the open car door. Tess nodded, dipping as she got into the car.

While Margaret walked around the car to get into the driver's side, Tess caught movement out of the corner of her eye and quickly turned to look out the window. She scanned the entire parking garage, looking around and between cars.

When Margaret got in and slammed the car door, Tess asked, "Did you see someone out there?"

"What? Someone in the garage?"

"Yes."

"I don't know. There are a few scattered people out and about right now. Why?"

Tess shook her head slightly. "I don't know. I thought I saw someone. It looked like Debbie, I thought."

"Well, she does tend to work late. I run into her leaving late occasionally."

"You don't think she saw us, do you?"

Margaret was silent for a moment. "No, probably not. People are often in their own heads, in their own little worlds."

"Okay."

Margaret reached out and caressed Tess's thigh, running her hand slowly higher. "Let's get out of here, all right?"

Tess nodded eagerly.

* * *

Students poured from the library. Kai, amidst the confusion, grabbed an evacuating student and asked what was happening.

"It's Dr. Morgan," the student replied. "She's on the second floor, shouting at everyone, a huge nightmare. I was on the third floor when I heard shouting, and then word spread to get out, the devil's temper is raging."

Tess pursed her lips. "That's hardly nice."

"Yeah, well, she was saying plenty of not nice things to others, trust me. If I were you, I'd stay clear."

Another wave of students burst from the library, and Kai placed her hands on her hips stubbornly. "Yeah, well, I need to print my paper, grumpy Dr. Morgan or not. And I promised Elle I'd grab that book for her, the one she needs to write her midterm paper."

"I know." Tess bit her lip, frowning slightly as she stared at the library. This temper, and her poor treatment of others, was something she greatly disliked about Margaret.

Kai looked pointedly at Tess. "I think we both know what's about to happen here."

"We do?"

"Yes," Kai stated emphatically. "Dr. Morgan is terrifying, but you like her. Most importantly, she doesn't scare you at all. So, therefore, you are going into the library, finding her, and getting her to chill out. While you do that, I'll print my paper and grab Elle's book."

"Okay, just because I'm not afraid of her doesn't mean I have any control over her mood."

"You do, literally. Her mood is always best on Monday, after meeting up with you over the weekend, and Fridays she's tolerable because she's too distracted to be mean."

Tess considered this. "Fine. Let's go."

Kai grabbed Tess by her backpack and shoved her forward like a human shield. They fought against the outward flow of students, all grumbling and gulping. As they made their way up the stairs, a library worker stopped them.

"Just to warn you, it's probably best you avoid the second floor. Dr. Morgan's up there, if you've heard of her, and she's in a nasty mood. It's probably best if you just come back later."

Feeling a growing sense of protectiveness over all the upset students they were encountering, Tess stood up tall, pulling away from Kai. "Thanks for the heads-up," she said, shoving her sleeves up as she marched up the stairs, ready for confrontation. Kai chased after her.

On the second floor, they encountered Margaret sitting at a table, while behind her, students cowered behind bookshelves, trying to plan their escape.

"Deal with that," Kai said, pointing at Margaret. Then she moved quickly in the direction of the printers.

A couple of boys went tearing across the room in a full-on sprint. Margaret's head snapped up and she shouted, "This is a library! Stop thrashing around like elephants." She then turned, noting several students gawking at her, and snapped, "What are you staring at?" The students quickly retreated into cover.

One girl crept forward, determinedly focused on the exit. However, as she passed Margaret's table, she mistakenly looked at the professor. Their gazes locked and the girl startled, banging into the table and toppling over a stack of books.

"Idiot!" Margaret screeched. "Watch where you're going."

"I'm so sorry."

Tess hadn't personally witnessed Margaret's public display of wrath in a long while. As an upperclassman, she was busy enough that she didn't linger around the STEM quad to overhear things, and when she was free, she was purposefully seeking out Margaret in the privacy of her office. But witnessing the professor shouting insults in the library, she felt transported back to her freshman year. Tess couldn't be friends with someone who treated others so poorly. It was hypocritical, went against all of Tess's morals. She clenched her fists and power-walked up to Margaret, her animosity mirroring how she felt when she first confronted her over her classmate's torn-up prelab several years prior.

Tess saw Margaret opening her mouth and she pointed her finger sharply at her, stalling any retort. "Don't." The abruptness stunned Margaret silent momentarily, long enough for Tess to turn to the student who was still shaking beside the table.

"Go on," Tess said, urging the girl away. Once she was gone, she turned back to Margaret. "You're behaving horribly. How dare you speak to students like that?"

"How dare you speak to me like that?" Margaret shot back. "They're interrupting me. I'm trying to get work done. And now my books are all knocked over and—"

"I can tell that you're upset, but that doesn't give you the right to shout like this." Tess reached out, collecting the toppled stack of books to help.

"Those were in order."

Tess's hand stilled on the book she was holding, and she sucked in a deep breath to maintain her own temper. "Alphabetical?" she asked, sensing a pattern.

"By title, not author. Excluding 'the.'"

Tess fixed the order of the book stack. She stopped on the last book, reading the title more carefully. She understood.

"Your drug failed clinicals, didn't it?" Tess whispered sympathetically.

Margaret's face contorted into a mask of anger. "Do you mind? I have a lot of work I need to get done, and you're being distracting, just like everyone in this damn library, using it as a social gathering hotspot."

Margaret's shouts cut deep into Tess. She thought that they, at least, had reached a level of understanding, of personal compassion. That if issues arose, or things were troubling them, they could talk about it with each other and not take their anger out on each other. But apparently that was asking for too much intimate commitment, as Margaret was currently snarling at Tess like she was any old student.

Clearly, this wasn't going to work.

"I'm just trying to help, and you're being a jerk," Tess said, stepping back. "I'm sorry your drug failed clinicals. I know how much effort you put into that project, and I know how excited you were about it. I'm sure this setback sucks. But just because you're struggling does not mean you can take it out on others, and it certainly doesn't mean you can take it out on me."

"You *don't* know! You're just an undergrad. What drugs have you had in clinical trials? What hours have you spent fighting for grant funding for your lab? Stop prattling on like you know anything about my situation, and leave me alone!"

Tess crossed her arms, frowning. "I thought you respected me more. Yes, I have less experience—I'm younger! But you know my academic merit. You know of my own commitment to science. I understand the gravity of this."

"You will never understand because you—you—"

"Because what? Because I'm not a real scientist? Because you don't think I'll ever be a real scientist? Just say it, Margaret. I know you're thinking it." Tess pressed her lips together firmly, tears welling up in her eyes. She pulled further in on herself.

Tess wanted to wait, hoping Margaret would realize how poor her attitude was, but she felt hurt. She started to turn, fearful tears would escape her eyes, ready to bolt out of the library just like all the other students. But as she turned, Margaret stood up and stepped toward her quickly, catching her arm firmly.

"Wait, Tess, no," Margaret frantically said. "I didn't—no. This has nothing to do with you. This is just me, and my issues, and—and yes, you're right. It's affecting my mood and I'm taking it out on others and—"

"You can't do that."

"I—"

"I'm serious," Tess stated more firmly. She sniffled and rubbed at her eyes furiously. Then she looked down at the floor, contemplating, before stepping closer to Margaret, lowering her voice. "I *know* that you're capable of being nice, that you're considerate and caring when you want to be. You're like a different person when it's just the two of us. But that's the problem. It's...hypocritical if I just ignore the way you treat others. You can't treat others like this. I can't be friends with someone who does—"

Margaret very abruptly stepped back. Her expression was hollow. She looked ghostly.

Tess rolled her eyes in annoyance. "Now is not the time for your stupid 'I don't have friends' bullshit."

Margaret's breathing was sporadic and heavy. "No, I... Please, sit for a second. I want to talk. I need to think."

Tess, still frowning, sat down at the table. Margaret sat a few paces away. They were close enough they could have a soft conversation just between them, unnoticed by the others around them. Several more students took that opportunity to run out of the library, though many were frozen, watching the heated exchange that was taking place, confused.

"Friends are...a new concept for me," Margaret started, and Tess patiently waited for her to say more. "I wouldn't want you to be friends with someone like me either. You're infinitely too good to put up with someone as cantankerous as me."

Tess heard an out. Though, it was self-sabotaging. Perhaps what Margaret needed most was loyal friends who would stand by her side and help her grow into a better person, not friends who fled the second things got rough. Still, Tess had standards. She crossed her arms stubbornly.

"You're right. I'm not going to put up with you," Tess declared. Margaret nodded slightly, melancholy. "I'm going to challenge you to be a better person." Margaret looked up at her. "Figure out less destructive ways to manage your emotions without taking it out on others. I know you're capable. You're good about it to both me and Dr. Greenwood. Now you need to start extending it to others—students, strangers, your coworkers."

Margaret nodded. "Okay." She glanced around the library. Students were still giving them a wide berth. "I'm...sorry."

"Do better."

"All right."

Silence stretched between them. "I...Where does this leave us?" Margaret hesitantly asked.

Tess contemplated this. On the one hand, she certainly didn't want to stop their weekly sex. She didn't even want to stop their personal hanging out. But she was trying to be a good role model, as a TA, and ignoring how Margaret made her students feel wasn't sitting right.

Finally, Tess answered, "I don't know."

Margaret slid forward, closer to Tess. "Let me try to make it up to you," she said. "I will try to do better at work, to be more open and less cold. If you find my behavior satisfactory, you can come to my office on Friday as usual."

Tess nodded in agreement. She could work with that.

"And...if you are not fully convinced that I am taking this as seriously as I should be, then perhaps Saturday, if you haven't already made plans, you could...stay."

Tess's eyes widened. She had been fighting with Margaret for months to get more than a single night with her. She wanted to feel less like a one-night stand and more like a committed fuck buddy, to reflect the nature and strength of their developed friendship. But like always, Margaret had been cold and opposed to any change in her routine. Now, Tess could sense how serious she was about improving her attitude and how sorry she was for her behavior, since she was offering up her Saturday to Tess as repayment.

"All Saturday?" Tess asked hopefully. "You mean, you'd let me stay? The entire day?"

"We could, if you're amenable."

Unable to control herself, Tess reached forward and grasped Margaret's hand. "Yes!" Tess eagerly agreed.

* * *

For Margaret, moderating her temper wasn't easy. It was difficult, at first, to catch herself and reel in her automatic responses. But once she took pause, she was able to think more critically about her words and how they would be perceived. She hoped her changes were noticeable and that Tess would appreciate the effort she was attempting to make.

She was on her best behavior for the codepartment meeting, knowing Tess would most likely ask her biology mentors for an update on Margaret's behavior. She bit her tongue when others made outlandish comments, smiled politely at others, and the only comment she made was a scientifically relevant, and kindly delivered, point.

Then, all Margaret could do was wait in her office and hope that it was enough, that Tess would come to her, and she could be forgiven. She nibbled nervously at her fingers as she waited, watching the clock, counting the minutes as they ticked by. Just as she started to lose hope, feeling depressed, her office door slowly opened.

Tess stepped in, folding her arms neatly together as she stood in front of Margaret's desk.

"Debbie and Kathy said the codepartment meeting went really well," Tess said. "Something about pleasant conversation and no petty derailments."

Margaret wasn't sure what to say, so she just remained quiet, waiting for Tess's conclusion.

"And the biology building has been peaceful. I didn't overhear a single student lamenting a bad encounter with any bio-chem professors."

Margaret swallowed hard. "I told you, I'm serious about this," she finally said.

Tess cracked a soft grin. "I know. I can tell."

Tess walked swiftly around the desk then, collapsing against Margaret in a hug which was returned eagerly. Margaret inhaled Tess's scent greedily and tried to not dwell on how much it felt like going home, returning to someplace safe, and warm, and comfortable.

From there, they hung out for a bit until Margaret confessed that she had a late meeting, and so Tess decided she'd drive separately to her house that evening.

Tess had procured a spare key over winter, after getting stuck outside in the cold waiting. When Margaret arrived home, she found Tess reclining on the sofa watching some dumb show. Margaret felt such relief that Tess was willing to give her another chance. She wasn't sure she'd survive losing this.

They made pasta for dinner. Tess chopped tomatoes and fresh herbs while Margaret watched the stove. They ate side by side at the counter, telling each other about their day.

"You know, Elle kicked me out the other day because Kai was coming over," Tess said between bites.

"Have they finally slept together, then?" Margaret smirked slightly behind a forkful of pasta.

"I can't get any info out of Elle, but Kai doesn't censor herself. I got plenty of details. But that's karma, I guess, since I've shared plenty about what we've gotten up to."

"I don't enjoy being the center of gossip."

"It's not gossip. I was bragging about how thoroughly you banged my brains out."

"How uncordial of you."

"Say one more big word like that and I'm telling Dr. Greenwood that your hatred of literature is all a guise," Tess warned. "I saw that novel on your nightstand."

"You wouldn't dare."

Tess shot Margaret a wink. "This is delicious, by the way." She snarfed down another bite. "How are you such a good cook?"

"Cooking is just chemistry, and I happen to be a leading expert in the field."

"I'd tease you more, but I heard you once made your own salad vinegarette in lab."

"It's called being resourceful."

"Speaking of your great chemistry mind, have you figured out how to fix your drug issues?"

"No...kind of. We can chemically manipulate a few functional groups, which might help. But we'd have to go through clinicals again."

"I know that'll take a while—"

"And a lot of money—"

"I'm sure you'll get it, though. That drug is your baby. You can't just give up on it."

"I appreciate your enthusiasm, but I do also need to consider it critically. Is the risk, the effort, worth the reward?"

"The reward for a drug is helping save one person. To that one person it saved, the drug is invaluable."

"Tell that to the drug companies that refuse to invest in drugs that don't yield high profits."

"Ooh, that reminds me of this documentary I want to watch with you."

"A documentary?"

"Yes. I think you'll have comments about their claims that I really want to hear."

"I suppose."

"Also, I just wanted to say..." Tess paused, picking at her food with her fork. "I'm...proud of you. About your behavior this week."

"I'm capable of admitting when I'm wrong."

Tess scoffed, but then laughed. "Thank you for trying, even if you are just doing it for me. I appreciate it. I just—I want everyone else to see how great you are, the way I see you, and if you're willing to be just the slightest bit more vulnerable around others, I think they'll see it too."

"Finish your dinner, Miss Stanford."

When they finished eating, Tess washed the dishes while Margaret dried them. Everything felt so domestic, like they lived together and they loved each other and they had dinner together every night. That, on top of the compliments Tess was rattling off while she scrubbed a plate, was too much for Margaret to handle.

Midsentence, Margaret cut Tess off with a searing kiss. Tess's soapy hands grasped at Margaret's shirt, and the plate she'd been holding shattered on the floor. Tess exclaimed about the broken dish, but Margaret shoved her more firmly against the sink.

"Leave it," Margaret said.

She pressed her leg between Tess's thighs, kissing her harder. Moments later, Margaret sank her hand into Tess's pants, and Tess came hard, trembling against the kitchen sink. She collapsed in Margaret's arms, panting.

"That…was unexpected," Tess uttered blissfully.

Margaret stepped back, pulling Tess with her. "Come on. The dishes can soak."

"Naughty," Tess teased as she skipped after Margaret.

That evening, Margaret was exceptionally rough. Tess clearly didn't mind; she adored the roughness and often asked for it. That night, though, it was a necessity. Margaret needed her brain, and heart, to accept that Tess was just a good fuck buddy, nothing more, and she never would be anything else.

Of course, that backfired, because after particularly rough sessions, Tess demanded more intimate aftercare. She wanted cuddles and sweet kisses to ease her aches, which Margaret couldn't deny. Tess's comfort was her utmost priority, and if that required her to risk her own heart, she had to.

Saturday, they woke lazily. Margaret usually got up first, but that Saturday, for whatever reason, Margaret's internal clock did not wake her. Instead, Tess had awakened first with an agenda in mind. She had hovered over Margaret, brushing featherlight kisses all over her face. Then she had dipped and sucked gently at Margaret's neck as she ran her fingers down.

Margaret woke blissfully and desperately turned on. She kissed Tess back with yearning need, sucking needily at Tess's bottom lip as Tess slid her hand lower. When fingers tangled in her damp curls, Margaret's mind abruptly caught up to what was happening.

Margaret did not have morning sex.

There was a reason why, even after breaking all her other rules with Tess, that she stayed true to only hooking up at night. In the evening, she was alert with time to plan and execute. Everything was meticulous and separate, ending the day with their romps. But sex in the early morning hours was softer, more thorough, and more intimate. That intimacy was what she wanted to avoid.

Tess stilled her hand when Margaret tensed. She leaned in, whispering, "Let me make you feel amazing, you wonderful, gorgeous, good girl. You deserve this after making such an effort to be kinder."

Margaret shivered. She nodded, giving Tess permission. She wanted, needed, Tess to touch her.

"Magnificent, thank you." Tess smiled. "Relax, Maggie. Allow yourself to feel."

And allow herself she did. Margaret drank in the feeling of Tess bringing her to the peak. She relaxed, feeling safe in Tess's arms, committing every movement to memory as if it were something precious that she'd never be allowed to experience again.

Afterward, when Margaret was panting and Tess had her head pulled close, Tess's stomach started growling. Margaret tried to pull away, but Tess held her in place despite her complaining stomach.

Eventually, Margaret said, "This is ridiculous. You're clearly starving. Let's go eat breakfast." And she forced them out of bed.

After breakfast, Tess said, "I need a shower."

They'd never stayed together long enough to reach that point, but now, Margaret had promised her an entire day together, which meant navigating this new experience.

A bit awkwardly, Margaret retrieved a towel from the hall closet. She followed Tess into the bathroom and meekly explained how the shower worked.

"I've used a shower before, Margaret, thank you."

And then pointed out the products she had.

"Again, I can read a shampoo bottle, but thank you."

Before Margaret could escape the bathroom, Tess stopped her. "Wait, there's something else I need."

"What is it?"

Tess jerked Margaret toward her, connecting their lips. When they broke apart, there was a glint in Tess's eyes.

"I might need help reaching my back. And I definitely need some company."

"I…um…"

Tess turned on the water and shut the bathroom door while Margaret just stood there gawking. Tess stared at her challengingly, stripping naked. Margaret's brain clicked onto autopilot. She stripped out of her own clothes, grabbing for Tess as she kissed her wildly. Tess tugged them both into the shower.

Just like morning sex, Margaret avoided shower sex. The bathroom was brighter, and everything felt more personal standing together in a shower. Gingerly they touched each other, taking turns lathering each other up. It was soft and compassionate. Tess was so gentle and caring.

Margaret tried to stop thinking, but it was so difficult. She caught herself at one point thinking that Tess had never looked more beautiful than she did in that moment, with water cascading down her body. Margaret nearly choked on her feelings then, but she shoved them away. Instead, she focused on making Tess feel as good as she possibly could.

Margaret pinned Tess against the shower wall, her fingers deep between Tess's legs. She listened as Tess sighed into her touch.

"Do you remember when I got this?" Tess asked, her voice breathy.

Margaret realized that Tess was holding up her arm, the one with the scar from the chemical burn. She ground her teeth together.

"Of course I do, you could have—"

Tess cut her off. "Do you remember when you jerked back the curtain of the safety shower? Because I remember. I remember your eyes tracing all over me when I was standing there in only my underwear, soaking wet…" Tess bit her lip. "I was wet in more ways than one."

Margaret inhaled sharply.

"You've been imagining this scenario for quite some time then, hmm?" She curled her fingers. Tess let out a pleased gasp. "Did you imagine me taking you in the shower? Did you ache for my touch? How often did you touch yourself in the shower, imagining it was me?"

"Countless times. I would have let you take me in the chemistry building. I didn't care. Your eyes were wild—you look at me the same way in the bedroom now. I would have let you do anything to me."

"Will you let me do as I please with you now?"

"Yes."

"Good."

Once they were clean and dressed again, they sat together in the living room. Tess grabbed the remote, paging through various streaming services.

"We're watching this documentary now…sorry if you had other plans," Tess said, but she didn't sound even remotely sorry. "I can't wait to hear all your snide comments."

"I'm sure it was adequately researched," Margaret said, unsure what she was getting dragged into.

It was well researched…kind of. The documentary team did good work but stretched the truth at times for shock value. Margaret commented every time they did, occasionally groaning dramatically. Every time she said something, Tess would giggle. So, Margaret started saying whatever she could just to pull that wonderful merry sound from Tess again. Once, she got Tess to laugh so hard she snorted, and embarrassed, Tess buried her face into her side. Margaret eased her out of her discomfort by saying it was cute, but Tess remained cuddled against her after that, relaxing into her body.

When the documentary finished, Tess pulled back slightly to look Margaret in the eyes.

"Thank you for watching that with me. I really enjoyed listening to your comments."

"I'll admit it was pretty enjoyable."

Tess smiled kindly and then she leaned forward and kissed Margaret. The kiss was slow and calm, deliberate. Another documentary started autoplaying. When they finally pulled apart, Margaret remained lost in Tess's eyes until she turned and regarded the television.

"This sounds interesting." Tess reached for the remote and turned up the volume.

At one point, Margaret made them lunch. Later, they played cards. In the evening, they watched a movie. Before Margaret knew it, it was dark outside, and Tess was yawning.

"Let's go to bed," Margaret whispered, turning off the TV while she urged Tess up.

She led Tess back to her bedroom as she had done many times before, but this time, it was entirely different. They kept their clothes on. They changed into their pajamas and Margaret urged a yawning Tess toward the bed, sliding in beside her.

Tess fell asleep quickly, but Margaret couldn't. She kept thinking about how full her heart felt, how wonderful it felt to have someone who cared about her challenging her to better herself. It was terrifying that she would lose this, that Tess would leave. To Tess, this was nothing more than casual—Margaret was sure—but Margaret wanted this every day, every night.

Something had changed. They used to just have sex. The goal was to elicit pleasure, and the end was pure exhaustion. What was the goal now, the finish line? They spent the day together, enjoying each other's company, and fell asleep in each other's arms without the exhaustion of sex. Margaret knew why she was allowing it. She liked Tess a lot…too much. It was more than just sex to her. But what about Tess?

Did Tess only seek company? Tess was social; she wasn't hurting for friends. Was she just looking to fill a void left by moving away from home? If Tess was still a freshman, and the transition to college newer, Margaret might have believed that. But Tess had three years to settle, and frankly, she was thriving. So, why, then? Did Margaret dare allow herself to think that her feelings might be returned?

No.

She dared not dream. Tess would never feel the same way. Because at the end of the day, Tess was wonderful and bright—no wonder Margaret had fallen for her, anyone easily could—and Margaret was nasty and bitter, not someone anyone fell in love with.

Especially not women like Tess Stanford.

* * *

At first, it was difficult for Tess to believe that Margaret and Amy were friends, but now that she knew them better, it wasn't so hard to believe. Their differences complemented each other nicely. Margaret was all sarcasm and snappy remarks, harmonizing with Amy's carefree attitude.

In public, on campus, Tess rarely saw the two professors together. Amy was a busy socializer, whereas Margaret preferred to maintain her "I hate people and have no friends" persona. But occasionally Tess would pop by Amy's office for a chat, and she'd find Margaret lounging in the eclectic office.

Tess spent all of Wednesday evening finishing a paper for Amy's class. She hadn't had time to bother Margaret, but she had noticed earlier that the lights were off in her office. She might have gone home early, but Tess suspected she was in the English building. After her final edits, Tess tracked over there as well.

"Hi, Dr. Greenwood," Tess said, still refusing to call her by her first name until she passed her class. "I just finished my paper, and I took all your comments to heart, so I hope it's—" When Tess turned toward the mismatched furniture, she gasped. "Oh, Margaret."

Amy smirked.

"You weren't in your office this evening." Tess's tone was lightly scolding. She braced herself on the arms of the chair, hovering over Margaret as she tried to look intimidating. "I thought you were hiding from me."

Margaret seemed more amused than scolded. "Amy wanted to chat."

Tess's eyes raked over her. "Is that a new blazer? It looks stunning on you."

"It's nice, isn't it? But do you mind? I'm trying to enjoy my evening, and you're cramping my space."

Per usual, Tess ignored her, instead leaning forward to whisper, "I'd rather like to take that blazer off you."

Amy cleared her throat loudly.

"Sorry, Amy," Margaret choked out, angling away from Tess. "Some of us clearly haven't learned any manners."

Tess just smirked, although she did turn from Margaret. But instead of sinking down onto the two-person couch, she wiggled onto the same chair Margaret was sitting in. Margaret complained loudly, although she shifted to accommodate Tess.

"There is an empty couch right there," Margaret said, gesturing wildly to the other couch.

"But Dr. Greenwood is going to sit there."

"Two people could easily sit there, Amy and you, and then I could sit comfortably here. Alone."

"Well, it's too late now. I'm already settled."

* * *

Amy finally took the offered invitation and joined them in the sitting area.

"So, what have you been chatting about?" Tess asked, glancing between the two friends.

"Various things," Margaret replied. "Students, work, dating apps."

"Dating apps?"

"I'm toying with the idea," Amy said. "I'm adjusting to the concept of remaining single, but perhaps I'm just being cowardly."

"I could help you set up a profile," Tess said excitedly. "Kai helped me set up one, and she ropes me into her matchmaking antics often."

"I'm worried my flirting skills are lacking." Amy laughed awkwardly.

"I could help with that too. I like to believe that I have a decent flirt game."

Margaret shifted uncomfortably. She'd been pointedly avoiding thinking about Tess talking to, flirting with, or even hooking up with other women. But it was inevitable. Someday, Tess was going to end what they had. She'd graduate and move away, or meet a woman and fall in love.

"I'm sorry, am I squishing you?" Tess asked, adjusting herself.

"No, um—my leg is just falling asleep, that's all," Margaret lied. She rested her hand on Tess's thigh, selfishly hoping to hold them together so that Tess couldn't leave...so that Tess wouldn't leave her.

"Sorry about that." Tess shot forward, kissing Margaret's cheek as a means of apology. It startled Margaret, and they both blushed.

"I—it's fine," Margaret replied hoarsely. She dipped her head to avoid Tess's eyes.

Despite Margaret's insistence that it was fine, Tess still perched on the arm of the chair. Margaret wished she hadn't. Tess felt too far away, even though they were only a few inches apart. She felt very emotional and needy, which she hated. Roughly, Margaret swallowed a lump that had formed in her throat.

It didn't matter. She didn't need Tess. Tess was never hers to have anyway. Margaret wasn't good enough for Tess. She would never be good enough for Tess.

Tess and Amy continued chatting, leaving Margaret to stew. But suddenly, Tess's hand slipped down and grabbed hold of Margaret's hand, gently running her thumb across her knuckles.

The calming effect was instantaneous. Margaret exhaled, coming back to herself. Once they finished talking, Tess got up, squeezing Margaret's hand before she slipped away.

"I need to get to my office hours," Tess said. "I'll see you in class, Dr. Greenwood. And, Maggie"—she turned and winked at Margaret—"I'll see you tomorrow. Bye!"

Amy turned pointedly to her friend once Tess was gone. "Maggie?" she questioned incredulously.

"Just another obnoxious habit she's picked up."

"I don't know. I think it's cute. Maggie..." Amy toyed with the nickname, grinning. "So, how are those feelings working out for you?"

Margaret groaned. "Horribly. I'm screwed. I hate feeling like this. Like there's this tugging at my chest, begging me to go after her, even though I know I'll see her again tomorrow. I can't stand to be apart from her, like it might be the last time I'll see her. I know she'll leave someday for good and all I'll have are these distant memories of her, bitter because I'll know that she's never coming back, but sweet for how she made me feel."

"Margaret! She's made a romantic out of you."

"What? No."

"She has! A year ago, you always denied caring and refused to let yourself feel. You would have been so matter-of-fact about it, like, 'We had a good run, but it's time to move on. The end.' You would have ended it and never spoken of it again. But here you are, allowing yourself to feel and putting words to your feelings. All because of Tess."

Margaret flushed, hiding her face behind her hands in embarrassment.

"I think it's beautiful, Margaret, really, I do. But," Amy declared warningly, "I don't like this sad attitude you're getting, this downer, 'oh woe is me' affliction."

"She doesn't care for me in that way, Amy, I'm being realistic."

"She told you so in as many words?"

"Well…no. But I know she never could."

"I can't speak for another person, but personally I don't think your feelings are as one-sided as you're claiming they are."

"Of course they are."

"Let's review some facts, shall we? Since that's what you nerdy science types love." Amy held up her hand to count off her fingers. "She entirely forgot about me when she saw you, immediately got right into your personal space. She whispered something raunchy to you and insisted on sitting on your lap despite there being ample other seating. She was aware of your discomfort and thanked you with a kiss but still moved off your lap because she didn't want you to be uncomfortable. She noticed you were pulling into yourself, and she took your hand. That's a comforting gesture, not something she would do if she didn't care."

"Okay, well, perhaps I can admit that she might care, but only because she is, in general, a caring person. She would have done the same for you."

"I doubt it." Amy crossed her arms and fixed her friend with a serious stare. "I think you should tell her that you're in love with her."

"In—in love is a rather strong statement. Love is…I mean…do I love her? Perhaps…yes. But to be in love, I don't—"

"You're in love with her," Amy repeated, more forcefully.

"I mean, but there's—"

"*In* love."

"But I just—"

"Margaret. You're in love with her."

"I…well, maybe…"

"You are. You're in love with her. And you should tell her."

"I can't."

"What about next year?" Amy asked. "What about when she's graduating and moving on? Are you going to wait until then to tell her, when it's too late, because she'd be leaving either way?"

Margaret's chest tightened at the thought of Tess leaving forever in only a year's time. It wasn't enough time. It would never be enough time.

"You're assuming that our little arrangement will survive another year." Margaret couldn't help sounding defensive.

Amy chuckled. "Oh, I have no doubt that it will."

* * *

One Friday, Margaret needed more desk space to spread out papers on, so Tess suggested they go work in the boardroom for a bit. This worked only briefly, as Tess was quick to distract the professor away from her work with a competitive game of hangman on the massive whiteboard.

Margaret sat on the boardroom table facing the whiteboard, Tess sitting in a swivel chair in front of her. She spun the chair away from Margaret and slapped the board intently with a dry-erase marker, right at the game of hangman written on the board.

"That is definitely not 'photosynthesis,'" Tess said. "Count. There aren't fifteen letters."

Margaret crossed her arms in a pout. "I told you I've never been good at spelling. And really, that was a good guess, considering it starts with a P and ends with 'thesis.'"

"But you already guessed T."

"And you're positive I've heard this word before?"

"Who here has the doctorate?"

"I didn't get my doctorate in spelling."

Tess laughed heartily. "I bet Dr. Greenwood could figure this out, and she certainly hasn't heard this word before."

"Okay, well, I suppose I have to guess another letter, then."

"Yes, finally. Be careful, though, because you only get one more wrong guess."

"What? You mean you don't draw on a face too?"

"Sure, if I'm playing with my baby cousins that need a handicap. Unless you're telling me that the big, mean, super scary, most certainly the most smartest—"

"It's just smartest—"

"Super big crazy smart genius, Dr. Margaret Morgan, is admitting that she needs help because she has a weakness and isn't good with words?"

"I'm fine with words. I write grants and papers all the time. Computers just happen to have spell-check."

"I'll draw on a face, but only if you admit that I'm a better speller than you."

"Let's see what happens with my next guess before we do anything drastic," Margaret said stubbornly.

"Fine. What letter do you want?"

"Y."

Tess nodded and turned back to the board, filling in the spaces.

"Two?" Margaret asked, scowling. "Well, the end has to be synthesis. But a Y in the beginning? And it starts with P?"

"Stop stalling and guess another letter."

"A."

"Wrong," Tess said triumphantly. "So, are you going to admit—"

"Just kill the guy and tell me what the damn word is."

Tess drew the final arm on the stick figure and gave him X eyes to signal his defeat. Then she filled in the remaining letters.

"Psychosynthesis?" Margaret questioned skeptically. "That's a made-up word."

"It's not made up, it's from psychology. It focuses on the self, like personal growth. At least, that's what I remember Kai telling me."

"Psychology?" Margaret scoffed. "I thought you said it was a science word."

"It is. Psychology. You know, the scientific study of the human mind?" Tess flipped around in the chair so that she was straddling it backward, regarding Margaret.

Margaret grinned mischievously. "Psychology isn't a real science."

"Yeah, right," Tess said, not accepting Margaret's stance for a second. "I saw all those psychology books at your house. You can't fool me."

"Yes, well, you cheated," Margaret said flippantly, sliding off the table. "You knew you couldn't beat me fairly, so you tricked me with misdirection."

"It's not my fault you didn't know a science word. Sorry for assuming that such a prestigious scientist would know something about science."

Margaret stalked toward Tess. "Cheater," she declared.

"You're just a sore loser," Tess replied smugly.

Tess watched intensely as Margaret approached her. Margaret's pupils were large and her look predatory. Tess reached out as Margaret stepped forward and grabbed her wrist, jerking Tess and the rolling chair forward. Then Margaret bent, grabbed Tess behind her head, and kissed her firmly and hungrily.

Margaret pulled back from Tess, tugging her bottom lip between her teeth. Tess let out a hiss that turned into an absolutely sinful moan. When Margaret released her, Tess looked up at her with hooded eyes.

"Time to leave?"

"Yes."

As they turned to gather their things, Tess caught movement through the window beside the boardroom door. She froze, staring.

"What's wrong?" Margaret asked.

"I just thought I saw something. Like, someone was at the window."

"Probably just someone walking down the hall."

"Um, yeah, probably," Tess replied, turning back to collect her things. But she was struggling to shake the uneasy feeling. She could have sworn it looked like Debbie again. She had noted the lights were still on in Debbie's office, so it was plausible that the biology professor was still in the building.

As they left, going down the hall, Margaret practically dragged Tess, easily pulling her out of her unease. Tess said something snarky, and Margaret spun with a fierceness, shoving Tess back and pinning her against the wall. Then she kissed Tess with reckless abandon, shoving her thigh between Tess's legs to create friction as she kissed and nipped from Tess's lips down her jaw and to her neck.

Again, Tess caught movement in the shadows. She pressed her palm firmly to Margaret's chest, stopping her.

"What?" Margaret asked her curiously.

"I just…what if someone sees?"

Margaret glanced in both directions down the hall. "Who else is here right now to see us?"

Tess pursed her lips. "If we're making out, I can't see around your big head to know if someone is there."

"You are so snarky tonight," Margaret stated, her voice low.

"Perhaps you'll have to punish me for it, then."

* * *

After their TA office hours, Caleb ran up to Kai and Tess, shouting, "I got a B on our last exam! That's pulled my grade up almost to passing."

"If you just keep up with homework and study well for the final, then I think you'll pass," Kai said happily.

"That's wonderful," Tess said. "Great work."

"Your extra tutoring has helped so much. I wish you could help solve all my problems," Caleb said, frowning. "I'm not sure how I'll survive the rest of the semester. My roommate and RA are being awful and spreading rumors, so the girl I was supposed to room with next semester got wind of everything and is already being awful about it."

"What's happening?"

"Well, they stuck me in the girls' dorm because I haven't legally changed my gender marker. It just costs time and money that I don't have. It's been weird living in the girls' dorm, but I've made a few good friends. My roommate is clearly uncomfortable, though, and she's being a jerk about it. She refuses to use the correct pronouns and makes a big stink about it. I don't enjoy the situation either, trust me. But I can't do anything about it."

"And your RA isn't any help either?"

"No. She's best friends with my roommate. They took it to Housing and Res Life, but they didn't do anything about it. But then my RA stalked me online and discovered my deadname, and she told my roommate, and they're spreading it around. It's demeaning."

"Did you try filing a complaint? I mean, to Housing, maybe, but—"

"Even if Housing moved me, they'd still stick me in a girls' dorm. Which I don't want. And I'm getting deadnamed all over campus now. There's this awful group of students that have made it their mission to harass me, I guess."

"Then file a harassment report, holy shit!" Kai exclaimed. "That is absolutely unacceptable."

"I—I mean, I tried. I met with someone in charge of claims, and she essentially told me that my problems weren't real harassment because legally, on my birth certificate, it says my deadname and that I'm a girl."

"That is total bullshit."

"I know, but no one will listen to me. I was trying to just tough it out until next semester, but the rumors are spreading, and I'm concerned that next year won't be any better."

Caleb clenched his fists and turned, rubbing at his eyes. Kai reached out a comforting hand. "Hey, breathe," she instructed calmly.

"It just fucking sucks. It feels like no one cares enough and has the power to actually do something about it."

"Did you try talking to Dr. Kemper or Dr. Marlow?" Kai asked. "They care. Trust me. They would be appalled to hear that this is happening to you."

"I thought about it. But I care too much about their opinion of me, I don't know. It's silly, probably, but—"

"It's not silly. I get it. Sometimes, it's easier to tell personal things to someone you don't see every day."

"So, we need to find someone in a position of authority who we trust but that you aren't really close to…" Tess said, contemplating out loud.

"I'm only really close to Dr. Kemper and Dr. Marlow," Kai said. "I mean, I like some of the neuro professors, but I wouldn't necessarily trust them with something like this."

"I…might know someone…" Tess said carefully. "Two people, actually."

"Who?" Caleb sniffed, sounding hopeful.

"Just, um…Caleb, could you step out into the hall for a second? I want to run something by Kai first."

"Sure."

Caleb slipped out of the classroom and Kai turned expectantly to Tess. "Who do you know? Would they really be able to help Caleb?"

"I'm sure they'll fight for Caleb, knowing their history," Tess replied. "It's just that…I'm not sure—"

"Not sure they'd be willing? Let's just email them and ask."

"I bet they're still on campus, actually. Do you trust me?"

"Of course I trust you, Tess."

"And do you trust my judge of character?"

"Of course, I mean—oh wait!" Kai flung an accusatory finger at Tess. "I know exactly who you're talking about. It's Dr. Morgan, isn't it?"

"She'd help."

"Like hell she would. She doesn't help anyone."

"I figured you'd react like this, but that's why I need you to trust me. Please?"

Kai scrunched her nose in disgust. "I do trust you. It's her I don't trust."

"But I trust her. Wholeheartedly."

"I know you do. And I know she doesn't mistreat you, but you're the exception. She still hates everyone else."

"It's not just her," Tess said. "I mean, yes, I fully believe Dr. Morgan will help Caleb. But I'm also talking about Dr. Greenwood, who I know will fight tooth and nail for every queer student here."

"Oh, Dr. Greenwood, Elle's favorite professor. Yes, perfect. Forget Dr. Morgan, let's just get Dr. Greenwood."

"Both of them."

"Tess, come on—"

"I'm saying both because I know Dr. Morgan's hanging out in Dr. Greenwood's office, and I'm sure they're both still there."

"Wait, what?"

"They're friends, Kai."

"You're telling me that Dr. Morgan, the world's most annoying and despicable person, is friends with an English professor Elle is obsessed with who is supposedly the light of campus?" Kai asked incredulously. "I don't believe it."

"Well, it's true, and if we hurry over, I can prove it to you. Come on."

Tess flung open the classroom door, and Caleb turned to her expectantly.

"Are you doing anything else tonight?" Tess asked the boy.

"You mean, other than avoiding going back to my dorm? No."

"Then I know some professors on the other side of campus that will help. We can go talk to them now. I trust these professors. I care about them, and they care about me, and I know they'll care about you and want to help you."

Caleb thought for only a short moment before nodding resolutely. "As long as you come with me, then yes, we can go."

"Perfect."

"I'm calling Elle," Kai said as they burst out of the biology building. "She's supportive and knows Dr. Greenwood."

"Yes, Elle is great."

As they speed-walked across campus, Kai detailed the situation to Elle, who met them in front of the English building. She gave her sympathy to Caleb and then they stopped at a closed office door.

"Is she still here?" Kai asked.

"Only one way to find out," Elle replied, knocking firmly on the door.

The door swung open, revealing Dr. Greenwood. Her eyes scanned the motley crew, and she frowned in slight confusion and concern.

"Oh, thank goodness you're still here." Tess sighed with relief.

"What's going on?" Dr. Greenwood asked.

"Hi, Dr. Greenwood. This is Kai—" Elle gestured to her girlfriend.

"Oh, the elusive Kai. I've heard so much about you," Dr. Greenwood said, teasing. Kai flushed.

"But this is Caleb," Elle quickly continued. "He's having issues with the school."

"Horrible transphobic things," Tess added with urgency. "No one's listening to him or taking his predicament seriously. But I figured that you, of all professors, would care and could help."

"Okay, yes, absolutely. Come in."

Tess stepped in first, immediately turning to face the mismatched couch and chair where her eyes landed on an otherwise silent Margaret. "I was hoping you'd be here too," Tess said, addressing her. Margaret raised a skeptical eyebrow.

Caleb then caught sight of the bio-chem professor and slammed to a stop, tensing.

"No, hey, it's all right." Tess turned quickly to reassure him. "She'll help you too, I promise."

"No, but—but she's—"

Tess grabbed Caleb's hand and held it firmly. "Caleb, I would never bring you to someone who would hurt you. I know how Dr. Morgan can be, and I know what others say about her, but trust me. She does care, and she will help you."

Dr. Greenwood pulled Tess back so she could fully regard Caleb herself. "Hello, Caleb, lovely to meet you," she said. "Dr. Morgan over there happens to be my best friend. I know she's got that scary reputation on the STEM side of campus, but in my office, she's just my friend. And I happen to only befriend good people."

"I can vouch for Dr. Greenwood. She's wonderful," Elle said. "And I trust Dr. Greenwood's judge of character. If she trusts Dr. Morgan, so can you."

"And speaking from experience Dr. Morgan cares about Tess, and Tess, for whatever reason, trusts Dr. Morgan above everyone else," Kai said.

"Well…I do trust all of you, so I guess I can trust Dr. Morgan too," Caleb admitted. "I mean, I need help. If they can get me that help, who am I to judge?"

"They can and they will," Tess resolutely declared.

"Help with what, exactly?" Margaret finally asked.

Caleb quickly detailed the misgendering harassment he was experiencing, to which Dr. Greenwood immediately barked out, "Absolutely unacceptable. We will certainly get to the bottom of this. Come sit."

"Yes, we'll sort this out," Margaret said. She gestured to the couch beside her as Dr. Greenwood walked Caleb over, and the three began discussing.

Elle shut the office door, and the three juniors huddled around Dr. Greenwood's desk, remaining close but not interfering. The two professors listened patiently to Caleb's situation.

Margaret, to the surprise of most everyone in the room, stated, "Caleb, your immediate safety is my biggest concern. If you don't feel safe returning to your dorm, we can find other arrangements. If you've nowhere else to go, I have a guest room you are more than welcome to stay in until this is resolved."

"Umm, thank you," Caleb said, sniffling between his words. "I, um, yeah, thanks for the offer, but I do have good friends on campus that I can stay with."

"Of course. But my offer always remains. And if you find that things are becoming too much for you to handle during the day, my office is always a safe space."

"As is mine," Dr. Greenwood said.

As Dr. Greenwood and Caleb chatted about final details, Kai harshly elbowed Tess.

"Ouch! What was that for?"

"I owe you an apology," Kai said. "You were right. Dr. Morgan is…not that bad."

"No, she's actually being really nice," Elle said. "She offered him her guest room. That's kind of insane."

"I just…I think you've been right all along, Tess. I don't think Dr. Morgan is as bad as everyone says, and I think the rumors have made everything worse. I guess I can see why you care so much about her. She's…kind of sweet."

"Yeah, she's not all that bad," Elle replied in agreement.

"Hey, can you walk me back across campus?" Caleb asked as Dr. Greenwood led him to the door. "I just don't want to walk alone."

"Yeah, definitely," Kai said, grabbing both Caleb's and Elle's hands as she pulled them toward the hallway.

"I'll head downstairs with you," Dr. Greenwood said, sliding out the door as well.

Tess, instead of following the posse, turned back to Margaret. Margaret dipped her head, pointedly avoiding Tess's eyes, and Tess smirked, realizing how bashful she was being. Tess knelt in front of Margaret, resting her hands on her knees.

"I knew you'd help, but I never dreamed you'd say such nice and reassuring things. And I never expected you to offer your office and home to him."

"He's in a bad situation," Margaret said, finally looking at Tess.

"It took a year of me barging into your office before you even tolerated my presence."

"Well…perhaps you helped me realize that letting people in isn't always such a bad thing."

Tess smiled, shooting up into Margaret's arms, where she kissed her firmly. Then she sandwiched Margaret's head between her hands and peppered kisses all over her face.

"I'm glad," Tess whispered, her eyes shut as she tipped their foreheads together. "I'm proud of you, you know? For learning to let people in—for letting people in, even if it's scary…"

"Maybe I just know what it's like to be berated in your own home, to not feel safe where you're living," Margaret murmured, pulling back. "And I mean, come on. I'm not a monster."

"I know," Tess said in a breathy whisper.

* * *

Summer was long; they wouldn't see each other for four months. Tess had an internship back home, hundreds of miles away in a different city.

Margaret realized she was going to miss Tess's companionship more than anything. Sure, she loved the sex. But if she had to give up sex in exchange for having Tess in her life forever, she would.

They were both physically spent, lying in bed cuddled together. Tess nuzzled needily against Margaret, practically purring. Margaret ran her fingers over Tess's bare skin, listening to the contented hums Tess released. Her fingers traced down Tess's arm, across the slight bumps where the scarred remnants of the chemical burn remained.

"Stop, that tickles," Tess said, giggling.

"This never should have happened."

Tess watched Margaret run her fingers over the scar again. "Yeah, I know. Kai and I were being careless idiots. It was entirely our fault."

Margaret's eyebrows tipped downward. "You just wanted to be done for summer. Who could blame you? I can hardly fault you for that."

"You…can't?" Tess asked, confused.

"It's as much the department's fault. Your lab coordinator should have been in the building. If I hadn't stopped by to drop off some mail…if Kai hadn't run into me…" Margaret grew quiet and contemplative. "This shouldn't have scarred so badly."

"Hey," Tess whispered, running her fingers down Margaret's cheek. "It's really not that bad."

"But it was entirely avoidable. It never should have—you could have—we need to update our lab safety policy."

"Margaret, I'm fine," Tess stated firmly.

Margaret pressed her lips together. "I know."

"You're just…worried about my safety…concerned for my well-being," Tess uttered, contemplative.

"It's just…a bad reflection on the chemistry department." Margaret fought to get her words out, swallowing her true feelings on the matter, deflecting.

"Well, a lot of good came from this scar," Tess said. "When you were fretting about me, I realized that you cared about me. I was furious with you that day. I thought you didn't care about me at all, but then I saw how worried you were, and I realized I was wrong. You do care about me. If this hadn't happened, we might not have ended up together like this."

"Why were you mad at me?" Margaret hesitantly asked. "I'm sure I've given you plenty of reasons, but—"

"I'm never mad *at* you, not really. Frustrated, maybe," Tess amended. "But I was irritated that day because you told me to switch to a bio-chem major. You said a chemistry degree is better. You're always shit-talking biologists because you think chemists are superior. But you're wrong. We're all scientists working to discover, and better humanity. We're the same."

Margaret frowned. "I might have looked down on the biology department because I was irritated that they moved me, but I don't think chemists are superior as a whole—"

"Not as a whole then, but as a part—"

"Listen to me and stop getting irritated," Margaret interrupted. "I only said you should switch majors because I was envious that the biology department got such a wonderful student. I wanted you under my wing. I've never realized such potential in an undergrad before. You…you're special."

Tess flushed. "You're only saying that because we're sleeping together."

"No, I mean it. You will make a fantastic scientist, Tess, a magnificent biologist, and someday when you win awards for your merit, I will read about your accomplishments and proudly smile because I always knew you were destined for greatness."

Tess shook her head, then responded by biting the depression of Margaret's shoulder.

"Oww," Margaret complained, although she didn't shove Tess away.

"You're maddening...so frustrating..."

"It's the truth, whether you want to hear it or not."

"Shut up."

"Don't you believe in yourself? Don't you see your accomplishments and realize that you're a spectacular woman?"

"Yes, no, I don't know. I'm still trying to figure out what I want to do. I'm going to be a senior already, but it feels like I just started college yesterday."

"Time does pass unfairly fast."

"It does...Maybe summer will pass by just as quickly, then."

"Will you miss me?"

"Of course. Always. Will you miss me though?"

Margaret cleared her throat. "You mean, will I miss having daily interruptions and no free time to myself? Hardly."

"Right..." Tess uttered, her voice dipping low and sad.

Margaret listened to the silence, no snarky remark meeting her own. She realized that Tess was a bit insecure. She didn't believe that she was a skilled scientist, and evidently, she didn't believe that Margaret would miss her. But she would. She wasn't even sure she'd survive four months without Tess.

"I will," Margaret finally whispered. "I mean, I'll miss you."

Margaret felt Tess smile. "Good."

* * *

As Tess was walking through the quad, she noticed Caleb ahead of her in a group of his close and trusted friends. She wanted to check in with him about how he was doing, so she started walking faster to catch up. As she neared, she overheard their conversation.

"I'm telling you, she's super nice." Caleb folded his arms defiantly.

"Dr. Morgan isn't nice."

"She is! No one else would listen to me, but she did. Dr. Morgan listened, and she got me help. If it wasn't for Dr. Morgan, the university wouldn't be letting me live in the boys' dorm next semester."

"She cares about trans kids?"

"She cares about students in general. That's what I'm saying! Dr. Morgan isn't bad, she's quite nice."

"Rumors do tend to get out of hand."

"I've actually heard various students defending her."

"Yeah, you aren't the first person I've heard claiming she's not all that bad. I mean, she's probably got some anger management issues, sure, but even I've seen her smiling from time to time."

"Honestly, I was expecting her to be way worse. She's disagreeable and hard to please, but past that, she's just a competent scientist."

"She compliments people now. I hear her saying nice things to her grad students every now and again. I don't think anyone left her lab this year, which is a first."

"Maybe being in the biology building has been good for her. Maybe our compassion is rubbing off on her."

Tess smiled slightly, happy to hear that Margaret was doing much better with her attitude and treatment of others. She slowed, hovering just behind the gaggle of friends, wishing to selfishly listen in on their conversation a bit longer before she intervened. She hoped to hear more accounts of Margaret's improved behavior.

However, then one of Caleb's friends said, "She likes Tess Stanford a lot."

Tess sucked in a sharp and abrupt breath.

"Why would you say that?"

"I just mean, Tess isn't really scared of her, not like other students. I heard from Jessica that Tess once defended Dr. Morgan, and Joshua said he saw them together in the library, you know that day when Dr. Morgan was freaking out? He said Tess came up to her and got her to calm down."

"Someone else told me they were friends, so I guess that kind of makes sense."

"Maybe she's not so bad, then, and it is just rumors, like you were saying."

"Well, I heard Dr. Morgan's sleeping with a student."

Tess froze then, completely stopping in her path. Someone who was walking behind her awkwardly leapt around her, nearly colliding with her after her abrupt stop. She felt panicked, her heart pounding in her chest.

"Whoa, what?" she heard one of Caleb's friends say.

"Now come on, that's just what I was saying, about rumors getting blown out of proportion—"

"I heard she's sleeping with Tess."

Tess's heart thudded again.

"Tess?" Caleb said.

"I don't think it's an unfounded rumor either, because Matt said he overheard Dr. Kemper and Dr. Marlow discussing it when he went to office hours for help. And I think the library incident only further confirms it, because Joshua said they were holding hands and gazing into each other's eyes."

"Tess Stanford and Dr. Morgan, really?" Caleb continued to question.

"Dr. Morgan is way less intimidating knowing she's sleeping with sweetly adorable Tess."

"Yeah, it's harder to take her seriously, knowing Tess has her wrapped around her pinkie."

"Let's start nipping all these horrible rumors about Dr. Morgan in the bud, then."

"She hasn't had a break from the gossip in years, but if none of it's true, we should start correcting people."

"Yeah, Dr. Morgan isn't scary and mean, she's just a regular professor with a soft spot for cute students."

"Students, as in multiple?"

"Is she sleeping with multiple students? Like regularly?"

"I did hear that she regularly goes to a gay bar and takes women home with her."

"She's kind of super hot…in like a 'I'd let her spank me' kind of way…"

"I think we're getting away from the point," Caleb said. "I was just saying that she isn't nasty, I didn't mean that she—"

"Dr. Morgan sleeps with students!"

"Do you think she'd sleep with me?"

"Oh god." Caleb covered his face with his hands and groaned.

Tess, feeling suddenly sick to her stomach, turned around and ran in the opposite direction.

* * *

Someone knocked on her office door. Confused, Margaret glanced at the time. It was early evening on Wednesday. Tess was currently at her TA office hours with Kai, although she didn't expect her interrupter to be Tess, seeing as she would have just burst in instead of knocking politely. But she was confused as to who could possibly be wanting her at such a time.

The knock came again, and Margaret, annoyed, went over and jerked the door open. In the doorway stood Debbie and Kathy, Tess's two biology mentors. They were both shaking, as if nervous and uncertain.

"Is this urgent?" Margaret asked, raising a skeptical eyebrow. The two professors stumbled over their words until Margaret raised her hand to silence them. "This is not necessary," she concluded, stepping back to close the door again.

Debbie reached out then and braced the door open. "No, we need to talk to you. It is urgent."

Margaret narrowed her eyes in distaste. Through clenched teeth, she forced out, "I'm busy. Leave."

"We do need to talk to you, though," Kathy restated, but Margaret was tired and now growing irritated.

"I figured, since you're interrupting my day. But I am very busy and—"

"We know you're sleeping with Tess!" Debbie said in a rush.

There was a pregnant pause. Margaret felt her eyes widen in utter shock, pure unabridged horror. Debbie seemed just as surprised by her own outburst, because she gulped, and Kathy wavered as if she might faint. Margaret glanced cautiously down the hall behind the two women, glad they had waited until after school hours to confront her about this.

Finally, Margaret stepped back. "I suggest you both come in," she said roughly, "seeing as this conversation is hardly fit for the hallway."

Both Debbie and Kathy nodded in agreement and tumbled into the office. They huddled near the coffee table as Margaret stalked around them.

"Now…" Margaret said, her voice low and pointed. "I don't know how you came to such an absurd conclusion, but I won't stand—"

Debbie, evidently feeling bolder, stood up straighter. "I saw the two of you kissing in the boardroom," she said, jutting out her chin. "And I've seen you leaving campus together a couple times now. It's hardly an absurd conclusion to draw, given the evidence."

Something akin to fear bubbled under Margaret's skin as she recounted the times Tess hesitated, insisting she'd seen someone, even sharing that she thought it was one of the biology professors. Margaret couldn't let them know this terrified her. So, she fixed Debbie with a death glare, refusing to budge. She worked her jaw before she continued her previous comment. "I won't stand to have you policing me over matters that don't involve you."

"We aren't policing you," Debbie said. "There's nothing in our contract forbidding professor and student relationships. We aren't here to scold or threaten you, nothing like that."

"Yes, we actually think it's kind of nice," Kathy said. Margaret's defensiveness morphed into confusion. "I mean, it's cute. Tess seems to make you happy."

"You've been in a much better mood lately. Tess evidently brings out a better side of you that we've all been benefiting from. However, because you're involved with Tess, we felt it was our duty to talk to you, because if you hurt her—"

Kathy cut off her friend as her tone turned guttural. "Tess is like a daughter to us," she explained. "It's just…we know how you can be. You don't have the most outstanding track record. But Tess, she has a very large heart. So…"

"So, if this is just something you're doing to occupy your time but you don't actually care about her, you're messing with the wrong girl."

Margaret remained silent, processing. Finally, she gestured toward the couch. "You best sit. It seems we need to discuss a few things."

Debbie and Kathy settled on the couch, and Margaret rolled over her desk chair, sitting down across from them.

"I gather from your accusations that neither of you have spoken with Tess about this," Margaret began.

"No, we couldn't, not yet at least," Debbie replied.

"We figured talking to you first would be best, since we're colleagues," Kathy said. "We're Tess's mentors, so it's different."

"Okay, well, then the first thing you must understand, since you insist on poking your noses into other people's business—"

"You were making out in the boardroom."

Margaret shot Debbie another glare before continuing, "The relationship that I have with Miss Stanford is casual. We approached the exchange as such, it began as such, and it will continue to be as such. We've communicated our feelings on the matter and there are no issues, so I hardly need this 'defensive parent' scolding. There are no feelings involved, just…itches to be scratched—"

"Oh, bullshit," Debbie barked.

"Debbie!" Kathy gasped, shocked.

"No, Kathy, it *is* bullshit!" Debbie held firm. "Look, maybe the sex is casual, I don't know. But you cannot sit here and claim that Tess doesn't care about you, because she does. She has a big heart, that's just how she is. That's why she makes such a great TA, because she'll help anyone, and she cares about everyone. You aren't an exception to that. But this attitude you have, this whole laissez-faire, I-don't-care attitude is going to end up hurting Tess because even if you don't care, she does. You're going to end up crushing her, and I can't just sit by and let it happen."

"I don't want to hurt her," Margaret said.

"It's not that I think you're inherently malicious, because I don't really think that. It's just that you don't ever think about the consequences of your actions. You don't think about how you negatively impact others. You're doing the same with Tess. You act like she doesn't matter to you, and that's going to end up hurting her, no matter your intentions—"

"That's not—I don't—"

"But furthermore, you don't deserve her anyway! She's too good for you," Debbie shouted, growing decisive. "You've made this side of campus a living hell for years. Tess is the good to your bad, the bright to your dark and ugly. I wish I realized it sooner so I could have stepped in before Tess got so invested. She comes to your defense all the time. But you aren't worth it. You're going to end up crushing her, destroying her, hurting—"

Margaret shot forward and slammed her fist down on the coffee table, causing both the bio professors to jump. Then she shouted out desperately, "I don't want to hurt Tess. I love her, damn it!"

Silence permeated the office space. Margaret's heavy breathing subsided, her anger falling away as she pulled into herself, crossing her arms over her chest protectively. Debbie and Kathy watched her, shocked to silence.

"I know I don't deserve her," Margaret said, softer, refusing to look either woman in the eye. "I know she's too good for me. I don't deserve someone who's willing to put up with my sour, cantankerous attitude. I don't deserve someone who can look past my flaws and embrace what little good I have, if I even have any good inside." She bit her knuckle and stood, turning her back on the women to further hide, and then she defensively snapped out, "You both need to leave right now. Get out."

Margaret, to her horror, began to shake uncontrollably. As she tried to school her emotions, she heard Kathy's tentative voice behind her.

"Margaret…We haven't gotten along too well in the past. We've locked horns at nearly every mandatory work meeting. I found you draining and exhausting, and you are mean at times, but I was quick to write you off. Everyone wrote you off, that's the thing. We all saw or heard something, blew it out of proportion, even if there were origins in truth.

"But you know, despite your actions and the rumors, Tess saw something in you worth saving. She saw this part of you, almost immediately, that was worth dealing with your daily abuse, because she knew there was a softness to you. She knew you were worth it. I really care about Tess. I respect and admire her. Since she cares about you, and she sees this part of you that's good, then I believe her." Margaret felt a hand rest very gently on her elbow. "Margaret, I want you to know that I'm here for you. It might take time, but I'm willing to put the past behind us and move forward."

Despite her best efforts, the choked-back whimper of a sob escaped Margaret. Kathy tugged gently at Margaret until she turned, revealing the tears streaking down her face. Margaret roughly wiped her face, gasping, "I'm s-sorry. This is unprofessional."

Kathy offered a shrug. "This all is, isn't it? But this isn't just work. I—well, come here." She opened her arms wide and didn't wait for Margaret to bolt, she simply pulled her into a hug. She grasped the shaking professor tightly.

Margaret couldn't remember the last time someone hugged her like this. She barely let Amy touch her beyond swift and brief greetings, and the way Tess caressed her was different. But this hug felt secure, tight, and grounding, like the way a mother might hug. She tried to remember what her own mother's hugs felt like, but that caused another wave of grief to wash over her when she realized she couldn't. Margaret didn't pull away from Kathy, but she remained rigid in her arms.

"I'm sorry I snapped at you like that," Debbie apologized. "I just…well, I guess I didn't realize that you were capable of caring, so I just assumed—"

Margaret pulled back in a jerk. "Well, I never gave anyone a reason to believe I had a heart, now did I?" she said, sucking in a deep breath to still her shakiness.

Debbie snorted, grinning slightly. "There's a bit of that regular Dr. Morgan sass we're all accustomed to."

"Can we sit back down for a moment?" Kathy asked.

"Yes, I want to cover a point of clarification," Debbie said, returning to their seats. "It's just…You said you're casually hooking up, correct?"

"Yes."

"But…you love Tess."

Margaret let out a choked laugh and rubbed at her puffy eyes. "It's…ahh…it's unfortunate, isn't it?"

"I don't think so," Kathy quickly said. "Truthfully, I think it's a miracle Tess melted your heart. Your whole 'being in love' look? It's a lot better than your old look, that's for sure."

Margaret rubbed her palms together as she avoided eye contact. Then she muttered out, "Yeah, so, like I said, I hardly need your 'protective parent' talk, because if anyone is getting hurt in this scenario, it's clearly me, not Tess."

"She doesn't know?" Debbie seemed confused.

"What?"

"Tess, I mean, she doesn't know that you're in love with her? Or—or she…rejected you?"

Margaret scoffed. "Tess doesn't know, of course not, and I'm not going to tell her. She might tolerate me, might see some good in me that others can't, but she would never consider me as a long-term partner. I'm worn out, hardly in my prime, and she's a young college student with her whole life ahead of her."

Debbie pursed her lips. "You're selling yourself a bit short, don't you think?"

"I would just hold her back," Margaret said woefully. She crossed her arms then sat up straight, fixing both biology professors with her typical glare. "But no, Tess doesn't know about my feelings, and I expect your discretion on the matter."

"Of course."

"But, Margaret, for the record," Kathy said. "Never assume you know another person's feelings."

SENIOR YEAR

They hadn't called, they barely texted. They were both busy, although Margaret wasn't too busy to regularly check her phone, hoping for a message from Tess. She could text Tess first, but she wouldn't. She couldn't seem needy.

Though Margaret tried to hide her misery, Amy saw through her. Between them sat an abandoned board game, half-empty wineglasses in their hands.

"Have you heard from her?" Amy asked casually.

"No. Radio silence all summer."

"I'm sure she's just been busy, catching up with friends, working at her internship, visiting—"

"I know that, Amy," Margaret forced out. She was a rational woman; she understood why. She just wasn't coping well.

"I think getting laid would help. You always used to get like this…Restless. Until you took a lady to bed."

"You're probably right."

"I know who you want to sleep with, but since she's MIA, maybe someone else could suffice in the meantime. Just a quick shag to get your libido in check."

Margaret scrunched her nose in disgust. "If you say another absurd thing, I'll kick you out."

"I know you're in love with her, but you refuse to tell her."

"Amy—"

"It's casual because you refuse to tell her your feelings. It's been three months, Margaret. You can sleep with someone else."

Margaret's back went rigid. She was about to shout, but before she could, they were interrupted by a desperate pounding on the door.

"Are you expecting someone?"

"No…" Margaret replied, slowly standing.

Amy looked at the time. "It's almost eight…a little early for serial killers, but a bit late for a delivery."

"It's probably nothing, a lost package or a neighbor," Margaret said, walking to the door. "Let's hope it's not someone wanting me to watch their pets."

She pulled open the front door, and before she could register what was happening, arms flew around her neck, followed quickly by the rush of golden hair, a comforting scent, and the press of familiar lips in a desperate kiss.

"God, I'm so glad you're home. I was worried you'd be out." Tess pushed into Margaret, sending her tumbling back, and Tess kicked the front door shut. "I'm on a road trip with my family," Tess explained, followed immediately by another kiss. "We're just passing through, only stopped for the night"—another kiss—"but I told them I wanted to visit some friends, that I'd spend the night with them. Lies." She raked her teeth along Margaret's jaw. "You're all I was thinking about…all I've been thinking about all summer—"

"Ahh…Miss Stanford?" Margaret managed to mutter out breathlessly.

Tess dropped her hands and pulled at the button of Margaret's pants as she sucked furiously at her neck. "Summers are the worst." She slid the zipper down. "I could barely go an entire week without seeing you, and now, months! It's been unbearable."

"Tess—" Margaret tried again to protest, gripping futilely at Tess's elbows.

"Please, Margaret. I want you. Please, Maggie, *please*, Dr. Morgan." Tess ran through every nickname in pure desperation. "I need you so badly, I—"

Amy loudly cleared her throat.

In a flash, Tess spun away from Margaret, her eyes landing wide with horror on Amy. "Oh my god!" she exclaimed. "Dr. Greenwood. Shit. I'm so sorry. I didn't even think you might have company."

Amy folded her lips together like she was trying to suppress a grin. She stood up from the couch. "That's all right, Tess, I was just heading out. And please, call me Amy, since you passed my class."

"No, I'm sorry I interrupted. You don't have to leave on my account. Please, I'll just go—"

"Oh, no," Amy said. "Reconnect and have fun. I'll see you both around."

Amy slipped out of the house then, and Margaret draped her arms around Tess, trying to pull her back to her.

"That was somewhat mortifying," Tess uttered into Margaret's arms.

"Forget Amy. I've got a list of a hundred dirty things that I'm desperate to do to you."

"You have me until morning, and I expect nothing but the best."

"Marvelous." Margaret dipped her head and sucked eagerly at Tess's neck, getting her to moan loudly. But then, Tess shoved at her sternum.

"No, stop, don't you dare give me hickeys. I am not going to be stuck in a car with my family with hickeys on my neck. No way. If you give me a hickey, you have to answer to my mother."

"Okay, okay," Margaret said, giving in. Then she grinned impishly. "No hickeys in visible locations. Got it."

Tess shivered happily.

* * *

Tess was anxious to return to campus for senior year, partly because she was desperate to see Margaret, but also because

Kai warned her about some rumors floating around that she refused to elaborate on until they were together in person. Kai was an RA again, so she had been on campus a month before the rest of the students. Tess and Elle moved into their on-campus apartment the earliest they could and ordered pizza for dinner.

When Kai arrived, she first fell into Elle's arms. After letting them tenderly reconnect for a few minutes, Tess directed Kai toward the leftover pizza.

"You two can fully catch up later, but I need to know about these rumors," Tess declared.

"It's huge tea, massive," Kai said. "And actually, it's about you, Tess."

"Wait, me?"

"Yes. I've helped with freshman move-in three years in a row now. All the gossip is the same, the same old advice: go to office hours, take care of yourself, the library is a great resource, and avoid Dr. Morgan at all costs. This year was basically the same except for the part about Dr. Morgan."

"What are they saying about her now?" Tess asked, frowning.

"They're saying she's *nice*," Kai stressed. "She's striking, a bit snappish but alluring, and she's approachable now because she's sleeping with a student."

There was a moment of pause and then Elle burst out laughing.

"Damn it, Caleb," Tess cursed, going red in the face. "I—I mean I know it's true, but they don't!"

"I mean, don't blame Caleb, but news got out about her helping him. Incoming students think it's neat when professors stand up for queer kids."

"As they should," Elle said.

"Well, she's not all bad, and I'm glad others are starting to realize it," Tess said.

"But also, several students saw Dr. Morgan chatting with, smiling at, and holding hands with a biology TA named Tess Stanford."

"Oh my god."

"I heard rumors saying she's just sleeping with you," Kai continued, "but I also heard rumors that Dr. Morgan regularly sleeps with many students."

"Oh no."

"It's not all bad. Everyone keeps saying how awesome Tess is, and Debbie told me that they have a record-long waitlist for their class."

"That's kind of nice…"

"But also, students are straight-up horny for Dr. Morgan. It's absurd. They're acting like it's a new trending challenge to bed the dominatrix of the bio-chem department."

"Correction, this is a nightmare," Tess said, feeling herself go pale.

It wasn't exactly a nightmare once classes started. Although the rumors were abundant, most turned a deaf ear. Tess did, however, develop a posse of "fans" that flocked to her after the first intro bio class. But beyond the first day, things mostly calmed down for Tess.

Margaret's life, however, was only getting more hectic.

The second Tess had an ounce of free time, she went straight to Margaret's office. She grabbed the door handle and shoved into the door, expecting it to give way easily, but instead she slammed into it. Frustrated, she jiggled the handle, confused as to why it was locked.

Margaret let Tess in a moment later, pulling the door open as Tess tumbled inside, huffing.

"Everyone knows," Tess said.

Margaret shut and locked her office door again. "Yes, well, good to see you too, welcome back," she said sarcastically.

"Everyone thinks it's true. I mean, they don't have proof. I've been playing dumb. But it is true, and everyone knows!"

"Yes, I'm well aware." Margaret's voice was an annoyed growl. "That's why my office door is locked. I'm tired of all the idiotic underclassmen tumbling in, trying to introduce themselves. And look at this atrocity Amy forwarded to me this morning."

Margaret extended her phone and Tess stared down at the screen. It was a social media app, an anonymous confessions page, and with abject horror she realized it was a student-created fan page for Dr. Morgan. Tess read through the anonymous confessions. *Her eyes are mysterious and striking*, and *She's alluring. I enjoy her strictness.* But then Tess read *I want her to bend me over a desk and choke me while she fucks me*, and Tess practically threw the phone back at Margaret.

"Unbelievable." Tess crossed her arms, huffing.

"I reported the page to the dean, obviously," Margaret said. "It'll be down by this afternoon, but I figured I'd show you while it's still up."

"It's disgusting."

"I'm not used to this kind of attention. It's so…aggressively forward. But surely it will die down, especially once classes begin and the freshmen see how I really am."

Tess glanced at Margaret, fighting—and failing—to hide a mischievous smirk. "You mean how you're a big sweetie who likes to cuddle?"

"No!" Margaret snapped, her cheeks reddening. "You are not helping this predicament."

Tess let herself smile fully then. She stretched out her arms, beckoning. Margaret resisted initially, but then she sighed, rolled her eyes, and dragged her feet as she walked over to the couch. She sat down and pulled Tess against her. Tess looked up at her fondly, slowly running her hand along her jaw before she pressed up and captured Margaret's lips in a tender kiss.

"Are you still free on Fridays?" Margaret asked when they parted.

"Always. And some Saturdays, if…?"

"Some Saturdays would be…agreeable."

"Fantastic."

* * *

It was oddly cryptic when Debbie pulled Tess aside and said she wanted to meet privately. It was the way she said it, a hushed whisper, with her hand clamped tightly on Tess's arm. Tess shoved off the eerie feeling and said, "Yeah, I was going to swing by and grade the worksheets. I assume Kai will come too."

"No, I'd like to discuss something with you privately. Without Kai." Debbie remained firm.

Maybe Tess was overanalyzing. Still, she felt uneasy.

When Tess went to Debbie's office later that morning, she found Kathy there as well. She trailed in slowly, sitting down across from Kathy, and Debbie circled back to the door and shut it. When Debbie sat down, both professors looked at her directly. Tess gulped.

Maybe she was getting fired. She didn't feel like she had done anything to warrant being fired, but it was early in the year—better to fire a team member at the start than halfway through the school semester. The thought made Tess sad. Getting fired would suck.

Debbie worried her hands and Kathy shut her laptop, pushing it to the side. Tess squeezed her fists together in her lap. No one said anything, and the silence in the room was deafening.

Eventually, Debbie cleared her throat. "I'm afraid this is, um…well, it's going to be awkward. Kathy and I tried to plan out what we wanted to say, but we couldn't find a way that wasn't awkward."

"We weren't planning on bringing it up at all. It isn't really our place, it's just…We've been hearing some things, and we thought we should talk with you about it."

Tess bit her tongue. This was about the rumors, then, about her sleeping with Margaret.

"You aren't in trouble, Tess," Kathy said softly. "Sorry, you're just looking awfully pale. I need you to know that none of this changes how we feel about you. We still care greatly about you, and we always will. That's why we felt the need to discuss this with you."

Tess nodded and released a long breath. So, not getting fired, then. Good.

"We just wanted to talk with you about—well, you've probably heard the rumors yourself," Kathy said. "It's about the, um, well, the—"

"What Kathy is trying to say is that…just that some students have been mentioning…that you've, well—"

Her mentors' struggle was only prolonging the extremely awkward conversation. Tess wanted it over and done with.

"You're talking about the rumor that Dr. Morgan is sleeping with a student, right?" Tess asked. "And that student is me?"

Both professors nodded curtly.

Tess ran her hand through her hair and forced out a chuckle. "Yeah, it's crazy the stuff that gets thought up and passed around. I mean, who would have even started a rumor like that? Super weird. But trust me, I'm being professional about it, ignoring it. It won't impact my work, and it currently isn't a problem, but if it starts to cause problems, I will let both of you know immediately."

With a flat and even tone, Debbie said, "Tess, we know it's true."

Kathy cringed.

"I—wh-what?" Tess stuttered.

"We know that you're sleeping with Margaret. I suspected something was going on between you two for a while now, but what really confirmed it was when I saw you two kissing in the boardroom last year."

Tess's eyes went wide, and she covered her face with her hands, completely mortified. "Oh, god."

"We talked to Margaret about it," Kathy said. "She confirmed our suspicions and explained what was really going on. We weren't planning on saying anything to you about it unless you brought it up first. But then, well…"

"The rumors are…a lot," Debbie explained. "I'm sure it will die down. But with everything getting passed around, we just figured maybe we should mention that we know the truth. And that we're here for you if things get to be too much. We care about you greatly and just want to make sure that you're okay."

"I am so sorry!" Tess exclaimed.

"Why are you apologizing?"

"I don't know, I just…well I admire you both and for you to know about…I just—it's just a bit embarrassing."

"Heavens, you needn't be embarrassed," Debbie said. "We're all adults. We've heard plenty about Kai and Elle's relationship, and you know plenty of tidbits about our relationships with our husbands. You're in college. Relationships happen. It's entirely natural. I mean, you have perhaps interesting taste, but—"

"Debbie!" Kathy gasped.

"You've made a big impact on Margaret's life," Debbie said instead. "We actually get things accomplished at our meetings now, and sometimes she even makes pleasant small talk. Four years ago, I would have thought that was impossible."

"She is kind of grouchy and…we're working on that nasty temper of hers," Tess admitted with a slight laugh, "but she's actually so sweet once you get to know her."

Kathy nodded, agreeing. "We realized that we let our bitterness get in the way, forgetting she's a person just like us, with her own hardships and feelings. We're trying to do better. I hope that our own relationships with Margaret will improve as well."

"I think it would be nice if she could be friends with more of her coworkers. She's friends with an English professor across campus, but I think it would be good for her to have some more 'local' friends."

"Margaret, friends with an English professor," Debbie said, smirking slightly like she was surprised.

"Well, so, that's all we wanted to discuss with you," Kathy concluded. "I mean, if you want to stay and talk, you're more than welcome. But we won't keep you if you're busy."

"She's supposed to be grading today's worksheet," Debbie said, scoffing. "She's still under our employ, you know."

"Yep, I'll be here grading." Tess, instead of moving to start on the task, just fidgeted in her seat. "Just, um…just one thing…"

"Yes?"

"You said you talked to Margaret, right?"

"We did."

"Did she tell you exactly what's happening between us? Because, well, it just felt like you were implying…but actually… We aren't dating. That's what I wanted to clarify."

Debbie nodded. "Yes, she was very clear that your thing is casual. We don't want details, but I understand the necessity of clarifying."

"Okay, yeah." Tess reached out and collected the stack of worksheets. "Can I actually take these with me? I'd like to grade them somewhere else, like the student center, or outside, maybe."

"Or in a certain bio-chem professor's office?" Debbie added, a sparkle of amusement in her eyes.

Tess flushed. "Or, um, yeah. That."

Debbie just laughed. "Yes, sure, go grade at your leisure."

"Awesome, thanks." Tess stood and headed toward the door. She reached for the handle but stopped and turned, looking back at the bio professors. "Hey. Thanks for being so cool about this."

"Of course, Tess," Kathy replied. "We just want to see you happy, and she does seem to put a smile on your face."

Tess grinned even bigger in response to that. "All right, I'll see you two later."

"Oh, and, Tess? One more thing. No more slipping out of our TA meetings early to meet with her."

Tess flushed profusely and jerked out of the room, slamming the door shut behind her.

* * *

"Where are you headed?" Debbie casually asked, abruptly stepping up beside Margaret, who was currently carrying a box of books from her car over to Amy.

Margaret glanced to her side, noting the interruption. "It's none of your business."

"That looks heavy. Let me help you," Kathy said, suddenly appearing on the other side of Margaret. She reached for the box, but Margaret jerked back.

"What is this, an ambush?" Margaret asked. "You're picking up bad habits from your TA."

"We just thought we'd say hi, chat while we walked. We're heading to lunch, if you'd like to join us."

"I'm heading to the English building, if you must know, which is a bit out of the way of the café, wouldn't you say?"

"The English building? What on earth for?"

Margaret shot Debbie a deathly glare.

Kathy peered around Margaret to address Debbie. "She's clearly going to visit her friend. Remember what Tess said?"

"Oh, right. You're friends with an English professor."

Margaret fixed her jaw and continued stalking forward, choosing to ignore the women.

They walked in silence for a few steps before Kathy said, "You know, we have lunch with our TAs every first Monday. You're more than welcome to join us next week if you'd like."

"I'd rather die."

"So dramatic," Debbie replied, rolling her eyes. "Surely you enjoy eating out from time to time. You can't be that much of a hermit. Besides, Tess will be there."

"So?"

"So, you like her."

Margaret, feeling cheeky and obstinate, declared, "Allegedly."

"God, dramatic *and* stubborn," Debbie said. "Can't you see we're trying to be your friend?"

"I don't have friends."

"Sure you do. What about the English professor—" Kathy started to say, but Margaret cut her off.

"I don't want friends."

"Feisty today. But actually—"

"Dr. Morgan," someone shouted.

"Well, would you speak of the devil," Debbie stated, smirking impishly.

"If you two insist on chatting, then by god, hurry up," Margaret said. She increased her pace, determined to ignore all further interruptions to her day.

"Hey, Dr. Morgan, wait up," Tess shouted even louder, cupping her hands around her mouth. Margaret continued forward, barely even flinching. With a huff, Tess trekked forward, shouting, "Margaret, stop ignoring me."

Margaret tensed at the use of her first name, but she defiantly continued. Debbie and Kathy kept pace, although they were glancing back over their shoulders and watching Tess.

Tess's voice rang out with, "Margaret Elizabeth Morgan, you stop right this instant!"

Margaret flinched fully then and pulled to an immediate stop.

"Margaret Elizabeth?" Debbie said incredulously just as Kathy asked, "Elizabeth?"

Tess stormed up behind Margaret and stated, "You have some nerve ignoring me like that."

Margaret spun, her body fierce but gaze affectionately soft. Her words, however, did have bite. "*You* have some nerve shouting after me like that."

"Your middle name is Elizabeth? Really?" Kathy asked. "That's my middle name."

"Never mind that," Debbie said. "Tess knows your middle name?" She fought back a laugh.

"This will not be repeated." Margaret scowled and gestured toward Tess. "Look at the spectacle you've made."

Tess crossed her arms defiantly. "I'm not going to stop talking to you just because everyone's gossiping about us."

Kathy jerked her head roughly in the direction of the nearby café and Debbie took the hint. "We're off to lunch. You two have fun," Debbie said, making their excuse. "Still, consider our invitation." She pointed seriously at Margaret. "Oh, and lovely chatting with you, Margaret *Elizabeth*."

Margaret let out a howl of frustration, Debbie laughing wildly. Margaret then turned toward Tess to protest further, but before she could, Tess snatched the box straight out of her arms.

"Geez, this is heavy. What's in here?"

"I don't need your help."

"No, but I'm carrying it for you anyway. What's in here, though? And where are you off to?"

"I'm going to see Amy," Margaret replied. "The box is full of books she loaned me."

"Explains the weight. Elle and I were going to swing by and catch up with Amy later today. We want to invite her out for drinks. You can come too if you'd like."

"Why is everyone suddenly inviting me out?"

"Is that what Debbie was saying? About considering their invitation?"

"Yes, your obnoxious biology professors invited me to your monthly TA luncheon."

Tess spun toward Margaret so quickly she nearly tripped. "You have to come. It'll be so much fun. You'll scare the pants off the juniors."

"It sounds like my literal hell on earth."

"Oh, you're so dramatic. I know you don't mean that."

"Just what Debbie said."

Tess hummed quizzically. "I didn't realize you'd gotten so friendly with them."

"Yes, well, it's not intentional, trust me. We just…there was a shift after they confronted me. Maybe this was inevitable."

Tess narrowed her eyes. "Oh, you mean when you told them we were sleeping together?" she said, her voice pitched low with accusation.

"I didn't tell them. Debbie knew, she caught us—"

"Macking in the boardroom, yes."

"How did you…?"

"Because they confronted me about it!" Tess gasped forcefully. "I mean, talk about an awkward conversation. But I guess it's good they know. Kai was bound to slip up sooner or later."

Margaret watched Tess for a moment before hesitantly asking, "Are you…upset? You seem tense."

"I'm not upset, just embarrassed. I liked it better when it was just us, before anyone knew. I just feel, well…"

"Exposed? Because that's how I feel. I did try to prevent this initially. Dropping you off blocks from campus, refusing your advances at school. But you're too persistent."

Tess shrugged. "It's your fault. You're too irresistible. Still, sometimes I wonder if people wouldn't talk so much if they knew it was true."

"You want everyone to know the truth?"

"No, I mean, that's not professional. It's just that the mystery perpetuates—wait. Do *you* want everyone to know?"

Margaret gasped. "Of course not. You know I'm a highly private person. I can't even fathom it, that we'd, what, shout to the whole campus that we're sleeping together? We aren't dating, so it's not even something you'd announce."

"Right, we aren't dating," Tess said forcefully.

"No…"

"So, it's settled, then. Glad we talked about it," Tess said, her tone no less harsh.

* * *

"We're going to be late," Tess said. She wasn't mad, just pointing out the obvious to prove she was right.

"Like, a minute," Kai replied.

"There's no parking."

"Here, I'll go down this street. There has to be something close."

"I told you we should have just walked."

"We'll be there with plenty of time. I know you're extra anxious today because your lover lady might come, but there's no need for you to be so uppity."

Tess felt her face color slightly. "Don't refer to her like that. I'm not even sure she'll come. I mean, a friendly get-together lunch with some biology professors and TAs? That's not really her cup of tea."

"But I think she might because you asked her to. Did you ask her while you were naked and flaunting? I'm sure that would have helped sweeten the deal."

"If you don't stop talking, I'm getting out of the car right now and walking."

Eventually, Kai found parking a few blocks from the café, and the two girls practically ran to make the lunch on time.

They crashed into the little local restaurant and spotted their professors and fellow TAs already sitting around a table chatting amicably.

"Sorry we're late," Tess said, approaching the table. "I would have just walked over, but Kai had to grab something from her apartment and then she insisted we drive, but we couldn't find parking."

"We're barely even late," Kai said. "Ten minutes? That's like…on time for us."

"Go order your food, so you aren't waiting around even longer." Debbie shoved them off toward the counter.

Tess and Kai stood in line at the counter, debating over the menu.

"You order next, I'm still deciding," Kai said, shoving Tess forward.

When Tess finished ordering, she turned to head back to the table but came face-to-face with Margaret. Excitement buzzed in her chest. She smirked. Margaret opened her mouth to say something, but before she could, Tess cut her off with, "You're late. By nearly fifteen minutes."

Margaret flushed a deep crimson. She crossed her arms stiffly and let out a huff. "I figured you biology bozos would be running at least fifteen minutes late, and I hardly wanted to be waiting around for you."

Tess stepped back into line with Margaret. "You're cute, you know, when you blush like that," she whispered, covering her mouth like it was some huge secret.

By then, Kai finished ordering, and she turned to face the pair. She fixed the biochemistry professor with a pointed stare and nodded swiftly. "Dr. Morgan."

"Kai," Margaret replied similarly.

"Glad you could make it," Kai said. "I'm excited to watch you scare the underclassmen."

After Margaret ordered, she and Tess headed back to the table. As they approached, they watched as one of the juniors grabbed Kai's arm.

"Is she in a good mood?"

"'Good' is a bit of a stretch for Dr. Morgan, but she seems fine. I'm impressed she even showed up...more impressed you two invited her out."

Debbie gave a slight shrug, but Kathy spoke up. "She has sour moods, but we've been too mean to her. Tess has always seen the good in her. We're just trying to do the same."

"Trying to befriend her, I think you mean," Debbie said.

"Hey, I figured I'd do some introductions," Tess said, stepping up to the table with Margaret. "The professors all know each other, and you know Kai and me, but these are the other TAs: Ila, Sage, Jessie, and Taylor. Everyone, as you know, this is Dr. Morgan."

"Hello," Margaret said, her tone pitched low.

"Cut the Doberman act, it's just lunch," Debbie said. "Here, take a seat. How's research going?"

"There they go, talking about work already," Tess said, rolling her eyes. "What all have the rest of you been up to?"

"Settling into classes."

"I'm taking a painting class. It's been pretty fun so far."

"Do you have any pictures of your work?"

"Yeah, here."

"Wow! That looks awesome."

"I've been getting back into running. I'm training for my first marathon."

"Where do you run? I've been trying to find a good running loop for a while now, but I haven't found one I like yet."

"Dr. Morgan's got a route she loves," Tess chimed in. She gently nudged Margaret to pull her into the conversation. "What's that route you run all the time? Taylor's looking for a good running route."

"Oh, it's through the neighborhoods south of Clyde Park. I can pull up a map and show you if you'd like?"

Taylor, wide-eyed, glanced around the table. When his eyes settled on Margaret, she was just staring at him expectantly. "Um, sure. That would be helpful," he said. "I, um, didn't know you ran?"

Margaret hummed as she pulled up her route. "I find it's a great way to clear my head, rethink experiments that didn't go well. Over time I built endurance, and I suppose I'm half decent at it now."

"She's great at it, actually," Tess supported. "She's placed first in several marathons."

"Do you have any marathoning tips?" Sage asked. "I've never run one before, but I'd really like to."

"Sure, I suppose I have a few pointers," Margaret said.

Tess saw Debbie and Kathy glance at each other and share a knowing grin.

* * *

When Margaret first settled into her big bad lone-wolf persona, she told herself it was to maximize efficiency, to limit interruptions and distractions. If others needed harsh words to get them on track, it was hardly her fault. But in truth, it was never about work. Margaret didn't like interacting with others because it was difficult to trust people and their motivations. Although her friendship with Tess proved that not everyone in the world was out to get her, she couldn't help the sickly feeling in her stomach as anxiety grasped her around the throat and tried to strangle her.

The rumors were annoying, and it was embarrassing that so many students were willing to vocally discuss a matter very private to Margaret. It was made even worse by the whispers behind her back. Everywhere she went, she felt eyes burning into the back of her head.

She tried to retaliate. She snapped at students and gave others the cold shoulder, but she'd fallen out of her nasty habits and her anxiety made her less sure of herself. Tess disliked the bitter and cold parts of her personality. She'd been working to change, realizing that she didn't want to be that kind of person anymore either. But there weren't clearly defined, written rules on behavior, and Margaret felt unstable trying to navigate all the new occurrences.

Tension, of a bad kind, grew between her and Tess. Margaret was getting anxiously attached, needy and desperate for her main source of warm stability, and Tess grew more distant, slightly bitter, avoidant. She was busy figuring out her future, balancing her many responsibilities, which meant she had less time to bother Margaret. On top of everything, their casual meetups felt more serious, with all the rumors and whispers going around, putting a type of pressure on them both.

It was the beginning of the end; Margaret could feel it. Tess was starting to pull away, because in less than a year, she would graduate and then she'd be gone.

* * *

"The entire world collectively decided to kill me this semester."

"Stop complaining and come on, or we'll be late. Besides, I don't know why you're dragging your feet. Your girlfriend is going to be there. Surely that's more than enough motivation."

Margaret shot Amy a ghastly look. "Tess is not my girlfriend."

"She's close enough."

"She's not—"

"You're acting like a few drinks is going to kill you, yet you used to do this every weekend."

"This is entirely different. I used to go to the bar for companionship, but now—"

"This is for companionship."

"Drinks with friends is hardly the companionship I'm referring to, and you know it."

"With friends, exactly. You adore spending time with Tess, I know you do."

"I'm not going for Tess, I'm going for you."

"You're going for Tess."

Margaret paused, then sighed loudly—dramatically. "Perhaps I am," she admitted. "I mean, I certainly didn't go to that biology TA luncheon for the biology professors."

"You went to a TA luncheon? For the biology department?" Amy asked, bemused.

"Yes, because as I mentioned, the entire world has decided to kill me. I'm getting invited out right and left. Now that Tess has…'befriended' me, a slew of others seem inclined to do so as well."

"It sounds serious—no, I'm not agreeing with your end-of-the-world monologue. I mean, it sounds like Tess's feelings for you might be serious. Does it not seem strange to adopt your fuck buddy into your friend group?"

"Tess just…likes me as a friend, so I assume she's trying to get others to see this supposed good in me, or whatever."

"I don't know. I think she might have feelings for you… romantically." Amy batted her eyelashes.

"Cut it out."

Amy stopped at the entrance of the pub and chivalrously pulled the door open. Though Margaret preferred O'Charlie's, she dreaded the look on Jimmy's face if he caught her bringing in a woman, even if she wasn't dating said woman. Ultimately, however, Elle had picked the location.

"Where shall we sit? A table?" Amy questioned.

They arrived before the others, scanning the menus while they waited. Shortly after, Tess dramatically flopped down next to Margaret, dropping her head onto her shoulder.

"I'm so happy I'm not third-wheeling again," Tess said. Then she sat up and turned fully to Margaret. "And I'm extremely happy that you've loosened up and are willing to be seen in public with me. Your cooking is fabulous, Maggie, but going out is fun."

Going out is reserved for dating, Margaret thought but voiced no such opinion.

A moment later, Kai and Elle both slid into the booth.

"If you want the wings, order your own plate, because I'm eating all eight, appetizer size or not," Elle said.

"But I don't want an order of wings, I want to steal your wings," Kai said.

"Stop flirting," Tess teased her friends. "So, you two are getting wings. Has the academic pair figured out what they're having yet?"

"Not quite," Margaret said.

"Oh, they've got that weird cheese pasta thing you like," Tess said to Margaret.

"That does sound rather appetizing. I assume you're going to have their grilled chicken sandwich."

"Of course."

Across the table, Elle said to Kai, "If you want a frozen margarita, I'll buy it for you. I know they're your favorite."

"Aww, how sweet," Kai replied, gazing affectionately at Elle.

Amy kicked Margaret under the table, causing her to look up at her and scowl. Amy shot Margaret one of her most obvious teacher looks, and Margaret could visualize her eye rolls in response to Kai and Elle's dating behavior mirrored in Margaret's behavior with Tess.

"That's *subtext*," Margaret imagined Amy saying to her students. "Read between the lines."

* * *

"She's absolutely gorgeous."

"I almost caught my shirt on fire in lab the other day because I was daydreaming about her…"

"You know, I heard she's a runner."

"That's literally so hot."

"I saw her take off her blazer the other day…Her arms are brilliantly toned."

"I'm not even gay, but I'd let her fuck me."

Tess was losing it. There wasn't a single place on campus she could go without overhearing students gush about Dr. Morgan. She was trying really hard to ignore it, but it was so difficult. She wanted to scream. Margaret was sleeping with her, not them. Margaret didn't sleep with students, she slept with Tess, singular!

Of course…they weren't monogamous. Margaret could sleep with other women, and she could sleep with other students. When Tess thought about Margaret sleeping around, she just got so mad. But why?

Maybe, if she humored her thoughts, Tess could admit that just a little bit, she kind of cared about Margaret…and not in the friend way she had been so adamantly insisting. But Margaret didn't do relationships, so it was pointless to consider. Also, Tess was graduating.

No part of Tess wanted to move away from Margaret and stop their weekly sexcapades, but she had to graduate. She had to move on. If they were dating, she'd consider Margaret's feelings on her postgraduation plans, but they weren't and never would be.

Tess wanted to go to grad school and get her PhD, so she was in the process of applying to various schools across the country. And, because maybe she was a bit of a masochist, she applied to two local schools as well, just in case.

But she hadn't told Margaret, and Margaret hadn't asked. Tess figured that if she really cared about losing her entirely, she would ask Tess about her plans because she cared enough to want Tess to stay. Or she'd want to stay in touch, anything. But Margaret never asked, and Tess never brought it up.

Instead, Tess grew more anxious, discontent about her uncertain future involving Margaret, and the mutterings around campus were not helping her mood.

* * *

Margaret was not faring much better.

She, too, was enduring the obnoxious rumors and the constant harassment from students who would have, in the past, left her alone entirely. Students asking her about chemistry were bad enough but easy to deal with. The blatant, unabashed flirting from certain bold students, however, was much harder to deflect.

"Dr. Morgan, nice blazer you're wearing."

"Flattery diminishes your character," Margaret barked out robotically.

She was ignored entirely. "Your blouse looks nice too, although I can't see it fully. Maybe if I helped you out of your blazer…"

Margaret's eyebrows shot to her hairline. "Get out of my sight immediately."

But the girl didn't run away. She simply shrugged as if it were barely an inconvenience to her.

Fucking freshmen.

A few of her particularly insistent groupies had begun to regularly congregate outside her office. "Get out of my way," she grumbled as she shoved past the girls.

"Dr. Morgan!" a chorus followed.

"I'm interested in—"

"Could you—"

"Would you like—"

"Enough!" Margaret hollered, her voice booming. "All of you, get out of here. I do not have office hours now, and the hallway outside of my office is not for social gatherings. Do I make myself clear?"

Motherfucking goddamn freshmen!

* * *

"Amy, I am going to kill someone."

Amy fought back a laugh. "It's a bit funny. You went from the unapproachable devil to campus's biggest bachelorette. Even you must admit that's funny."

"I can't even think on campus," Margaret continued ranting. "They're festering, crawling out of the woodwork like a bad infestation of bugs. So, the whole school hears a rumor that I'm sleeping with a student. Fine, let them think what they want. But that doesn't mean I'm looking for more students to sleep with. Especially freshmen—by god, they're only eighteen!"

"If that."

"I don't know how I'll survive. I'm interrupted constantly. I don't know how professors with open-door policies survive, although maybe class-related interruptions are rarer than... than the gross and pathetic moves these children are trying to make. I can't stand it."

"Look how much you've changed. A few years ago, you would have been soaking in the attention, happily taking girls up on the offer."

"At the bar, maybe, but never at school. It was bad enough that Tess got to me."

"Oh, you adore Tess, don't lie. But speaking of Tess, how's she feeling about all the attention you're getting?"

Margaret's mood fell as she contemplated Tess's recent distance. She picked at her finger. "I haven't actually seen Tess all week. She's helping Dr. Logan write a paper, so she's been busy."

"Have you texted?"

"No. I didn't want to bother her."

"It's unlike Tess to give you radio silence during the school semester. I mean, she usually does all her homework in either your office or mine."

"I suppose it is uncharacteristic."

"Maybe something is bothering her. Maybe you should talk to her. It drives me crazy how both you and Tess internalize everything."

"I've been contemplating it," Margaret admitted. "Having all these students flirt with me has only made me realize even more profoundly that I don't want anyone else other than Tess. That's terrifying. But I can feel her starting to pull away. She isn't thinking about me long term, and, well, I suppose that hurts a bit."

"You aggravate me, Margaret," Amy said. "Maybe Tess is moving on. Maybe she won't want anything to do with you beyond this year. But how will you know if you don't talk to her?"

"This whole…being emotionally vulnerable thing is foreign to me."

"All you can do is try."

"But what could I possibly say to convey all these feelings when I can't even put them into words to appease my own mind?"

"Just say that you know she's planning her future and that if she'd be willing, you'd like to be in that future with her. Tell her it isn't just about sex, that it never was—"

"It was at the start—"

"I'm not entirely sure I believe that, but fine. The point is, it's not just about the sex now. You care about her. You want her, Margaret, and you have to tell her that. I know it could end in heartbreak and I know you're scared, but you have to go for it. Love is such a beautiful thing. I don't want you to miss out on this just because you're scared. You're braver than that. I know you are."

Margaret rubbed at the back of her neck, shifting uncomfortably. "She doesn't feel the same way, Amy."

"Stop putting words into her mouth and get your information straight from the source."

"Fine, you're right." Margaret gave in. "I was just afraid to upset the balance, but now she's distant, and everything hurts, so I suppose I'm no longer risking losing her, but rather I'm desperately hoping to keep from losing her."

"Okay, yes, tell her that!"

* * *

Tess felt territorial. Every time she overheard someone gushing about Margaret, *her* bio-chem professor, she wanted to rear on them and snap that Margaret was *hers*. Except she wasn't Tess's. Tess would leave, and Margaret would find a new student to shag every week. But until she graduated, Tess would make a point to be the only woman in Margaret's bed.

All week, Tess had been busy, but Friday, she was determined. She was going to fall into Margaret's arms, fuck her senseless, and suck every inch of skin, leaving too many marks to cover. Because Tess wanted everyone to know that Margaret was off-limits.

As was now commonplace, several girls were loitering outside Margaret's office when Tess arrived.

"Don't bother," one of the girls said. "She didn't even open her door for office hours."

"I'm waiting until she leaves for the night," another said.

"Maybe we could convince her to get dinner with us?"

"Oh, totally."

"Move," Tess harshly said, shoving past them.

"She's not going to answer, you know. She hasn't come out in hours."

Tess knocked incessantly until the door yanked open. Margaret pulled Tess in by her backpack straps, immediately slamming the door shut again.

"I don't know how to get them to leave. They're driving me crazy." Margaret ran her fingers through her hair, clearly stressed.

"Forget about them," Tess said, dropping her backpack as she went after Margaret. Out of view, she pinned Margaret against the wall. "Let's get out of here," Tess said into her mouth.

"I, well...I need to finish this," Margaret said, gesturing loosely toward a stack of papers.

"Can't you finish it later?"

"Maybe...it would be nice to get some work accomplished together, like we always used to."

"I don't want to sit around and do homework, I want to be doing *you.*"

Suddenly decisive, Margaret crossed her arms. "I'm finishing my work before we leave. Either stay and do homework, or don't. I'm not your keeper."

Tess pursed her lips, irritated, but did as she was told, sitting and pulling out homework. Every time she glanced up, though, she caught sight of the girls in the hallway.

"Can't we cover the door window with something?" Tess asked.

"It's against university policy," Margaret replied, clearly annoyed by the rule herself.

"Like anyone would notice the covered window on a Friday."

"If they're bothering you so much, come sit at my desk."

Tess graciously took the invitation and immediately took advantage of their newfound closeness. She slid up, biting her lip as she whimpered needily. Tess could tell she was distracting Margaret, as the professor's hands gripped her pen tighter, but she wasn't budging.

"Please can we leave?" Tess begged, unable to contain herself.

"Actually, first, I want to discuss something with you," Margaret said, her gaze fixed on the pen in her hands. "About your plans after graduation."

"Why do you care?" Tess snapped defensively, disguising her hurt as anger.

"What, is it some big secret?" Margaret snapped in response, matching Tess's tone.

"You just didn't seem to care before. I mean, you never asked. I figured you mustn't really care."

"No, I've just been preoccupied."

Tess scoffed. "Sure, preoccupied with all these students throwing themselves at you. I bet you love the attention. You're probably ecstatic to sleep with more women. What are you waiting for? Go ahead and bed them, unless you already have—"

"Tess—"

"You don't need my permission. This is just casual, like you've said a hundred times. You don't do relationships—"

"You said you didn't want a relationship either—"

"Yeah, exactly, so go sleep with those girls!" Tess snapped. "Far be it from me to stand in your way. We've never been exclusive."

"Is that what you want? You want to see other people?"

Tess crossed her arms. "We probably should. It's not like this was ever going to be serious anyway. Since I'm moving on, Maggie—Margaret. I'm graduating. And you're not going to follow me to grad school, that's ludicrous—"

"You're going to grad school?"

"Yeah, I am, to get a PhD. Not that you care enough to even ask, because you don't do relationships, and you *don't* care, period."

"I—"

"I know you want to sleep with those girls, and it's fine. Do it. See if I care." Tess stood quickly, suddenly, and stormed to the door. "Have a good weekend, *Dr. Morgan*."

Tess jerked into the hall, ignoring the girls. She hugged her arms close, mad and hurt, and stormed off.

* * *

Tess threw her things down and looked up at the ceiling, letting out a raging scream. Elle and Kai, who were cuddled on the couch playing video games, startled at Tess's intense interruption and paused their game.

"What on earth happened?" Elle asked.

"Yeah, and why are you here?" Kai asked. "Don't you always get laid on Friday?"

Tess turned, her gaze fiery. "Dr. Morgan wants to sleep with other women."

"Oh..."

"Which...is fine. We aren't dating. She's not mine." Tess forced out a pained laugh. "Obviously she can sleep with whoever. I mean, weekends are only so long. Clearly, I'd have to share."

"Oh, Tess," Kai said, her voice a whisper, disentangling herself from Elle to catch Tess in a tight hug. "I'm so sorry."

"Why? I don't care. I mean, that was the nature of our deal. It was just sex. I can sleep with someone else too, it's not a big deal."

"You seem pretty upset about it, though..." Elle said.

"It was only casual. I've known from the start that she doesn't do relationships. I don't want a relationship either. It's fine."

"Is it fine, though? Is it really?"

"Yeah. Of course it's fine. I don't care. I mean, it's not like I have...feelings for her or anything. That's ridiculous."

Both Elle and Kai eyed her incredulously.

Tess scoffed. "Come on. How could I fall for someone like her? Someone who can be so mean, and distant, and who can never talk about her feelings and have a serious conversation about...about..."

Tess couldn't talk about her feelings either, but she wasn't ready to face that hypocrisy just yet. She bit her tongue.

"Even if we pretend that's true," Kai said, "you coming in yelling hardly seems like the reaction of someone who doesn't care. Are you sure you aren't upset because you secretly, deep down, like her?"

"No, I—I don't have feelings for her. I'm just...irritated that I'm not getting laid, is all."

"You're a shit liar," Elle said.

"Can this be a three-player game?"

"Sure. I'll start up a new match," Kai said, admitting defeat and dropping the topic.

* * *

When Margaret woke, her head was pounding. Everything hurt. Physically, she hurt from crying herself to sleep, and emotionally she hurt because Tess was gone. Tess had erupted in anger and stormed out, calling her by her formal doctorate title. That stung the worst…that Tess had given her that stupid nickname and then taken it away, just like that.

In the past, Margaret would have gone to the bar, eager to find someone to occupy her mind. Now, that thought made her physically ill. Plus, it was far too early. To pass the daylight hours, she would have poured herself into her work. However, the thought of writing sounded exhausting.

Finally, she understood. She understood why other members of her lab would complain about working late. They had more in their lives than their work. They didn't need to use science as a coping mechanism. They had people in their lives that they cared about, who loved them in return. And now, Margaret had people like that too. Decidedly, she grabbed her keys and left her house.

Margaret mustered what strength she had and marched up to Amy's door. She rang the bell once, twice, and then started pounding furiously.

Finally, she heard her friend shout, "I'm coming, damn! Way to wake the dead on a Saturday."

Amy, wearing a house robe, jerked open the door. Her hair was messy, and her feet bare. When she saw who was on her front porch, her expression grew immediately concerned.

"Margaret? What are you doing here? I—you look horrendous. Are you okay? What happened?"

Margaret's face folded in on itself and she rubbed one arm, pressing her lips together. She gave the tiniest, painful shrug.

Amy, now more awake, seemed to take in the miserable state her friend was in. Quickly, she pulled Margaret into a hug.

"Oh, darling, come here. You poor thing." She patted Margaret's back. "Come here, let's get you a coffee."

Amy sat Margaret down on the couch, then made them both coffees. She passed a steaming mug to Margaret, who cradled it like a comfort blanket, and Amy sat beside her.

"It's Tess, isn't it?" Amy asked.

"Intuitive," Margaret mumbled.

"It's not difficult to guess. Are you going to tell me what happened? Did you tell her about your feelings?"

"I…tried to. I was nervous, so I was stalling…I was thinking about what I was going to say and how Tess might react, I didn't—well I told her I wanted to work. That was my excuse to stay longer while I collected my thoughts. Tess just wanted to leave. And of course, I did too! I always want to sleep with her, I—"

"Spare me the details," Amy interrupted gently. "Tess was… eager, we'll say, and then likely displeased by your insistence to wait."

"Yes, but we still stayed. Eventually, I got up the courage to talk, to discuss what she was doing after graduation."

"If she told you she was moving out of state, goodbye, done-zo, would you have cowered out and not told her how you really feel?"

"Well, probably, because that's what happened. She didn't say she was done, but she got mad and told me how she really felt, and I just let her go."

"Mad?"

"I think she thought I didn't care because I hadn't been asking about her plans. It hurt too much to consider a future where we weren't together, so I was avoiding it. But I guess that hurt her. Maybe I was just never a good friend, so she didn't tell me her plans either."

"Do you know about her first kiss? With the boy, behind the skating rink?" Amy asked. Margaret nodded. "And do you know about that time in middle school when she got sick with stage fright and puked?" Again, Margaret nodded. "She's shared some of her most embarrassing, deeply personal parts of her life with you—not even including the intimacy of sex. Something else must be going on."

"Maybe time just changed things. There's been so much strain, all the worry about the future, and the rumors on campus. I'm exhausted. I'm sure it's even harder on Tess."

"Please, dear god, tell me you told her that. You're so sentimental and caring now, Margaret. I hope you share that side of yourself with Tess, because it's beautiful."

"I...couldn't..." Margaret said in a whisper. "I couldn't because Tess said we should see other people. She said we were never going to work long term, so we might as well see other people."

"But you don't want that."

"No. But Tess is moving on, so we might as well cut ties now."

"I'm sorry."

"Why? This is hardly your fault. It's no one's fault, just life."

"No, I'm sorry that you're hurting and that I can't just magically fix everything," Amy said. "I love you, Margaret, in all your silly, cantankerous ways, and I really thought Tess did too. I was rooting for you, you know. I thought it could be the real deal."

Margaret let out a heavy sigh. "Yeah, I thought so too."

* * *

Without the concern of upsetting and losing Tess, Margaret felt no need to censor herself or consider how her words might affect others. For a few days she stalked around, letting out her pain and frustration on undeserving individuals. But it felt wrong. She felt like she was doing Tess a disservice. She felt scolded by Tess, even though she wasn't there to scold her. She knew better. Though her initial wrath helped quiet the rumors, she began to pull in on herself, avoiding others entirely.

In the afternoon she went to the mail room to retrieve her mail. She stood near the cubbies, flipping through her papers.

She saw Debbie and Kathy enter the mail room in her peripheral vision, watching as they froze and stared at her.

"Stop gawking and get your mail," Margaret grumbled, eyes averted toward the floor.

"What happened?" Debbie immediately asked.

"What happened is that you two are engaging me in pointless conversation. Get your mail or get out."

"What happened between you and Tess?"

For a split second, Margaret felt vulnerable, but immediately tamped the feeling down and scowled. "What an absurd conclusion."

"We've barely seen Tess, and your mood hasn't been this bad in years."

"Tess is a senior. She's busy. She'll graduate and move on, as all seniors do. You've both taught long enough to understand the system."

"So, you're bitter Tess is leaving?" Debbie asked. "She's got the rest of senior year. She's hardly leaving tomorrow."

Margaret let out a huff. "You two won't let this go, will you?"

"Not when you're being a righteous pain in the ass. We're friends now, we can call you on your bullshit. What happened? You can talk to us."

Margaret contemplated before dejectedly muttering, "Tess broke it off."

Kathy stepped forward, her arms wide open. "Come here, have a hug, you don't have a choice," she declared, pulling Margaret into a tight hug. "I helped my daughter through her first heartbreak, so I can sure as hell help you through yours."

"Yeah, come here," Debbie said, joining the hug as well.

* * *

Tess couldn't stand to look at Margaret, and unfortunately Margaret was everywhere. She was around every corner, down the hall, across the quad, always there. It was fine that Margaret wanted to sleep with other women. She could do as she damn well pleased. But Tess didn't want to hear about it or see evidence of hickeys or smell the scent of another woman's perfume, nothing.

Tess was miffed. She had every right to be—and she had no right to be. Were they still fuck buddies? Were they still friends? Why did it feel like a breakup when they were never together to begin with?

Tess wanted to stay friends, but she couldn't play nicely when all she wanted to do was pin Margaret in bed and make her scream, hold her close, and tell her how amazing and beautiful and sweet she was. She wanted to feather kisses all over her face and tell her that she loved her. And she desperately wanted Margaret to break her no-dating rule.

But Tess wasn't a moron. Margaret didn't do relationships. There was no point in pretending.

Tess sat on her bed, knees pulled close to her chest. Usually, at this time, she'd be in Margaret's office, bothering her about pointless things, laughing with her, spending time with her. Was that how she fell in love with her? Was it through the daily interruptions, not when they were sleeping together, but when they were laughing together?

Tess thought they had something special. Margaret didn't easily tolerate others, but she was vulnerable around Tess. It had to mean something. But it didn't. Because Margaret hadn't texted or called. Tess hadn't either, but it didn't matter.

Tess missed her. She just wanted to be close, snuggled against her or sitting beside her.

Had she always been in love with Margaret, from the second those icy eyes first locked with hers? Did she keep Margaret at arm's length because the professor demanded it, or because Tess was afraid? She got hurt anyway. Still, it was worth it because she got to know the real Margaret. Plus, her temper lessened, no longer the villain of campus. Tess was glad others were seeing the true Margaret too, but Tess was realizing she wasn't good at sharing.

"You all right in there?" Elle asked, knocking softly on Tess's closed bedroom door. "Kai's worried...I'm worried too."

"Y-yeah," Tess choked out hoarsely. "I'm fine."

"You don't sound fine." Tess didn't offer a response. "Can I come in?"

"Sure."

Slowly, Elle pushed open the bedroom door. She crawled up beside Tess on the bed and picked at some lint on Tess's bedspread, contemplating. Finally, she said, "You know, Kai says you're heartbroken…I think I agree with her."

Tess scoffed.

"You don't have to lie, you know, and act like you don't have feelings. I mean, I knew you had a crush on Dr. Morgan the second you first saw her. I don't look down on you because you caught feelings. The heart wants what it wants. And yeah, she was kind of bad at the start, but she's not too bad now."

"I didn't really mean to, but you're right. At some point, I caught feelings for her. And this break really sucks. Like, I can't stand it."

"Then go tell her how you feel."

"I don't think she feels the same way. She cares, but not for the long run. I'll graduate, and she'll just find a different student to sleep with."

"You want to know if there's even a chance that Dr. Morgan likes you back, right? And you'd like to know if she immediately jumped into bed with another girl, yeah?" Tess nodded. "Okay, so, who beside Dr. Morgan would know these things?"

"No one. She doesn't share her personal life."

"Wrong. You're forgetting about her best friend and the absolute best professor."

Simultaneously, both girls stated, "Dr. Greenwood," Elle with triumph and Tess with dawning realization.

* * *

Tess, feeling meek and entirely too hesitant, knocked on Amy's office door as confidently as she could.

"Can we talk?" Tess asked when Amy opened her door.

"Of course, Tess, come in. I haven't seen you in a while."

"I know…Things have been weird. I don't know if Maggie's talked to you…"

"I know you two had a bit of a spat. Why don't you tell me what happened?"

They settled in the sitting area and Tess kicked her feet, looking at the floor. "I haven't talked to her since then," she deflected. "Has she…been fine?"

"Do you think she's fine?"

"No. Well, I hope she isn't. Not that I hope she feels bad, I wouldn't wish her ill, I just…" Tess sighed deeply. "*I'm* not fine, so part of me hopes she doesn't feel fine either, because this is killing me."

Amy raised a curious eyebrow. "Tell me what happened, Tess," she urged again.

"I got jealous and angry. We hadn't talked about the future, if we'd stay in touch, or what it meant. I should have brought it up, but I thought if she really cared, she would ask about it. If she wanted me to stay in her life, she'd tell me. But she didn't. And, well, it wasn't fair of me to put all that on her, but I did."

"She told me that you wanted to see other people."

"I did say that, but I didn't mean it. I don't want to see anyone else, and I certainly don't want her seeing anyone else. But I know she doesn't do relationships, and I was hurt because I thought that I was an exception, or that I could be. That what we had was special and she would change her mind…"

Tess trailed off, rubbing furiously at her eyes as tears she didn't want threatened to fall.

"If you want my unsolicited opinion," Amy said, "I think you should be having this conversation with her, not me."

"I know, I just…I can't face her if she's—I need to know. You're her best friend, so if anyone would know, it'd be you, and—"

"You want to know if she slept with anyone else?" Amy asked incredulously.

"Yes."

"You can sleep with anyone without having feelings for them."

"I know, which is why I'm such an idiot for thinking she might have feelings for me—"

Amy cut Tess off. "I also believe it's nearly impossible to sleep with someone regularly, and spend time with them often, and not develop feelings. I think Margaret feels the same, and that's why she always kept her distance and why she refused to sleep with the same woman twice."

Tess swallowed hard.

"Under any other circumstances, I would not tell you this. I believe you should ask Margaret yourself and I hope she gives you the truth. But to boost your confidence so that you will talk to her, I'll tell you. She hasn't slept with anyone else, not since you two first started seeing each other, and certainly not now that you two aren't talking."

Tess nodded, accepting that information. Then she looked straight at the English professor. "I'm in love with her, Amy," Tess confessed.

Amy's gaze softened as she smiled. "I know you are, Tess. I figured that one out a long time ago."

"Do you think there's any hope for me?"

"All I'll say is that it's amazing you were able to get through to her, pull her out of her shell, and she was willing to put up with you. It speaks volumes."

"You know, I applied to grad school in town because part of me always hoped I'd be lucky enough to have her in my life for a long while…longer than just four years of undergrad."

"Go talk to her and let me know how it goes. I'll be here for you regardless."

"But you're her best friend—"

"And I'm your friend too. Now go on. Get!"

* * *

"You look better," Kai said as she walked with Tess to class in the morning.

"You might have been right about something…I talked to Dr. Greenwood about it."

"This 'something' wouldn't happen to be the 'fact' that you're in love with Dr. Morgan, is it?"

Tess playfully smacked at her friend. "Do you have to be so loud?"

"You've been depressed and melancholy, and she was being a jerk again. But she calmed down quick. I do want to warn you, though, that there are still murmurings. I know that's what made you jealous in the first place, so just be careful."

"I wasn't—okay fine. I was jealous, and I still am, but only because I thought that what we had was special. But…if she's calming down again, maybe she has moved on."

"Or maybe you changed her for the better for good, and she couldn't maintain her horrid attitude because she's actually nice now. Debbie and Kathy said they talked to her. I think they're all friends now."

"Well, I plan on talking to Maggie this Friday. Hopefully it goes well."

"Best of luck. In the meantime, let's enjoy baby bio."

Tess and Kai trailed into the lecture hall building. Immediately, they noticed a massive crowd buzzing with electric energy, which was unusual. At best, such energy happened the morning before an exam, but they just finished a unit, and the intro chemistry classes, housed in the same building, gave their exams in the evening, so it wasn't a chemistry exam either.

"What's going on in here?" Kai questioned.

"Hurry, hurry," a student said, shoving past. "I want to get a front-row seat. Hurry!"

"I have no idea," Tess replied.

It took a bit of effort to push through the overactive crowd. Once they slipped into the bio lecture hall, the classroom was buzzing as well.

"What's going on out there?" Kai asked one of the junior TAs. "It's a madhouse."

"I'm surprised you didn't hear. Dr. Morgan's teaching the intro chem lecture this morning, and the freshmen are just bonkers over her. I don't get it."

"Wait, she's lecturing to the freshmen? She hates freshmen."

"Well, I doubt she's happy about it," the junior said. "There's some chemistry conference, and the entire chem department is out of town. I guess because she's bio-chem, Dr. Morgan didn't go. But she's the closest they've got to a qualified person to sub, and you know they'd never cancel class for a day. But I'm sure she's in a foul mood. I would have skipped class, personally."

Tess scowled. "All this commotion over a chem lecture is ridiculous, regardless of who's teaching." She crossed her arms with a huff and stalked off, sulking.

Commotion settled as class began. Occasionally, Tess heard a slight uproar coming from the massive auditorium-style room where the chem lecture was happening. She tried not to picture Margaret standing front and center, wearing a microphone, describing chemistry concepts...imagining the power in her stance and how goddamn attractive she was when she showed off her genius.

When ten minutes of the session remained, Tess stumbled into a couple of girls as they snuck out of class. They had no obligation to stay, and Tess wasn't going to stop them, but she was curious.

"Where are you off to?" Tess asked.

"Hey, shh, shh. We're going to sneak into the chem lecture. We want to see Dr. Morgan teaching."

"Yeah, it's a once-in-a-lifetime opportunity."

"All right, sure, have fun."

Tess stood by the door for a minute, contemplating, then she caught Kai's attention across the room.

"Hey, what's up?" Kai asked, sliding up beside her.

"I need to run something over to Dr. Logan before next class," Tess lied. "Cover for me so I can slip out a few minutes early?"

"Sure, no problem," Kai said, her smile growing mischievous. "Tell Dr. Morgan hi for me."

"I said Dr. Logan—"

"I know what you said, and I know what I heard. Go, get out of here."

Tess nodded, slipping out into the now empty hall. She walked swiftly toward the other auditorium, the noise rising as she neared. Taking a deep breath, she pulled open the lecture hall doors.

In the back of the room by the doors, a standing crowd of extra students had gathered to witness Dr. Morgan's teaching. Tess noticed the girls from baby bio craning their necks to see down to the front of the room. Tess pushed her way through the crowd, scanning the hundreds of seats, watching the students take notes. Then her gaze shifted to the front.

Margaret wore black dress slacks and a white button-up blouse, her short brunette hair half pulled up in a style that drove Tess mad. The professor was mic'd, pacing at the front of the lecture hall as she explained orbitals. Tess loved watching Margaret in science mode. She adored hearing the passion in her voice and witnessing the spark in her blue eyes.

"She's a genius," someone uttered wistfully next to Tess.

"And so gorgeous," another said.

"Do you really think she sleeps around with students?"

"Definitely. I heard she's already slept with five girls in our year. College is a time for experimenting, right?"

Tess's nostrils flared, but she focused on what Amy said. She watched Margaret, thinking about how much she missed her and how badly she wanted to be back in her arms. Only the two of them mattered, not everyone else in the lecture hall, not the hundreds of increasingly obnoxious underclassmen.

"We will conclude there," Margaret said, noting the time. "Any questions before you're dismissed?"

A hand shot up in the front and the student immediately asked, "Dr. Morgan, are you busy tonight?"

Murmurs broke out. Students were shocked by the girl's boldness.

"*Chemistry* questions, please," Margaret said, pinching the bridge of her nose.

"It is a chemistry question." The girl doubled down. "A question about our chemistry, that is."

The lecture hall erupted in a fit. Margaret attempted to maintain decorum, but the mob was lost, gasps and shouts filling the room.

Tess realized two things in that moment. First, Margaret had changed. She was voluntarily teaching undergrads, mainly freshmen, even. She willingly offered to answer the students' questions, something she previously found to be a waste of time. She also said please and didn't immediately snap, even though the classroom behavior had fallen away from the science topic at hand. Margaret was nicer. She was acting like a truly caring— although perhaps a bit exhausted—professor. Tess could spend the rest of her life with that woman. She wanted to.

Second, Tess wasn't going to stand for freshmen unabashedly flirting with *her* Margaret. With a scowl, she shoved through the crowd, storming down the incline of the lecture hall toward the front of the room.

"Class dismissed!" Tess hollered, her voice booming over everyone else's. The harshness of her tone cut off the chatter immediately. Heads snapped in her direction.

Margaret's head turned as well. "Tess?" she questioned softly, though her voice was amplified by the microphone. That broke something in Tess, because so rarely did Margaret call her by her first name, and never in public.

When Tess noted that none of the students were leaving, she angrily shouted, "I said, class is dismissed. All of you, out, now!"

Her voice matched Margaret's original signature harshness, and the mob of students stood, scrambling for their things as they exited. Margaret pulled the mic off and stood with her arms crossed, watching Tess. Tess waited until the classroom doors shut behind the last student, then she turned and faced the professor.

"How dare you?" Margaret beat her to the punch. "How dare you barge in here while I'm teaching and order my students around?"

In lieu of a verbal answer, Tess grabbed Margaret by the shirt and fiercely smashed their lips together. When she jerked back, Margaret opened her mouth to retort, but Tess silenced her by pressing her thumb to her lips, holding her jaw.

"I don't want you to sleep with other women," Tess said. "I have feelings for you. I don't want to see other people. I want to see *you*."

Metal clanged as someone opened the classroom door. Both women turned sharply, jerking apart. It was a student, wearing headphones, absorbed in their own world, filing in for the next class. Another student followed, seemingly oblivious to the pair at the front of the room.

Margaret harshly grabbed Tess's wrist and jerked her out a side door, into the maintenance hallway. The space was dimly lit, dusty, and smelled vaguely like mold, but it was desolate. Margaret shoved Tess against the nearest wall and reconnected their lips with a desperate, feverish passion.

Tess relaxed into the familiar touch even as her body lit on fire. She pawed at Margaret, whimpering, moaning into her mouth. Margaret responded by pressing against Tess more firmly, and Tess's mind went fuzzy in ecstasy.

When they broke for air, both were panting.

"You have a lot of gall interrupting my lecture like that," Margaret said.

"You have a lot of gall letting that student flirt so openly with you," Tess retorted, fixing her jaw. She stared into Margaret's eyes, waiting for a response to her earlier confession.

Margaret bit her lip nervously, glancing down, afraid to meet Tess's eyes. "Did you mean what you said?" Margaret hesitantly asked. "Did you really mean you have feelings? Feelings...for me?"

Tess swallowed hard. "Yes." Though her statement was soft, she nodded confidently.

Margaret nodded then too, sagging forward as she pressed her head into the side of Tess's. She let out a choked sort of laugh. "That's good—very good—because, well, I have... feelings for you too."

Tess's heart stuttered and her eyes went wide. Immediately she jerked forward, spinning them, pinning Margaret against the wall. She reconnected their lips and Margaret kissed her back with equal desperation.

"Are you busy the rest of the day?" Tess asked.

"No, but you have class—"

"Not anymore. Take me home."

"All right."

* * *

Margaret fucked like an expert. She was deliberate with intent, and anything short of perfection was unacceptable. However, she made love like a goddess, innately attuned to intimacy with an overwhelming desire to be close. Tess had slept with her hundreds of times; she figured she knew every part of Margaret. Yet the sweet tenderness of lovemaking after their admission of feelings caught her by surprise. It was overwhelming and nearly brought her to tears.

Tenderly, Margaret ran her hands along Tess's sides, nibbling at the swell of Tess's neck. Tess pressed her head back, groaning at the sensation.

"I thought I'd lost you," Margaret said. Her grip tightened. "I always figured I would once you graduated. But I wasn't prepared for it to happen."

"I'm an idiot."

"Hardly." Margaret gently tugged Tess's shirt off, kissing every inch of bare skin. "Let me show you how much you mean to me." She punctuated her words by sliding her hand between Tess's thighs.

"Happily." Tess obliged, sighing blissfully.

Margaret laid Tess bare against the bed and Tess eagerly leaned up on her elbows to watch as Margaret stripped herself, unbuttoning the buttons of her blouse. Tess's hands were restless, so she pushed up from the bed and reached greedily toward her. She was used to Margaret's stubborn unwillingness to give up control, so she expected to be immediately shoved back down. However, this time, Margaret let Tess reach her. She let Tess help her with the buttons, let Tess push her shirt off her shoulders, and let Tess undo her pants and slide them off her hips.

Tess pulled Margaret closer and kissed her breastbone, reaching around to undo her bra. Tess reveled in her scent and her warmth, having missed her terribly the last several weeks. Once her bra was off, Margaret bent and tipped Tess's head back, reconnecting their lips. As they kissed, she slowly lowered them, hovering above Tess.

They rocked together, their lips only parting so Margaret could suckle at Tess's neck. She ground her hips down, pressing her thigh between Tess's legs. Tess whimpered, her breathing growing needier. Just when she was about to beg, Margaret slid her arm between them. Tess gasped into her mouth.

Tess wasn't used to the closeness. Margaret had always been somewhat distant when they slept together. Either she was behind Tess, or at the foot of the bed, or kneeling on the floor with her head between Tess's legs. Or she would sit up, or tie Tess down, and Tess was kept at arm's length. Never had Tess come undone in Margaret's arms, held close and tight, their bodies fully touching. She could feel every twitch and quiver of Margaret's muscles, could feel her warm breath tickling her neck, and she knew Margaret could feel every part of her body as well. When Tess came, she came hard, shuddering, gasping, and clawing at Margaret's back, desperate for purchase as her body melted into the pleasure.

"You are radiant, beautiful, absolutely stunning." Margaret peppered kisses everywhere she could reach while still desperately clinging to Tess. "I need to taste you."

Tess tightened her grip on Margaret's shoulders. "No, I want you close," she uttered, her voice needy.

"I need to witness your undoing again."

Tess scoffed but laughed. "Fine, give me a moment, and you can fuck me with the strap. But missionary, because I need you close, just like this."

"Done."

Feeling Margaret thrust inside her when they were so close was everything Tess had ever needed. It didn't take long before Tess was crashing over the edge again, crying out, shaking, and moaning.

After Tess lazily recovered, she flipped their positions. Margaret went willingly, not even putting up a pretend fight, and Tess could tell she was already close with need.

"You're beautiful," Tess whispered. "Are you going to come quick for me, you gorgeous, wonderful, good girl?"

Margaret's whimpered cry answered Tess completely.

Tess curled her fingers and sped up her motions, listening and feeling as Margaret jolted through her orgasm, crying out. She let her calm for a moment, then pulled her into a tight, all-encompassing hug.

"Are you still scared to lose me?" Tess asked after a moment. "I could go to grad school anywhere in the country."

Margaret pressed her short nails into Tess's arm in warning. "I should hope you'd at least call."

"I'm not sure either of us would do well with a long-distance relationship."

"Relationship?"

"I—" Tess's voice caught in her throat.

Margaret let out a nervous breath. "I know what I said when we first started this, how I was back then. But time's passed, and things have changed. I never thought I could feel this way about someone, yet here I am, feeling things for you."

Tess laughed then and relaxed again into Margaret's embrace. "I applied to two schools in town, just in case. I always hoped I could be the exception to your no-dating rule. I think my top choice will be staying here in town with you."

"See where all you get accepted, and we can talk from there. There are always weekends and plane flights."

"You'd travel just to see little ol' me?"

"Only if you promise to be on your best behavior."

"You like me better when I'm not."

"Touché."

Tess nuzzled against Margaret's neck. She ran her fingers through Margaret's hair, scratching gently at her scalp. She practically purred under Tess's ministrations.

"So..." Tess began, mustering courage. "When did you, um...know you had feelings for me? Was it not until recently, or...?"

Margaret hummed, collecting her thoughts. "To be entirely truthful," she said after a moment, "I think I knew right away... after we first slept together. That's probably why I was so adamant to hold you at arm's length, because I knew it was dangerous."

"Dangerous to let yourself feel because I might hurt you?"

"Yes…"

Tess sensed hesitancy, but instead of pushing, she eased back into her previous question. "So, you knew after the first time we slept together…What made you know?"

Margaret turned away slightly, sucking in fresh, cool air, contemplating. Eventually she whispered, "Because I let you touch me."

Tess pulled back, propping herself up. "Because you let me touch you? Do you not—Did you never let the women you slept with touch you?"

"No," Margaret confirmed, her cheeks tinted pink. "My priority was their pleasure. I liked being a woman's undoing, bringing her pleasure. I didn't need, didn't want, anything in return."

"Is it…like a kink? Like you're a touch-me-not top, or it didn't suit your dominatrix persona?"

Margaret flushed further and refused to comment, wiggling away from Tess. Tess had never known Margaret to shy away from anything related to sex, so she knew something was off.

"What's going on?" Tess muttered softly, pulling at Margaret until she sat up next to her. Tess cupped the sides of Margaret's face and kissed her gingerly. "Can you talk to me?"

"I was…assaulted when I was younger. It's made it difficult to—I don't feel like I deserve it."

Immediately, Tess jerked Margaret into a tight hug. She held her close and rocked her slightly.

Then slowly, with dread, Tess asked, "I didn't—I never touched you against your will, did I? I never—not when you didn't want it, I mean…?"

"Oh, no, of course not," Margaret replied immediately, cupping Tess's face and kissing her for reassurance. "When I slept with other women, I never felt safe enough, so I couldn't relax. It wasn't pleasurable or fun, so I never wanted them to. But with you…you made me feel safe. That's why I could relax and why I wanted you to touch me. And god, are you attentive. That's how I knew I was fucked, immediately—"

"Yes, I thoroughly shagged you. Thanks for the ego boost."
Margaret swatted lightly at Tess. "You're unbelievable. But
either way, I knew that I already had feelings for you because I
felt so safe with you. I haven't been able to trust another person
like that in so long. It was wonderful and refreshing, but also
completely and utterly terrifying."

"I'm sure." Tess watched Margaret for a minute, then smiled
softly. "Do you want to talk about what happened to you? I'm
more than willing to listen."

"Well…it started back in high school. I skipped a few grades,
so I was younger than my peers. Most of my energy was dedicated
to school. Science was extremely fascinating, and math came
easily, so I excelled. My parents were my biggest cheerleaders. I
didn't have many friends, from the age difference, I assume, but
I always had my parents. We were very close."

"Were you an only child?"

"Yes, just the three of us. They were so proud of me and
my accomplishments. I was really happy back then, but then we
found out my mom had stage four breast cancer. She didn't live
very long after that."

Margaret looked down and gripped the bedsheets,
swallowing hard.

"My dad couldn't handle the loss. I took her death hard, but
he—he scared me. He um…drove his car into a cement wall
on the highway, headlong. We found a suicide note. Part of me
wishes I'd never read it, so I'd have my memories of him before
then, untainted. I wish loss didn't bring out the worst in people.

"But, um." Margaret cleared her throat. "I was an orphan. I
was nearing the end of high school, but I was young, so my aunt
and uncle took me in. I'd always loved them. They had older
kids, but they were out of the house by then, so I was there
alone with my aunt and uncle. It was a hard adjustment, but I
thought they really loved me. I thought I could heal with them,
you know?

"I went off to college, supported by academic scholarships
and life insurance money. That was when I realized I like women.
I met a few great women in my early college days."

"Like Amy?"

"Yes, but I didn't meet Amy until the end of undergrad. Before Amy I met someone I thought I could be with forever, but my aunt and uncle didn't take it well. I was eighteen when they found out. I—I thought they loved me. I thought I was safe with them. I was wrong."

Margaret pressed her lips together in a faint line. Tess pulled her closer. "You don't have to tell me if it's too hard. I'll care about you the same no matter what. I want to ease your pain, but if talking about it hurts too much, you don't have to. I'll never make you."

Margaret choked back a sob. "I'd forgotten what real compassion felt like. But you showed me it again. I'm so angry they took that away from me."

"I'll spend the rest of my life making sure you never lose it again, if that's what you want."

Margaret sucked in a deep breath, like her emotions were too strong. They were silent, just rocking gently in each other's arms.

Eventually, Margaret spoke again. "My dad loved me," she said. "I loved him so dearly, and I know he loved me. But even so…my uncle said I was a disappointment, a disgrace to my father, that being this way would have killed him, like in some perverted way it was my fault that he was dead. And—and maybe it would have. Maybe my parents would have hated me if they'd lived long enough to know. But I want to live in a world where they would have still loved me, unconditionally. I wish my uncle didn't get into my head like that."

"I'm sure they would have still loved you," Tess said. "From what you said, it sounds like your parents loved you very much, and I can understand why. You are an amazing and wonderful person, and I'm so sorry that life has been this hard on you. Also, fuck your aunt and uncle for contributing to your misery. You didn't deserve that."

"It wasn't just their harsh words, their homophobia. It was…I mean, my uncle, he was the one who—" Margaret heaved in a breath, like she was on the verge of hyperventilating, and Tess pulled her closer, holding her tighter.

"He…was the one who assaulted you?" Tess asked, her voice barely more than a whisper, hoping it wasn't true but fearing it was.

Very minutely, Margaret moved her head in a nod. "It was impossible for me to fully heal from that…They kicked me out, I fell into a depressed state, broke off all my relationships because I felt disgusting and unlovable. I didn't want to get close to anyone because I was afraid of getting hurt again. I didn't feel like I could trust anyone anymore."

"That's why you kept everyone at arm's length…"

"Yes. I didn't let myself get close to Amy either, that's why we went our own ways. She wanted love, but I didn't think I'd ever be able to give her that. I'm glad we've reconnected now as friends, though. I'm lucky to have her in my life."

"I'm glad you have a best friend too. And I'm glad you let me in as well."

"I hardly had a choice. You wormed your way in like a bad rash I couldn't get rid of."

Tess gasped in mock offense but hugged Margaret affectionately. "Thank you for sharing all of that with me. I know it wasn't easy, but it helps me understand you better. I always figured you must have been hurt terribly to be so cold. It's just a defense mechanism. So, I figured something must have happened to you, but I never knew what. So, thank you for sharing. It means so much that you trust me like that."

"I know I haven't been the best at communicating my feelings to you, but…I hope you understand."

"I understand that it means you trust me, and you care deeply for me. I'll admit there were many times that I questioned if you really did care for me, but you proved you do in your own ways."

"I'm so grateful you understand me."

"I would, however, like some specific confirmation…" Tess uttered sheepishly. "I mean, I care about you so much. And you're hot and amazing in bed—obviously I've been sold on that for some time now. But it's more than that. I care about you. I like you. I want to be around you constantly. I want to share my life with you. I'm hoping you feel the same?"

"I do, yes."

"And I know you've got this silly little rule, something about how you 'don't do relationships,' but I'm hoping you've changed your stance on that by now?"

Tess shot Margaret a goofy little grin that she could tell melted her heart, as her happiness was reflected back at her.

"Why, Miss Stanford, are you asking me to be your girlfriend?" Margaret's tone was laced with humor.

"I'm barely asking. I'm more so demanding."

"Then yes. Let's date," Margaret said, sealing it with a kiss.

* * *

The following morning, Margaret drove Tess back to campus as she had done countless times before. However, this time, Margaret drove straight past her normal stop. Tess eyed her curiously.

"Where are you going?"

"I'm driving you to campus to drop you off," Margaret replied, as if Tess's question was silly.

"But you passed—" Tess's words cut off as Margaret pulled up next to the on-campus apartments. "Really? So close? I thought you didn't want anyone to see us together?"

"What's so wrong with dropping my girlfriend off at her apartment before class?"

Tess dove at Margaret, frantically. "Call me your girlfriend one more time and I won't want to get out of this car," Tess warned.

"You're going to be late for class."

Tess jerked Margaret forward and kissed her pointedly. "I'm coming straight to your office after class this morning."

Margaret rolled her eyes. "Come on, get out," she said, shoving Tess back.

"See you later!" Tess called as she slipped out of the car.

Tess's first class lasted an eternity. She normally loved the advanced biology class, but she could barely focus knowing that just down the hall was her girlfriend—her *girlfriend*—who she could see the second class let out. She was ready, having already packed up her backpack while the professor was still lecturing, and she burst out the door the second the minute rolled over.

Tess had tunnel vision for Margaret's office. All she cared about was getting back to the woman she had very reluctantly left that morning. However, a figure stepped straight in front of her, blocking her view entirely, forcing her out of her head.

"Hey, Tess." Kai grinned impishly. "The biology building has been surprisingly peaceful today, and I heard from Elle that you spent the night out and came back glowing."

"Hi to you too," Tess said.

"You're still glowing, by the way."

"I would love to catch up, but there's somewhere I need—"

"Uh-huh, darting off to Dr. Morgan's office. I know. But we need to grade the baby bio exams, and I am not doing that by myself. So, come on."

"Ugh, fine, you're right."

The pair headed to Debbie's adjoining lab space and set up at the table, spreading out the exams they needed to grade. They worked in silence, focusing on their task, until the hour shifted over and Debbie came in to check on her grad students.

"Tess, Kai, hello to you both. Getting the exams graded, I see. Good, good."

"We're nearly finished."

Debbie's gaze fell on Tess. "Tess, you look slightly less dour than before."

"W-what?"

"You and Margaret have both been in piss-poor moods. It just looks like you're doing better now, is all."

"That's because they made up," Kai spilled.

Immediately, Debbie fell onto a chair beside the girls. "You did? Really?" She gasped excitedly.

Tess flushed. "Yes," she replied. She made a point of picking up another exam, avoiding eye contact. Debbie wasn't having it, however.

"Now, Tess, you know that I care about you deeply. And of course, you are your own person free to do as you wish, however—"

"She's a good person." Tess felt immediately defensive. "I know she hasn't always been the nicest, but she's a good person and she deserves happiness."

Debbie leaned back in her chair, raising an eyebrow as she crossed her arms. "I was going to say as much, actually. Thanks to you, I consider Margaret a friend now, which is how I know she's been hurting. What did you think I was going to say?"

Tess flushed. "Sorry, I thought you were going to scold me for going back to her."

"I am going to scold you, but only slightly. If you're happy, that's what's important. But Margaret's happiness matters too. I want to make sure you're considering her feelings as well."

"Wait…" Tess narrowed her eyes suspiciously. "Did you know?"

Debbie smirked.

"Know what?" Kai asked eagerly.

"That Maggie has feelings for me," Tess declared.

"I'm glad you finally figured it out," Debbie replied. "I hope you're considering her feelings as you move forward."

"You're being so analytical," Kai scolded the professor. "Tess, Dr. Morgan has feelings for you? Why didn't you tell me? Oh my gosh, are you—did you—*ahh!*" Kai grabbed Tess roughly and shook her. "You have feelings for her too! Did you tell her? Are you dating?"

"Stop shaking me, let go," Tess said. She turned toward Debbie and pointed an accusatory finger. "How did you know?"

"We forced that confession out of her a long time ago, none too gracefully," Debbie admitted. "I'm surprised it took you so long with how miserable she was, dreading your graduation."

"Well, I'm not leaving," Tess declared stubbornly. "I don't know where grad school will take me, but I do know that I intend to remain in Maggie's life for a long time."

"So, you *are* dating," Kai accused.

"Yes," Tess finally admitted, blushing profusely.

"It's about damn time," Debbie said.

* * *

Meanwhile, down the hall, Margaret was recalibrating contaminated equipment. In the past, this would have annoyed her, but today she was elated beyond souring. Not even the interrupting knock on the lab door could bring down her mood. She spun, catching herself smiling before she forced the grin down, realizing it was Kathy standing in the doorway.

"Can I help you?" Margaret asked the biology professor.

"You're in a good mood," Kathy said. "The ladies in the office said you were doing better. I thought I'd come see for myself."

"My lab isn't a zoo, and I'm not a monkey on display for your entertainment," Margaret shot back.

Kathy, evidently, did not take this as a serious threat as she stepped into the lab anyway and pulled the door shut. "There's only one thing that could have lifted you out of your funk…You made up with Tess, didn't you?"

Margaret nodded, unable to suppress her grin any longer.

"You look good when you smile. However, how is it that you made up? If you're just continuing your casual romps, I'm going to have to step in—"

"It isn't casual. We've confessed to each other."

"Both of you? Tess, in return—"

"She likes me back, yes. It's unbelievable. I never thought someone as wonderful and sweet as Miss Stanford could like someone like me."

"Ahh, good on you both. I'm afraid now you have to come to our regular game nights."

"Your…what?" Margaret was aghast.

Kathy laughed at her pained expression. "Yes, our game nights. Our husbands come, and Kai and Elle come together. Tess never seemed to mind, but games are easier with even numbers."

Margaret rubbed her eyes. "Another reason I always avoided dating."

"Oh, you're being dramatic. You'd do anything for Tess, and I know it."

"Speaking of Miss Stanford, have you seen her around? She told me she'd come to my office after her first class, but she never showed up. I'm sure she just got busy, but—"

"I think she's grading exams, probably in Debbie's lab. I was about to head over there myself. Would you like to walk together?"

"No, but I suppose we can."

"You're being dramatic again. Come on."

When they shoved into Debbie's lab, Debbie immediately said, "Kathy, they made up. They're—"

"Dating, yes, I just heard."

The biology professors glanced at Tess, but her focus was on the bio-chem professor. Tess smiled contentedly, and Margaret gazed fondly as well.

"Are you two always hoarding Miss Stanford?" Margaret asked, looking at the bio professors. "She's more than just your TA, you know."

"Kai abducted me to grade, I'm sorry," Tess replied, her smile growing larger. "I swear I was heading straight to your office before I was diverted."

"We have work to do during work hours," Kai said. "Keep your pining for after work hours."

"I will do no such thing," Tess declared stubbornly. She stood, tossing the last graded exam onto the pile before she walked over to Margaret. "Let's go to your office," she suggested.

"Don't forget about game night!" Kathy shouted after the pair.

"Oh, now that's a great idea."

Margaret couldn't help but grin as she heard Debbie's approving tone.

* * *

For the past several weeks, Margaret had been nothing short of depressing, refusing to go out, refusing to meet up, and insisting on staying at home moping. Well, she read scientific journals and ran theoretical calculations, but for Margaret, that was moping. However, with her heart healed and Tess back in her life, Margaret couldn't wait to share the news with her best friend. She texted Amy, requesting they meet for their regular Sunday mimosa-heavy brunch.

When Margaret arrived at the restaurant embarrassingly late, she quickly walked up to the table Amy was already sitting at. "Hi, Amy," she said, trying to not sound too sheepish. "Sorry I'm a bit late. Someone didn't want to get out of bed this morning."

Immediately, Amy gasped. "Are you and Tess sleeping together again?"

"Don't shout," Margaret scolded.

"Are you?"

"We are," Margaret confirmed. "And we're doing more than that too."

"More than—are you two together then? Officially? *Monogamously?*"

"You don't have to say it like that. But yes, we're together, and yes, we're exclusive."

"She did it, then, that brave girl," Amy concluded in awe. "She was so afraid that you'd reject her—of course, I knew you wouldn't, but I couldn't tell her that."

"You talked to Tess? When?"

"Last week. She came to me and told me she was in love with you."

Margaret choked on her spit. She grabbed Amy's drink to soothe her cough, and Amy gasped, appalled at the thievery.

"*In love?*" Margaret wheezed once she could breathe again.

"Whoops," Amy muttered. "I guess she was more sparing in her confession to you. It's silly, as if liking someone is less substantial than loving someone. But I know you feel the same way, so I'm hardly worried."

Margaret's initial shock morphed into a warm feeling of contented happiness. She couldn't believe her luck, that Tess cared about her so greatly.

"Well, are you going to tell me the details?" Amy asked facetiously.

"The only details you're getting is that Tess and I are dating and that I'm very, *very* happy."

"Does it feel wonderful? The love? I think that's the point of human existence—to love. Romantic love, but other love too. I cherish our friendship, and I love you, as a friend, obviously."

"I know. I love you too, Amy."

"Ahh!" Amy squealed. "Remind me to send Tess a thank-you card because she made you capable of sharing your feelings."

"Cut it out. You're being ridiculous."

GRADUATION

Margaret watched as Debbie elbowed Kathy in the ribs. "Kai's next," the biology professor whispered.

"I know, I can see," Kathy said.

They sat in the massive gymnasium, which had been converted into a graduation venue at the end of the year. They were all dressed in their own doctorate gown regalia, celebrating the success of the graduating class.

Kai walked across the stage and took her diploma, excitedly waving to Elle, who was on the floor, having walked several minutes earlier.

"I bet they get married in a year," Debbie said, watching the pair.

"I'm positive they will," Amy said, leaning forward from the row behind the science professors. "Elle already bought her a ring. She wanted to wait until after graduation to propose. I'm sure Kai will say yes."

"No doubt in my mind."

"You gossip too much," Kathy scolded. "I know they're like our adopted children, but stop speculating about their lives."

"They're hardly children," Margaret said from beside Debbie.

"Speaking of"—Debbie harshly elbowed Margaret in the ribs—"your sweetheart is walking next."

"Yes, I can see," Margaret said, repeating Kathy's earlier words.

The announcer called Tess's name, and she walked across the stage. When she received her diploma, she paused and looked straight at Margaret, winking.

"She could have gone to Harvard, but she decided to stay here with you," Debbie muttered whimsically to Margaret.

"She didn't apply to Harvard," Margaret retorted. "Our university has a leading biochemistry program—I wonder why. She chose to remain here for that."

"And you aren't allowed to mentor her because of fraternizing rules," Debbie said, laughing slightly.

"They'll be cute, a little bio-chem power couple," Amy cut in.

"All of you, shush, they're doing closing remarks," Kathy said.

The graduation ceremony closed, and the students all processed out, followed by the professors. Outside, students were running every which way, throwing hats, shouting to friends and family as they went. Everything was a whirlwind.

"We need to get to the biology building for the celebration," Kathy said, tugging Debbie toward the science quad. "Margaret, are you coming?"

"She's a goner already," Amy said.

Margaret had locked eyes with Tess across the flood of people and was no longer listening to the other professors' conversation.

"Maggie!" Tess shouted over the crowd. She weaved between people and fought through the crowd so she could run and jump into Margaret's arms. She caught her and spun her, pulling her close.

"I'm so incredibly proud of you," Margaret said, kissing Tess lightly on the temple. "I can't wait to grill you on biochemistry for your qualifying exam."

Tess jerked Margaret close and whispered in her ear, "I can't wait to get you into bed."

Margaret pulled back humorously. "Now, now, you have to go to lunch with your family, and this evening we're meeting up at O'Charlie's, remember?"

"Of course I remember, it was my idea."

"I'll see you tonight, then, all right?"

"I guess if I have to."

"Go. Have fun," Margaret said, sending Tess off in the direction of her friends. Then, Debbie grabbed the professor by the elbow and tugged her toward the biology building.

* * *

That evening, Amy and Margaret met Tess, Kai, and Elle at O'Charlie's. The professors arrived first, and Jimmy spotted them, waving them over to the bar.

"Mad Dog, it's been a few years," Jimmy said, watching Margaret. "You look good. Life's been treating you well?"

"It has. She's got a girlfriend," Amy supplied.

"Ahh, then I understand why I haven't seen you around. I wasn't sure if you'd ever couple up, being such a loner. I hoped you might, but I wasn't sure you had it in you."

Margaret flushed slightly. "I have Tess to thank for that."

"Speaking of—"

"That's why I told him animal behavior is the best," Elle said, bursting through the door with Kai and Tess. "And he was like, 'Isn't that just a glorified dog trainer?' No! There's so much that goes into animal behavior, and beyond just dogs, you know."

"I think you should intern at the zoo," Kai said. "I'd come visit you every day on my lunch break, assuming I can escape the hospital for a bit. They like to keep us med students on our toes."

"I'd come visit too, but they keep grad students pretty busy too," Tess said.

"Busy, my ass. You'll always find time to sneak off and see Dr. Morgan."

"You're not wrong." Tess waved at Margaret across the bar.

Margaret flushed, although she offered a small wave in return. "What would you like to drink?" she asked as Tess approached. "It's on me, to celebrate your graduation."

"Thanks. I'll take a vodka Coke."

Jimmy poured the drink and passed it to Tess. "So, you're the famous gal that stole Mad Dog's heart."

"Mad Dog?" Tess asked, looking between the bartender and Margaret.

Margaret rolled her eyes. "Tess, this is Jimmy. He owns the place. We're old friends."

"Another friend you've been hiding?" Tess gasped. "How many secret friends do you have?"

"It's nice to meet you," Jimmy said. "You must be something special, taming the lone wolf, Mad Dog."

"Why do you call her that? Mad Dog?"

"It's an old nickname," Jimmy explained. "I always considered her a lone wolf, and there's the saying 'you dirty dog.' Then mad, because she is mad, a damn mad scientist. She'd crush women's hearts, a damn terror in this bar, yet the women kept chasing. That was the most maddening part of it all. So, I called her Mad Dog, and I still do. Tame Mad Dog now or not." Jimmy then said, "I hope you aren't the jealous type. Mad Dog tends to turn heads around here."

"There are other people in this bar?" Margaret hummed, her eyes locked on Tess.

Tess shivered. "Can we sit at a booth?"

"Sure. It looks like my favorite booth in the back is open."

"Guys, we're grabbing a table," Tess shouted to their friends.

"Enjoy your evening," Jimmy said as he bid them off. "I can mix some damn good drinks if you're feeling adventurous. Just let me know."

* * *

The crew crowded into the back booth, chatting amicably as they drank and celebrated. Elle continued talking about dog training and animal behavior. Kai debated what she wanted to specialize in in med school. Amy mentioned a new queer book she'd recently read, which Elle jumped in on. Margaret and Tess kicked each other gently under the table, the promise of more lingering in the air between them.

Eventually, a few more drinks in, Kai convinced Elle to dance with her. They moved onto the dance floor, laughing, spinning, and jumping around. Amy smiled, soon excusing herself to go chat with Jimmy at the bar.

Alone together, Tess slid closer to Margaret.

"I love you so much," Tess whispered.

Margaret's heart swelled. For the longest time, she thought she was completely unlovable. Now she had so many supportive friends and a deeply caring lover. Still, it was difficult to voice her feelings. She worried Tess would grow impatient with her inability to voice those words in return, but she'd yet to find the confidence to speak them.

"You're going to do great things in graduate school," Margaret stated in lieu of a reciprocated confession.

"Do you think I should work in industry, or stay in academia?" Tess asked. "I did enjoy being a TA. Maybe I should teach, like you."

"Maybe one of us should earn more than a teacher's salary."

"What? Do you intend on making a wife out of me or something?" Tess asked. "I'm kidding, kind of. I know feelings aren't easy, and I know this is a lot for you. As long as I have you in my life in some capacity, that's all I care about."

"You know…you never asked me why I became a professor instead of going into industry."

"I've wondered plenty, trust me. You staying in academia was partially why I was so adamant in breaking you in the first place. It takes a lot more heart to teach. That's how I knew you even had a heart." Tess smiled, chuckling lightly. "But I'll ask. Why did you become a professor?"

"Well, you know, despite my bitter attitude and asshole façade, I am capable of love."

"Of course I know that."

"I've fallen in love twice. The first woman I ever fell in love with was a TA."

"Really?" Tess asked, bemused.

"I'm entirely serious—my sophomore year of undergrad. She taught a chemistry lab...I guess you could say that she ignited my passions in multiple ways. She supported my curiosity in the lab, and we spent long hours just discussing science for fun. Then she kissed me and brought me home with her, and I fell in love. I thought I might run away with her, but then..."

"Your uncle..." Tess squeezed Margaret's hand tightly.

"Yes, I just couldn't trust anymore. I distanced myself. But she's the one who inspired me to remain in academia. She made me fall in love with science. I wanted to do that for others, cultivate a love for science in them. I haven't been the best at showing my students that I care, but I do, truthfully, and I'm incredibly proud of them when they succeed."

"You're a good teacher, honestly. Maybe you had a bit of a rough patch where you got too grouchy, but that's not you anymore."

"You taught me the value in being tender."

"I didn't teach you that. Your parents taught you that, and maybe even this chemistry TA. I just showed you tenderness again because you'd forgotten it—no. Life treated you poorly and broke your trust in humanity. I just brought it back. So, good. I'm glad you fell in love with this TA. I'm glad that she made you the fantastic scientist that you are. And then, I'm sure the second person you ever fell in love with was Amy."

Margaret grinned impishly, squeezing Tess's thigh. "Nope. You're wrong."

Tess thought for a moment, her eyes widening with dawning realization. "Wait, Maggie! Are you saying what I think you're saying?"

"That I love you? Yes, completely, one hundred percent."

Tess inhaled sharply, pulling Margaret into a solid kiss and a tight embrace.

"Oh, I love you, Maggie. I love you so much."

"I love you too, Tess."

Bella Books, Inc.
Happy Endings Live Here
P.O. Box 10543
Tallahassee, FL 32302
Phone: (850) 576-2370
www.BellaBooks.com

More Titles from Bella Books

Hunter's Revenge – Gerri Hill
978-1-64247-447-3 | 276 pgs | paperback: $18.95 | eBook: $9.99
Tori Hunter is back! Don't miss this final chapter in the acclaimed Tori Hunter series.

Integrity – E. J. Noyes
978-1-64247-465-7 | 228 pgs | paperback: $19.95 | eBook: $9.99
It was supposed to be an ordinary workday...

The Order – TJ O'Shea
978-1-64247-378-0 | 396 pgs | paperback: $19.95 | eBook: $9.99
For two women the battle between new love and old loyalty may prove more dangerous than the war they're trying to survive.

Under the Stars with You – Jaime Clevenger
978-1-64247-439-8 | 302 pgs | paperback: $19.95 | eBook: $9.99
Sometimes believing in love is the first step. And sometimes it's all about trusting the stars.

The Missing Piece – Kat Jackson
978-1-64247-445-9 | 250 pgs | paperback: $18.95 | eBook: $9.99
Renee's world collides with possibility and the past, setting off a tidal wave of changes she could have never predicted.

An Acquired Taste – Cheri Ritz
978-1-64247-462-6 | 206 pgs | paperback: $17.95 | eBook: $9.99
Can Elle and Ashley stand the heat in the *Celebrity Cook Off* kitchen?

www.ingramcontent.com/pod-product-compliance
Ingram Content Group UK Ltd.
Pitfield, Milton Keynes, MK11 3LW, UK
UKHW041325310125
4394UKWH00009B/15

9 781642 476286